# THE ECHO AT ROOKE COURT

*By Harriet Smart*

The Butchered Man: Northminster Mystery 1
The Dead Songbird: Northminster Mystery 2
The Shadowcutter: Northminster Mystery 3
The Hanging Cage: Northminster Mystery 4
The Ghosts of Ardenthwaite: Northminster Mystery 5
The Echo at Rooke Court: Northminster Mystery 6
The Fatal Engine: Northminster Mystery 7
The Witches of Pitfeldry: Northminster Mystery 8
Moonshine and Mercury: Northminster Mystery 9
Tarleton's Coffer: Northminster Mystery 10
Mummer's Night: A Northminster Novella
Carswell's First Case: A Northminster Novella
Emma Vernon's Northminster Ghost Stories
The Dolls at Heron's Reach
The True Value of Pearls
The Daughters of Blane
Green Grow the Rushes
The Wild Garden
The Lark Ascending
Reckless Griselda
A Tempting Proposal

# THE ECHO AT ROOKE COURT

by

**Harriet Smart**

Published by Anthemion



Second Edition



ISBN 978-1-907873-59-1

Made with Jutoh

# Chapter One

## August 1841

"Farewell, Caledonia," said Eleanor, as the steamer passed the twinkling lights of Berwick-upon-Tweed.

They had sat on the stern deck since after dinner, watching the coast of Scotland dwindle into the fading light, to the accompaniment of the industrious thud of the paddles. Now it was almost dark. She leaned closer towards Felix, seeking comfort from him.

"We should go to bed," Felix said, reaching for her hand and kissing it.

"Not yet."

"You're not cold?"

"Not at all," she said. "Not with my plaid."

She was wrapped in the vast tartan shawl that had become her constant companion ever since Felix's mother had presented it to her. She had learnt how to wind it about her, in true Highland style, and had declared that she would wear it when she had her portrait painted. This had delighted his parents and Felix too, although he suspected his vision of the portrait would differ somewhat from theirs. They probably had in mind a half-length in an oval, and modest attire. For Felix, Eleanor would be painted in full length, sitting in rural glory in the Birks of Pitfeldry, wrapped in the shawl with nothing much more than her chemise under it, her feet bare and her hair unpinned and flowing over her shoulders. He had thought of attempting such a sketch himself, but he did not think his limited skill with the pencil could ever capture the potent charm of the real Eleanor in delicious disordered dress.

"I shall want to go to bed quite soon," Felix said, kissing her hand again, and then her wrist.

"You always want to go to bed," she said, "don't you?"

"Not always," he said, "but often, certainly. Any man would, in the fortunate position of being your husband." Now he folded back her glove and began to stroke her wrist. "And I have happy memories of that cabin. As do you."

It was where they had spent their first night together, a hot-breathed, surprisingly successful adventure. He had been afraid of her innocence, but she had discarded it readily.

"Yes, I do," she said. "But regrettably, I find I am *unwell*," she added, with the last word whispered.

"What?"

"Unwell," she said again quietly.

He would have queried this again, but then he realised what she was implying.

"Oh, I see," he said. "Well, that's a shame, but it's for the best. I was beginning to worry, actually, that –"

"To worry? About what?"

"That –" He hesitated. "That we had been reckless and it would catch up with us. Rather, that I had been reckless, for it is my responsibility and I have been foolish, but I promise you, from now on, I will begin to be more careful. I do not want to endanger your health and ruin everything."

"What do you mean?" she said, twisting out of his embrace and facing him. "What are you talking about? Be more careful? In what respect?"

"When we are..." Now he lowered his own voice, so that the other passengers who remained on deck should not overhear. "Intimate. I will take care that there is no risk of your getting with child."

Even though the light was dim, and her face was shadowed by her bonnet brim, he sensed her surprise.

"Marriage and parenthood are not inevitably linked," he

went on, quietly. "We can spare ourselves the trouble of all that, for a while at least. I certainly don't feel ready for it, and surely you don't?"

"Perhaps I will go in," she said after a moment's silence. "It's getting cold." She stood up, pulling her wrap about her, and said, "Will you find Stevens for me?"

"Yes," he said, also getting up. She went towards the cabin and he went to look for her maid.

Her lack of answer began to nag at him as he searched for Stevens. Had he offended her? Surely he had not. She could not want to be a mother yet. She had never said anything to him to that effect. It had been preying on his own mind that he had been foolish in giving in to temptation as he had done, and the subject was one that ought to be dealt with, sooner rather than later.

He had intended to have a frank and honest conversation with her at the first opportunity about the benefits of avoiding conception. But the appropriate moment had never arisen. From the moment they were first alone together in the carriage, driving from the wedding breakfast to the railway station, he had felt his resolutions evaporate like dew on a fine summer morning. The sheer excitement of being alone with her at last, the possibilities of untrammelled intimacy, had made him drunk and weak. Her beauty, her high spirits and her enthusiasm for all things sensual had made him a slave to congress. How could he speak to her of French gloves or coitus interruptus or any of that clumsy, ugly stuff when all she wanted to do was lie in his arms and return each kiss, each caress? He had never imagined a woman could be as hungry or eager for congress as a man, and yet Eleanor...

Such temptation it had been, and such pleasure. Caution had gone entirely to the wind. But now it was time to be rational, and he felt sure that she would see it, once it was all explained properly to her. Why on earth would she want children so soon, after all?

Having found Stevens and sent her to Eleanor, he took his ease on the deck, elbows on the rail, gazing out into the darkness. Of course, he knew that this idea was not conventional, but neither was Eleanor. She did not think or behave as ordinary women did. She had a rebellious, spirited mind – it was one of the things he adored about her.

Stevens was just leaving as he returned to the cabin. Eleanor was on her knees by the bunk, saying her prayers, which she did every night with child-like sincerity. She had finished just as he was pulling on his nightshirt, and she got up from her knees and climbed into the bottom bunk, without another word.

He picked up his book and wondered if, in light of her indisposition, he ought to climb up into the bunk above. She had curled herself up in a ball, and seemed to be feigning sleep rather than making space for him to join him as usual. He stood there, in a state of indecision, remembering all too vividly that first night alone together in the cabin, and then waking with her in his arms as they steamed into Leith Harbour.

"I'll just read for a while," he said, and climbed up the little ladder. He opened his book – it was an anonymously published novel that he had turned up at one of his favourite booksellers in Edinburgh. It had a peculiar, frank and passionate tone which had charmed him, and the shop man had told him it had caused a great stir at Oxford, for it contained a savage critique of the University and the Church, and many other shocking things besides. Felix had not yet read anything in it that he found remotely scandalous, but he had not got beyond the first few chapters where the hero was still a boy at home, with a beautiful but sickly mother. He was thinking that the mother would not last much longer when he heard Eleanor say, "Felix?"

"Yes?"

"I'm cold," she said.

So he abandoned the novel and got into the bottom bunk with her, and she gratifyingly pressed herself against him, shivering in his arms.

"About what you said earlier," she said. "You did not mean it, did you?"

"Yes," Felix said.

"But," she said, "doesn't the Prayer Book say that marriage was ordained for –"

"Yes, but we don't need to abide by that, do we?"

There was a pause and she said, "Do we not?"

"No, not really," Felix said. "At least not to the letter. When that was written no one had any notion of how procreation might be limited, and perhaps they could not see the benefits of it either, though I am sure there were plenty of women in the past who would dearly liked to have been spared the endless misery of childbearing."

"Is that not immoral?" she said.

"No, not at all. Physical love is an appetite that needs to be satisfied, by both men and women. You have found that for yourself, yes? And now we have the means to limit its consequences. What possible harm is there in that?"

"It is taking pleasure for the sake of it," she said. "And it is interfering with natural law, surely – with what Providence intends! It is not our business to do that."

"Natural law?" he said. "What is that, precisely? And as for interfering, you might say that of vaccination. That has been of the greatest public benefit. Think how many lives have been saved by it!"

"And you are proposing to destroy lives by never allowing them to begin," she threw back. "That is what you are saying."

"No, no, I only think that if we could regulate conception then the lives of many people would be improved immeasurably."

"The lives of men especially," she said, sitting up. "For they would feel freer than ever to seduce women if they knew there would be no consequences to their actions! Yes?"

"Yes," he was forced to concede, admiring how she had gone on the attack. "That might be a result. But one might hope that relations between men and women –"

"And you would not even exist," she went on. "Think of that. You are here, surely, because of the natural consequences of physical love?"

"Yes," he said, "but my not existing is not necessarily a terrible thing in the grand scheme of things. How can I regard my own existence as important?"

"I'm not sure your parents would see it that way. For them you were a gift from God – as much as if you had been their own flesh and blood. Your mother prayed for a miracle and there you were!"

"She said that to you?"

"Yes. And it is a miracle, is it not? For if Lord Rothborough had done as you are suggesting then there would be no Felix Carswell. How can you suggest we meddle like this, Felix? I don't understand."

"Meddle?" said Felix. "It is not meddling. It is behaving rationally."

"I think it is meddling, plain and simple. I cannot agree with what you suggest. It feels absolutely wrong! I'm sorry to disagree with you, but really, it's horrible!"

"It is not," Felix said. "It only feels that way because it is a new idea to you. You must think about it a little more and then you will see it, I'm certain of it."

"Will I?" she said. "How can you be so certain? Do you think my opinions are so weak and changeable?"

"No, of course not, but this is simply common sense! I know you have plenty of that."

"If this is common sense, I would rather be thought silly," she said, lying down again, with her back to him. Due to the tight space in the bunk, she had her face almost pressed against the bulkhead, in her uncomfortable protest.

"I think I will go up again," said Felix after a moment's silence in which he rehearsed various arguments and then put them to one side as being too inflammatory. "We will never get any sleep like this. You can have my blanket if you are cold."

She turned now and regarded him.

"I suppose you had better," she said.

"I would rather not," Felix said. "I'm not sure I can sleep without you near me, Nell, to tell the truth." Now she wriggled round and they lay facing one another. "And I'm sorry my ideas offend you," he said, pushing back a mess of hair that covered her face. He leant forward a little and kissed her forehead, feeling the ache of quickening desire, and at the same time the annoyance that he would not be able to satisfy it.

"Is this our first quarrel?" she said.

"Is it even that?" he said. "No, we shall never have quarrels. Those are for commonplace husbands and wives."

"We will quarrel," she said, touching his cheek. "People always do."

"Not if we are careful."

"If one simply agrees with the other, irrespective of what she really believes? For the sake of peace?" she said.

"It need not come to that. Not if we are honest with each other and agree to disagree, when necessary. With luck it will not be often. If ever."

"But what we just discussed...?" she said.

"I promise I will think about what you said, and you shall think about what I said, and we shall talk again about it, and I dare say it will all seem perfectly straightforward what we do then." As he spoke, he was confident that she would still come around to his point of view, but at the same time he felt ashamed of his promise. He knew he would only be thinking of better ways to refute her arguments. "Does that seem reasonable?"

"Yes," she said. "But you must not imagine I will not be ready to fight you point for point, Mr clever Edinburgh man." This was as stimulating as it was terrifying and he wished again that she was not indisposed. He settled instead for kissing her with some warmth and then pulling her against him, letting the motion of the steamer send them to sleep.

# Chapter Two

"Who could not love an ancient house like this," Emma said, "where every creaking board tells a story?"

"Creaking and sloping," said Giles, squatting down and observing the way that the floor fell away from them. "But beautiful, yes."

"Oh, come and see this, Giles!" Emma exclaimed as she walked into the next room.

He followed her into a large, well-proportioned drawing room. It had panelled walls painted a pale yellow, and a shallow, domed ceiling that was wreathed with garlands of plaster fruit and flowers.

"We could have quite a few couples standing up in here," said Emma from the centre of the room. She dropped a curtsey to an imaginary partner while Giles went about the room tapping the plaster above the panelling. "And there is enough room for waltzing."

"Waltzing?" said Giles. "In the Minster Precincts? You will need permission from the Dean and Chapter."

As he spoke he realised that his words were being strangely amplified and directed.

"I wonder if this is a whispering dome," he said, this time facing the wall and speaking more quietly.

"What was that?" Emma said.

"Go and stand opposite. I think –"

She obediently positioned herself, and he whispered, "Can you hear me?"

She gave a shriek of delight and clapped her hands. Then she turned to the wall and Giles at his wall heard her say: "A wonder! I have heard of these things before, but – oh, how deliciously eerie!"

He saw her shudder, her shawl and flounces shaking.

"I wonder why it was built this way," he murmured into the wall. "It cannot have been an accident."

"Nothing ever can be an accident with you, my love," Emma said to the wall, and then she turned and smiled at him across the room.

"Perhaps," he went on, again to the wall, "it was so that two lovers could talk discreetly?"

"Oh yes, when the match had been forbidden by some stuffy old parent. But love triumphed," she said.

"Love will always triumph," said Giles, and unable to resist any longer, crossed the room to her side, took her hand and kissed it. "You have fallen in love, by the look of it."

"Have you not?" she said.

"I admit to having admired this house for some time. You can see the garden from upstairs at my sister's house, and that little arbour has always intrigued me."

"Yes, I noticed that. Clematis and honeysuckle, and later in the year there is a damask rose on it," she said. "But it is too expensive."

"Yes, it is rather," Giles said, letting go of her hand. He strolled into the adjoining room, a smaller, more old-fashioned parlour, with latticed windows. It was easy to imagine sitting there by the fire on winter evenings.

"Perhaps we should suggest to Mr and Mrs Carswell that they take it," Emma said, following him. "Then we will have some of the pleasure of it, without the responsibility. She would love it, certainly."

"Only because she has no knowledge of practical housekeeping and would be blind to its faults," said Giles.

"Quite," said Emma. "It will be a task to manage such a house as this. I feel my good sense coming on. We should take that villa near Captain Lazenby's. The stabling was better, not to mention the kitchen. Why are you frowning?"

"Did you really like it?"

"It was the right price and something might be done with it. The garden was pleasant – and large."

"The garden was a field," said Giles. "So, did you like it?"

"Not as much as this, but that is not at issue. We have to be practical. And that villa – well, many people would not sniff at such a place, and neither should we in our circumstances."

Yet at the same time, she brushed her hand across the panelling, and the sight of her doing so put Giles at war with himself. The villa on the Exford Road had been built a year ago and had all the latest conveniences. The terms it was to be let on were excellent but it was an ugly, lumpen house of yellow brick and utterly lacking in any sort of character. Watching Emma drifting about Rooke Court, empty of furniture as it was, with layers of dust on every ledge and sill, made him want to give her her heart's desire and more. Seeing how she had willingly resigned herself to the ugly and the sensible for the sake of practicality and economy was depressing. He loved her common sense, but at the same time he wished she did not have to exercise it.

"I'm sorry," she went on. "We should never have come. I gave in to temptation and curiosity. We cannot take this house. To ask such a price for it when there is so much wrong is frankly insolent of the owner, don't you think?"

"Somewhat, yes," said Giles, who was making rapid mental calculations, wondering what he could sacrifice to make the house possible. "But it is a good address, unlike Exford Road. It strikes me that Lord Milburne's mother ought not to live in Exford Road."

"If you are worried about his being ashamed to visit me there," she said, "do not. He probably will not visit me at all."

She said it carelessly enough, but Giles sensed the unease in it.

"He will if I have anything to do with it," said Giles. "Has he said that to you? Did you have another letter from him?

What did he say?"

"Perhaps I am only reading between the lines. He did not say so in so many words. It was just rather cool – at least it seemed to me. I suppose he is preoccupied with his reading party and his Oxford friends, and I am a mere dot on his vast horizon these days. Which is as it should be."

"No," said Giles. "He owes you too much for that. Let me write to him."

She laid her hand on his arm, and shook her head.

"You know what he is like," she said. "He will get there in his own good time, I am sure of it. A lecture from you –"

"It would not be a lecture," said Giles. "You know that. I would be civil."

"Yes, but in his present state he will perceive anything from you as the heavy hand of the patriarch on his collar. He will resent it, and we must not stoke that fire."

"He may resent me all he likes," Giles said, "but I will not have him treating you unkindly. That I cannot accept."

"It does not hurt me so much," she said.

"I don't believe you," he said.

"Our paths are diverging," she said. "That is all." She walked away and gazed about the room again, and sighed. "Now, I suppose we should go and tell Mr Hopkins that we shall not take this house."

"He might consider putting the price down if we pointed out some of the faults."

"Are you sure?"

"It's worth trying, surely?" said Giles. "At the moment he takes us for besotted fools."

"Which we are," she said.

"Possibly," said Giles. "But I cannot face the thought of that blasted heath in Exford Road for a garden. I like the thought of my own mulberries, not to mention apples and walnuts. And I can walk to work from here." He took out his notebook. "Now, what did you say was wrong with it? Let us make a list. You said there was damp in the attics, didn't you?"

"You never fail to surprise me, Major Vernon," said Emma, smiling.

"I don't like to give up without a fight," said Giles.

They made their list and went downstairs to speak to Mr Hopkins. They had left him waiting in the large, stone-flagged entrance hall that was deliciously cool even on such a warm morning. However, he was no longer there, but had gone out into the garden and was standing at the end of one of the paths, looking up at the façade. He had been joined by a tall, white-haired gentleman of impressive appearance whom Giles recognised.

"Who is that?" said Emma.

"That is Sir Morton Hurrell. I have seen him on the bench from time to time."

"Oh! As in Hurrell of Hurrell Place? I have heard a little about that family. Hurrell Place is supposed to be the most magnificent property. What does he want with Rooke Court?"

"Perhaps he wants a house in town," said Giles.

"I am sure he can afford it better than we can," said Emma. "He has a proprietorial look, don't you think? We have already lost it. He has outbid us! How wicked of Mr Hopkins not to say. He did not say there was anyone else interested. Really!"

She swept out into the garden and, before Giles could stop her, went up to Mr Hopkins.

"Mr Hopkins," she said, "it was my understanding that – please excuse my interruption, sir," she added, turning to Sir Morton. "But you should know that we are also interested in this property, and that perhaps Mr Hopkins has misled you, as he has misled us!"

"Oh no, ma'am, no, not at all," said Mr Hopkins. "This is the owner of the property, Sir Morton Hurrell. He wanted to meet you. When I said Major Vernon was looking over the property –"

Emma flushed, and Giles felt her agony.

"Then forgive me, Mr Hopkins, will you?" she said. "It is simply that this house... I never saw such a beautiful house," she went on. "And I could not bear that anyone else should get it. And please forgive me, Sir Morton, for casting you as an interloper in your own property!" With which she dropped him a graceful curtsey, and looked up at the distinguished old gentleman with a winning smile. The effect, with her blushes, was delightful.

Sir Morton took her hand, and made an equally courtly bow.

"Mrs Maitland, I understand?" he said. "Of Woodville Park?"

"My son's property," she said.

"I hear you have been active there, in his minority."

"One does what one can," said Emma.

"That land is a challenge, I should think. I heard that you began an extensive drainage scheme."

"Oh dear, what a reputation to have!" said Emma.

"Then forgive me, ma'am, for mentioning it," said Sir Morton.

"Necessity, sir," said Emma, "forces us along paths that we were not bred to take. I merely took the best advice available to me. Lord Rothborough's man, Mr Tranter, was the real force behind it."

"There was no criticism intended, ma'am, none at all. I had heard only good things. That a mother should act so decisively for the welfare of her son," he said. "It is noble."

"Thank you, sir."

Now Sir Morton looked at Giles, and putting out his hand, said, "Major Vernon, I presume? You are to be congratulated. A sensible wife is a prize above rubies."

"Oh really, Sir Morton," said Emma. "When you have just seen me blunder so, how can you say I am sensible?"

"That was no blunder, ma'am, that was the action of a

lioness. Yes, Major Vernon, congratulations, indeed! When are you to be married?"

"In September," said Giles.

Sir Morton took Emma's hand again and raised it to his lips. "Ah, that we had met sooner, ma'am –"

"I am glad we have met," said Emma, "in this most charming garden! How can you bear to let such a place?"

"I am no townsman," said Sir Morton. "But it is a fine house, and I'm anxious to have some good tenants."

"Of course," said Emma. "But it is..." She glanced at Giles, giving him his cue.

"A little more than I can afford," said Giles. "Unfortunately."

"That's why I am here," said Sir Morton. "You are exactly the sort of tenant I am looking for."

"That's flattering," said Giles. "But the terms as they stand, I regret to say, are beyond my means. Especially since there is a certain amount of work to be done." Sir Morton nodded. "For example, the plaster in the scullery and the kitchen..."

"A small job, really, sir," said Hopkins. "It is nothing."

"I fear that ceiling might come down at the slightest provocation," said Emma, "if you will forgive me saying so, Sir Morton? We had the same thing at Woodville in the south parlour. It was distressing, but I know the signs now. I took the liberty of standing on a chair, and that ominous bulge in the right-hand corner – it feels spongy to the touch. Not that I would touch it again, for it is likely to come straight down. This dry weather gives a false picture. May I show you?"

"Certainly, ma'am. Please?" said Sir Morton, and offered his arm.

Together they went back into the house, followed by Giles and a flustered-looking Hopkins, who was clearly on a percentage and did not wish the rent put down. But Emma now had command of the situation, and was taking Sir Morton step by step and showing him the dangerous defects of his fine old house. She did this with an artful mixture of flattery and humility.

"Major Vernon and I were wondering, for we do like the house very much," Emma was now saying, "if an improving lease might be of any interest to you?"

"An improving lease, ma'am?" said Sir Morton. "That is an idea, certainly."

This was the first Giles had heard of it, but he was prepared to let Emma's improvisational talents win the day for them.

"It would depend for how long," Sir Morton said. "Ten years, Major Vernon? Would you undertake that?"

"At what cost?"

Sir Morton looked about him for a long moment, considering.

"Seventy-five guineas a year?"

"Goodness," said Emma. This was a considerable reduction on the advertised price.

"On condition that you see to the repairs," said Sir Morton, "in a satisfactory manner."

"But done to our taste?" Emma said.

"Very sharp, ma'am, yes, to your taste. Major Vernon, what do you say?"

Seventy-five was ridiculously cheap, but Giles had no idea what the cost of the repairs would be, and how much would need to be done at once to make it habitable.

"That is extremely generous, and of course tempting," he said. "However, might I have an hour or two to think it over? I am not sure of the liabilities yet."

"Take as much time as you wish, Major Vernon," said Sir Morton. "It is not something to be rushed into. That is my offer, though. Let me know when you decide."

"Thank you, sir," said Emma.

"A pleasure, ma'am," he said. "And if you do take it, you

must let me come and drink tea here when I am in Northminster."

"That is a delightful prospect," said Emma. "We can discuss drainage at length."

Sir Morton laughed at that and said, "In fact, I have a better proposition. Will you both come to dine and sleep at Hurrell Place tomorrow night? It is short notice, I appreciate, but we are expecting Lord Rothborough and his daughter. I think you know them?"

~

"What a wonderful specimen," said Emma when they were walking back across the Precincts. "A fine old English gentleman of the best sort."

"And an incorrigible flirt," said Giles. "I shall have to be careful."

"Oh no, not at all," said Emma. "That was all my doing. I bewitched him."

"With your talk of green mould and warped casements?"

"Yes, quite."

"A remarkable achievement," Giles said.

"So shall you take it?" she said.

"How much is a new kitchen ceiling?" he said.

"I shall look into it. More here than in the country, I suppose. Then we can decide."

"But you would like me to take it?"

"I have a good receipt for apricot jam. I should like to have a chance to use it. Did you see that tree?"

Giles nodded. "The plums looked promising too – we might risk it for that alone." He took her hand and kissed it.

"But we should sleep on it," Emma said.

"Sleeping at Hurrell Place will hardly help," said Giles. "It will only tempt us further."

"But how pleasant to be asked," said Emma. "I am beginning to enjoy the consequences of your consequence, Major Vernon."

"Oh, that was all your doing. You have the power of enchantment over him."

"I had better reign that in for the sake of Lady Hurrell," she said. "If there is a Lady Hurrell. For isn't he a widower?"

"I think you are right."

"Yes – I remember what I heard about her now – she was supposed to be a great beauty and an even greater wit. It was a tremendous love affair, apparently, for she had no fortune. And now he has lost her – oh, poor man!"

"I think he has lost quite a few of his children as well," Giles said, at which Emma winced.

"That, of all things..." she said, and then shook her head.

They had reached the gate to the Treasurer's House, where Giles took his leave of her with a discreet kiss. He watched her go along the stone path, her summer muslin fluttering about her, and her air purposeful. She would go and make lists and plans, he knew. It was true that Rooke Court would be a challenge for them, and perhaps a great expense, but the thought of coaxing it back to life was irresistible.

He walked back to the Northern Office and returned just as two large boxes were being delivered. They were addressed to F.J. Carswell MD, and bore the imprimatur of a bookseller in Edinburgh. He had them taken down to Carswell's laboratory and went up to his own office, amused at this herald of Carswell's imminent return. It was clear that there had been time on his wedding journey for extensive shopping.

Inspector Rollins was waiting for him. The most pressing business of the day was the circumstances of a fire at a cotton warehouse three days previously. Mercifully no one had been injured, but the fire had caused the loss of many hundreds of pounds of stock, for which the owner was apparently well insured. There was nothing overt to suggest that the fire was begun deliberately, but Captain Lazenby had asked him to pursue the matter because it had emerged that the owner, a Mr Howard, had experienced some recent business difficulties, and no one had yet been able to identify how exactly the building had caught fire. So it was this puzzle that lay on his desk, and he was glad to know that Carswell would soon be back at work to help him with it.

# Chapter Three

"Welcome back! You look well for your travels," Giles said, seeing Carswell climb out of a conspicuously new carriage that had drawn up outside the Infirmary. "I'm sorry to have to pull you from your bed at such an hour," Giles added as they shook hands. It was a little after six in the morning.

"What's happened?" Carswell said.

"There's been a serious fire in Jebb Street. Mr Harper needs your assistance – but I wanted to brief you first. It started just after midnight as far as I can gather, but it's under control now, thank God."

"How many injured?"

"One family at Number 7 have taken the brunt of it – but it would have been much worse had the young man from the bank offices next door not run in and got them all out. Unfortunately he's in a poor way, but Mr Harper has hopes of his pulling through. He wants your opinion."

"I'd better go in, then," Carswell said, starting up the steps.

"I'll be in Jebb Street," he said. "If you can spare a moment later to look over the scene with me, I'd be grateful."

"Do you suspect arson?" Carswell said.

"Four nights ago, Hale's cotton warehouse went up in circumstances that are not fully clear yet. We have to ask that question, given there is another cotton warehouse in Jebb Street."

"I'll be there when I can," Carswell said, and disappeared into the building.

Jebb Street was only a few minutes' walk away from the Infirmary. As Giles walked towards it, the air began to fill with smoke and cinders. Considering how warm and still the night had been, it was something of a miracle that the fire had been contained so swiftly, and with relatively little damage. A brisk wind could have changed everything. The sluggish air had saved a great many lives and much property. Even as it was, the fire insurance company and the Constabulary were still hard at work, saturating the smouldering remains of Number 7. It was a curious and depressing sight.

The ancient and timbered house seemed to have sustained most of the damage, while the buildings on either side – the house to the left at Number 9 and the Bank office to the right, at Number 5 – showed scarcely any signs of it. It might be that as the morning light came on, some scorching would be more evident.

At first glance, however, it was tempting to assume that the fire had begun at Number 7, probably as the result of a commonplace household accident – an upturned lamp or an ill-made fire. Yet in the light of the recent fire in Hale's Warehouse, the presence of a cotton warehouse at Number 3, two doors down from this fresh conflagration, could not be ignored.

Having ascertained from the Brigade Superintendent that it was safe for him to approach, he went to the door of the warehouse. The front door was firmly locked, as he would have expected, but the handle was hot to the touch. Just as he was trying it, a man called out behind him, "You there, what do you want?"

Giles turned and saw a man striding over to him. Clearly agitated, he had a bunch of keys in his hand.

"This is your property, sir?" Giles said.

"Yes. And you are?"

"Major Vernon from the Constabulary, Mr...?"

"Cartwright. I only just heard. I live out at Barbury but you'd think the company would have sent someone given the money I put down for insurance –" He gazed up at the façade of his warehouse. "But it looks sound enough, thank God."

"After what happened at Hale's the other day?" Giles said.

"Thank the Lord, yes," said Cartwright. "That was a business. Do they know why that started yet?"

"It has still to be determined. Perhaps this case might help us. Do you have a night watchman, Mr Cartwright?" said Giles.

"Of course!" said Cartwright, unlocking the door.

"He may be a useful witness," said Giles, following him into the darkened building.

"He should be about," said Cartwright. "He has a hut in the back yard. I wonder he didn't send someone to me, come to it! You cannot trust anyone to do what's right these days."

While Cartwright sought out the watchman, Giles lit a candle stub in a lantern to augment the grey light of dawn, and looked about him. There were no immediate signs of fire, though the air was thick with smoke.

"Noakes! Noakes! Where are you?" Cartwright was shouting in the yard, as Giles climbed upstairs.

It seemed to him that the smoke was far thicker here, and he went warily. This was where the stock was kept – rows of raw cotton bales: a tinderbox that had, by some good grace of the fates, remained untouched by the fingers of the fire. It could be, he supposed, orientating himself to the street, that the solidity of the bank building had protected the warehouse and that the fire after all had its origin in Number 7.

Yet Cartwright was still shouting for his watchman, and it seemed strange to Giles that he should not be about at such a crucial time.

Then he noticed the form of an old fireplace in the wall, hidden behind a pile of hemp sacking, clearly not in use. However, it was the wall adjacent to the bank, and Giles wondered where the chimney went, and indeed how thick the wall that divided the properties was. The warehouse building seemed about the age of Rooke Court, where Emma had given a fine demonstration to Sir Morten of the flimsiness of such walls, inviting him to poke his fingers into a crumbling partition.

He pushed away the sacking and crouched by the old hearthstone, lighting another candle to help him see better, convinced now that this chimney was the source of the smoke that was making him cough and splutter. He was not mistaken. He could feel the heat; venturing to look up the chimney, he saw that its contents were glowing ominously, for it had been stuffed at some point with waste material.

He backed away, taking a scant moment to glance at the base of the chimney where the fire would have been laid. There was a heap of cinders, the remains of a material he could not at once identify. The chimney made an alarming crack and groan as if from pain at its smouldering innards, and he judged it best to get out of there as soon as he could.

The quickest way out was down an external staircase leading to an irregularly shaped yard, where the watchman's hut lay suspiciously empty. Cartwright met him at the foot of the stair, anxious to go up.

"You can't, sir," said Giles. "There is a blocked chimney burning away up there. We need to get the brigade in here at once before your stock goes up."

Cartwright needed nothing more to persuade him, and went running back to the street. Giles was about to follow him but noticed a scrap of white cotton material lying on the floor of the yard: a carefully cut strip, like a ribbon. He picked it up; it was greasy with lamp oil.

~

"So you think the fire was set deliberately?" Felix said,

examining the strip of cotton.

"It looked to be the case," said Major Vernon, "as far as I could see in all that smoke. My examination was necessarily rather cursory. Perhaps once the fire is out, we will get a better idea."

"Perhaps," said Felix.

"And there may be witnesses. The young man from the bank – how is he doing?"

"Not well. We are trying a new treatment involving the irrigation of burns, but it may come to nothing. He is very weak."

"Do we know who he is?"

"Yes, the old woman from Number 7, Mrs Sedley, whom he brought out of her house, says he is Frederick Pierce, the son of one of the bank's directors."

"And what was he doing there at midnight?" Major Vernon said.

"Do you think he may have something to do with it?" Felix said.

"It's very late to be at work."

"Not for you," said Felix.

"True," said Major Vernon.

At this moment a lady and gentleman came into the entrance hall of the Infirmary.

"My son, Frederick," the man said, "I am told he has been brought here."

"Mr Pierce?" Felix said.

"Yes, and this is my wife. What has happened? Is he –"

"Perhaps you would come this way," Felix said. "Mr Harper will explain everything."

"Yes, yes, of course." Mr Pierce looked at Major Vernon. "Major Vernon, is it not? Is this police business?"

"I'm afraid so," said Major Vernon. "But that can wait. You must talk to Mr Harper. My best wishes, sir, and to you, ma'am."

Mr Harper had the gift of a supremely reassuring manner, but in the circumstances there was little comfort for Mr and Mrs Pierce. The grave extent of the injuries could not be concealed, and although the young man was not conscious, there was no serenity in his oblivion. The pain of his wounds made him thresh about as if in a fever; the constant cooling and dampening of the affected areas would no doubt have a good effect later, but in the short term the scene was distressing. His breathing was also painfully laboured, for he had undoubtedly inhaled a great deal of smoke. As his mother sat holding his hand, Mr Harper said, "If he had not acted as he did, it is clear that the occupants of the house would all have perished. He seems to have gone in quite without any concern for his own safety – only for the welfare of others. You have much to be proud of."

"That is so typical of Fred," said Mrs Pierce. "And although I know it is selfish and wrong of me to say it, I wish he hadn't been so brave." She seemed to be on the verge of a complete breakdown, and then she got control of herself, rose from the bedside, and went to Mr Harper. "What can I do? My daughter and I, we are ready to do what we can. I have some experience in nursing."

"Then you are more than welcome to stay, ma'am," said Mr Harper. "Your presence will be excellent for him."

"John," she said to her husband, taking off her bonnet, "will you go home and get Margaret? I suppose you will have to go into the bank, though –"

"Yes, yes, I will," said Mr Pierce.

"What was he doing there so late? That is what I do not understand," she said, turning back to the bedside. "I assumed he had gone out to see Mr Gray, when he was not home for supper. He did say something about going there. What was he doing at the bank?"

"I asked him to stay and look over some figures for me, for some companies we were looking at as prospective investments for our depositors," Mr Pierce said. "I never expected him to stay so late. I expected him home for supper, of course, but you know how conscientious he is, my dear." He turned to the others. "Frederick has a brilliant actuarial mind, you see, and once he is engaged on an analysis, he will not let it go."

"Oh, my darling," Mrs Pierce was murmuring at her son. "How you do like to please everyone, how much good you like to do, and now this..."

"Mr Gray, is that the clergyman at Raythorpe?" said Mr Harper. "The famous cricketer?"

"He has taken Fred up," said Mrs Pierce. "Fred is a good cricket player, but it is certainly not just about the cricket. Mr Gray is forming an association for all the young men in the city, a sort of guild, to encourage them not to fall into vice, but to do good works, educate themselves and help one another, and so forth. He had picked Fred out as one of his officers."

"I am not sure I like Gray's ideas. It all seems a shade too radical for me. But..." Mr Pierce sighed heavily and went to the door. "I will go and get Margaret. And I shall be back as soon as I can. I do not know what I shall find at the bank, though!"

~

The smouldering chimney of Cartwright's warehouse had been successfully doused by the time Giles returned to the scene, but they had almost run out of water in the process. The river was low because of the season and there was little to spare. The exhausted brigade men were staggering about, waiting to be dismissed, while those who worked in Jebb Street arrived to find everything changed. Giles spoke to the chief bank clerk who showed him upstairs where there was some damage to an empty storeroom in the attic. They were just examining the extent of this when Mr Pierce arrived.

"It's a miracle, sir," said the clerk, "when you think what might have happened. But how is Master Fred?"

"I cannot say. It does not look good," said Pierce, looking around him.

"I shall pray for him, sir," said the clerk. "But he is in good hands at the Infirmary. They say that Mr Harper is the best in the country. We are lucky to have him here!"

"Yes, certainly," said Mr Pierce. "You had better get things in order downstairs, Brown. Business as usual, if you please!"

"Yes, of course, sir." The clerk went away, and Pierce looked over the damage.

"It was a near thing," he said at length.

"Yes, given that the fire seems to have been started on the other side of this wall," said Giles.

"And you think it was started deliberately?"

"It's possible," said Giles. "What do you know of Cartwright and his business dealings?"

"He is perfectly sound, as far as I know," said Pierce. "He is not a customer of ours, though, but I have not heard any complaints about him."

"He had a watchman called Noakes whom we have not been able to locate. Do you have any knowledge of him?"

"Yes, I did see him about. A dirty, low person. Not one to whom I should have given such a responsible job, but I suppose he was cheap, and a man like Cartwright will always be thinking of his margins. Cotton is such a volatile business."

"Unlike banking?" Giles said, thinking of the recent provincial bank failures which had caused great alarm and distress.

"There are banks and there are banks, Major Vernon," said Mr Pierce. "And Wytton's Bank is of the soundest sort. We cannot even be touched by the hand of fire, you see!" he added, tapping the scorched plaster. "Your money is safe with us."

"Do you know why your son was here so late?"

"He was looking over some figures for me. He is a conscientious boy, unfortunately. I wish I had not asked him to do it now, as you may imagine."

# Chapter Four

Noakes was easily found, not far away. There was no sense of flight or concealment. He was heavily intoxicated and in no state to be interviewed. Major Vernon had him put into a cell to sober up.

"The barmaid said he was being free with his money and that he had a pocketful of shillings," Major Vernon explained to Felix. "He doesn't now – you can only wonder how much he drank."

"Or someone filched the rest off him," said Felix, who had come from the Infirmary to join the Major at the Northern Office.

"More than likely. The barmaid herself, perhaps? However, the point is that he was not accustomed to having such largesse."

"Then it was a bribe to make him stay away?"

"It does seem that way. In the meantime, Coxe is looking over Cartwright's books. He was more than willing to surrender them to us, which suggests he has nothing to hide. I don't think he has any part in the fire, but I may be wrong. I am told that account books can conceal all sorts of interesting situations. How is young Pierce doing?"

"You won't be able to interview him for some time – if ever."

"From what the other witnesses said," Major Vernon said, "he showed extraordinary courage. There is no doubt that all the occupants of that house would be dead if he had not acted as he did."

"And there is no clearer picture yet of why the fire took hold there?"

"The building was old and in a poor state compared to its neighbour the bank. My feeling is that a spark, or a piece of burning matter from the chimney fire at Cartwright's warehouse – perhaps one of those oil-soaked ribbons – was blown across and landed on the roof of Number 7 where it flourished unchecked. Does that sound plausible?"

"So entirely accidental?"

"Yes, in the sense that Number 7 was not the target for our fire-setter."

"Who intended to burn down Cartwright's?"

"Perhaps," Major Vernon said. "It seems the likely target, but why? If Cartwright is solvent, what benefit is there for him? Every bale of cotton in that warehouse is spoken for, he told me. A fire would have been a disaster for him."

"Then he has an enemy. An old employee with a grudge?"

"That may well be. Fire-setting often goes hand in hand with revenge. Greedy farmers find their hayricks going up when they cheat their labourers of what is due to them. We shall have to look into that. And then there is the matter of Wytton's Bank. Given where the fire was started, we cannot ignore the possibility that the bank may have been the target, not the warehouse."

"Or it may be that it is simply a coincidence, and the easiest available place to set the fire," Felix pointed out. "Have you heard a rumour about Wytton's? With all these banks going under, I suppose it is a question that must be asked."

"I have not," said Major Vernon, "and that will not be our first area of investigation, but it is worth bearing in mind. I'm still curious about what young Mr Pierce was doing in the building so late – his father tells me he was doing some work for him."

"Mrs Pierce was wondering about that too," Felix said. "And Mr Pierce said the same thing to her. But he seemed a little confounded, to tell you the truth."

"It won't hurt to enquire a little more closely about what exactly he was doing," Major Vernon said.

"But in the first instance this is a grudge gone wrong?" Felix said. "Executed by someone reasonably competent, but not entirely so?"

"And someone unlucky," said Major Vernon. "That may help us a great deal, for either they may attempt to do it again, or when the full story of the damage gets about, their conscience may get the better of them. If they hear that a man is dying in the Infirmary it may bring them to their senses. I'll have Tom O'Brien put out the details in The Bugle."

Felix nodded.

"And you should go home," Major Vernon went on. "Mrs Carswell will be wondering what has become of you."

~

Felix arrived at Hawksby, which did not yet feel like home. One night's sleep there in a strange bed, with nothing yet unpacked let alone arranged to his satisfaction, could not qualify it as such; but as Felix climbed out of the carriage and looked up at the commodious white-walled house, he felt the pleasure of return. Eleanor considered the house woefully ugly and lacking in any romance, and he had been inclined to agree with her, but there was much to be said for comfort and convenience, especially after such a morning.

An enquiry of a servant whose name and face he did not yet recognise told him his wife was in the tea-house in the garden. He made his way there, remembering it well from one of his previous, strictly-supervised courtship visits. He and Eleanor had taken shelter there for as long as they dared, stealing kisses and a little more. That she was there today filled him with pleasure, and the sight of her, sitting on the long bench under the thatched eaves, made him run towards her, calling out that he was back again.

"I have a full two hours," he said, sitting down beside her. "And then I must go back."

"Only two hours?" she said, laying down her book.

"One hundred and twenty minutes," he said, and gathered her into his arms and kissed her. "How are you feeling? I hope I didn't disturb you too much when I left this morning. Did you get back to sleep?"

"Yes, I did. I am only just up. I feel very... oh, this business is wretched, Felix – it is so unfair what women are made to suffer!"

"It certainly is," said Felix. "But in a day or two more you will be free of it."

"Yes, but it is called the curse for a reason. It makes one feel so... stupid. I so wanted to ride."

"You could drive me back to Northminster later," said Felix, "perhaps? Those new ponies of yours could do with a showing."

"Perhaps," she said, with a smile.

"What are you reading?"

"Oh, your shocking anonymous novel."

"What do you make of it?"

"I'm not sure."

"I'm hoping it will be extremely scandalous," said Felix, taking it from her and beginning to look through it.

"You are wicked," she said. "I don't think it can possibly be that sort of scandalous, or that bookseller in Edinburgh would never have dreamt of stocking it."

"What a pity," said Felix, and threw the book down. "Do you remember that afternoon when we were last here?"

"I do," she said.

"And now we can stay here as long as we like and quite alone," he said, stroking her cheek. "Think of that! And one day when you are better, then we will do exactly what we wanted to do then..." He finished by kissing her.

"Yes, you are wicked," she said.

"So are you," he said, and kissed her again. "But since we are married, it does not matter. We are absolved!"

"I am not so sure," she said, disentangling herself from his arms a little. "Not if we proceed as you would like. It seems so wrong, Felix. I have been thinking so hard about it, and I cannot..." Then she pressed against him once more and sighed.

"Give it a little more time," said Felix. "When you are well again, it will seem clearer." He felt very confident of this.

"You must think I'm such a fool," she said.

"No, no, never. I just think we have a lot of nonsense crammed into us by society and it is difficult to get rid of sometimes."

"If it is truly nonsense?"

"It is," Felix said. "Believe me."

She straightened and gazed at him.

"I will try," she said. "I promise."

"And you will drive me into town after lunch?"

She nodded and smiled. "Why not? That will annoy Mama excessively!"

# Chapter Five

"Another early breakfast, Mr Carswell?" said Lady Blanchfort the next morning at six. She had come into the dining room, and found him at his coffee and bacon. He staggered up from his seat, rather astonished by the sight of her. She was wearing a green silk dressing gown, her hair loose and flowing over her shoulders, unadorned by a cap, and in her arms was a large, long-haired marmalade cat, with a distinctive white ruff. "No, no, please don't get up!"

"I'm needed at the Infirmary," he said, sitting down again. "And I'm taking over Mr Peterson's duties so that he and his family can take some leave."

"Oh yes, I remember now," said Lady Blanchfort, dropping the cat onto the floor. "It is a rude return for you both."

"I'm glad to be back," Felix said, with perfect honesty. "There is a lot to be done."

"Very commendable," said Lady Blanchfort. "Many men in your position would succumb to idleness. May I join you?"

"Yes, of course," Felix said, surprised at her conciliatory manner.

"I take it Nell is breakfasting in her room," said Lady Blanchfort.

"She is indisposed," said Felix. The cat had now padded up to his chair and was determined to jump onto his lap.

"As she was for most of yesterday," said Lady Blanchfort. "I take it this is – you will forgive my frankness – that regular condition experienced by women?"

"Yes," Felix said.

"That is just as well," she said, pouring herself a cup of

tea. "She is still so young."

"Quite," Felix said, most surprised that she should share his opinion. The cat was now on his lap, waving his tail in Felix's face and sniffing at his empty plate.

"Oh, excuse me, sir," said Felix, lifting him off and putting him back on the floor.

"I hope you do not mind him," said Lady Blanchfort.

"No, he is magnificent. It is just that his claws are a little sharp."

"I will clip them. Forgive me. He and I have become rather good friends while you were away. He wandered in from the farmyard and is so handsome that I have let him become lord of all he surveys." She bent down and picked him up again. "Have I not, Byron?"

"Byron?" said Felix with a laugh. "That is quite a name."

"I know – it is foolish, perhaps, but I thought he had a touch of the Corsair about him," said Lady Blanchfort. "But please do say if you find him objectionable. I do not want you to feel that you are not master here. You must tell me all your quirks and fancies so that we can bend to them."

"Should I be encouraged in that?" he said. "And really, you should not have to trouble yourself when –" He shrugged and got up from the table. Byron jumped from his mistress' lap and came to wind himself about Felix's legs.

Felix might have said that it was Eleanor's business to make his tea to his liking and see to his slippers and his shirts, but she had not shown any inclination so far. And if she were not there, who would order the dinner or indeed see to his breakfast? That Eleanor would think of these things seemed most unlikely.

"I should go," he said.

She nodded, and then suddenly got up from the table and followed him to the door, where she gently caught his arm.

"Excuse me," she said, "it is only that Byron has –" And she reached out to brush some cat hair from his lapels, before stopping abruptly, as if conscious she had been overfamiliar.

"Thank you," he said, but she had turned away to scold the cat.

~

At Constabulary Headquarters, Felix was presented with the usual ragbag of ailments and injuries to deal with, both among the constables and the occupants of the cells. In the latter, he was called to examine a woman, Agnes Williams, who had assaulted her lover and several other men in a pub brawl. She had been committed to the cells to cool off. She was heavily pregnant and had been complaining loudly of labour pains since the small hours. The duty sergeant had taken this for a ruse, for it had happened many times before that female prisoners faked the symptoms of labour to secure their liberty. Felix began to examine her – no easy task, for she was wary of him – and soon found she was in labour after all. It did not look as if it would be a simple delivery – he could not detect a heartbeat for the child – so he decided to take her to the Infirmary, and supervise the delivery there.

His suspicions proved right. The child was dead in the womb and he was tasked with the miserable business of removing it as safely as he could. By this time, Mrs Williams had lost what little command of her emotions she had left, and was fiercely resistant to his help, screaming at the sight of the knife. She had no confidence in anyone's opinion, certain that her strong pains meant the child was well, and that time would do its work as with her other children.

"I'll not have you meddling! You will kill it, sure as sure!" she said, pushing him violently away, as he attempted to help her.

"I'm sorry to say the child is dead already!" Felix said,

with as much grace as he could manage. "And you will be too if you don't let me help you."

It would have been better if he could have knocked her out, or perhaps, as he had read in some cases, mesmerized her into submission. In the end, they had to resort to restraints, and a large measure of brandy. She lay there, howling and bellowing more loudly than anyone could have imagined possible in such circumstances, and no doubt putting the fear of God and the Devil into every other patient in the building. She was only silenced by the sight of the dead child which Felix had, due to its small size, been able to bring out intact. She demanded to hold it, so he had the restraints removed while he delivered the placenta (which mercifully presented no complications) and allowed her to take the child. However, Mrs Fletcher, the matron, was certain she would try to run away with the little corpse and that such maternal sentiment should not be indulged.

"Just makes it harder for them, sir," she said.

"Five minutes, then take it from her," said Felix, feeling sick as he said it.

"I want her christened!" screamed Mrs Williams. "I want a parson!"

Felix left on this pretext, glad to get out of the room. He always found himself unequal to such cases. He was attempting to compose himself in the passageway, his hands still sticky with blood, when a giant of a man, fashionably dressed in loose pale linen riding clothes, a soft straw hat and a turned-down collar tied with a jaunty red kerchief, came striding along towards him.

"Are you Mr Carswell?" the man said. "I was told I would find you here."

"Yes, but I am busy, as you can see," said Felix, holding up his hands to him.

"I understand, sir. Henry Gray at your service. I have come in to visit Mr Fred Pierce."

"Gray?" said Felix. "You are a clergyman?"

"Yes," said Gray.

"Will you baptise a stillborn?" Felix said, indicating the door. He was not sure that this was an orthodox procedure, but Gray did not look like an orthodox clergyman. He looked like a progressive and prosperous farmer.

"Of course," Gray said, and sailed in ahead of Felix.

If he was shocked by what he saw, he gave no sign of it. Instead, he went straight to the bedside, put his hand on the woman's shoulder and fixed his gaze on her as if there were no one else in the room. Astonishingly, the woman gazed back at him, as if enraptured. This was the sort of mesmerism that Felix had been wishing for earlier.

"My name is Gray, and I am a priest," he said in a soft voice. "What name will you give her?" he said.

"Mary-Anne," said the woman, still looking up at him. Meekly, she offered up the child, and he took the little form into his arms.

"A cup of water, if you please, nurse," he said, and then, having been given it, he poured the water over the child's head and said, "Mary-Anne, I baptise thee in the name of the Father, and of the Son, and of the Holy Ghost. Amen." He handed the child back to the mother, folding the cloth around it more closely, carefully covering her face. Taking a prayer book from his pocket and quickly finding the place he wanted, he went down on his knees and said, "Let us pray! O, Almighty God with whom do live the spirits of just men, made perfect, after they are delivered from their earthly prisons, we humbly commend the soul of this thy servant, our dear sister, into thy hands, as into the hands of a faithful Creator."

Are you a faithful Creator? Felix thought. He had bowed his head from habit, rather than conviction, and although the words were comforting and familiar, he struggled with them as he always did. The brutal tragedy of what had preceded this, from the sight of the blood-stained straw in the woman's cell to the perfect tiny feet of the corpse, could not be washed away unquestioningly in a tide of divine love. He wished for a moment that Eleanor could have seen it. Then she would have understood what he meant. But perhaps that was too severe a lesson for her.

He noticed that Mrs Williams was shaking violently now, mostly from shock, and he took up a blanket and draped it about her shoulders, as Gray finished the prayers. She flinched slightly at his touch but allowed him to do it.

"Get her some good mutton broth, Mrs Fletcher; get her clean and comfortable, and give her some laudanum," he said. "And let her keep the child with her as long as she sees fit."

Mrs Fletcher frowned at him.

"If you say so, sir," she said.

Gray followed him into the passageway.

"A sad case," he said.

"I found her in the cells at the Constabulary. She took a broken gin bottle to her husband in The Fox and Grapes last night. I think he might have kicked her in the stomach, given the bruising on her abdomen. We will need to get hold of him."

"You think the assault killed the child?" Gray asked.

"It's possible. I'll know when I have done a post-mortem. Do you want some coffee, Mr Gray, or perhaps some whisky?"

"Whisky?" said Gray with a smile. "Certainly."

He took Gray to his narrow slot of a room and sent for some coffee and hot water.

"Excuse me, won't you?" Felix said, pulling off his shirt and starting to scrub himself.

"Of course."

"The whisky is on the shelf there. Help yourself."

"Thank you," said Gray, and proceeded to pour out two drams. "I am glad to meet you at last. I have heard a great deal about you."

"That's always alarming," Felix said, pulling his shirt back on.

"Not at all, in your case. All good, I assure you. Slainte!" Gray held up his cup. "You are just back from your wedding journey, I believe?"

"There are no secrets in Northminster," Felix said.

"Forgive me," said Gray. "Mr Harper mentioned it. May I offer you both my best wishes! The crown of matrimony is a glorious thing, is it not? And now I have met you, you and your wife must come and dine with us. It is an easy road between Hawksby and Raythorpe, especially at this time of year. We are neighbours."

"Yes, I suppose we are," said Felix, taking up his whisky and sipping it. "I'm not used to the fact of living at Hawksby yet."

"This is regular fire-water!" Gray said admiringly, having sipped from his own glass.

"It comes from near my father's parish in Pitfeldry," said Felix. "It is a trifle rough."

"Your father's sermons are great friends to me," Gray said. "His vision of what parish life should and can be – he is one of our great men, in my opinion."

"I am afraid he will not like that," Felix said.

"That I can believe. But his tenets – a practical ministry, for the needs of all God's people, no matter how humble – that is true wisdom. I will not take preferment, I will not climb that ladder. That is not the way to the Kingdom. I have found my lot at Raythorpe and I will serve out my days there, God willing."

"You came here to see Frederick Pierce, I take it?" Felix said, wondering if this was how future bishops were wont to speak. "His mother mentioned your name. I have not been in to see him yet. How is he today? Mr Harper –"

"He was not entirely hopeful," said Gray, sitting down. "And I suppose you are not either?"

"The damage is extremely extensive. There are things that can be done, but whether he is strong enough to endure them is another matter."

Gray pressed his hands to his face for a moment, and then said, "When I last spoke to him, a day or two before this happened, he was troubled by something – that is why I wanted to speak to you, given your connection with the Constabulary."

"That's interesting," Felix said, sitting down opposite him. "Do you think that Fred may be connected with the fire in some way?"

"It was about something at work."

"To do with the bank?"

"It was hard to tell. It was a most frustrating conversation, and I am struggling to know if I am recalling it correctly, especially in the light of what happened. I tried to draw him out; he would not say what precisely, but he seemed deeply troubled. It was to do with his father, but what that might be I cannot imagine. And then I heard the building next to the bank had burnt down, and Fred had been so late at his desk there. It puzzled me."

"You don't think him capable of setting a fire?" Felix said.

"Why would you think that?"

"The circumstances are peculiar."

"Fred Pierce would not set a fire," said Mr Gray. "That I can assure you. But he was worried about something in the bank, that is all I can say with certainty."

"That's useful to know, Mr Gray," said Felix. "Thank you. And if any details come back to you, then please do not hesitate to tell me or Major Vernon."

"I only hope Fred survives to tell us the whole tale for himself," said Gray, getting up. "But I fear that despite all your care and skill here, God's will may be that He takes him at this time, rather than later. It is hardly surprising. Fred has a pure heart and a good soul. He will be in my prayers!"

~

"So it was something to do with the bank and his father?" Giles said, finding Carswell at the Infirmary.

"Yes. Gray was adamant that Fred would never set a fire, but he is a man who always thinks the best of everyone."

"That's a useful talent," said Giles.

"Not in our business," said Carswell. "But in his, I suppose it is."

"So your theory is that Fred perhaps discovered something that discredited his father, and set the fire to conceal it?"

"And burnt the wrong building down," said Carswell, "having paid off the watchman."

"It's a possibility. We need to talk to Mr Pierce again. It is difficult in the circumstances to press him, but if he has something on his conscience then he may be persuaded to unburden himself. We'll talk to him tomorrow. I am going to see what the watchman tells us first. He should be sober enough now."

Giles left the Infirmary and went down to Constabulary Headquarters where Noakes was waiting to be interviewed.

"It was a woman that gave me the money," Noakes said, with little prompting.

"Just like that?"

"Just like that, sir, yes."

"Out of the goodness of her heart?"

"I suppose so, sir."

"How much?" Giles asked.

"Fifteen shillings or so."

"All coin?"

"Yes, sir."

"And she came to you at the warehouse? Where and when was this?"

"Well, I was in my hut, just having a dish of tea, a bit after seven, and she came in, just like that."

"Do you often have visitors?"

"No, sir, not often."

"And it never occurred to you, at any time in this transaction, that it was rather strange for her to come in there and offer you fifteen shillings to desert your post?"

Noakes rubbed his chin and considered.

"Yes, but – well, fifteen shillings is fifteen shillings."

It was depressing, Giles thought, how easily a man could be bought. He had no loyalty to his employer.

"How much does Mr Cartwright pay you?"

"Twenty shillings a week."

That seemed a wretched amount, even by Northminster standards. Cartwright obviously felt that the security of his premises was not important.

"And she asked for the key," Noakes added, as if that excused him entirely.

"You gave her keys as well? For fifteen shillings?" Giles said. "Come on, Noakes, tell me how much she really gave you."

Noakes looked around, his anxiety palpable now.

"May have been a sovereign or two," he said.

"For which you gave her the key and left the building?"

There was a long pause.

"Aye, sir," he said, "and I remember this, now you ask me – she did say Mr Cartwright sent her."

This struck Giles as a likely falsehood.

"Does she have a name?"

"Nay, no name."

"Can you describe her? Was she young, old, fat, thin?"

"Young," Noakes said, "but not a lass. Younger than I.

She had a wedding band on and she had a way about her, as if she were the missus somewhere. Not high-born like you, sir, but she had a way of saying a thing that would make a man jump to it, if you know what I mean."

"And her clothes? Anything distinctive?"

"She had a red pinny on, with stripes on it," said Noakes. "And a bit of white stuff here," he added, touching his neck. "Oh, and a leather bag tied about her waist, like a pocket. She took the money out of it."

"And was she wearing a cap or a bonnet?"

"Bonnet. I couldn't see her face for it, now you mention it. She had a little, you know what, covering her eyes." He passed his hand over his face to indicate a veil.

Giles frowned. How many women in Northminster wore striped aprons and bonnets with a veil? This was hardly going to help him. The leather pocket was perhaps the most useful observation he had made.

"And you had never seen her before, Noakes?"

"No, sir. She just came."

"She was lucky you were such a fool," said Giles, getting up. "If you had done your job as you should then there would not be a young man at death's door at the Infirmary."

"I didn't know she was going to burn the place down!" he said. "Did I?"

"What did you think she was about, then, Noakes?" said Giles. "In all honesty? Giving you money to absent yourself?"

"Folk like me," said Noakes, "we can't be picky. We take the money and do as we are told. She said Mr Cartwright had sent her, so I didn't think any better of it. I did what I was told, that's all! Ain't that what the likes of me are supposed to do?"

He ended with a defiant shrug, and Giles wondered if there was anything else of use he might get from him.

"If you see this woman again, I want to hear about it, Noakes. In the meantime you can go, but you may be sure one of my men will be keeping a close eye on you."

When he had gone, Giles asked Sergeant Coxe, who had been sitting with them in the room, what he thought.

"I think he is playing the simpleton, sir."

"Yes, I think so too."

Coxe was looking through his notebook.

"I have the door to door enquiries here, sir," he said. "There was a woman seen passing through one of the yards at the back some time after one, but the description of her is sparse. I will go and talk to that witness again, see if it might be the same one. At least then we might know which way she came and went."

"Excellent plan, Coxe," said Giles. "I look forward to hearing what you find."

# Chapter Six

They arrived at Hurrell Place at a little after six.

"How delightful this is," Emma murmured to Giles, leaning on his arm as they went up the grand staircase which led from the ancient hall to the drawing room. "To be travelling about together like an old married couple!"

"Soon enough it will be true," said Giles.

"It cannot be too soon for me," she said.

"Yes, but we will need a little time to repair the house."

"Indeed. I have the estimates to show him, by the way."

"Of course you do," Giles said.

The servant announced them.

"My dear Mrs Maitland, and Major Vernon, how do you do!" said Sir Morten, striding over to them. He was dressed in an old-fashioned plum-coloured coat and was accompanied by his lurcher dogs. "How good of you to come!"

Sir Morten was enthusiastic in his greeting. He insisted on kissing Emma's hand several times, and Giles felt his own arm was like a pump handle after filling a pail with water, such was the heartiness of the handshake.

They were then presented to Sir Morten's widowed sister-in-law, Mrs Edward Hurrell, a pale shade of a woman all in grey, thin and fragile-looking, who timidly whispered her how d'you dos. Lastly they met Arthur Hurrell, the son and heir, and also the clergyman of the parish, who looked bored, despite his perfectly correct manners.

"Now, Mrs Maitland, come and sit down by me, and tell me all the news," Sir Morten said.

"What news might that be, sir?" said Emma.

"Oh, you are a woman with information," said Sir

Morten, patting the space beside him. "Did I not say so, Mrs Hurrell? Mrs Maitland will keep us fresh. We are so dull here in the country."

"I am not sure what you want of me, Sir Morten," said Emma, hesitating a moment longer before going and perching beside him. But she turned herself carefully to face Mrs Hurrell. "I have a little nonsense about the shape of sleeves, Mrs Hurrell, but I am sure that is of no interest to Sir Morten. If you want the news from town, Sir Morten, you must ask Major Vernon."

"I hear there has been a fire," said Arthur Hurrell.

"Another one?" said Sir Morten.

"Yes, unfortunately," Giles said.

At this moment Lord Rothborough and Lady Maria were announced.

"It is a great pleasure to be here again," Rothborough said, shaking Sir Morten's hand. "I'm only sorry the pressure of business has prevented more intercourse between our families. It has been too long – five years, I think?"

"It's a pity that Lady Rothborough cannot be with us tonight," Arthur Hurrell said. Giles thought this was a sharp thing for a young man to say given the general speculation that went about on the state of the Marquis' marriage, but Lord Rothborough showed no sign of being wounded.

"You will see her soon enough, if you will honour us with your company at Holbroke, Mr Hurrell. She and my daughter Augusta are travelling back from Italy as we speak. She will be glad to see you there, at any time you desire, will she not, Maria?"

"Yes, certainly," said Maria. "We have great plans for this autumn. Do you like to dance, Mr Hurrell? We have been thinking of a ball, to celebrate – well, may I mention it, Papa?"

"Of course. My eldest girl, Charlotte, is to be married," said Lord Rothborough. "To Lord Dunbar."

"Oh, how delightful," said Mrs Hurrell.

"I think you were at Oxford together," Lord Rothborough said to Hurrell.

"I don't recall meeting him," said Hurrell.

"A ball at Holbroke," said Emma. "That will be a sight."

"It has been some years, yes," said Lord Rothborough. "So you must not disappoint us, Mr Hurrell. We do not wish to be short of gentlemen who dance. For the sake of the ladies."

"I am not sure I am much of a dancer," said Hurrell.

"He will be there, sir," said Sir Morten, "white-gloved and ready to do his duty. As will I, if an old man is allowed such a liberty, Lady Maria?"

"It would be delightful, Sir Morten, to see you dance," she said.

"Then you will reserve one for me, my lady?" he said.

"Of course, sir," she said.

"And perhaps one for my son?" he added, with a glance at Arthur Hurrell. Hurrell looked less than pleased at this.

"It must be difficult for a clergyman to think much of dancing," Lady Maria said, and got a thin-lipped smile from Mr Hurrell. "Tell me, is Mr Mark Hurrell at home at present? I remember him distinctly from when we were here last. He had just finished at Westminster and was about to go up to Ox–"

"No, he is not here," cut in Mr Hurrell.

"Oh, how disappointing," said Lady Maria. "I wanted to thank him. He was so kind to me that day. It is silly, but I cannot forget it," she went on, turning to Sir Morten. "He rescued me from a fractious dog – a bull mastiff. I don't think I was in any real danger, but he was very chivalrous."

"I am sure that is the family tradition," said Lord Rothborough. "I remember him too. A bright young fellow. Maria would talk of nothing else for days. What is he up to?"

There was silence, and Sir Morten began, in a tone of great regret, "Unfortunately my son –"

"Can no longer be received here," said Arthur Hurrell.

Another silence fell, which was broken finally by the timid voice of Mrs Hurrell: "Perhaps we should go and dress. Lady Maria, Mrs Maitland, might I show you to your rooms?"

~

Giles was just taking stock of his room when Lord Rothborough's man, James Bodley, appeared with a message from his master. Would Major Vernon object to his Lordship waiting upon him?

"No, of course not, if he does not mind my dressing?"

Mr Bodley said that Lord Rothborough would not mind in the least, and a few minutes later, when Holt had arranged Giles' cravat to his exacting standards and helped him into his evening waistcoat, Lord Rothborough came in.

"This is an odd roof to find ourselves under," he said. "Poor Maria – I hope she is not afraid to come down to dinner. Why are you here, Vernon?"

"I am currying favour with a potential landlord," Giles said. "I must say I was curious when he mentioned that you would be here."

"Yes, and I am still wondering why I agreed to come," said Lord Rothborough, going to the window and gazing out at the prospect. "Still, this is a sight worth seeing. I've not been here for years, and it's the finest house in the county, Holbroke notwithstanding. My mother always said so and I'm inclined to agree with her. Just look at that stand of timber – it's magnificent. I wonder how much it would be worth."

"Surely one would never want to sacrifice it?"

"No, of course not, but it's so well planted you might take your pick, get a good profit, and never notice anything had gone. I wonder if Sir Morten will let me speak to his forester. There is some dark art involved in that and I should very much like to know the secret!" He smiled and glanced back at Giles. "Landlord, you said?"

"Rooke Court in the Minster Precincts," Giles said. "Mrs Maitland and I went to look it over, and she beat him down to an improving lease at an outrageously low price."

"Ah, yes, but of course she would!" said Lord Rothborough.

"The problem is, seeing all this, I think the expense of the improvements done to his standard will bankrupt me. But it is a charming house, and the only one we have seen that we like."

"Yet he has let the place decay? He can't be too demanding. He should be grateful to have you. I'm only sorry I have nothing to offer you at present. All my suitable properties are let. There seems to be a demand for good houses in Northminster. The fruits of prosperity! I thought of throwing up a suburb myself, but the matter needs a little more consideration and more time than I have at the moment, unfortunately. I should hand it over to Maria. She has her model cottages, after all. They have become quite a thing with her. She argues beautifully for them. Speaking of our ladies, we should go and find them! They may need to be rescued."

They went into the long gallery, a spectacular room some sixty feet long and commanding magnificent views of the country in all directions. Tall, latticed windows filled the room with the golden light of the waning afternoon, making the great curtains of crimson damask appear a soft rose while the dark wood panelling glistened. The walls were crammed with portraits: a host of Hurrell ancestors looking down at them as they walked along; some stiff, some beautiful, some benign and others decidedly suspicious.

At the far end, two boys were crouching on the floor setting out a game of ninepins, when Arthur Hurrell strode into the room. He grabbed the smaller of the boys by the collar, almost lifting him from the floor.

"There you are, you dirty whelp! What are you doing in here? How dare you?" he said.

"He has finished," said the other boy, jumping up and attempting to stay the man's hand, for he was about to box the smaller boy's ears. "We have both finished!"

"That is not what Mr Willoughby says!" said Arthur Hurrell.

"It is the truth, Uncle Arthur, I swear it!" said the boy who had been captured. "I finished the lesson. I know it all, I swear I do!"

"And I am to take your word over his, am I? When we all know what you are, Lewis Hurrell?"

"He had finished," said the other boy. "I made sure that he had. I made him repeat it. I swear I did."

Arthur Hurrell released the boy, though whether it was because of the boy's words, or because he had caught sight of Lord Rothborough and Giles coming along the room, was not clear.

"Gentlemen," he said, straightening. "Good evening!"

"And who are these fine lads?" said Lord Rothborough, indicating the boys.

"My nephews," said Hurrell, "who should not be here, alas."

"I told you, Uncle Arthur," said the older boy, "we had finished –"

"Be quiet, Morten!" said Hurrell. "And get back where you belong. I shall come and hear your lesson, Lewis, so beware! If what you say is false then there will be consequences for both of you."

Having made hasty bows to Giles and Lord Rothborough, the boys scurried away, leaving their ninepins behind them.

"Excuse me," said Hurrell. "They are little better than savages at the moment. They need to be kept on the shortest leash or it is nothing short of chaos."

"It will not be long before they are back at school," said Lord Rothborough, wandering across to the ninepins and surveying them. "The sweet pleasures of the summer holidays always felt too brief, to my mind. One cannot blame them for making the most of it! I am sure we have all made mischief in our time."

"Yes, certainly," said Giles.

"Unfortunately, we are past the point of clemency," said Mr Hurrell. "They are not to be trusted. A firm hand now will save them later. I was the same – wild, ill-disciplined and indolent – but my father took pains with me, and I am now grateful for it."

At this moment, the ladies entered the far end of the room, and Giles had the pleasure of seeing Emma take stock of her magnificent surroundings and stroll towards him, in her silvery skirts. She was accompanied by Lady Maria and Mrs Edward Hurrell, the mother of the savages.

He supposed she was effectively the mistress of the house, but there was nothing about her manner that suggested she was at ease with her position. When Emma and Lady Maria complimented her on the large vases of flowers about the room, she seemed to find it remarkable that they had been noticed.

"We do not entertain much," she said. "I did not know what would be right. And I have probably made our gardener cross by taking so many."

"He will be pleased – you are showing all his good work," said Emma. "What is a cutting border for, but cutting? And in August – it is always tricky. But these combinations – the roses with the cornflowers and this one – now, what is that one, pray? I never can remember its name. And I have never seen them put together like this – have you, Lady Maria?"

"No, it's charming. I must remember it. And the smell of this rose is heavenly – oh, Papa, have you smelt this one?"

Lord Rothborough then turned the full dazzle of his

charm on Mrs Hurrell and her roses. On pretence of smelling another flower, Giles was able to slip his hand into Emma's for a moment and squeeze it.

"Are you well-lodged?" he asked.

"In utter magnificence," she said. "It must be the best bedchamber. Blue velvet with silver spangles. I was astonished. Lady Maria has much less state. I suppose being an old woman has some compensations; or maybe it is my future husband who gives me the consequence here?"

"It's all your doing," said Giles. "My room is nothing to speak of, though the views are beautiful."

"That is the case everywhere," she said. "This place feels like another Eden, does it not? And what are they doing to produce such roses? Is it witchcraft?" she added in a whisper before moving away, for Sir Morten had come in accompanied by another lady and gentleman. As she drifted away and he felt his blood warm with longing for her, he reminded himself that it was only six weeks until their wedding.

"Lord and Lady Wytton!"

The names startled him and he paid attention to the new arrivals. A young couple – he, broad, solid, rosy-faced and genial; she, half his size, elaborately tricked out, jewels at her throat and in her hair. She seemed to sparkle and tremble at the same time as she shook hands.

"Forgive me, have you any connection with Wytton's Bank, my lord?" Giles asked, having been presented.

"Yes, the same. I am one of the directors."

"Then you and I should have met soon enough. I wanted to speak to you. I am working on the cause of the fire in the premises adjoining the bank."

"A fire?" said Lady Wytton. "My goodness! What happened? Was anyone hurt?"

"Unfortunately, yes," said Giles. "One of your husband's employees, Mr Frederick Pierce. He was rescuing the family on the other side."

"No!" she exclaimed. "Not Fred Pierce? Oh, how terrible – how badly hurt is he?"

"He is in the Infirmary," said Giles. "I don't think they are very hopeful. He was almost foolhardy in his courage. So you know this young man, Lady Wytton?"

"Yes," she said.

"How?" said her husband, clearly surprised.

"Through Mr and Mrs Gray," said Lady Wytton. "He is often there. He is a charming young man. Oh, this is awful, truly awful..."

"I'm sorry to bring bad news," said Giles.

"Mr Gray thinks the world of him," said Lady Wytton. "He wants him to go to Oxford and become a clergyman. And now he is –" She broke off, and then turning to her husband said, "Why did you not tell me this, Edward? You must have known about it. Mr Pierce would have told you, surely?"

"Yes, of course he did, but I didn't wish to distress you," said Wytton. "After all, the fire did no damage to the bank. And I didn't know that you knew Fred Pierce. I'm a little astonished that you should. But the Grays seem to entertain the multitudes." He shrugged. "It is, of course, terrible news."

"We must do something for him!" Lady Wytton said. "You say he is in the Infirmary, Major Vernon?"

"Yes, Mr Harper has him under his care, and Mr Carswell, my colleague, is assisting."

"I have heard good things about Mr Harper," said Lady Wytton. "That is a blessing, I'm sure of it."

"Yes, yes, certainly," said Wytton. At this point, Lady Wytton excused herself and went to speak to Mrs Hurrell. When they were alone together, Wytton asked, "So you have not fixed on a cause of the fire yet, Major?"

"No," said Giles. "The evidence does suggest that it was begun deliberately. The watchman, Noakes, had been paid to absent himself that night."

"Good God! Pierce did not mention that. I suppose the

warehouseman – I am sorry, I do not recall the man's name –"

"Mr Cartwright?"

"That's the fellow – I suppose he was in trouble. That's the usual way with these things, isn't it? The cotton business is a risky one, and it attracts the speculative types, and when things get desperate – well, we are lucky it did not spread, very lucky indeed."

"Did Mr Pierce tell you where the fire was started?"

"No."

"It was in an old fireplace in the warehouse, the flue abutting your bank's upper rooms. That is what is puzzling me, my lord. If the intention had been to burn down the warehouse, then there would have been much easier ways to accomplish it. The room was stacked from floor to rafters with cotton bales, like a well-laid fire in a grate. Why not just set the fire at the foot of them?"

"I can't imagine," said Lord Wytton.

"How involved with the day-to-day affairs of the bank are you, my lord, if you don't mind me asking?"

"Not a great deal, I must confess. Mr Pierce is so capable, and I'm not really suited to office life. But I go in once a week to attend to any necessary business."

"And you have complete confidence in Mr Pierce?"

"Oh yes."

"How long has he been with the bank?"

"He became a director when my father was still alive. It was after my uncle died. He replaced him as a director. He had been working for us for some time before that, and had amassed sufficient capital to buy my uncle's share. We are most fortunate to have him – and Fred too, for he is in the same mould. Very accurate and utterly trustworthy."

"You don't happen to know why Fred was working there so late that night?"

Wytton shook his head.

"As I said, I don't have any real knowledge of the day-today running of the bank. Fred was diligent – that is all I can tell you."

"His mother seemed surprised that he was there."

"Womenfolk do not always have the clearest idea of what business requires," said Lord Wytton, glancing at his wife who was now talking to Emma and another young man who had come in after the Wyttons. "I see Willoughby is still here. The rumour hereabouts is that he was on his way to Rome."

"I'm sorry?" said Giles.

"He's a friend of Arthur Hurrell. Staying with him at the Vicarage – although monastery would be a better name for it, from all I have heard. And a crowd of young Oxford men staying there to sing the virtues of Rome! It's disgraceful. I am amazed that Sir Morten lets Willoughby tutor those nephews of his. I should not let such a crypto-Catholic near my children, but then again, perhaps Sir Morten is still partial to the old religion. It would not surprise me – there are priest holes in this house, after all!"

"And Arthur Hurrell has the living here?" said Giles.

"Yes. In his father's gift. I wish I had such discretion in our village. Instead we have Mr Gray, no thanks to the Bishop."

"Mr Gray seems to have the reputation of a radical," said Giles.

"He is a red hot one! What has happened to clergymen these days? When I was a boy they were perfectly reasonable people, to whom one could talk about hunting and so forth, but nowadays –" He broke off. "Excuse me, I do not like Willoughby talking to my wife."

With which he left Giles and went to interrupt the conversation. Seeing him, Willoughby took flight. To Giles' delight, Emma returned to his side.

"Tell me about Mr Willoughby," Giles said.

"I know that he looks as if he lives on nothing but weak tea and bread and butter," said Emma. "But he has caused a great stir at Oxford. I never expected to find him here."

"Lord Wytton just alleged that he is a crypto-Catholic."

"One might infer something like that from his preaching, certainly," said Emma. "And he had a great many of the undergraduates in a sort of rapture."

"And Mrs Maitland?"

"I was interested, but not moved," said Emma. "He has a rather quiet, sweet voice, almost womanly. It was an odd experience. Charles did not like it either, but whether that was the natural prejudice of a Salvator's man against an Oriel man, I don't know."

At this moment, Lady Maria joined them, looking somewhat flustered.

"I wish to go into a cupboard and die," she said. "How am I going to bear this? Mr Hurrell keeps staring at me as if –"

"I'm sure that is not the case," Emma began. "I think he may be staring at you because he is unused to handsome young women."

"How was I to know that Mark Hurrell had disgraced himself? He is the only one of them I remember. It was a perfectly innocent enquiry and now I'm sure Sir Morten and Mr Hurrell think I am malicious."

"No one could think you malicious," said Emma.

"I could feel it. It went cold as ice all of a sudden. Did you not feel the temperature drop?"

"It is not your fault!" said Emma. "Rather it is the fault of whatever it is Mark Hurrell has done – which would seem to be quite extreme."

"Perhaps Papa will know," said Lady Maria. "He generally knows everything."

"Perhaps it is not something fit for us to know," said Emma, taking her arm.

"I hope it is not very bad. He was so kind to me – that is why I remember him. But then, the kindest people can turn out to be the most horrible villains – is that not so, Major

Vernon?"

# Chapter Seven

Dinner passed off without incident, but it was tiresome. The conversation rarely moved beyond the banal. For all the grandeur, there was an undercurrent of restraint, which seemed to subdue even Emma and Lord Rothborough, both of whom were usually fearless social performers. For his part, Giles found himself thinking back to his unsatisfactory conversation with Noakes, as he watched Lord Wytton across the table. Why had the fire been set in that fireplace and not under the cotton bales? Was the real intention to burn down the bank and not the warehouse?

The ladies withdrew, and mercifully there was no concerted move to prolong the male conviviality, despite the excellence of the port. Wytton drank the most, while Arthur Hurrell filled his glass and then pushed it away, as if attempting self-denial. Willoughby did not drink at all. It was a great relief to rejoin the women in the drawing room and find Lady Maria at the piano, playing some lively Mendelssohn.

Standing near him, Arthur Hurrell was listening with interest, and when the piece was finished, he turned to Giles and said with some surprise, "She does play well."

"Why don't you ask her to play again?" said Giles, wondering that he had not already gone straight up to her and demanded it. In such circumstances he would not have hesitated. "That would please everyone." He hoped too that it would please Lady Maria and make her feel forgiven.

"I do not want to be misinterpreted," Hurrell said, after a moment.

"Ah, but your father has beaten you to it," Giles said as Sir Morten went up to the piano.

"We are not a musical family," said Hurrell. "It is a novelty for us to have a good performer in the house. She is –" He broke off. "You must know her quite well, sir. I understand that you and Lord Rothborough are friends?"

"I know that she is a charming, intelligent young woman."

"And is she – is there anyone...?"

"The field is clear, as far as I know," Giles said. "But I would advise you speak to Lord Rothborough."

"Yes, yes," Hurrell said, and moved away to where he might get a better view of Lady Maria. Giles went to sit next to Emma, and together they listened to the music. Lady Maria had chosen to play a long and clever arrangement of famous airs from Handel, and when she had finished, Emma murmured, "She has saved us all from the misery of conversation. But she will be exhausted."

"You should carry her off to bed. Lord Rothborough might prefer that. Especially as Arthur Hurrell asked me –"

"If the field was clear?"

"How did you know that?" he said.

"I had a hint from Sir Morten at dinner – well, more than a hint. He wants him married. That is why they were asked."

"I'm not sure Arthur Hurrell is entirely to Lady Maria's taste," said Giles, thinking of how he had threatened his nephews.

"No, certainly not. And not to Lord Rothborough's taste either," she said, getting up. "I had better intervene. She looks as if she needs to be rescued."

For Arthur Hurrell had found his courage and was talking to Maria, or rather at her. He towered over her while she sat on the piano stool and it did not look at all comfortable for her. Arthur Hurrell was clearly not a practised flirt. He seemed intent on giving her his latest sermon.

Emma crossed the room, and at the same time Giles looked about for Lord Rothborough. He was not in the room.

He found him sitting in the passageway outside, drinking a glass of water.

"I had a curious little turn while Maria was playing," he said. "I needed a glass of water and some air."

"Nothing serious, I hope?" said Giles, sitting down beside him.

"No, I think not," said Lord Rothborough. "Perhaps the result of a trying evening. I had not suspected matchmaking when I accepted the invitation. It was naive of me."

"Emma – Mrs Maitland – is rescuing Maria as we speak," said Giles.

Rothborough smiled at his correction.

"You are a lucky man, Vernon," he said. "She is –" He sighed. "To have such a person in one's life, a real equal to share the road with – that is something I suppose I will never know. I can only hope that my children..." He smiled, for Maria was coming along, arm in arm with Emma.

"I have excused us," Emma said.

"We had better go and make our own excuses," said Lord Rothborough, getting up and kissing Maria. "You played beautifully. I liked your phrasing in the last section of the Handel. You have not done that before. Most effective."

At that moment a manservant passed them and went back into the drawing room. Lady Maria and Emma had just set off towards their rooms, and Giles and Lord Rothborough were about to go back in, when the servant came out again with Arthur Hurrell hard on his heels. Hurrell seemed to be pushing the manservant from the room.

"Can you not take a simple instruction, Martin?" Hurrell exclaimed to the servant. "Tell him to leave at once!"

"But sir, he says he was asked to come. That the Master asked him."

"Which you know cannot be true."

"I don't know that, sir –"

"Don't be insolent! Go and tell him to leave!"

"We have done, sir. Mr Lightbody has told him, but he says he will not go until he sees the Master."

"Where is he?"

"In the great hall, sir."

Arthur Hurrell hurried on, with the servant just behind him, and went down the stairs to the great hall. Emma and Lady Maria had stopped and turned to see what the commotion was, for he dashed past them, almost tripping over their hems in his hurry.

"Goodness," murmured Lord Rothborough, and went over to the balustrade that overlooked the hall, and Giles joined him. The same urge clearly took Emma and Lady Maria, for they also went to their side of the balustrade, as if moving to the front of an opera box for a celebrated aria.

A young man, dressed in a brown velvet coat, was sitting at the long refectory table. He got up when Arthur Hurrell came towards him.

"You know you are not welcome here!" Arthur Hurrell shouted at him.

"I know that. But since Papa wrote and asked me to come, I thought it would be –"

"You are lying," said Arthur. "As you always do."

"I am not."

"Show me this letter, then!" Arthur Hurrell demanded.

"I do not have it with me."

"How extraordinarily convenient. Because it does not exist!"

"Because I might expect the courtesy of being taken at my word!"

"Your word, sir, is worthless! And as for courtesy, you have forsaken any right to that."

On the landing above, they now exchanged horrified glances. Emma began to steer Maria away, but the girl remained rooted to the spot, even as her father came to her side.

"That is Mark Hurrell, Papa," she said, in a whisper.

"We had better retire," said Lord Rothborough. "This is not for our ears."

And so they began to move away, but the argument still rang out.

"And why on earth would Papa ask you here?" Hurrell demanded. "Tonight of all nights when we have half the county here to dine?"

"I don't know, but he wrote and I came, as requested. No, as ordered, for it was put in his usual manner. Where is he?"

"You shall not see him."

"You shall not deny me, Arthur. He wrote to me!"

"You have come here to make trouble, but I shall not allow it. Get out! Or shall I have to throw you out myself?"

"I have an invitation. I shall stay until I see him."

"No, you shall not!"

Now came the sound of furniture crashing to the floor, and Giles left the others and ran downstairs to see the long bench overturned and Hurrell and his brother clearly on the brink of doing each other violence.

"Gentlemen!" Giles said, attempting to separate them. "This is no way to settle a dispute. Step back from each other and clear your heads!"

"Who are you?" said Mark Hurrell.

"Major Vernon from the Northminster Constabulary."

"Ah," said Mark Hurrell and retreated, his palms raised. But Arthur Hurrell glared at Giles, angry at his intervention.

"He is trespassing!" he said. "This man is trespassing."

Mark Hurrell took another step back and made Giles a slight bow.

"No, sir, I am not. I have called here in vain, that is all. If you might convey to my father that I was here, I would be grateful. Tell him I obeyed his wishes, that is all I ask. Good night."

He picked up his hat from the table, turned, and walked from the hall. Hurrell went after him a few steps and then thought better of it. The door shut behind Mark Hurrell and Arthur turned back to Giles and said, "Thank you, sir, but this is a family matter. There is no need to mention it to anyone."

~

Giles had just finished writing a brief note to Emma, when Holt came in.

"So, Holt, I hope you and Bodley and Mrs Patton had an agreeable time downstairs."

"It was pleasant enough. Good food, certainly. And I learnt a lot about the family," said Holt. "Would you like to know the ins and outs, sir? I thought you might, what with Mr Mark Hurrell arriving."

"You know me too well, Holt. So tell me the tale. What did he do?"

"That's the funny thing. It did not seem so bad to me. He wrote a book they did not like at Oxford, but he did not even put his name to it, so what can be the harm in that?"

"It must be an offensive book."

"They told me that Sir Morten bought as many copies of it as he could and burnt them all. A hundred of them at least. Think of that. Like burning money, that is! I mean, how much harm can a book do, in all honesty?"

"Clearly Sir Morten felt strongly about it. Did the servants say anything about Lord and Lady Wytton, their neighbours?"

Holt shook his head.

"Nothing, sir. Shall I take that to the mistress?" he said, indicating the note to Emma.

"If you would, Holt," said Giles, amused at Holt calling Emma 'mistress' already. They had been worried that Holt and his bride would look for work elsewhere, but Holt had pronounced himself perfectly content to remain in his service if they could find a post for the future Mrs Holt. Given that she was a professed cook, trained in the kitchens at Holbroke, this request was easily accommodated, although Giles worried that the costs of their new household might prove excessive if she continued to cook in the style of Holbroke. He consoled himself with the thought that Emma would surely, with her exquisite tact and practical economy, keep things in check.

Holt took the note, and said, "And the house in the precincts, sir, Rooke Court – is that settled? Mrs Patton was saying it was as good as, but –"

"Yes, and here is another letter, for Sir Morten, telling him I will take it," said Giles. "Though we may have to rough it there for a while. It's not in a good state."

"It's a fine address," said Holt. "That is the main thing. Will that be all for tonight, sir?"

"Yes, thank you, Holt."

Holt carried off his letters.

Giles reflected for a moment, wishing he could have gone in person to Emma, and sat with her to talk over the events of the evening; or better yet, joined her in bed. Still, it was only a matter of six weeks until such pleasures would be his to enjoy.

# Chapter Eight

"We have been asked to stay on," said Emma the next morning.

"I cannot, it's impossible," Giles said. "I have to –"

"No, not you. Just Maria and me," said Emma. "Mrs Hurrell begged us. She wants us to help with a feast for the local children. She declared herself out of her depth with it. At least that is the pretext. I suppose this is matchmaking."

"It's rather clumsy," said Giles.

"Yes, but it is born of desperation. Arthur will be thirty next month, and there has been so much misfortune in this house, they are anxious to get him settled. We must excuse their clumsiness."

"But Lady Maria cannot like it?" said Giles.

"She does not. But we have made a pact," said Emma. "We are determined to help poor Mrs Hurrell. She seemed to quiver with misery as she asked us – one could not say no to her. She must be unhappy, and if we refuse I fear she will be in trouble for it."

"Oh Lord, I hope not," Giles said.

"This is a strange house," said Emma. "So Maria and I are resolved to help her. But Maria will not give Mr Hurrell any encouragement. She will stay in my shadow at all times, and be perfectly indifferent if he attempts any lovemaking. But we will have done our duty by Mrs Hurrell, and Sir Morten will not be offended, which is the most important thing as far as we are concerned."

"Especially since I wrote to him last night and said I would take the house," Giles said.

"Oh, Giles, how wonderful!" She pressed her hands to

his face and kissed him. "Oh, thank you! It will be the most perfect house when we are done with it, I promise you."

He caught her in his arms, and returned the kiss, but only for a moment, because Maria joined them.

"I have spoken to Papa," she said. "He is willing to let me stay if I promise to box Arthur Hurrell's ears if he attempts any nonsense."

"The trouble is that with some men that would only encourage them," said Giles.

"Not Arthur Hurrell," said Emma.

"And I will have a most cunning chaperone," said Lady Maria, taking Emma's arm and wrapping hers about it. "I shall be quite safe."

"The cunning chaperone?" said Emma. "That sounds like the title of something, don't you think? A comic opera in three acts, perhaps?"

"I wish I could stay and watch it," said Giles.

He had arranged to meet Carswell at the Infirmary at eleven, with the intention of talking to Mr Pierce again.

He found him at Frederick Pierce's bedside, along with Mr Harper and several nurses. Their patient was in a high fever, and thrashing about in the most distressed state. They were on the verge of plunging him into an ice bath as Giles came in, and it might have been a pool of flaming oil, such was the agony it evidently caused the poor man.

From the way Carswell and Harper were acting, this was a desperate measure. It was soon clear that the outcome of this scene could only be a tragic one.

Pierce grabbed Carswell by the shoulders, as if he wanted to use him to drag him from his fiery torment, and shrieked into his face. It was not just an expression of pain. He was attempting to speak.

"ST... ST.... STOCKHOLM!"

He continued to grip at Carswell's shoulders, and stared about him with his bleary, red rimmed, exhausted eyes. His gaze rested on Giles.

"Yes, Mr Pierce?" Giles said, coming forward a little.

"Stock –" he said, and then with great effort so he was sure he could be understood: "Stock Holm."

And then he collapsed and ceased to breathe.

~

"Stockholm," said Felix again. "Stockholm? Why Stockholm?"

"Mr Pierce may know, but I don't think this is the moment to talk to the Pierces. They will be too distressed," said Major Vernon. "Perhaps tomorrow we will attempt it."

"I should tell Gray," said Felix.

"Ah yes," said the Major.

"He will probably want to go to them. He will do them good, I should imagine."

"We had better go and see him. He may have remembered something else, and then I want to talk to Lord and Lady Wytton. She seemed to be concerned about Fred Pierce. She may have some confidences about him. We can go by way of Hawksby – it is much the best road."

"As you wish," said Felix.

"I should pay my respects," Major Vernon said.

Lady Blanchfort was in the house, and received them as if they had done her the greatest favour in the world by calling so unexpectedly. Her character reformation was still puzzling Felix, but he could not deny it gave him pleasure.

"Shall we go and find Eleanor?" she said, and they crossed the lawn together.

Eleanor was again stretched out on her chaise in the Tea House, intent on her reading, and she scarcely stirred until she noticed them approaching.

"This book!" she said. "It's both terrible and compelling."

"Which one is it?" Felix said. "Oh, the scandalous Mr Anon. Have you finished it?"

"Yes, just. And I can't begin to know what to say about it. It's so strange."

"I bought it in Edinburgh," said Felix. "The bookseller told me it had caused a scandal in Oxford."

"And so you gave it to my daughter, Mr Carswell?" said Lady Blanchfort, with something of her old froideur.

"It's not really scandalous," Eleanor said. "And I may read what I like now I am married. Well, it is, but – it is quite outspoken about the Church, and I can see why everyone in Oxford would be upset, because of what he says about the University."

"But it is a good tale?" Major Vernon asked.

"It must be, because I have been reading it all day," Eleanor said.

"May I see it?" said Major Vernon.

"Of course," she said, offering him the book.

"I may know who wrote this," he said, having examined it for a few moments. "And it is a wonder you got hold of it. I have been told most of them were burnt."

"Goodness!"

"The person who burnt them would be distressed to know a copy is in the hands of his neighbours," Major Vernon said.

"You are being mysterious," said Eleanor.

"I meant to be discreet and yet I have failed, haven't I?" He turned the book over several times and then handed it back to Eleanor. "I would be careful where you mention that you have read it, that is all."

"You don't think I should burn it, though, Major Vernon?" Eleanor said. "Out of loyalty to the neighbourhood?"

"Even if he were to recommend that, I would entirely forbid it," said Felix, taking the book from her. "I am vehemently against the burning of books, under any circumstances!"

"And you know I would never recommend that, don't you, Carswell?" said Major Vernon, much amused.

"No, you are too pragmatic. You would say it only draws attention to the matter that they are trying to suppress."

"Quite," said Major Vernon.

"In some ways," Lady Blanchfort said, "I find it more shocking to imagine a neighbour – presumably a gentleman – doing something so –"

"Barbaric!" said Felix, and offered the book to her. She shook her head.

"I don't think I should. We are relative strangers here, after all. I hardly know anyone and I do not like to be prejudiced against my neighbours. You should probably forget what you have read, Eleanor."

"I can never forget anything I read," Eleanor said.

"Wait until you are older, Mrs Carswell," Major Vernon said. "And my apologies, ladies, for raising this spectre."

"I suppose you can't bear to leave such puzzles unsolved," said Lady Blanchfort, "and since you do so much for justice, sir, we will forgive you. And now, may I offer you some refreshments, before you go on your way? I shall not insult you by calling it luncheon, which I know is a thing despised by any man of action."

~

"So, you are now a man of action in your mother-in-law's eyes!" said Major Vernon, as they rode away after the refreshments, which might easily have been described as luncheon, and a lavish one at that. "A high compliment."

"That was directed at you," said Felix. "I have not done

anything to make her love me, I'm sure enough of that."

"Except make her daughter happy?"

"I hope I have," Felix said. "I feel –"

"You are still adjusting – both of you," said Major Vernon. "You have to allow for a little uncertainty."

"Yes, yes of course," said Felix. "And it is a blessed relief that Lady Blanchfort has become –"

"An ally?"

"Quite," said Felix. "And I have to admit, that in her present state, I'm glad she insists on living with us, because we would be in chaos otherwise. Eleanor is not practical, truth be told. Nor am I. We are not ready for our own establishment."

Major Vernon smiled at that, and said, "I wonder if I am. Given I'm about to sign the lease on a house which is half-collapsing."

"You found somewhere you like, then?"

"Rooke Court. It's in the Precincts and has a beautiful garden, and if one was being strictly objective, that is all one can say is good about it. The rest is a list of imperfections that I am sure are going to cost me dear over the years."

"Good grief," Felix could not help saying. "I know the one you mean. It's visibly crumbling, is it not?" That Major Vernon and the equally pragmatic Mrs Maitland were prepared to take on such a project seemed astonishing.

"The rent is tiny," Major Vernon went on. "We are obliging the landlord, really."

"Who is?"

"Sir Morten Hurrell." He laughed. "My alleged book-burner, if you must know."

"Ah, I wondered if you were ever going to tell me that. Heavens. I have heard something about him from Lord Rothborough. He is a dyed-in-the-wool reactionary, is he not?"

"I ought not to tell you to have any secrets from your wife, but it would be better if that goes no further."

"That will be difficult. I'm no good at lying."

"That is to your credit. Then if she must know, she must, but please caution her to be discreet. He is an important man in the district."

"Indeed, he is your landlord!" said Felix, much amused. "Whom you now suspect of the most illiberal behaviour possible. Burning books! Unforgivable."

"Yes, 'suspect' – please remember that. I'm only hypothesising, as you know well that I often do, and I'm probably wrong. But from the pages I read – I should have to read the rest to prove my case."

"Well, I have the only copy in the district, if you are correct, and I shall read it first, if you don't mind. I only got as far as the death of the hero's beloved mother and I should like to know what happens next. Anon can certainly tell a tale, whatever the rest of it contains."

"You should read it and then lock it away. Certainly I should not be allowed near it. After all, as you said, I cannot offend my landlord. Mrs Maitland would never forgive me. She is already making extraordinary sacrifices for the cause."

"Locking away is as bad as burning," Felix said. "However, I would not like to disoblige the future Mrs Vernon. For her I shall do it."

"Thank you," said Major Vernon. "I wish I had not even thought of it. It is simply the way my mind works – I'm constantly looking for connections. I wonder if it is not an over-developed and pernicious sense of curiosity that has led me into this profession."

"It's your great strength," said Felix. "That eternal 'why'. It underlines what we both do. It is necessary for progress, surely?"

"Yes, but it can make trouble in one's private life," said Major Vernon.

They reached Mr Gray's rectory, a handsome house set in pretty gardens, and found that Mr Gray, predictably enough, was not at home. However, Mrs Gray was pleased to receive them.

They found her sitting in an arbour – it was clearly a day for arbours and tea houses – with another lady, whom Felix learnt was Lady Wytton. Nearby, various small children and their nurses were playing on the lawn. Given the number of children involved, it had to be assumed that they belonged to both ladies, but it still struck him as an excessive amount of childbearing for two women who were still so young. Neither of them was much above his own age. He knew how strong maternal instinct was, but it did not fail to astonish him that women of the educated classes seemed to embrace it, rather than put some check upon it. He wondered whether they would have adopted a rational alternative had they been offered it, or turned away in disgust as Eleanor had done. Society rewarded them for it, crowned them as mothers when they were admired for little else, but at the same time, he could not help feeling that it abused them. Mrs Gray was heavily pregnant and not far from her delivery, as far as Felix could judge, and, although pregnancy sometimes made a woman bloom, she looked faded, as if all her young health and beauty were soon to desert her.

Major Vernon sketched out the details to them and they were both at once distressed. It was clear enough that Fred Pierce had meant something to both of them.

"Oh, Harry will be –" Mrs Gray said, choking back her tears. "He is so fond of him. He had such hopes for him. We all did, did we not, Lavinia?" said Mrs Gray. Lavinia Wytton nodded, apparently unable to speak.

"And did either of you know if anything had been troubling him?" Major Vernon asked.

There was no time for them to answer, for at this moment a nursemaid, little more than a girl herself, came running up and said breathlessly, "Oh, madam, madam – Master Johnny's fallen down on the fernery and he can't get up. He's lying there all twisted up!"

"What!" exclaimed Mrs Gray, and began to struggle to her feet. "The children are not allowed in there, Mary-Anne –"

"Yes, madam, but he ran off. Like he always does."

"Stay there, ma'am," Felix said. "Major Vernon and I will go and see to it."

"Yes, yes, a good plan," said Lady Wytton. "You stay here."

"It is probably nothing," said Major Vernon.

So they followed the maid back across the garden.

The fernery lay in a hollow and had its own gate, which the nurse swore was closed.

"He must have climbed over it," she said. "I turned my back for a minute and –" She hurried along the path.

A superficial glance showed that the place would have been irresistible to adventurous small children. It was full of rocks and low-hanging branches, a natural playground, but a dangerous one. A turn in the path revealed the small figure lying in the cleft between two enormous rocks, and in a most alarming posture.

Felix ventured down. Some careful scrambling was required until he was able to crouch beside him. Mercifully the child was conscious, so Felix could set about testing which limbs he could still feel. The boy managed to nod and murmur his responses. Then for good measure he rolled over and vomited profusely over Felix. Felix scooped him up in his arms and carried him back to the path. There, with the child laid flat on the grass, he could make a more thorough examination. As far as he could judge, there was a fracture of the lower right leg.

Major Vernon had not been idle and had found one of the gardeners, and a hurdle on which to carry the child back to the house. Felix followed them, composing himself for the grim and delicate work ahead of him. Bone setting was never pleasant, and risky for a child of that age.

One of the other children, a little girl, escaped her nurse

and came running up to him. She thrust a wilting flower into his hand and said: "To make Johnny better."

# Chapter Nine

It was impossible to speak to Mr Gray about Fred Pierce while his son lay in such a dangerous condition.

The sight of the boy in agony as the bone was set had been a distressing one. Carswell had banned Mrs Gray from the sick room until he was done, so it was left to Mr Gray to comfort and sustain his son, while Giles and the nurse served as dressers, helping Carswell with setting the leg as best they could. Carswell contrived a box made of splints for the child's leg, so that nothing could be disturbed, and told them that the box would have to stay in place for at least two months. That looked to Giles like a terrible torture for the child, but the alternative was amputation.

"He has a better chance of recovery from this, as a child, because he has the power of growth in him," Carswell said to Gray, when the task was finished and the child was sleeping in a pleasant cloud of opium. "He will heal."

"God willing," said Gray.

"John willing," Carswell said. "The power the patient has over his condition is never to be underestimated. He is to be encouraged to believe in that at all times, even when he is very low."

"Yes, yes, of course," said Gray. "I must go and speak to my wife. May she come in yet?"

"Yes, but only for a little while. Her strength must not be taxed. She does not look strong – I hope you do not mind my saying so. Has she had many difficulties with this last pregnancy? What has your usual physician said?"

"She has been more than usually tired," Gray said, "that is true. But it will be hard to keep her from her duty here."

"Her duty is to herself," Carswell said. "I can tell her so, if you like? I would prescribe absolute rest, and that is even on the most superficial observation. You have help enough to nurse your son? Perhaps you could send for someone else? A female relative or some such."

"John will want his mother," Gray said.

"And he may have her, but in the smallest doses."

"I must defer to your knowledge," said Mr Gray. "And perhaps you should see her. Another opinion would not go amiss. I think she has been worried, although she will not tell me that directly!"

They went off together, leaving Giles in sole possession of the sunny family morning room, and a pleasant window seat. He took out his notebook and began to look at it.

He had written STOCKHOLM in capitals, and he turned the word over in his mind. Had Pierce simply been referring to the place, or had he meant something else by it?

He looked up and saw Lady Wytton standing in the doorway.

"I'm glad you are still here. May I have a word alone, Major Vernon?"

"Of course."

"It's about what you asked earlier. About Mr Pierce."

"Perhaps we should sit down?" he said, and led her to the window seat.

"I hope you will not misconstrue what I'm going to say to you in any way. It is just that given the circumstances, I feel I have to tell someone. You see, I think Fred was a little in love with me..." Her voice trailed away. "As a young man sometimes is with a married woman. Not in the way of a French novel, but – perhaps you know what I mean, Major?"

"Yes," Giles said. "As in the old tales of chivalry?"

"Exactly so. I knew I could count on your understanding," Lady Wytton said. "I have heard you are a perceptive person. I should never have dared broach this otherwise." She glanced around as if she were afraid of being overheard. "So he did confide in me a little."

"Thank you for being so frank," Giles said. "Anything you tell me will be very helpful."

She studied her nails for a moment, nodding, and then said, "The fact of it is, that it makes no sense – the thing he was trying to tell me. Necessarily, he was not direct. He felt he could not be, I suppose."

This seemed to be nothing but riddles, so Giles said, "Perhaps you could just repeat his own words?"

"Yes, yes, I shall try and remember it exactly: he said, 'I have discovered something that makes me afraid for you,' and he said it so gravely. What could he have meant?"

"He did not clarify?"

"There was no chance. We were alone for only a few minutes and it took him a while to get to the point, and then we were interrupted. And I never got the chance, and now – oh..." She looked away, tears overcoming her. "What did he mean?"

Giles asked himself again why Fred Pierce had been in the bank so late at night.

"Stockholm means nothing to you, ma'am?" he asked.

"Stockholm?" she said.

"Fred never spoke of Stockholm or Sweden to you?"

"Not that I remember. Why do you ask?"

"It is what he said before he died," Giles said after a moment. This was too much for her and she began to cry. When her tears had subsided a little, Giles asked, "One last question, if I may, ma'am?"

"Yes, of course. Anything!"

"Did Fred like puzzles and riddles? Word puzzles, in particular?"

"Yes, yes, he did!" she exclaimed. "Very much. And he was clever at them. Rhymes, riddles, that sort of thing."

Carswell came into the room. He was still in his vomit-stained shirt sleeves, and he looked dishevelled and grim-faced. Seeing him, Lady Wytton took flight.

"Anything interesting?" Carswell said, pointing to Giles' open notebook.

"Possibly. Stockholm may be an acronym or an anagram or a riddle. Or not. It may just be Stockholm, which is interesting in itself."

"Good God, what a tangle," said Carswell, sitting down. "I shall have to stay here. The boy is in a shaky state, and as for the mother – may I beg a favour?"

"I was about to suggest that I ride back by way of Hawksby and send your man – Jacob, is it not? – with some clean clothes."

"That is exactly what I was going to ask," said Carswell. "Yes, please send Jacob. And I need a few things that Lady Blanchfort or the housekeeper might have to hand."

"Put them down here," said Giles, offering his notebook. Carswell scratched down his list. "And what message shall I give Mrs Carswell?" he added.

Carswell stared at him, as if the question was a shock to him.

"I don't know. What should I say?" He tugged at his filthy shirt front. "I have had one patient die today and now I have a child at death's door. What am I supposed to say?"

Giles hesitated to answer, knowing how easy it would be for him to fill a page or two to Emma outlining the day's events and telling her how he wished he might be with her. Writing to her was always his greatest pleasure.

"Excuse me," he said.

Carswell ripped his list from the notebook and said after a moment, "Tell her I will be back as soon as I can."

"Of course," said Giles, folding the list.

~

Lady Blanchfort was resting, and so it was Mrs Carswell who received him, in an impressive library, shuttered and so deliciously cool that Giles found himself envying Carswell's married quarters.

Mrs Carswell was sitting at a desk surrounded by books, looking most industrious and charming. He could not help remembering the first days of his own marriage to Laura, how she had been waiting to greet him in the stuffy little sitting room and how another man telling him he had been delayed would be a grave disappointment. But Mrs Carswell showed no sign of that.

"I have been trying to work out which neighbour you meant, Major Vernon," she said, jumping up. "I have the county gazetteer here, you see, and the Peerage and Baronetage, and from what I can gather from the novel itself, I have solved it. Is it Hurrell of Hurrell Place?"

"It is only a hypothesis," said Giles.

"I can tell by your expression I have hit the mark!" she said, smiling and clapping her hands together. "May I explain my reasoning to you? I must say it has been diverting."

"Of course," he said.

She picked up Anon's novel, which now had a host of paper markers. "It is this passage here that I found telling. The description of the house – well, read it for yourself." She offered him the book, open at the page. "From here," she added, pointing out the passage.

> Mr Breakbridge was the youngest son of a country gentleman, bearing an illustrious and ancient name which he no longer felt able to use, such had been the quarrels in the family. He had grown up in his father's house, a fabulous mansion, one of the most famous in the North of England, situated at the centre of an extensive and valuable estate. His father, though a mere baronet, considered the family far superior to any other in the district, for his forefathers had been on those lands since before the Norman Conquest, without the slightest doubt. In-

> deed, there was some talk of them being there at the time of the Romans, leaders of an ancient noble tribe of British warriors. This intense family pride kept them apart from their neighbours. Mr Breakbridge's father did not care to dine anywhere except at his own table, and he schooled his children in the same creed. Breakbridge Place and the company of their own kin were to be sufficient for them. The other great noble families who lived within calling distance were counter-jumpers at best.

Giles could not help smiling at that.

"Hurrell of Hurrell Place. It can only be," Mrs Carswell went on. "The county gazetteer has the line about the family being there at the time of the Romans. And then, there is the description of the house –"

"Yes, yes, I see it. It is clear. I can see why –"

"Sir Morten was moved to burn it? It gets far worse, I assure you."

"Well deduced, ma'am, I must say! But I must also counsel discretion. You may meet Sir Morten soon enough. Mrs Maitland and Lady Maria are at Hurrell Place at the moment, as a matter of fact."

"So you know the monstrous baronet?"

"Monstrous? Is the book so plain as that?"

"Yes. Monstrous and cruel. Poor Mr Breakbridge suffers terribly at his hands – especially as a boy. And there is a dreadful older brother too."

"That explains a great deal," said Giles, thinking of the scene in the hall he had witnessed and the palpable anger of Arthur Hurrell. "I advise you not to take it at face value. People with grievances are liable to exaggerate. And being scrupulous and fair makes for a dull story."

"It is certainly not dull," she said. "You must read it and see what you think, given you know the players."

"Your husband wants to read it first – if he has time. I'm afraid I have tied him up in a net of work already, Mrs

Carswell, and now there has been an accident at Raythorpe Rectory which will keep him there tonight. A little boy of five – a horrible accident. It was fortunate that Mr Carswell was to hand, and he must stay there tonight in case of complications."

Mrs Carswell frowned and said, "How wretched. He is very clever at such things, though, so I am sure the boy will mend beautifully. But it is a pity he will not be home."

"That is something, I regret to say, that will be your lot to bear, Mrs Carswell. Our business is an inconvenient one for domestic life. Speaking as one about to establish my own hearth."

He made what he thought was a sympathetic gesture, but she did not look reconciled to her loss or her lot.

Then inspiration struck him. "In the meantime, ma'am, perhaps I can ask a favour of you. I have a riddle on my hands. I have not made any progress with it. May I?" he said, indicating a stand of ink and paper.

"Of course. What kind of riddle?"

"I don't know," he said, taking up a sheet of paper and folding it in four, and then dividing the paper using a letter knife. "That is part of the difficulty." He did the same with another two sheets and then wrote each letter of STOCKHOLM on his quarter scraps. Then he went over to a large baize-covered table in the centre of the room, meant for spreading out maps, and laid them out.

"Stockholm?" she said.

"The young man who died this morning from the fire had a love of puzzles and riddles. This was the last thing he said to us, and he seemed eager to say it. It may have been a product of delirium, but I want to see if there may be more to it than that. These trifles can sometimes mean a great deal. Perhaps you would like to help me?"

"Stockholm," she said again, and after a moment began to rearrange the letters. "Oh, how interesting," she said, "most lock – but that leaves the h... moths lock?" And she began rearranging them again. "Cloth leaves us only skom... now I wonder –"

When Lady Blanchfort came in a little later, Mrs Carswell was completely absorbed in the task, drawing up grids of letters and talking authoritatively of ciphers and substitutions. Giles, still a little astonished how she had taken to the task, was about to compliment Lady Blanchfort on her daughter's accomplishments, but she seemed displeased by what she saw.

"Eleanor, you must take care you do not tire yourself with that," she said.

"I will not be tired," Mrs Carswell said. "Besides, I must help Major Vernon."

"And we all know how these things go with you," said Lady Blanchfort. "You will work yourself into a frenzy."

"Of course I shall not, Mama!" Mrs Carswell said. "What nonsense!"

"Please take care, I beg you," she said. She turned to Giles and said quietly, "Perhaps we might have a word in the garden, Major Vernon?"

So he went out onto the terrace with Lady Blanchfort.

"That sort of thing is dangerous for her," she said. "I know I may sound foolish and old-fashioned, but I have learnt the hard way. When I discovered she had such a prodigious talent for mathematics, I was eager to encourage it, and I hired the best tutors for her. Unfortunately –" She sighed. "It disturbed her. I do not know why, but it was alarming the effect it had on her. I do not believe my sex to be weak and incapable, sir, but there are things that our temperaments are unsuited to bear, no matter how strong the appetite."

"My apologies. I had no intention of stirring her up. It was simply to give her a distraction while Mr Carswell is elsewhere. If I had known –"

"You were not to know," she said. "And perhaps I am being over-cautious. It is simply that this is a difficult time for her. The first days home as a wife. I remember all too well how bewildered I was!" She looked away, clearly embarrassed by her frankness. "Excuse me, sir."

"I will attempt to persuade her to stop, then," said Giles.

"Thank you. She may listen to you. I pray that she does. I do not want an episode developing. And you will stay and dine with us? We have no one to eat Mr Carswell's portion, after all."

He went back into the library and found Mrs Carswell still at her desk.

"It makes no sense," she said. "I cannot find any sense in it."

"That is because there may be no sense in it. He had a high fever. It was uttered *in extremis*. Perhaps it was nothing, or something private and personal. Perhaps we shall never know what it meant."

"How can you, of all people, bear not to know?" she said, laying down her pen and gazing up at him. "All I have heard of you from my husband, is how you will worry at a problem until the answer emerges."

"That makes me sound like a terrier after a rabbit," said Giles. "But I often let things go. To be careless is a delicious condition, especially on a beautiful evening like this. Would you show me the gardens?"

"What did my mother say to you?" she said. "You are trying to make me stop."

"Yes, to be frank – and I hope I may claim that privilege with you?"

She stood up and looked him over.

"Your frankness is famous too. Felix has told me all about it. I should expect to be scourged if I permit it."

"It can be mutual," Giles said. "No, it will be." He made a slight bow and she smiled.

"Very well. I will show you the gardens. How could I dare disobey you?"

# Chapter Ten

Both Johnny and Mrs Gray passed a comfortable, uneventful night, much to Felix's relief.

He was taking his breakfast with Mr Gray the next morning when a servant came in to say that Mr Braithwaite was waiting to see him.

"Show him in, Jane," Gray said to the servant, and turned to Felix. "We are honoured. Braithwaite is our village blacksmith and a splendid man. I wonder what he wants."

He entered a moment later, and from his powerful physique and sturdy clothes one might have guessed his profession. He seemed ill at ease.

"Sit down, won't you? Will you have some breakfast?" said Gray.

"No, sir, I couldn't eat. The thing is –"

"You must not mind Mr Carswell, Braithwaite. Come and sit down."

Braithwaite sat down awkwardly and Gray poured him a cup of tea.

"Now, what is amiss, Braithwaite?" Gray said.

"It's the missus, Parson," he said. "She's gone. Clean gone."

"Did you quarrel?" Gray asked.

"No, sir, certainly not. She's just gone."

"When did you last see her?" Gray said.

"Four nights ago. I've been hoping she'd be back by now."

"So she has gone off like this before?" Felix asked.

"Nay, nay, nothing like that, sir, but she is a strange one. She has her notions and I'm not one to question them, for she has been the making of me, Parson, you know that – and you know what's she's like – queer, right queer at times."

"But never a bad wife or mother," said Gray, "from what I have observed."

"You'd be right about that, Parson. She sees us all to church on Sundays."

"She does, and you are all a credit to her."

"Then where is she?" he said. "And why's she gone?"

"Tell me, did she vanish on her way somewhere, Mr Braithwaite," said Felix, "or was she gone from your house?"

"From the house. I went up to Pennings to look at his gates – he wants them replacing – and when I came back she was gone. She'd got our neighbour's girl to mind the children. She gave her a ha'penny to do it, and off she went along the high road with her Sunday bonnet on."

"Her Sunday bonnet?" said Felix. "That's interesting. Are you sure?"

"Aye, for it's not in its box. I gave it her at Easter and it cost me a pretty penny."

"Can you describe it?" Felix said.

Braithwaite looked stumped for a moment and then said, "It was – you know, like this," and gestured about his face to indicate the shape of the brim. "Black it was, with a lot of what-cha-ma-call-it on it – Esther told me the proper name. She knows all the names. She wanted to be a milliner and have her own shop. Point of something. Nay, I can't remember."

"Perhaps Mrs Gray will know," said Gray. "She will have noticed, for Mrs Braithwaite is a handsome woman and knows how to choose a handsome bonnet."

"That's true enough," said Braithwaite.

"But she did not put on her Sunday dress?" said Felix. "Just the bonnet?"

Braithwaite nodded.

Felix tried to form a mental picture of the missing blacksmith's wife. What did Gray mean by her being handsome? That was a compliment reserved for a woman who was neither a classical beauty nor sweetly pretty.

"And it has been four days since you saw her?"

"Aye, sir, and I have asked all about the neighbourhood and no one has seen her. I am at my wits end, Parson. I am beginning to think something terrible has happened to her."

"No, no, I am sure that is not the case. Mrs Braithwaite is able to take care of herself."

"True, Parson, true."

"And you had no hint of her being unhappy or troubled by anything?" said Felix.

"No, sir."

"Does she get letters?" said Felix. "There was nothing unusual in that regard? Or a visitor that you did not expect?"

"No, sir."

"And in which direction was she headed, did the girl notice that?"

"Northminster, sir, though why the devil she would want to go there, I cannot say. There is nothing there for any of us."

"Have you spoken to your village constable about this, Mr Braithwaite?" Felix said.

"No, not yet, sir."

"Then you must give a full description to him and he will send it about the district," Felix said. "And I will take a copy to Major Vernon at Constabulary Headquarters. They keep a list there of people who have gone missing, and it is often the case that they are found again without much difficulty. Likewise we have a list at the Infirmary."

Braithwaite looked downcast at that, and Mr Gray said, "Come, Braithwaite – I am going to say Morning Prayer. That will be a comfort for you."

"Aye, Parson, maybe so."

"Will you join us, Mr Carswell?"

Felix shook his head.

"I must get back to Northminster. I will arrange for the

nurse to come out to you straightaway and I will be back in the afternoon, as I said. In the meantime, you must send Jacob with a message if there is any change. I will just look in on him before I go."

~

Felix met Major Vernon as arranged. Felix was waiting for him in his laboratory in the basement of the Northern Office, among the crates of unpacked books.

"You did not buy anything on the nature of fire, by any chance?" Major Vernon said.

"No. Nor on the treatment of burns," Felix said. "I could have done with some up-to-date information. But it is not much studied, unfortunately. Mr Harper was saying one of us ought to write a paper on it, for just that reason."

"Will you do the post-mortem here or at the Infirmary?"

"At the Infirmary. Mr Harper expressed a wish to assist me, and I don't want to inconvenience him. He is forming a hypothesis about smoke inhalation. Do we have permission from the family yet?"

Major Vernon shook his head.

"I thought we would go and ask Mr Pierce in person. He may need a little persuasion, and we need to set matters in context for him."

Together they walked to the Pierce's residence in St Anne's. As they did, Felix told him of the missing blacksmith's wife.

"When you go back to the Rectory you must get Mrs Gray to give you a full description of that bonnet," said Major Vernon. "Did Mr Braithwaite say anything else about her clothes – her apron, for example? Or a leather bag hanging from her belt?"

"No. He just said her work clothes."

"A red-striped apron?"

"I'm sorry. I should have pressed him. He was going to speak to the village constable and give a detailed description. Is it urgent?"

"It might be. Our fire-setter was most likely a woman. Noakes described the woman who bribed him to go away as wearing a lace-covered, half-veiled bonnet. In fact, I will go and see the blacksmith myself when you go back to the Rectory."

The Pierces lived in an expansive, expensive villa, set behind high walls with a large front garden. Mrs and Miss Pierce received them in the drawing room, where the blinds were down and the looking glasses had been draped with gauze. The ladies themselves were wearing fresh, elaborate mourning but their eyes were red from crying and their faces grey and drawn. The prayer book and the Bible lay open on the table.

"Is Mr Pierce at home?" said Major Vernon.

"He is... indisposed," said Mrs Pierce.

"Would you like Mr Carswell to see him?" said Major Vernon.

"I don't think that will be necessary," she said after another pause.

Then Miss Pierce, who had been studying her hands, looked directly at Felix and said, "Perhaps he should, Mama." Mrs Pierce gave her daughter a searching glance. "He would never send anyone for himself, you know that, and he might be quite unwell. It is not like him, to lock himself away as he has done. We should let Mr Carswell see him."

Mrs Pierce thought for a moment and then rose from her seat.

"I shall go and ask him."

She left the room, and Miss Pierce at once leapt from her place and went to close the door behind her mother. She stood leaning against it, so that no one might come back in.

"You must see him," she said. "Something is very wrong. Very wrong. Ever since Fred was injured – well, to be honest, long before that he has not been himself."

"Your father, you mean?" said Major Vernon.

"I think he is going insane," said Miss Pierce, in a whisper. "I know that is a terrible thing to say, but I cannot think of any other explanation."

"Did Fred think this too?" Major Vernon said.

Miss Pierce nodded.

"We were going to talk to Mama about it. It seemed so difficult to say anything, though, for she is blind to everything. Of course she must be because she could not bear it if this were true, but sometimes –"

"What makes you think he is losing his reason?" said Felix. "Was there anything specific?"

She leant back on the door, closing her eyes for a moment.

"Where do I start?" she said. "It is a hundred little things. He has developed a terrible temper, and I think he has been drinking immoderately. I know he cannot sleep. Some nights he is pacing about the house, or rather upstairs – there is an old lumber room upstairs and he has on occasion shut himself in. He may be up there now. He was there last night. He was pacing all night. I feel we are losing him. First Fred, and now this! I have hidden his razors, though I dare say he will be storming about demanding them."

"That was prudent, Miss Pierce."

"And you discussed this with Fred?" said Major Vernon.

"Yes, a great deal. How could we not? When one's own dear father..."

"I think I should go up to him," said Felix. "This sort of restless agitation can be an indication of mania."

"Would you? Can you help him, do you think?"

"I don't know, but I will do my best," Felix said.

"Perhaps you would take us up?" Major Vernon said.

So they climbed to the top of the house, which seemed intolerably stuffy on such a day, and found Mrs Pierce standing in front of a closed door, tapping almost imperceptibly, and saying, "George, George, can you hear me?" so quietly that he might only have heard if he were a supernatural being.

"Mama," said Miss Pierce, "we must let Mr Carswell see him. It is beyond concealing now."

She gently steered her away from the door.

"I will take her to her room," said Miss Pierce. Mrs Pierce consented, but she seemed enveloped in a veil of shame and could not look either of them in the face.

The door was latched, but a sharp shove by the Major soon dislodged it.

Felix went in, expecting at least a corpse or a man on the verge of suicide, and was relieved to find neither. However, the sight was miserable enough: Mr Pierce, dressed in his nightshirt, was on his hands and knees, rocking back and forth in a piteous paroxysm of grief and anxiety. His agitation was so profound that it was with great difficulty that Felix attempted to examine him. He had scraped his hands and knees to a bloody mess on the bare boards, he had a high temperature, his pulse was highly irregular and he was showing signs of dehydration. Felix managed to get him to drink a little brandy and water, laced with laudanum, and then after some struggle, they got him to bed in a servant's garret across the landing, keeping him calm by means of tying the bed sheets around him, like swaddling about a baby. There his agitation seemed to diminish a little.

Mrs Pierce was beyond speaking to and so Felix was forced to give the bad news to Miss Pierce.

"Confinement – at least for a short period – would be the best for him," Felix said. "At least somewhere where he can be kept from damaging himself and where they are used to dealing with such cases."

"A mad house," said Miss Pierce. "You mean a mad house, sir, do you not?"

"Yes, but it would not be for long. Such cases often resolve themselves. It is a question of adequate supervision, which cannot be provided here. Dr Hall has an establishment out at Blatherton. It is the best in the county," Felix said. "He can be trusted to be careful with your father."

She nodded and said, "Then you had better arrange it. We will do whatever is needed."

~

"So what may have caused such a collapse?" Major Vernon asked as they walked back into town. "I know that these things do not always have obvious causes, yet in this case –"

"That's true enough. The circumstances can be everything or nothing."

"Would some serious difficulty at the bank be enough to send a man to distraction?"

"I don't know. His son's death might be a more immediate cause."

"I shall have to go and see Lord Wytton," said Major Vernon. "I need to know what the real condition of the bank is. And I also need to know that this attack of his is genuine."

"I think it was," said Felix. "Why on earth would he feign madness?"

"To cover some wrongdoing at the bank. Fred Pierce seems to have attempted to warn Lady Wytton that she was in danger of some sort. Did he mean financial ruin?"

"You think the bank is going to collapse?" said Felix.

"We shall see. In the meantime, I am going back to Raythorpe to talk to the blacksmith, and you must get Mr

Pierce taken to Blatherton."

"I will see you there later," said Felix. "I have to go to the Rectory."

# Chapter Eleven

Braithwaite the blacksmith was at his work assisted by two strong lads, the forge blasting out heat and sparks flying this way and that, but catching sight of Giles tying up his horse, he left the fire.

"Afternoon, sir. How can I help you?"

Giles explained why he was there.

"I would go and look for her myself," Braithwaite said. "I have been on the verge of going a hundred times, but I cannot think which way to go, how to begin, and besides there is the matter of the children and the business." He shook his head. "I'm glad to know that you are looking into it, sir."

"I hope we may find her, and with some happy conclusion," Giles said.

"I pray to the Lord that you do."

"Tell me a little more about your wife, Mr Braithwaite. You said to my colleague, Mr Carswell, that she was strange. I was wondering what you meant by that?"

"It's hard to say. It's what other folk say of her, you see – and she herself says it too. 'I'm a strange one, husband,' she says to me. 'I'm not one of you.' She says she has the heart of a gypsy."

"But no gypsy blood as far as you know?"

Braithwaite shook his head. "Nay. But maybe, long ago, for she has the look of it. Perhaps that's what makes her feel it. You can see it in our children: black hair and dark eyes they all have, and they are handsome like her. Nothing of me in them, at least not in their looks."

"Is your wife from these parts?"

"Yes. Her father had the forge here. I was his apprentice

and we ended up wed, and I took over the forge when he died."

"And how long have you been wed?"

"Ten years, sir."

"And no serious quarrels between you, if you do not mind me asking, Mr Braithwaite?"

Braithwaite gave an emphatic shake of the head.

"Why would I quarrel with my sweetheart?" he said, spreading out his great hands. "And why would she go? I cannot stop asking that, and the children are asking it too. Why has she gone? When will she be home? I swear that the Devil himself, or the Fairy King, has taken her – for that is the only sense I can make of it."

"Does Mrs Braithwaite know much about the business of the forge?"

"Aye, she knows a fair bit. And no one can lay a fire like her. She learnt it from her father – how to get a quick, hot fire first thing. Time is money, she says, and the forge is away and ready, just like that!"

"How does she do it?"

"She has some special rags – she makes them, soaks them in – well, I don't know what, but they burn as hot as hellfire!"

"May I see them?"

"She keeps them in here." He took down a glazed jar from a shelf and offered it to Giles. "Strange but sharp as a knife is my Esther." Inside were strips of white cotton soaked in some greasy substance, just like the one he had found at the warehouse.

"May I take a few of these?"

"Yes, sir, as many as you like," said the blacksmith.

Giles put them in his pocket and took out his notebook.

"If I could just confirm with you the description of her clothes that you gave to Mr Carswell – a red apron, a black lace bonnet and a leather pocket, worn over her skirts."

"That's right, sir. Red check on the apron. Her favourite."

"And does she have any money on her, do you think?"

"She's taken nothing. I looked in the box where we keep what we can, and she has not touched it."

"And she has no secret store of her own, as far as you know?"

"No, sir. She would never do that. We have no secrets."

~

Lord Wytton was not at home when Giles called at Raythorpe Hall. His sister, Miss Wytton, received him instead.

"We should have met the other night, Major Vernon," she said. "I was supposed to go and dine at Hurrell Place with my brother and sister-in-law but I was not well. My sister-in-law is at the Rectory now. Poor little boy! It is so fortunate that Mr – Carswell, is it? – was there. I don't suppose I can help you with anything."

"You might, Miss Wytton, as a matter of fact. I have been at the forge, speaking to Mr Braithwaite. Perhaps you have heard that his wife has gone missing." She nodded. "The circumstances are rather strange. I wonder if you might be able to tell me anything about her. I understand she is the daughter of a previous blacksmith here?"

"Yes," said Miss Wytton. "That is so. I had heard about it and I do know her."

"And what do you think about it? Did it surprise you, from what you have observed of her?"

Miss Wytton thought for a moment and said, "A little, but there has always been something about her. But you really should ask my brother. He was put out to nurse with the family. They grew up together, so to speak. Ah, here he is."

Lord Wytton had come in.

"You want to speak to me, Vernon?" he said.

"He wants to know about Esther Braithwaite and why she has gone missing," Miss Wytton said. "I was just saying that you practically grew up with her."

"My sister overstates it. I don't know her in the slightest," said Lord Wytton. "And why are you still here, Peggy? Did Aunt Chatham change her mind?"

"I changed my mind," said Miss Wytton. "It's too hot for travelling."

"She will be offended," said Lord Wytton. "And why do you think you may change your mind at such short notice?"

"Because I'm not a package to be sent about the country at your say-so!" said Miss Wytton. "Excuse me, won't you, Major Vernon?" At this she left the room abruptly and her brother glared after her, with the look of a man about to lose his temper.

"I must have a drink," he said. "Will you join me, Vernon?"

"No thank you, my lord, but I do have some more questions for you, if you don't mind?"

"To what end?"

"About the fire in Jebb Street."

"Very well, if you must. But I must have a drink. It has been a damnable day – another damnable day."

Lord Wytton led him to his study, which showed few signs of study and more of sporting pursuits. The butler was setting out a bottle of champagne and a bottle of porter, which Wytton himself then mixed to his liking in a large silver tankard. He threw himself down on the sofa and drank deeply.

"You are sure you won't join me?" he said.

Giles was tempted, but shook his head again and sat down opposite.

"You've been at the bank, I suppose?" he said. Wytton nodded and took another draught of his concoction. "Then you know what has happened to Mr Pierce?"

"Dear God, yes!" said Wytton. "What a business. I had

not thought that he, of all people..."

"So you have seen no signs of undue stress in him?"

"No, but as I said, I don't really have much to do with the day-to-day business of the bank. Each time I have seen Pierce of late he seemed entirely in charge of himself. I had no idea! And now they have carted him off somewhere! Lord, what a fate!"

"He may recover."

"I hope so, for without him – and of course Fred Pierce, as well..." He groaned.

"It is hard to imagine the management of the place without him, I suppose?"

"Very," said Wytton. "But thankfully the bank's affairs are in good order."

"You are certain of that?"

"Absolutely."

"You don't think that Pierce's breakdown might be due to some difficulty in the business?"

"No, not at all," Wytton said, shaking his head. "The bank is in perfect order. In fact, if you are interested, Major Vernon, I can offer you a rate on any deposit that might surprise you."

"I'll bear that in mind," said Giles.

"We are rock solid. Poor Pierce's afflictions are nothing to do with the bank."

"Nor Fred Pierce being troubled?" Giles said. "Several people have mentioned that to me. What do you suppose that might be about?"

"His father's health?" said Wytton. "Perhaps he saw signs that we did not."

"Perhaps," said Giles.

"It's a wretched business," said Wytton, getting up and refilling his tankard. "I suppose Fred's death was the last straw. Terrible. Terrible."

"I wonder if I might raise the business of Esther

Braithwaite again, my lord?" Giles said.

"And why would I know anything about that?" said Wytton.

"Your sister –"

"My sister is a feather-head," said Wytton.

"But you were put to nurse there?"

"Yes, I was a child. What would I know of her now?"

"Because sometimes bonds are formed in such circumstances."

"Only in ill-regulated families," said Wytton. "I have no special knowledge of this woman because of that. I don't think I was there above a month or two."

"Yes," said Giles. "But it is a puzzle, none the less, that a woman happily settled, with children, would simply vanish. The consensus is that she is a fine-looking creature."

"Yes, and the lure of another man is the obvious answer to your puzzle, Major Vernon. She's a bored wife – common enough, I should say. No mystery there, with a dolt like Braithwaite for a husband. What else can explain it?"

Giles got up and said, "I dare say you are right, my lord."

"Women are fickle at the best of times," said Wytton, finishing his tankard and lolling back on the sofa. He did not make an attractive picture, and Giles could not help remembering his wife's blushing confession about Fred Pierce's affections.

"Thank you for your time, my lord," he said.

He walked down to the Rectory, considering Lord Wytton's denial of intimacy with the family that nursed him. Giles had himself spent his first two years out to nurse, as had his siblings. His mother had no fashionable notions of nursing and his father had been a firm believer in the old system. When he had come back home, he had not been made to neglect his milk siblings and had often gone to play with the boys in the cottage. He knew what had become of them subsequently, but perhaps the Vernons had been peculiar in that regard.

Carswell was still busy with his little patient and Mr Gray was with him. Instead, he was shown into the drawing room where Mrs Gray was resting on the sofa.

"May I distract you until the consultation is done?" he asked.

"I wish you would, Major Vernon. It is hard to be made to do nothing in such circumstances, but Mr Carswell is right, and I must submit."

"I wanted to talk to you about Mrs Braithwaite and her Sunday bonnet."

Mrs Gray smiled at that, but only for a moment, saying, "Oh dear, I hope she will be found soon and safe, and I hope there will be no scandal!"

"Do you think there might be?" Giles asked.

"I don't know. It is just that so often when you hear of this sort of thing it's all a question of an unhappy wife succumbing to temptation – yet..."

"Yet?"

"Mrs Braithwaite is the last person one would imagine doing something like that. I have known other women where you might believe it, but not her. And leaving her children! It is a platitude to say that no woman could ever leave her children, but sadly it does happen, and far more often than one would think, but Mrs Braithwaite was truly devoted to them, and to her husband. That is why it is such a puzzle."

"It must have been something very out of the ordinary, from all I have heard of her."

"I am glad to hear you say that," said Mrs Gray. "I did not think it could be anything wicked or commonplace. Neither of those things strike me as being in her nature. She is such a fine creature, so naturally noble and really something quite extraordinary."

"Could you be more specific?" Giles asked.

"I wish I could. It's just that she has an air about her, as if she is a lost princess or something. As if she is from a fairy tale – oh, how ridiculous that must sound, but if you had met her, you would know what I mean."

Giles nodded and said, "And that Sunday bonnet?"

"Black straw, trimmed with broad, pinked black ribbon and with a black tulle veiling, trimmed with just the right amount of lace – not too much and not too little. It was most fetching and so nicely done, all in all. I'm ashamed to say I took in all the details and envied her it! And on a Sunday!" She made a grimace that was half a smile.

"It is excellent that you did," said Giles.

At this moment, Carswell and Gray came into the drawing room.

"How is he, Mr Carswell?" she said.

"Much improved and eager to see his mama," said Carswell.

"Oh, thank God!" said Mrs Gray, clasping her hands together. "So I may go to him?"

"For a while, yes," said Carswell.

"Oh, thank you, thank you, Mr Carswell," she said, as she got up from the sofa, assisted by her husband. "And I do promise absolutely to follow all your prescriptions to the letter."

"She looks better already," said Carswell, when Mr and Mrs Gray had left the room. "How did you get on at the forge?"

"I have something for you," said Giles and took out the piece of paper in which he had folded the rag strips. "These were made by Mrs Braithwaite to light the fire. Soaked in some mixture of whale oil, lard and perhaps something else. Would it be possible to match this with the rag I found?"

"Maybe," said Carswell, sniffing the rag. "It's certainly similar. And ingenious."

"It still might be a coincidence," Giles said.

"Noakes was bribed by a woman in a fancy bonnet,"

Carswell said. "That adds greatly to the idea it was the missing Mrs Braithwaite. And I ought to be able to see if these are of the same ilk."

"We need to find her," Giles said.

"Are you going back to Northminster, then?"

"Not just yet. I want to make a few more enquiries here. There is a vexing lack of gossip about Mrs Braithwaite. Perhaps the village inn will supply some."

~

Felix settled with a tankard of ale in the pleasant garden of The Lamb Inn and watched while Major Vernon encouraged a variety of village stalwarts to weigh in on the mysterious disappearance of the blacksmith's wife. He came back from his conversations frowning.

"This becomes more and more curious," he said, sitting down next to Felix on the bench. "I cannot get a shred of criticism about her. They are as puzzled as her husband. The King of the Fairies is the principal candidate, and who am I to disagree with that? So I have no clear leads to go on."

"Well, the beer is good," Felix said.

"You have left me some, then?" said Major Vernon, peering into the almost empty jug.

He poured the scanty remains into his own tankard.

"It's this heat," Felix said. "It has made me uncommonly thirsty – and tired." He yawned.

"It may be stronger than we anticipated," said Major Vernon, sipping his own beer with caution. "I wonder if they can make a decent cup of coffee here."

"I doubt it," said Felix.

"So do I," said Major Vernon. "We will try tea instead."

The barmaid came up and asked for Major Vernon's

order.

"Do you know Mrs Braithwaite?" Major Vernon asked the girl, having ordered a pot of tea.

"Known her all my life," she said.

"Do you have any idea where she has gone?"

"No, but it doesn't surprise me she has, not one bit. I was only saying to my sister that she was always bound to come to trouble, so proud of herself and her only a blacksmith's daughter."

"But you have not heard where she might have gone?"

The girl shook her head. "No, sir. Will that be all, sir? No more ale?" she added with a glance at Felix.

He shook his head.

When she had gone, Major Vernon said, "That is the nearest thing to criticism I have heard. I shall have to press her."

"And I ought to go home. But I ought to look in at the Rectory before I do."

"Then drink some tea first, perhaps?" said Major Vernon.

"A good idea," said Felix. "How did you enjoy dinner at Hawksby, by the way?"

"There is something I have been meaning to tell you about that. I fear I may have upset your mother-in-law."

"That is as easy as breaking an eggshell," said Felix.

"I asked Mrs Carswell to put her mind to work on Stockholm. I hope you don't mind that I did – I thought it might amuse her, and as you know, another pair of eyes is always valuable on any such problem – but Lady Blanchfort was very concerned, and told me to persuade her not to continue with it. She considers such puzzles dangerous for her daughter. So I told Mrs Carswell that it was not necessary to proceed with it. We went for a delightful walk in the gardens instead."

"Dangerous? What does she mean by that?"

"She said that Mrs Carswell might easily be overwrought

by such things. Yes, it was a little strange, but she was perfectly sincere."

"That sounds nonsensical," said Felix.

"I am sure she has Mrs Carswell's best interests at heart. It was not lightly done."

"Perhaps," said Felix. "It still seems odd. Eleanor does have a talent for such things. I have never seen anyone work out an acrostic as fast as she. She had my parents astonished. There can be no harm in it. What nonsense! To discourage her daughter from rational thinking – what a peculiar woman she is!"

"As I said, it was not lightly done," Major Vernon said.

"The sooner we are free of her and can live as we wish, the better!" Felix said.

"Even though she orders your house so pleasantly for you?"

"That is as maybe, but I do not like such interference. And to take such a line with you!"

"Oh, my pride can take it," said Major Vernon, smiling. "It was her concern that moved me. It was, as I said, quite genuine, and she must know her daughter's mind pretty well."

"She has sought to control her overly in the past," said Felix, "and Eleanor has a ragbag of silly notions in her head, which I am sure are all her mother's doing, and this business only confirms it. To tell her not to think! How absurd!"

# Chapter Twelve

Felix got back to Hawksby a little before seven, the butler informing him that dinner would be at eight.

He went straight upstairs and into their bedroom, throwing off his coat. The door to Eleanor's dressing room was open, and he saw she was sitting at her dressing table in her underclothes, her hair falling down over her bare shoulders. She was not gazing in the glass but bent over some piece of writing. Since she was completely unaware of his arrival, he could not resist stealing up behind her and putting his hands over her eyes.

He regretted doing so a moment later, for she screamed with genuine distress. At the same time she was so startled that her hand flew out and she upset the ink pot.

It was all a great mess. She had been scribbling letters and numbers on scraps and strips of paper, and the ink had gone all over them. He attempted to mitigate the damage with his handkerchief, a Turkey red one that Sukey had made for him. Seeing it sopping up the ink, and ruined forever, he was filled with unexpected sadness. What had it even been doing in his pocket? Jacob had surely put it there, and he was not to know its history. To him it was simply a handkerchief.

Eleanor began plucking up her papers with great haste, as if they were about to be consumed by fire.

"What is all this?" Felix said, stooping to retrieve one that she had dropped.

"Stockholm," she said, as if he were a fool, "of course!"

"Oh, that."

"And it is a cipher," she went on. "I am certain of it, and I was so close – and now you have ruined everything!" She flung out her hand towards the sea of ink on the dressing table.

"I'm sorry. It was irresistible. You looked – irresistible." He put out his hands to her but she batted them away. "I'm sorry, truly. And I am sure it can be sorted."

"I will have to start again! It is all ruined, utterly ruined."

"Let me see – perhaps I can help you? I know a little about these things."

But she shook her head and clutched the papers to her. At this moment Stevens knocked at the door and came in.

"Mr Carswell has upset the ink pot," Eleanor said to her, as if she were reporting a transgression to the schoolmaster. Stevens began to clear up the mess without a word, gathering up the ruined muslin cover and Sukey's handkerchief with it, while Eleanor swept into the bedroom. Felix followed her and closed the door behind him.

She opened her commonplace book and began to tuck the little papers away.

"Will you let me see?" he said, carefully calm. "We could look at them together."

But she closed the book and pursed her lips. There was a knock on the door behind him.

"Yes?" said Felix.

"Your bath is ready, sir," said Jacob.

"Thank you, that will be all for now," said Felix. When Jacob had gone, he said to Eleanor, "Will you keep me company?" On their wedding journey they had frequently indulged in this delightful intimacy, but now she shook her head. "I suppose you need to dress," he said. She opened the commonplace book and began to sort through the pieces of paper. "How long have you been doing this?" he said.

"What did she say to you?"

"Who?"

"My mother."

"She said nothing." She frowned as if she did not believe

him. "I have not seen her."

"You will not tell her about this," Eleanor said.

"I am all at sea," Felix said, sinking onto the sofa at the end of the bed, suddenly feeling exhausted. "What has been going on? Major Vernon asked you about Stockholm and you have decided it is some sort of elaborate cipher?"

"It's not my decision. It's a fact. Why else would Pierce say it?"

"Because the man was in a high fever and at the point of death? People say strange things. They do not necessarily mean anything, and I am sure the Major was very clear on that point."

"Yes, yes, he was – after my mother had got to him."

"What do you mean?"

"She has the ridiculous notion that a simple puzzle like this will make me ill. So she told him to dissuade me."

"He told me that. But why on earth does your mother think it would make you ill? In what way?"

"Because she is ridiculous," said Eleanor. "Simply ridiculous." She held up a strip of paper and gazed at it. "It is a cipher, I am sure of it. Give me a few more hours and I will have your answer for you!"

Felix gazed at her. Standing there in her chemise and stays, her red-gold hair cascading down and catching in the beautiful dusk light that now filled the room, she made him ache with longing. But at the same time, he was uncomfortable, feeling that Lady Blanchfort's caution had some odd truth in it. It certainly no longer seemed ridiculous.

"Have you thought of Occam's razor?" he said, getting up and taking off his waistcoat.

"What?"

"The simplest answer is usually the correct one," he went on. "At least in the practice of medicine that is a useful guide, and often enough Major Vernon and I have discovered that in our peculiar line, the theory holds good. A code, delightful though it may be to the imagination, is perhaps stretching it a little far."

"Major Vernon told me that Fred Pierce liked puzzles. And when I have this solved, you will see I am right."

"And if you cannot solve it?"

"Of course I shall!" she said. "Do you think I can't?"

"No," he began. "It's just that sometimes there is no answer to these things. It would be better to forget it, perhaps."

He stretched out his hand to her, but she did not take it. Instead she reached for a shawl and wrapped herself tightly in it, concealing all her charms from him.

"You had better have your bath," she said, and went back to her dressing room.

He went into his own dressing room and took his bath, feeling thoroughly wretched. He got out of the bath and knotted the towel about his waist; dripping a little still, he went to find her. To his relief, she had not gone back to the puzzle but was lying on the bed, her shawl still wrapped tightly about her, her back to him.

He went around and crouched down by the bed so that they were face to face. He ventured to stroke her cheek and she did not flinch. She moved a little to make space for him.

He climbed onto the bed and pulled her into his arms. To his great relief, she relaxed there and soon permitted the intimacies he had learnt she was fond of. She liked nothing better than for him to pet and fondle her, and he was happy to oblige her. The abstinence of the last few days had spiced the sauce.

"It's all right now," she murmured. "I am quite well again, you know."

Even as she said it, he knew he must restrain himself, however deliciously eager she was and how hungry he felt for her. He carefully detached himself and got off the bed.

"Perhaps we should dress," he said.

"Do you not want –?"

"Not just yet," he said. "Perhaps later? To be frank, I feel we cannot until we have decided how we will go on."

"Do you mean until I have decided to go along with you?" she said. This he could not answer. He reached for his towel and knotted it about himself again. "And I know I'm supposed to obey you, Felix, but I find that idea so difficult," she said. "But if I don't obey you, then it will spoil everything between us." She gave a sob. "That's not what I want." She curled herself up and rolled away from him again, dissolving into tears.

"And that's not what I want," he said, sitting down beside her and turning her to face him. "I do not want anything spoilt, believe me. And I don't want you to have to obey me – please, please do not let us talk in those terms!"

"But you do want me to do what you want," she said, "don't you?"

"Because it's good sense! And why you can't see that, I don't know!"

"It is not. It's disgusting, and if I were to tell anyone about it, which I might feel obliged to do, they would be shocked. If I were to tell –"

"But you will not," he said. "This is a private matter. Why would you even think of doing it? Do you think you can bully me into agreeing with you by threatening that?"

"And neither can you!" she said. "And I know it's my duty to submit to you, but how on earth am I to submit to something so unnatural and immoral, something so disgusting? No nice woman could be expected to – and I shall not!"

"Then that will be your loss!" Felix said. "And you will regret it soon enough. I know what you are like! I'll sleep in my dressing room – it's just as well your mother had it fitted out so comfortably for me."

"That's because she didn't expect you to make me into your mistress! She expected you to treat me with discretion, like a gentleman! And no gentleman would ever suggest such a way of going on with his wife as you have. It's disgusting! You are disgusting! Get out!"

She flung her hand out towards the door.

"With pleasure, ma'am!" said Felix, and left.

Jacob was laying out his evening clothes. Felix, still clad only in his towel, lit a cheroot and sat down on the window seat trying to calm himself.

"Will that be all, sir?" Jacob said.

Felix wondered how much Jacob had overheard and how long it would be before the quarrel between the young master and mistress would be the talk of all those unknown servants. The thought of that was appalling to him and he wondered if he should tell Jacob to keep quiet on the matter. But he decided that would only draw attention to it, so he dismissed him without another word and sat for some minutes smoking his cheroot, and not enjoying it in the least. He hauled himself into his evening clothes and found that Jacob had put out another of the handkerchiefs Sukey had made for him, this one not Turkey red, but embroidered with a heart. He did not put it in his pocket, but under his pillow, remembering how at least on that issue they had not quarrelled. They might have disagreed about everything else but never that. Why on earth did Eleanor find the idea so repulsive? He could not begin to understand it.

His only hope was that a good dose of abstinence would bring her round to his point of view. He knew she would not enjoy it, just as he would not. The only question that remained was who would give way first.

# Chapter Thirteen

Although she was a frequent correspondent, a letter from Emma was always something to delight in.

The sight of an envelope addressed in that familiar hand, sealed in blue, the pattern pressed in the seal from the ring he had given her, always lifted his spirits. Giles had snatched this one up on his return from Raythorpe and tucked it into his waistcoat, saving the pleasure of it for when he had the time to fully appreciate it. That time had come, as he sat alone in his room in The Black Bull in the comfort of his dressing gown.

> Hurrell Place, Tuesday
> My Dear,

He could not resist rubbing that familiar salutation with his fingertip. As ever, she had underlined it for emphasis.

> The grandeur of my bedroom has been matched by the generosity of my host with candles. I am sitting up at eleven at night, in a blaze worthy of a ballroom. But with no company – I have seen my charge to her bed. You may be sure she has exhausted herself in the acquittal of her duty for the village children's feast, and I must say I do not think my own performance was in any way deficient. We came to the conclusion, just now, in our counterpane conference, that Mrs Edward Hurrell would have been lost without us. She is a sweet, kind woman but the vicissitudes of such an occasion were beyond her. She does not have the instincts of a chatelaine although she is that, de facto, in the absence of a Lady Hurrell, or perhaps even a Mrs Arthur – if that were to happen, and on further observation I am not convinced that it will, despite the strenuous efforts of Sir Morten. (Or perhaps not strenuous enough. One would have thought that given the size of the estate and the title, more at-

tention would have been paid to the matter a little earlier, surely? But then I think of Charles and I wonder when would be the moment to interfere. Perhaps in the normal course of things we do not need such encouragement. People are better at managing these things for themselves and it is usually too much haste rather than too much leisure that is the problem.)

We were assisted today by a pair of pleasant young Oxford men, Mr Stapleford and Mr Powell. They are staying at the Rectory, on a sort of reading party with Mr Willoughby and Mr Hurrell. It all is rather a hot-house. Mr Powell, a touch robuster than his companions and certainly Mr Willoughby, seemed glad to be released from his books and made to be useful in the matter of running races, quoits, greasy poles and the grand tug of war. Perhaps he was inspired by a sudden admiration for Lady Maria? He was certainly more obviously attentive than the others, which I found surprising – what have our young men become? Mr Hurrell did nothing in the way of wooing, and although he was the clergyman supervising the feast, he seemed out of humour to be there. One child told me the sports at Mr Gray's were far more the thing, although the tea was deficient in comparison to that of Hurrell Place.

Maria is of the opinion that Mr Hurrell has a cold heart. I'm inclined to agree with her, even at such a slight acquaintance. She has the conviction of passionate youth and one cannot help warming to that, as to a good fire. She has confided a great deal to me, and she will not mind me speaking of it to you. She is afraid that when Lady Rothborough returns she will be forced to choose which parent she must go to, because it seems most unlikely that the Rothboroughs will ever be able to live under the same roof again for long. The détente that had been achieved has finally been broken by her remaining so long in Italy. Her doctors thought it perfectly safe for her to return, but she chose to stay. Although poor Maria is under no illusions about the nature of her parents' marriage, she is suffering from all the pain this final break has brought. She is longing for her own establishment, for then she will not have to take a side, but the prospect of marriage is daunting after such an example. Her sister Charlotte has been labouring under the same disadvantage, though I must say Lord Dunbar does not sound like a reasonable man, but I only have Maria's account of him. Given Lord R has approved the match, he cannot be as abrasive as she suggests. I think it is the fear of losing a dear sister to marriage, and all that will mean.

After the sports were done we had another small adventure. Maria and I took ourselves off into the magnificent groves of trees that you so admired. It is really the pleasantest thing imaginable – if I were the mistress of the house I should never go anywhere else to walk. We thought we might find some autumn crocuses and wild cyclamen but we did not have a great deal of success – it is still too early.

However, we did come upon a picturesque huntsman who turned out to be none other than the wicked Mark Hurrell of the previous evening. He was wearing a countryman's smock and a broad hat with pheasant feathers in it, and carried a longbow and arrow by which means he had just brought down a hind. This was almost too theatrical to be believed, or at least worthy of a mezzotint. It is apparently the family custom to hunt game with the bow and arrow. Whether or not, given the quarrel with his father, he ought to be taking down game in the park, is another matter, and he was a little uneasy to be caught by us, red-handed so to speak. The hind was a beauty and there was probably a bereft fawn not far away, which Maria did not fail to point out. He excused himself by saying it was not for sport that he had brought her down – he had wanted meat for his own table and to repay some kindnesses amongst the villagers. Prettily said, and he was readily forgiven by Maria. We did not speak long. He had the decency to know that he ought not to be talking to us at all, but I sensed that Maria and he would have stood there until dusk came on. Five years since she last spoke to him, and they were talking as if it were the day before. What that means – well, I leave the question with you, for I know you like such puzzles.

By the time you read this, I will be at Holbroke.

Your own,

E. Maitland

# Chapter Fourteen

Three days later, on Saturday morning, Giles received a visit from Carswell in his office.

"It's calico, soaked in a mixture of lard and lamp oil," Carswell said, laying a cotton ribbon on the table. "It took some time to work out the exact proportions but I managed to make a duplicate."

Giles took up the strip and examined it.

"And the one I found at the warehouse is an exact match for those I took from the forge?"

"Without a doubt," Carswell said. "The same cloth soaked in the same mixture. The same batch."

"And how do they burn?"

"Efficiently. Steady and hot."

"So an excellent tool."

"Yes; as I said, ingenious."

"She's a clever woman," Giles said, thinking of how her family and acquaintances had considered her strange. Did that mean a bold, creative mind, not at all trammelled by expectations of how a woman of her class should behave?

"Mrs Braithwaite, you mean?"

"We have to suppose that her hand is at work here. Why else would she go missing from a loving family? I have not been able to find any reason for her going. So unless it is on some criminal enterprise, and the fact she has not yet come back –"

"There is no sign of her in the city?"

Giles shook his head.

"It's frustrating. Our last possible sighting was of a woman broadly similar in description taking the Axworth

Stage on the morning after she had dealings with Noakes. I've sent Coxe to Axworth this morning. He may be able to pick up the scent there."

"There is a rumour of Indian cholera in Axworth," Carswell said. "Mr Harper told me the other day. He thinks we should be considering our options here."

"We haven't had an outbreak here for years," said Giles, "thank God. Caution is probably in order. What does he suggest?"

"He wanted to talk to you and Captain Lazenby. He had been reading up some continental cases and the opinion seems to be that a policy of quarantine can be quite successful, if enforced properly."

"So we should lock the gates and herd everyone back inside the walls?"

"Not far off. It is the very devil of a thing to control, after all. And what the cause of it is – there is such a difference of opinion, even amongst the most eminent men. Mr Harper advised me to read all I could on the subject, which I have done, but I do not feel much wiser for it." Carswell grimaced and went over to the window, and looked out at the rain-soaked street. "And now we have a deluge to add to our woes!"

"That storm last night was impressive, certainly," said Giles. "I can only hope it will send Mrs Braithwaite back to her hearth and children. Perhaps it will make her think better of her actions."

"Is it ever that simple?" said Carswell, with a bitter laugh.

"No, but it is unusual for a woman to desert her children. Husbands are deserted frequently, of course," Giles said. "But a child is an anchor and she was regarded as an exemplary mother. It is puzzling why she should take off on such a bizarre endeavour. I have talked to nearly everyone in that village and they have nothing to offer me that could indicate why."

"An endeavour at which she singularly failed," Carswell pointed out. "Assuming she meant to burn down the warehouse –"

"Or the bank," Giles said. "I will not rule that out. Especially in the light of Fred Pierce's behaviour. Speaking of which, the post-mortem – did that reveal anything of interest?"

Carswell shook his head.

"Unfortunately not. Oh, and I have called on Dr Walker to see Mr Pierce senior. He is a little calmer but not yet in a state to be interviewed. They are attempting to keep him rested. It is a miserable case, all in all."

"You have been industrious," said Giles. "That's a ten mile round trip."

"I felt in need of the exercise, after my thoroughly futile endeavours to understand cholera," said Carswell. "And it is just as well I went when I did – it was before the weather turned so filthy."

Giles was on the verge of enquiring if all was well at Hawksby, for he had been a little surprised to find Carswell at the office on Saturday, but there was a knock on the door, and Saxon, his chief clerk, came in.

"I have a young gent here, sir, Mr Stapleford, who would like to see you at once. Says it's urgent."

Giles went out and saw a handsome, well-dressed but sodden young man fretting in the outer office. He caught sight of Giles at the door and said, "Major Vernon?"

"Yes?"

"John Stapleford, sir," he said, putting out his hand. "I have come from Langdon Rectory. It's about Mr Hurrell. He has been found dead, and I do not think it was an accident."

~

Stapleford laid out the facts for them as they drove to Langdon in Major Vernon's carriage.

"When Mr Hurrell did not appear for Morning Prayer today, my friend Powell and I were alarmed, although Mr Willoughby said we should not be. He supposed he had stayed over at his father's house."

"At Hurrell Place?" said Major Vernon.

"Yes. It happens often enough that he does, he said, but Powell and I could not help wondering, for all the time we have been here, which is almost a month now, he has never been absent like this from his own church for Morning Prayer. So we decided to go and look for him, or perhaps meet him on his return from the big house."

"You say you were alarmed, Mr Stapleford – was there any particular reason for that?" Major Vernon asked.

"It is the atmosphere that has developed there. A feeling – I cannot define it – but since the great quarrel with his brother, it struck me that there was something about his not coming back that morning, that was unsettling. Perhaps alarmed is too strong a word, but I had an uncomfortable feeling. Mr Hurrell had been so provoked for the last few days, and – I am sure I am not speaking with hindsight."

"Perhaps we should step back a day or two," Major Vernon. "When did this sense come on you, Mr Stapleford?"

Stapleford considered for a moment.

"It has been here the whole time I have been here, now I think of it. It has not been as I thought it would be. Mr Hurrell is not as he was in Oxford, certainly."

"And why are you here, Mr Stapleford?" Felix said.

"Mr Hurrell was a fellow of St Anthony's, and he was my tutor," Stapleford said, "but he took over the living at Langdon at Whitsun, and he asked a few of us Anthony's men to come and join him and Mr Willoughby over the long vacation. We all have certain interests in common, you see, and some of us are preparing to take orders. The intention was to form a community for the summer in order to undertake a period of spiritual purification and reflection, as well as pursuing our scholarly work."

"A reading party, in effect?" said Major Vernon.

"Yes, but without the frivolity and indulgence that those usually entail. Our business is serious – the fate of the established Church – well, perhaps you have read some of Mr Hurrell and Mr Willoughby's tracts?"

"Tracts?" Felix said. "No, I'm afraid not. Unless there is one on cholera."

"I have heard something of your ambitions," Major Vernon said mildly. "You feel that the established Church is under attack –"

"It is not just a matter of feeling, sir," said Stapleford. "It is a fact. The evangelicals and the dissenters are seducing people away from the established Church with their gaudy emotional –" He broke off. "I am quoting Mr Hurrell," he added.

"So he has been your guiding light?" said Major Vernon.

"Quite so, and I don't know what wickedness it is that has taken him from us at such a time. I cannot yet see God's hand at work, I am ashamed to say." He looked across at the Major with damp eyes.

"You said he quarrelled with his brother? And that was the cause of his being provoked?" said Major Vernon. "Can you tell us anything more about that?"

Stapleford hesitated for a moment.

"There was a distressing incident on Tuesday night. Powell and I saw something which – well, that was why we were alarmed today. There was violence between them that night."

"A fight?"

"Of sorts. It was after the party for the village children. We had gone for a walk to the village, and Mr Mark Hurrell was sitting in the garden of the inn there – The Hurrell Arms.

Powell wanted to go and speak to him – I did not, but Powell insisted and so we went in and talked to him for a little while."

"About anything in particular?"

"About shooting or hunting or some such. I did not pay much attention, nor take part much. I did not want to be seen talking to someone with such a reputation, if I'm honest. Powell was all for sitting and drinking with him, but I managed to dissuade him from that and we left some ten minutes or so later. We turned back towards the Rectory and then we saw Mr Arthur Hurrell cantering down the street towards us. He passed us with the barest acknowledgement, but it was clear from his expression that something was amiss. We stopped and turned, and saw him dismount and go storming into the garden where Mark Hurrell was still sitting, and they had words, and then –" He broke off. "Then Mr Hurrell struck his brother across the face with his whip."

"Just the once?"

"No, three or four times, at least. I have never seen him in such a state before. He is – was – the mildest, sweetest of men, the first person to move for forgiveness and understanding, and yet – what his brother must have said to drive him to that, I cannot imagine! It was savage. We went down to attempt to intervene but by the time we got to the garden, they were both gone."

"And you did not see either of them again that night?"

Stapleford shook his head.

"Tell us about this morning," said Major Vernon. "You were concerned about Arthur Hurrell's absence and went looking for him, am I right? How did you decide where you should look?"

"There is a ruined chapel where I know he likes to pray," said Mr Stapleford. "It is in an area of woodland called the Hermitage. It is a wooded ravine, with a stream running through it. The chapel is a medieval fragment left over from the days before the Dissolution of the Monasteries. It is dedicated to Our Lady and I know that Mr Hurrell had hopes of restoring it to its former glory; but I believe it is on land that does not belong to him. I heard the land there belongs to Mark Hurrell, but that is odd, given he is only the youngest son, and Mr Hurrell is the heir."

"So you went to the chapel?"

"Yes, and we found him – well, not there, but down the slope on the other side of the path. We nearly did not see him. It is only because Powell had his terrier with him. Mr Hurrell had been urging him to give up his dog, as an unsuitable indulgence for a priest in Holy Orders, and Powell would not, and if he had – well, we might never have found him."

"And he was dead?"

"Yes. Powell went down – he kept calling to the dog to come back because he was barking, and Powell was worried that he had been caught in a trap or some such. So he climbed down the slope to get him, which was not easy because it was raining so heavily and the slope had turned into a river of mud, and suddenly he was shouting back that he had found Mr Hurrell. I could scarcely believe it, and I scrambled down myself and nearly turned my ankle doing so. And there he was, lying there in a heap, all twisted about and caught up in the roots and the branches..." He pressed his hands to his face for a moment.

"If it is any comfort to you," said Major Vernon after a moment, "there is nothing you have described that means this death is in any way suspicious. An accident can produce the most disturbing effects, can it not, Mr Carswell?"

"Certainly," said Felix.

"I understand what you are saying, sir," said Stapleford, straightening, "and I have tried to think that myself, but the more I consider it, I am sure..." He shook his head again, and gazed out of the carriage at the rain. "May God and you gentlemen prove me wrong!"

~

Arthur Hurrell's corpse had been brought back to Langdon Rectory where it had been laid on the dining table.

The room was consciously austere, as if Hurrell, on taking over, had attempted to make a monkish refectory out of the previous rector's dining room. However, the cheerful yellow and white wallpaper with Italian ruins and lounging shepherds remained, a curious contrast to the large and graphic crucifix hung above the sideboard. Someone had lit candles and arranged them on the mahogany board as if it were an altar.

"Why could they not have left him where he was?" said Felix, pulling back the sheet that covered him.

"In this rain?" said Major Vernon, pulling open the shutters and putting up the blinds.

"True," said Felix, surveying the body.

Arthur Hurrell lay in shirtsleeves and black waistcoat. His face was covered in mud, as was his white clerical stock and shirt front.

"What happened to his coat?" said Major Vernon, joining Felix at the table. "Did he go out without one?"

"It's here," said Felix, spotting a black coat draped over two dining chairs in the corner. He felt the sleeves. "It is soaked through. He must have been lying there for some time." He turned back to the cadaver. "We need to undress him. And some water and rags would be helpful."

"I'll go and arrange it," said Major Vernon. "And make sure no one disturbs us."

Felix continued with his superficial survey until Major Vernon returned, servant-like, with a jug and ewer and towels draped over his shoulder.

"Anything?" he said.

"We have wounding of a sort," said Felix. "But it is rather curious. Can you help me with this, and the shirt? I want to keep them intact."

Together they set to the awkward business of removing the dead man's clothes.

"Rigor well set in, you will note," Felix said. "Which means we can hazard a guess that the time of death was yesterday. Perhaps in the afternoon."

"Before the rain came on?"

"Perhaps," said Felix, reaching for his hand lens. "These are our culprits." Now the shirt had been taken off, the two abdominal wounds he had identified earlier were clear to see. "Here and here."

"Knife wounds?" said Major Vernon.

"I would have said so at first, but there is something about them –" He crouched and peered at them. "A knife wound is usually elliptical, with the sharp side – the cutting edge of the blade – quite evident, but the flesh is torn all about here. Do you see?" He passed the lens to Major Vernon.

"Yes. And the other the same?" Felix nodded. "A dagger?" Major Vernon went on.

"Perhaps. And turned about and then pulled out," said Felix. He mimed the motion, trying to picture it in his mind.

"But you cannot say for certain?"

"Not at this stage. It may become clearer," he said. "But that is certainly the cause of death. There is a great deal of post-mortem bruising and bleeding, as you can see – a result of the body rolling down the slope."

"So he was dead before he was pushed down the slope?"

"I should say so. After being wounded at close quarters."

"A face-to-face attack?" Major Vernon said. "Or if he were on his knees, I suppose his attacker might have come up behind him and reached over? Is that possible?"

"That's an interesting idea, and plausible," said Felix, "given that the wounds are on the left side."

"Kneel down," said Major Vernon.

So Felix did as he was bid and found himself gazing up at

an old painting of the Virgin Mary and an extremely ugly Christ Child. A moment later, the Major came up behind him, hooked his left arm about his neck, restraining him and pulling him back, exposing him perfectly for an attack on the abdomen.

"More than plausible," said Major Vernon, sinking back on his own heels, having mock-stabbed Felix twice. "So this is efficient and ruthless. To take a man at his prayers – that says something about the character of our murderer, does it not?"

"And these fellows will make a martyr of him, given their tastes," Felix remarked.

"A nest of Romans," said Major Vernon, looking about him at the paintings. "They are talking of crypto-Catholics in the neighbourhood."

"I cannot imagine," Felix went on, getting back on his feet, "what possesses an apparently sensible, not unintelligent man like Stapleford to get involved in this sort of" – he gestured about him – "business. Yes, we need our clergymen, but can they not be calm and civilised about it, like your brother-in-law?"

"Enthusiasm is the fashion," said Major Vernon.

"When the benefits of science are laid out for them! Why the devil must people retreat into mere superstition? I cannot comprehend it! To throw back all the benefits of knowledge in favour of –" He broke off.

"They would probably say the Devil is at the heart of it," said Major Vernon.

"The Devil is a construct made to keep us in servitude," said Felix. "I have never believed in him!"

# Chapter Fifteen

The rain came on strongly again as they made their way into the Hermitage woods. They took with them Mr Powell and his terrier. Powell seemed to Giles an unlikely addition to the 'monastery' at the Rectory; he was as handsome in his way as Stapleford, but unlike him, he was dressed in the sensible clothes of a countryman and clearly not much bothered by the intense downpour. He had good command of his sturdy little dog and went striding along the narrow, twisting path ahead of them.

"I tied my handkerchief about the nearest tree," said Powell. "I thought you might want to see exactly where he fell."

"Thank you, Mr Powell," said Carswell.

"What did you think of Mr Hurrell?" Giles asked. Powell did not seem noticeably upset by Hurrell's death.

"Everyone will tell you he was a saint," said Powell, "and I suppose it depends how you define such things. But I don't know – one ought not to speak ill of the dead, but I was beginning to feel uncomfortable here. My parents did not want me to come, and –" He broke off and gestured up to the right. "The old chapel is up yonder; there is a sort of a path and we had just come down it, to this spot here, and Billy set up barking and went hurtling down there." Now he pointed out an opening on the left hand side of the path and took the eager dog in his arms to restrain him. "I assumed he was after a rabbit."

"And presumably all this undergrowth was hacked down when you brought him up on the hurdle?"

"Yes, that was Joe's doing – he's the gardener at the

Rectory. He helped us get him up, which was no easy task. I wondered if we should have left him there," he said, turning to Carswell. "I think that is what you fellows prefer, from what I have read, but Stapleford said it was disrespectful. But what is disrespectful about trying to find out the truth of the business? Still, I let him have his way."

Carswell nodded, and then squatted down at the edge of the path, peering into the undergrowth.

"In all honesty," he said, "I don't suppose much would have been gained in leaving him in situ. He was dead before he got down there, that much I can say."

Giles glanced at Powell, who had covered his mouth with his hand, as if disturbed.

"Who would do this?" he said. "I know he wasn't an easy man. I was angry with him, I will be the first to admit that, and I don't suppose I was the only one."

"Why were you angry with him?" said Giles.

"It was about Billy," said Powell, fussing with the dog in his arms. "He didn't care for Billy and Billy didn't care for him. A man is entitled not to like another man's dog, that I can't quibble with, but to dress it up as a spiritual reproach! Are we not supposed to care for all God's Creation? Billy is as worthy of my love as my fellow man, surely? But Hurrell was all for fasting and self-denial and taking it a sight too far, if you ask my opinion. And celibacy – that was another thing. He was pushing us all towards Rome, that's the truth of it, and I for one was not ready for that. Stapleford might be, but I am not! I was going home today. I had had enough. I would be on my way already if we had not –" He turned away. "You'll want to look over the chapel, there's a bit of shelter there," he said. "Shall we?"

And he started energetically up the path.

"When did Billy start barking?" asked Giles, following him. It was a steep, tight climb up to the chapel, and the undergrowth was showing some signs of damage. He found himself wondering how a fatally-wounded Hurrell had got down the path. Had he been escaping, staggering down away from his assailant, or had he already expired and been pushed down?

"In the chapel, now I think of it," said Powell.

"Damn this rain," said Carswell, coming up behind them. "How is one to see anything?"

"Fortunately, we have a smart dog," said Major Vernon. "Put Billy down, would you, Mr Powell? Let us see if he can still pick up the scent."

Powell obliged; Billy began to run about energetically, and then started to bark excitedly and scrabble at the earth.

"What have you found there, you clever boy?" said Powell. "What is it?"

The dog had a piece of white material, heavily muddied, between his teeth. Powell detached it and handed it to Carswell.

"Man's handkerchief," Carswell said, shaking it out and studying it. "Those patches might be blood."

"Any markings?"

"M.H.," said Carswell, passing it to Giles. It was a fine linen handkerchief, with the initials beautifully embroidered. At the other corner was a rose, equally neatly done.

"Property of a gentleman, would we say?" said Giles. "Made by an affectionate woman, perhaps?"

"And discarded as too incriminating," said Carswell, taking it back from Giles. "I am certain that is blood."

"Then you had better take it back to Northminster and see if you can make any more sense of it with your microscope. And let us get out of this rain."

They returned to the Rectory, thoroughly sodden. Here Mr Stapleford informed them that Mr Willoughby had been taken ill. Carswell went up to see to him while Powell chivvied the servants into making up fires and bringing refreshments.

"There is no reason why we should be uncomfortable,"

he said, "is there?"

"None at all," said Giles.

"You and Mr Carswell can take your ease in here," he said, opening the door to a small sitting room. "You will need to talk privately, I expect. I had better go and see to poor Stapleford. He looked wretched. He has taken this hard, but in the end it will all be for the best. All this –" He broke off, shaking his head, and left Giles alone.

Carswell came in a while later and was glad of the coffee, the fire and Powell's good sense.

"What is wrong with Willoughby, then?" Giles asked.

"It's nothing serious," Carswell said, stripping off his wet layers. "He has a predisposition to acute dyspepsia and the situation has brought it on. He is a strange fellow, though. He was almost enjoying the pain he was in, or at least enjoying the chance to suffer. He did not want my advice on how he might avoid it in future. He wanted me as an official witness to his suffering. Ridiculous. Well, that is his choice, I suppose." He bent over the fire, now in his shirt sleeves. "To be a slave to something like that when –"

Giles spread out the handkerchief on the table. Carswell glanced round at him.

"Mark Hurrell, do we think?" he said.

"Morten Hurrell?" Giles said.

"Who would embroider roses on his handkerchief?" said Carswell.

"His late wife or one of his daughters?" said Giles. "Poor man. To have to bury six children and a wife."

"And only the black sheep left," said Carswell. "Who will inherit everything now, I imagine."

"Mark Hurrell," said Giles. "Yes, true. And he was violently and publicly humiliated by our victim. That would be a serious provocation for a certain kind of man. I shall have to go and talk to him – but perhaps we should wait until the rain clears a little."

"I'll go and have another look at the body while there is still some light," said Carswell. "There may be something I missed earlier."

# Chapter Sixteen

Alone with his thoughts, Giles took out Emma's letter and began to re-read her description of the village sports and of Mark Hurrell. He was interrupted soon after by a knock at the door.

"Major Vernon?" It was Mr Willoughby, arrayed in an elaborate and gorgeous crimson damask dressing gown with pointed red slippers to match. "Forgive the intrusion. I must talk to you."

"Of course," said Giles, folding up Emma's letter and wishing she were there to see the sight of the pale, slight young man in such a splendid raiment. He looked like a boy cardinal from some dark Italian intrigue. "I'm glad you are feeling better."

"A little. It is a habitual condition with me. The slightest anxiety sets it off – and this day has been –" He closed his eyes and put his head back, clearly attempting to master himself.

"Come and sit down, Mr Willoughby," said Giles, setting a chair for him opposite his own. "What do you wish to tell me?"

The young man shut the door behind him and settled himself, with some care for his silken skirts. Then he leant forward and said quietly, as if afraid of being overheard, "I wish to tell you – that however shocking this event has been, I cannot say I am wholly surprised. I have been afraid for some time that Arthur's life – Mr Hurrell's, I mean – has been in danger."

"What makes you think that, Mr Willoughby?" said Giles, reaching for his notebook.

"You are going to make notes?" said Willoughby.

"Yes?"

"I cannot allow that," said Willoughby.

"I'm afraid I am not so young and nimble-minded as you," Giles said. "It's a necessity."

"No, no," said Willoughby. "This conversation must be entirely off the record – as if it had never happened, so to speak."

"And why is that?" said Giles.

"Because – it is a little difficult to explain to a layman, but the importance of what has been occurring in the Church recently cannot be overestimated. We are at a great moment in history, Major Vernon, and the forces at work here – they are stronger and more dangerous than you can imagine. I therefore insist that this conversation is entirely off the record."

"I'm afraid I cannot agree to that," said Major Vernon. "My professional experience has shown, many times over, that when a person asks for no record to be made of a conversation, it is to avoid incriminating himself. Now, I don't think that is your intention, Mr Willoughby, is it?"

"No, of course not!" said the young man, flushing a little. Then he drew himself up and said, "My intention is to protect Mr Hurrell's legacy, and it is my strong belief that the forces against us are powerful ones. It does not do to let certain information into the wrong hands, and I wonder if I am wise even to speak to you –" He crumpled up his face and bent forward a little. "Oh, excuse me, sir –" he gasped.

Giles attempted to push aside the idea that this was an elaborate feint, and feel a little pity for him, but he could not. There was something about Willoughby that struck the wrong note.

"Do you need something?" he said, wishing he had Carswell there to examine him again. He was an expert in detecting confected illnesses.

"No, no," said Willoughby. "It will pass, God willing."

So there was an uncomfortable interval while Willoughby writhed and muttered to himself.

"Excuse me," said Willoughby at last. "It is just that when I think of what may be at work here – and I had hoped to make you understand how grave the situation is, but it seems –"

"Then make me understand," said Giles, closing his notebook. He felt it necessary to concede that.

"Thank you, sir. I am sure that when you hear what I have to say to you, you will understand my caution, and I thank our Lord for your wisdom and patience." He closed his eyes for a moment, made the sign of the Cross and then fixed his large, pale blue eyes on Giles with a watery but curiously intense gaze. "The difficulty for you is that you only knew Mr Hurrell slightly. If you had more acquaintance with the man and his ambitions then you would understand what has been lost. So I shall try in the first place to address this, though it can only be an imperfect sketch. However, I can say with some confidence that Arthur Hurrell will be remembered in the coming centuries as one of the great men of England – no, he will be seen and loved as one of the saints. He was a man who, had he not been taken from us, would have brought England back to the loving embrace of Rome."

"I see," said Giles.

"I sense your disapproval, sir," said Willoughby. "That is to be expected. Your eyes are not yet open to the necessity of this. But with time, because of God's grace, you will see it too, and join us in our crusade. As you come to know what and who Arthur Hurrell was, you will see him as a saint martyred to a great cause, a cause to which every loyal and truth-loving Englishman must turn if he wishes to save his country from the Devil!"

He spoke softly and earnestly, just as Emma had described his preaching. Giles decided he would let him carry on without interruption, although he had many questions. It was clear that Willoughby's intention was to push a particular line about Hurrell's death and that Giles was supposed to swallow it whole, like an enthralled undergraduate in the University Church at Oxford. So he sat and listened.

"We have fallen, Major Vernon, fallen," Willoughby went on. "Far from the state of happy faith that existed in this country three hundred years ago, when Henry VIII was still content with his devout Spanish Queen; where, in every parish in England, the Mass was celebrated every day and the ordinary people felt a living, joyous sense of devotion to their Lord God and his Lady Mother. Those bright altars and flower-decked shrines spoke of a simple but true faith. That is the England that Mr Hurrell and others, myself included, are struggling to bring back, but there are many against us."

Giles considered this for a moment and said, "And you think this may have something to do with Arthur Hurrell's murder?"

"Why else would he have met such a violent, terrible, unshriven death? As I said before, if you had known him as I did, then you would know that there could be no commonplace reasons for his murder. This was not an ordinary murder, in short."

"I do not think murder is ever ordinary," Giles said.

"I take your point, Major, but you must understand me. This was not a base undertaking. It was an act of war."

"So who do you propose as a suspect, Mr Willoughby?" said Giles. "These powerful forces, these enemies, who are they?"

"They are everywhere," said Willoughby. "And they are well hidden. That is the difficulty."

"Then it is just as well that I have some experience in finding out such people," said Giles, feeling a little tried by Willoughby now.

"Yes, yes, that is true," said Willoughby.

"However, a few specifics would not go amiss, Mr

Willoughby," Giles said. "I heard he had quarrelled with people."

"People had made quarrels with him, sir," said Willoughby. "People who were not ready for the truth, or rather were its sworn enemy."

"For example? Friends, relations, lovers?" Willoughby frowned at that, as the idea of any such persons surrounding Hurrell's already sainted presence offended him. "Mr Stapleford and Mr Powell saw him horsewhip his brother Mark. Did you see this?"

"They have overstated it."

"Did you see it?"

There was silence for a moment. Willoughby then shook his head.

"Mr Hurrell told me of it."

"What did he say happened?"

"He said that he was provoked by what his brother said to give him a few cuts with his whip. I do not suppose much damage was done."

"But he did not say what it was that Mark said to him?"

"No."

"And do you know what the general nature of their quarrel was? Why had Mr Mark Hurrell been banned from his father's house?"

"Mark Hurrell is an apostate and a troublemaker. He is not a fit person for the society of the young men under this roof, nor for anyone in this neighbourhood. He has forsaken his right to be received by decent people."

"What exactly did he do?"

"He wrote a book. Of course, he calls it a novel and hides, like a filthy coward, behind a mask of anonymity and fiction, but in reality it is a piece of libellous trash. He has taken the trouble to insult everyone. As I say, he is a troublemaker and an apostate. I pray for him. He has a great mind, but he has put all his talents at the service of the Devil."

"But he was of your party at one time?"

"Yes, and we had great hopes of him. He is quick-witted and an excellent scholar, no one can deny that. He had the sense in him then to know what his brother could accomplish and wished, quite sincerely at that point, to serve under him, as we all did. But then –" Willoughby sighed. "Arthur always said he had the Devil in him, that even as a boy he was wild and wilful and seemed to delight in provoking everyone, merely for the sake of it. There was a strange tale he told me once. When they were children, they had been taken to Swalecliffe for their health and were sea bathing there. Apparently Mark had, in his usual foolish fashion, gone out too far and Arthur brought him back to safety – clearly preserving his life. Yet Mark always claimed that Arthur had urged him to swim so far, taunted him into a foolish venture, and had threatened not to bring him back to safety. What an extraordinary piece of ingratitude! But that is the way with the man." He hesitated a moment. "It would not surprise me if he were behind this. He has clearly lost all sense of what is right. From there, it is a small step to murder."

"More than a small step, usually, Mr Willoughby," said Giles.

"Not for Mark Hurrell," said Willoughby with a solemn air, reminiscent of a liveried footman placing an elaborately dressed dish on the dinner table for all to admire. "Now, if you will excuse me, sir, I must rest."

# Chapter Seventeen

The rain had cleared a little, so Giles decided to waste no more time. He called on the kitchen boy from the Rectory to take him through the winding paths of the Hermitage woods and show him the way to Hermitage House, the property of Mr Mark Hurrell. He went without Carswell, for a message had come by tortuous means from Northminster that Mr Gray was concerned about his wife and so he had gone to Raythorpe to attend to her.

The Rectory kitchen boy was not a boy at all, but an elderly man who had worked for the Hurrells for many years. When Giles enquired what he thought of his late master, all he would say was that it was "very sad, very sad, and he was right sorry for the Squire to have to bury another child, after he had already put five in the earth."

"There you are, sir – just over yonder. You can find your way from here." At which he turned and began to make his way back to the Rectory.

It soon began to rain again, and Giles continued along the path to get a better view of the house.

The Hermitage House was small and consciously picturesque. Set under a thatched roof, it had pointed, latticed windows set in rusticated stone. Charming though it might be, it sat uncomfortably on a narrow strip of land resembling a ledge. Behind was a densely wooded cliff, and in front the ground fell away precipitously. It had, he realised, been placed so as to catch a magnificent view through the tree tops to the river flashing in the gorge below, but the house itself looked ill at ease. The thatched roof had in places been supplemented by tarpaulins, and the dark stone looked damp and less than welcoming in the rain.

A young woman, her neat bonnet, crisp print dress and ruffled apron suggestive of an upper servant, was sitting on a bench outside, with water cascading from the overhanging roof in front of her. She had risen and appeared to be on the verge of retreating from the rain as Giles approached.

"Is Mr Hurrell at home?" he asked her.

"Well, yes, I suppose so, sir," she said, making a slight curtsey, "but I don't know, really, I'm only waiting on my mistress."

"I see. Who is your mistress, may I ask?"

"Miss Margaret, sir. I mean Miss Wytton."

"You are a fair way from home in this weather," said Giles.

"I know, sir. Miss Margaret did insist on our coming. We were lucky to escape the rain, but now –" She sighed. "She had to come when she heard the news."

"I think we should go inside, Miss –?"

"Agnes Baker, sir," she said.

"The news being about Mr Arthur Hurrell, I suppose?"

"Yes, sir. The very thing. You know about that too, sir?"

"I am from the police in Northminster," Giles said.

The girl put her hand on her chest for a moment. "Then it's true? That he was done away with?"

"It does seem so."

"Lord save us all!" she whispered. "And I'm glad you are here, sir. I don't reckon the constable here would know what to do with a murderer, let alone find one out." She looked at him for a moment and said, "Excuse me for asking, sir, but you aren't Major Vernon, are you?"

"I am."

"We have read all about you in The Bugle!" she said. "Mr Owen the butler reads it to us after dinner. That last business – so shocking! And you are here now – what a blessing to know, for everyone at Raythorpe has been so, so –" She laid her hand on his arm for a moment. "We shall all be safe in our beds now you are here."

"I hope so, Miss Baker," he said, rather surprised at his fame. "Now, perhaps we should go and find your mistress?"

She looked a little fearful at that.

"She told me to wait outside," she said.

"I am sure nothing improper is going on," he said, and knocked on the door. "Good afternoon, Mr Hurrell!" he called out. "May I come in? It's Major Vernon."

He half expected Hurrell to come to the door in a state of undress, but he was perfectly respectable in his appearance. In fact, he looked pleased to be interrupted. However, since Giles had last seen him, his face had acquired an unpleasant tangle of scars.

"Major Vernon – how good to see you again," he said. "And Agnes, will you come in and look to Miss Meg? She needs some salts. And some tea."

He led them into an ill-lit chamber with a bare flagstone floor. It was furnished with old furniture of the plainest sort with the addition of a great many books heaped about in no particular order. A square piano was open in the corner, and there was a mess of writing things on the table as if some great literary undertaking was under way.

Amidst all this Miss Wytton was sitting on a low stool by a smoking, smouldering apology for a fire. Dressed in full mourning, as profound as any widow's, she turned her veil-framed face to stare at Giles, as if she were a prophetess who had just seen some vision in the grey fog of the hearth.

"Oh, it is you," she said, her voice a husky whisper.

"I'm afraid so, Miss Wytton."

"You are the herald of everything miserable," she said. "First Fred Pierce, and now –" She could not go on, and buried her face in her hands.

"We really should go back now, Miss Margaret," said Agnes Baker, attempting to comfort her. "Before the rain comes on too heavy again. If we make haste we should be all right. Otherwise you will catch cold and –"

"Die, Agnes?" said Miss Wytton, pushing her away. "Oh, I should welcome that!"

"Meg, Meg, come now," said Mr Hurrell, taking a greatcoat from a hook on the door. "If you wrap this about you, you will escape the worst. Agnes is right, you really should not be here."

"You are so cruel," she said. "Let me stay, for pity's sake, Mark, let me stay!"

"It is bad enough that you have been here as long as you have," said Hurrell. "If you go now, your reputation –"

"It is only your reputation you care about!"

"I have no reputation left," said Hurrell. "But you do. Please, Meg, I know it is hard for you, but you must go home. I will come and call tomorrow, I promise."

"And my brother will not let you into the house," Margaret said.

"Given all that has happened, he may."

"He will not!"

"Mr Hurrell is right. You should go home, Miss Wytton," said Giles. "In fact, I will take you myself, given the circumstances. What happened to Mr Hurrell may not be the end of it."

"Oh dear God, you do not think so?" said Miss Wytton, rising and staring at him.

"We do not know what has happened. At the moment, I do not think these woods are particularly safe for anyone, and especially not two women alone."

"Here, Meg," Hurrell said, coming forward and attempting to drape the coat about her shoulders. She pushed him away.

"I will go, but only because Major Vernon says I must," said Miss Wytton, "though he need not look far for the culprit."

"What do you mean?" said Hurrell.

"You, Mark," she said. "After all, you have everything to gain, and you always hated him, for no good reason – and you have the hardest, blackest heart! A murderer's heart."

"I did not hate him!" Hurrell said. "You will not say that! I will not have you put that about, Miss!"

"So defensive!" she said. "Yes, I can see it now. Everyone knows how much they loathed each other, Major Vernon. It would not surprise me at all that –"

"You don't know what you are saying," Hurrell said. "You know nothing about how it was between us."

"I know exactly what I am saying!" Miss Wytton said. "If you cared one jot for Arthur, if you felt this loss truly in your heart, you would not send me away like this."

"It is only for your own sake," said Hurrell. "And I will come with you now, and attempt to speak to Edward. Will that satisfy you? And please, I beg you, do not throw around such foolish accusations. I know you are wretched, but you get yourself absolutely no credit by it."

She was at last persuaded, and they began a long, sodden and uncomfortable walk, a good two miles on a bad path made extremely imperfect by the rain. They reached Raythorpe Hall and at the gates, Miss Wytton suddenly rejected her escorts and went running into the house, followed by her anxious, loyal Agnes.

Mark Hurrell stood watching her, shaking his head.

"The inn here is a decent place, Major Vernon," he said. "Perhaps we should take refuge? I have to admit I cannot face a run-in with Edward Wytton just yet. Let me buy you a brandy and hot water, if it does not sully your good name to be seen with a wretch like me in such a place. I imagine you want to talk to me about Arthur's death?"

"I am afraid I must, Mr Hurrell," said Giles. "And the inn will do as well as anywhere."

~

Felix sat staring at the empty grate in the private room in The Lamb Inn at Raythorpe and wondered, as the rain beat on the lattices, if he might order a fire to go with his dinner. He had got thoroughly soaked walking from Langdon to the Rectory.

"Mr Carswell?" It was Major Vernon. "May I come in? The landlady told me you were here."

"Of course," said Felix, opening the door to him. "Mrs Gray is not quite at the stage of delivery so I thought I would get myself some dinner here first."

"Then I apologise for intruding. This weather –"

"No, it's not an intrusion at all. I'm glad of company, to be honest," he said, glancing at the other rain-drenched figure standing behind the Major.

"This is Mr Mark Hurrell," Major Vernon said.

Felix nodded and indicated that they should both come in.

"I was about to ring for a fire."

"A good plan; and perhaps some coffee?" said Major Vernon.

"I was thinking brandy and hot water," said Hurrell.

"As you wish, Mr Hurrell," said Major Vernon, "but I am afraid I must keep my wits straight."

Hurrell nodded.

"Perhaps you are right, sir," he said. "This business..." He sat down, and turning his wet hat in his hands, said, "I must go and see my father – if he will see me. He must see me now, after all this. He will be broken, though he will not show it. And these circumstances – it will be seen as a great humiliation. He is already traumatised by the stains I have inflicted upon the family honour."

The servant came in and Felix gave her orders, and a few minutes passed in silence as she made up the fire and brought in the tray of refreshments. When she had gone, Major Vernon sat down opposite Hurrell and took out his notebook.

"Perhaps we should get down to business, while matters are still fresh in everyone's mind." Hurrell nodded. "Could you tell me when you last saw your brother?"

"That was on Tuesday evening. It was when he attacked me." Hurrell put his hand up to indicate the scars on his face.

"And this took place where?"

"In the garden of The Hurrell Arms at Langdon."

"What happened?"

"I had gone there at about six to see Fuller, the landlord. I wanted to have a piece of game butchered. I had brought down a hind in the woods that afternoon and I wanted him to deal with it for me. So I was sitting in the garden with a glass of ale, having delivered it to him, when my brother came riding down the high road and saw me there, and after that –" He gave a sigh. "We were not civil with one another. I suppose I provoked him, as I always seemed to do, and he lost his temper with me."

"And after that?"

"I let the landlady dress my wounds and then I staggered back to the Hermitage, without my haunch of venison."

"Was that the hind that you killed with your longbow in the woods below Hurrell Place?" Major Vernon enquired.

"Yes. May I ask how you know that?"

"Mrs Maitland mentioned it in a letter to me. She told me how she and Lady Maria met you that afternoon."

"You know those ladies?" Hurrell said.

"Yes," said Major Vernon.

"You killed a hind with a longbow?" Felix said, sitting down next to Major Vernon on the settle.

"My father taught us all to hunt with longbows. He is the master of it – well, he was, until he got a rheumatic affliction in his shoulder, so he can no longer draw a bow."

"And when you make a kill," Felix said, "you draw out

the arrow and use it again?"

"Yes."

Felix had an urgent desire to ride back to Northminster and examine those curious abdominal wounds again. An arrowhead was a weapon he had not considered.

"I should be interested to see a demonstration," said Major Vernon, and Felix felt sure that he was pursuing the same line of thought.

"It's good sport," Hurrell went on. "Far superior to rough shooting with a gun, no matter how expensive and new-fangled your gun might be. One misfire from a rifle alerts every living soul that there is a hunter in the neighbourhood, but an ill-judged arrow is soundless and allows you to take a second shot, or even a third, if necessary."

"You would expect to have a kill with a second arrow, then?" said Major Vernon.

"I would be irritated with myself if I did not. I spent a lot of time as a boy practising my aim, and it was a point of honour. I wanted to be better than my brothers and as good as my father, as if that were ever possible. No one could ever shoot as accurately as he."

"So that was definitely the last time you saw your brother, Mr Hurrell?" said Major Vernon.

"Yes, I took to my bed after that. I have only been out of it today when Powell brought me the news that Arthur –" He clasped his hands together, looking down at his boots for a moment.

"When was this?" Major Vernon said.

"A little after ten. It was kind of him to come and tell me."

"You knew each other at Oxford?"

"Through Arthur. Powell, however, was growing a little confused by the whole business, and had asked me for advice – though I am hardly the person to ask for that! He is far too sensible a man to throw away a promising career in the Church by taking such an extreme position, but at the same time, the whole thing seduced him thoroughly. My brother could make an acolyte of the most unpromising material. I have felt that siren call for myself. That is why Arthur is – was, I should say – regarded with such fear in Oxford. Willoughby is a shadow in comparison when it comes to such things. In fact, I wonder how long their movement can continue now."

"Sometimes a martyr can assist such a cause," said Major Vernon.

"You have been talking to Willoughby," said Mark Hurrell, and laughed uneasily. "He will make a great deal of this, if we are not careful."

"So you took to your bed from Wednesday until this morning?" Major Vernon asked.

"Strictly speaking I was not entirely in my bed, but I did not leave the house. I was in no fit state to do so. Fortunately Mrs Fuller came down and looked after me. And I had other visitors who can attest to my being in the village – that is what you want to know, I think, sir?"

"Yes."

"Because, I suppose, my violent altercations with my brother make me look less than innocent?"

"I am not making any suppositions at this stage, but I thank you for your frankness, Mr Hurrell."

"My father came to see me," Mark Hurrell went on. "That surprised me. Yesterday, just before the rain came on. And Miss Wytton came three times: on Wednesday, Thursday and again yesterday. Quite unbidden, you do appreciate."

"Yes," Major Vernon said.

"She is in a wretched state of mind. She was before, and this will only make things worse, though the point is now settled, so to speak."

"What point is that?" Major Vernon said.

"My brother's behaviour towards her has been – oh, I know I'm not in the position to accuse anyone else of poor behaviour, but how he treated her – it was not decent. I cannot use the whitewash of death to excuse him."

"So there was the understanding of an engagement?"

"More than an understanding. It was all settled years ago and with some enthusiasm on both sides, as well as the consent of the elders and betters. When Arthur was first at Oxford, he was an attentive lover. He drew her portrait badly and wrote dreadful poetry to her. She was a loveable, beautiful girl, after all. But waiting for him to name a day has faded her. A decent man would have told her years ago that he wished to be released from his obligation, but Arthur never did. Even on Friday when she was here, she was convinced that he would at any minute tell her that he was ready to call the banns. She had based her supposition on the most ridiculous thing – he had apparently told her he did not like Lady Maria Haraald and considered her frivolous. She took that to mean that his preference was still for her. I tried to tell her it was hopeless."

"Why were you certain he would never marry her?" Major Vernon asked.

"He took a vow of celibacy. He and Willoughby both did. I witnessed it myself. They tried to make me take one too, in preparation for my ordination. But in the end, I could not, just as I could not go through with my ordination. I think it was that suggestion that made the scales fall from my eyes – as it has done with Powell. It is a step too far. It is akin to abandoning the English Prayer Book for the Missal."

"And your father was with you on Friday?"

"Yes, for some time. He wanted to talk to me about emigration."

"He wants you to emigrate?"

"Yes," said Hurrell. "It had occurred to me that I should, even before he mentioned it. It seems that New Zealand or some such might be a more accommodating place for a scoundrel such as myself. And yet, when one thinks of it, how hard it would be to leave!"

"And after this conversation with your father, you did not leave the house?"

"No. I thought of going out but I was still very sore, and the conversation with my father had been demanding, one might say. Then Margaret came and it started to rain, so after that I went back to bed and contemplated my sins through a haze of laudanum." Shaking his head, he sighed and got up from his seat. "And now I really must go to him. Are you done with me, sir?"

"For the present," said Major Vernon.

"Then I will go and see if I can find someone to drive me home."

When he had gone, Felix said, "That business with the arrows –"

"Yes, it's interesting," said Major Vernon.

"And he seemed collected, given the circumstances, don't you think?"

"Perhaps," said Major Vernon, leaning back and gazing into the fire. "I think we need to read that scandalous novel of his."

"I will get it when I next go back to Hawksby," said Felix, getting up and putting on his coat. "I had better go and see how Mrs Gray is doing."

"I'll come with you," said Major Vernon. "I want to know what Mr Gray thinks of Arthur Hurrell's theological capering."

# Chapter Eighteen

Mr Gray was sitting with his injured child, who was sleeping peacefully.

Carswell made a brief examination, and being satisfied with his progress, left to attend to Mrs Gray.

"My wife's sister is with us now," Gray said to Giles. "She tells us how fortunate we are to have Mr Carswell to hand. He has quite the reputation as an accoucheur. Mimi – that's my sister-in-law – met Mrs Yardley in Florence and heard all about Mr Carswell from her."

"I understand there are twins on the way?"

"Yes," said Mr Gray. "They run in my family, but it is still a fraught passage. It always is, even with the most skilled attendants."

Giles nodded, remembering – without wishing to – the night when Laura's pains had come on in the sultry heat of a Canadian summer. He had been at her side the entire time. He had sent for the regimental surgeon, but the message had come back from his servant that he was drunk and beyond use. Fortunately they had the assistance of a local woman, part Indian, who had coaxed Edward into the world with a wonderful mixture of cunning and magic.

"Let me distract you a little," Giles went on, in truth wanting to distract himself now. "May I ask you about Arthur Hurrell?"

"Arthur Hurrell," repeated Gray with a nod. "They are saying it is murder. It must be, or why would you be here, Major Vernon?"

"It is," Giles said. "How well did you know him?"

"Not well. I have to confess I did not want to know him.

There was something about him that I could not like. I understand why everyone thought him brilliant. His writing certainly is, and his mind was sharp, but there was nothing there I could warm to. A failing on my part, but –" He glanced at the bed. "Perhaps we might talk elsewhere?"

"Of course."

They went downstairs to Gray's study, and were just crossing the hall when a piercing female scream ripped through the air.

"Perhaps you should go –" Giles began, thinking of how feverishly Laura had clutched at his arm through each wave of pain and how her nails had dug in, leaving marks on his skin, as if she meant him to feel something of it for himself.

"She does not like me there," Gray said, showing him into his study and carefully shutting the door. At the same time, there was another heart-rending scream.

"You have the same taste in engravings as Mr Hurrell," said Giles, noticing that the same image of the Virgin ascending into Heaven hung above the fireplace, just as it had done in the Rectory at Langdon.

"I do?" said Gray with some surprise. "I'm very fond of that picture. It reminds me a little of my wife. It is engraved from a painting by Murillo."

"What does it mean in theological terms?" said Giles.

"It represents the Assumption of the Virgin," Gray said. "It is the Roman Catholic tradition that the mother of Jesus did not die an ordinary mortal's death, but was assumed into Heaven, like her son, and there she reigns as Queen." Gray shook his head. "Both Hurrell and Willoughby were active in the promotion of such Marian devotion with the Church, but it is not really part of the Church of England."

"I have heard some talk about Willoughby converting to Roman Catholicism. What do you think of that?"

"It would not surprise me. In fact, I have often heard that of Arthur Hurrell. In Oxford they have been talking not of 'if' but 'when', which is a great sadness to some, but I say: good riddance! What would Hurrell have done if he had become a bishop? He was regularly spoken of as a future Archbishop of Canterbury." Gray shuddered. "No, it is better that a man is true and open and submits to whatever tradition he thinks represents the truth instead of trying to undermine the church of his birth from within. If the pair of them had had any honesty they should have walked away years ago. For Hurrell to have taken the living here – it is not what that parish needs! I tell you, Major Vernon, there are people who no longer go to Sunday service at Holy Trinity in Langdon because of Arthur Hurrell's antics. Some of them have gone to the Methodist chapel, and one or two actually come here, which I take as a great compliment, but it is an inconvenience for them, and why should they be turned from their own place, where their ancestors worshipped?"

"Do you think he should not have taken the living?"

"Not without some moderation of his views. Nor without marrying. Marriage is essential for a parish clergyman."

"Do you know about the business with Miss Wytton?"

"Oh yes, and that is another reason I could not take to Hurrell. He has treated her abominably. From what Mark says –"

"You know the younger Mr Hurrell, then?"

"Yes. We were at school together. He is younger than me. He was my fag, of all things, but we soon became friends. I have him to thank for this living. He introduced me to the present Lord Wytton's father. I should be in a far worse situation now if he had not gone to such trouble on my behalf. I was not the first candidate, but Mark argued my case tirelessly. I am greatly in his debt."

"What do you make of the quarrel between the brothers?"

"It is a complex business. Mark is not one to make quarrels, but he is both stubborn and rash, which is a dangerous combination – mind, he would be the first to say so. But he loved Arthur, indeed he idolised him, and this will be agony for him. His only living sibling gone – there were seven children once, and now only Mark remains! It is a dreadful thing."

"And do you know what this latest difference between them was all about? Why he had been banned from the house?"

"It has been growing for some years. I cannot excuse Mark, because he has been beyond foolish in publishing that disgraceful novel. I take it you know about that?" Giles nodded. "I told him he should not, but he said he must – he had written it and must publish it."

"Do you have a copy?"

"Unfortunately I do. He insisted on giving me one."

"Might I borrow it?"

"Yes. You are welcome to it. Please forget to return it. It is an outrageous thing, and I know Mark will regret it soon enough. I think he regrets it already." He went to his desk, unlocked the bottom drawer and took out a small volume which he handed to Giles. "He had it bound especially for me," he said. "I think he has been suffering from a brain fever. He will come to his senses and he will ask me to add this to Sir Morten's bonfire. Perhaps, indeed, Arthur's death will remind him of the fragility of his mortal soul and bring him back to the fold! I pray it will be so! That some good might come of this."

"Do you think Mark would be capable of murdering his brother?"

"What a question!"

"I am sorry if it shocks you, but I must ask it. Violent feelings nursed over many years can have dire results, and he has been provoked."

"Not Mark," Mr Gray said. "He is too sweet-natured. There is a tenderness about him that would keep him from such an act. I am sure of it. He may have suffered a great deal and be angry, but I do not think that he –" Mr Gray broke off, as if he doubted his own words. There was a knock at the door. "Enter!"

"Mistress wants you now, sir!" said the breathless maid. "It's two little girls!"

~

Felix returned to the inn and found Major Vernon reading in a blaze of candlelight.

"Mrs Gray is doing well?" he said.

"Very well, considering. And both children were large ones, and thrawn, but healthy," Felix said, sitting down.

"Thrawn? Is that Scotch?"

Felix nodded. "Stubborn. A term often applied to myself by my father." He found himself yawning. "I could sleep until the end of Christendom," he added, and began to pull off his boots.

"You're staying here?" Major Vernon said.

"Too late to go back," Felix said.

"I suppose it is," said Major Vernon.

"I want to see Mrs Gray first thing," Felix went on, "and I may be wanted overnight. Then I shall go back to Northminster and look at those wounds again. What are you reading?"

"Mark Hurrell's novel," said Major Vernon. "Mr Gray's copy. Inscribed by the author himself on the title page. Gray wanted to burn it too but he could not, out of sentiment. They are old friends, it seems, and Mark Hurrell even got the living for Gray."

"What do you think of it? The part I read was compelling, and Eleanor, of course, could not stop reading it."

"I'm no literary critic," said Major Vernon, "but it does draw you in. Everything is a trifle overstated and clumsy but there is a great deal of passion in it, which is attractive. Perhaps if he writes another one it will be more accomplished."

"Do you seriously think he will?" said Felix. "That he is not facing the gallows?"

"Perhaps. Perhaps not. Can it really be as simple as that? That the pariah of the family murders his brother in a fit of pique?"

"Hot weather like this provokes people. Makes them violent and unpredictable, especially if there is strong drink involved. There are always more brawls and riots at this time of year. And everyone seems happy enough to accuse Mark Hurrell. He practically accused himself, which is a novelty."

"But you would not have said he was on the verge of a confession, would you? He seemed very cool to me. Perhaps too cool. It's all a great puzzle," said Major Vernon, laying down the book. "Perhaps it will become clearer after a good night's sleep."

He got up and began to get ready for bed.

Felix picked up Hurrell's novel and flicked through it, trying to find the place he had reached before Eleanor had taken it from him. But he was too tired to do anything with it. Major Vernon was already in bed and there was nothing to be done but undress and get in.

"I wonder if it is not too late to go back to Hawksby," he said, his cravat in his hand.

"It's an easy mile," said Major Vernon, propping himself up on his elbows. "You could walk there. There is enough moon and it is drier now."

"I could," Felix said.

"To an infinitely preferable bedfellow, I should say," Major Vernon said.

Felix pictured Eleanor, curled up in the embrace of the sheets, half-asleep. Would it be possible to go home and broker some sort of peace? In that moment he wanted nothing else but to return to the simplicity of a few weeks ago; but how was that to be managed? Humbling himself to her would not make the difficulty go away.

He hesitated, his cravat still in his hand.

Major Vernon said, "Has something happened between you? Forgive me for saying this, but a quarrel is like a wound. It ought to be dealt with promptly, wouldn't you say?"

"What makes you say that?" Felix said.

"You have been avoiding Hawksby as if cholera has broken out there."

"Would you rather I neglected what needs to be done?"

"No, of course not, but you ought not – excuse me if what I say is unwelcome, but for a newly married man it is a little unusual to be so preoccupied with his work."

"We have not quarrelled," Felix said after a moment. "It is just that we have a difference of opinion that I must negotiate a sensible way about, but I am not sure at this moment quite how it is to be done. So it is good for me to cool my heels and be distracted, to be honest. It is not that I do not want to go back, it is just better for a while that I do not. I do not trust myself at present. I will stay here."

"As you wish," said Major Vernon, moving over to make room for him.

# Chapter Nineteen

On Monday morning, Giles rode out to Hurrell Place.

A servant took Giles upstairs to the long gallery where every ancestor had been draped in black gauze. Here Sir Morten and Mrs Hurrell were sitting, as stiffly as the effigies of their ancestors in the parish church, on high back chairs with the family arms behind them, draped with even more black. It was sombre and impressive.

Willoughby was standing before them, as if in an audience with royalty.

Sir Morten rose as Giles entered the room and came to shake his hand. "Good morning, Major Vernon. I hope you have some news for us."

"We hope that your son's body will be returned to you shortly."

"This examination by the surgeon – is it absolutely necessary?" said Sir Morten.

"Unfortunately, in the circumstances, yes," said Giles.

"And it is certain now that my son met an unnatural death? That he was murdered?"

"Yes."

Sir Morten put his hand on his chest and turned away. "Then we must trust God that justice prevails and the villain is brought to light. I am grateful that we have a man of your reputation at our service in this," he said. "Won't you sit?"

So Giles sat down beside Mrs Hurrell.

"I have told Sir Morten," Mr Willoughby said, "of that which we discussed the other day."

"In cases like this," Giles began, "there will inevitably be many theories and rumours going about."

"You have no clear candidate yet?" Sir Morten.

"No, I am afraid not. These are early days in the enquiry."

"But you are not disregarding what I told you?" Mr Willoughby said.

"I am not," Giles said, "but when a man's life is taken in violent circumstances, the cause is usually raw anger, not some subtle conspiracy."

Sir Morten closed his eyes for a moment. "Such as a violent quarrel between brothers?" he said quietly.

"You think that possible, sir?" said Giles.

"What else can I think, given all that has passed between them? Though it is unbearable to think my own flesh and blood would be capable of such an act, given the events of recent months, I cannot –"

He broke off, got up from his chair and went to stand in the great oriel window, looking out across his lands. "Sometimes, one has to acknowledge that there is corruption in something one loves."

"I understand you paid a visit to your son Mark at the Hermitage on the day Arthur Hurrell was murdered," Giles said.

Sir Morten shook his head. "I did not," he said.

"Are you sure about that, sir?" said Giles. "On Friday, before the rain came on?"

"No, certainly not."

"Perhaps you have mistaken the –"

"I don't know where you have acquired this notion, Major Vernon, but I can assure you I have not been anywhere near the Hermitage. I have not set foot in that building for many years. Since my wife died, in fact, in 1828. It is not a place I care to visit. I would have demolished the place, if I still had title to it, but unfortunately I do not."

"Might I ask, then," Giles said, "how your son Mark comes to be living there now?"

"It is a sorry tale. In the first instance, a foolish lawyer made a mistake with my wife's will. I gave the house and the land about it – barely an acre – to her as a gift after Arthur was born, because she so loved the house and its situation. That is why I cannot bear to go there. She loved the place so much. The understanding was that the property would revert to the estate at her death, but for some reason, at the end, there was a misunderstanding with her affairs and in her will it was left to John, our second boy, who was then fifteen. Why she did so, I do not know exactly. She did unfortunately display episodes of tragic confusion at the last, and perhaps that is where the accident arose."

"And then John left it to Mark," said Mrs Hurrell. "And that was all Mark's doing."

"We cannot say that for a fact," said Sir Morten.

"I know, I was there," Mrs Hurrell said, getting up. "I nursed John to the last. And Mark was there, attempting to wring every last shilling from his dying brother because of his debts at Oxford! I do not think you need to look far, Major Vernon, for the person who did this. I saw Mark begging John to make him his heir, and John, poor sweet John, could not refuse him. That was always the way between them. And now Mark will inherit everything because of the entail. And where will he stop? He might be thinking of you next, Sir Morten!"

"You are being hysterical, Susan," said Sir Morten.

"But is it not the case that some murderers get a taste for it?" Mrs Hurrell pressed on. "I have read –"

"You should not read servants' trash, ma'am," said Sir Morten. "And I will not have you rehearsing such idle speculation. If Mark is involved in this terrible business, then – then that alone is –" He shook his head. "No!"

He went and sat down again, with a defeated air. "I pray to our Lord God above that this is not the case, but all my instincts –"

There was silence, and then Willoughby said, "Neither should we discount the possibility that Mark was a tool of those forces who seek –"

"Enough, enough!" said Sir Morten, putting up his hand to silence Willoughby. "Will you please leave us in peace, sir? Do my nephews not need you? You are supposed to be their tutor, after all."

"As you wish, sir," said Willoughby. He left with the air of one enjoying a martyrdom.

Sir Morten turned to his sister-in-law and said, "And Susan, do you not have duties that require your attention?"

Mrs Hurrell obediently left the room without another word.

When the door had shut behind her, Sir Morten rose from his chair, indicating the great gallery stretching out in front of them, and said, "Shall we walk?"

So Giles joined Sir Morten in his progress down the room.

"You must disregard her story, Major Vernon," said Sir Morten. "I do not believe it to be the truth. John did not leave that legacy because Mark asked for it. John did it of his own free will. He spoke to me about it – it was because he wanted to redeem his brother. Unfortunately it was a misguided act. Mark was surprised to receive it, and for a short while it seemed to do him some good, but then –"

"I understand that this is a painful subject, Sir Morten," Giles said. "But can you give me some idea of why there was such animosity between the brothers?"

"I fear it was all my doing," said Sir Morten. "When my wife died, I took it very badly. I found it difficult to be with my children, especially the younger ones. They were left a little too much to their own devices, and Arthur being the eldest took to filling my shoes and commanding them in my stead. And now I think he was over-zealous. Being young, strong-armed and sincerely concerned for his brother's welfare, he took his duties too seriously. He did not temper the necessary discipline with love. Mark certainly considered him monstrous and cruel, for he, with his high spirits, bore the brunt of it – deservedly, I must point out; there was nothing done that was not earned. Mark had the very devil in him and Arthur attempted to thrash it out of him. It was unfortunate. Mark, having the unhappy disposition to cherish grudges, has let it spoil his relationship with his brother."

"Causing him to write the book, do you think?" Giles said.

"You have heard about that?"

"I'm afraid I have, sir."

"I destroyed as many copies as I could. Such a piece of malice and libel. At the time, I struggled to believe he could do such a thing to us, but now, with Arthur found dead in such appalling circumstances, I fear Mark has finally succumbed entirely to the wickedness that has always been in him. Must I now face the fact that my only surviving child will likely end his days on the gallows? Dear God, I hope that is not the answer to this business, Major Vernon! I pray you may turn up some other candidate, but I am afraid that –" He turned away. "Excuse me, sir."

"I will take my leave now, Sir Morten," said Giles. "Thank you for being so frank. Might I ask one favour of you before I leave? I understand that you and your sons are all experts with the longbow."

"It has been something of a sport with us, yes, but alas I cannot indulge any more. My shoulder, you see."

"Of course. Do you still have your bow and arrows?"

"Naturally."

"Might I borrow the arrows?"

"Yes, but to what end?"

"It is merely to establish what kind of weapon killed your son. My colleague Mr Carswell is anxious to match the wound to the weapon."

"You think he was shot with an arrow?"

"We do not know what weapon caused the wounding."

"Mark would be capable of that," said Sir Morten after a moment. "He is the best shot of us all. Yes, you must have some arrows, though I pray to God that you are mistaken!"

~

On Monday morning, Arthur Hurrell's corpse was delivered to Felix's laboratory and he began on the post-mortem, grateful to have a substantial piece of work in hand.

Sunday at Hawksby had not been comfortable. He had been glad of the piety of the ladies who went to church twice. He went in the morning and sat with his wife and mother-in-law in the well-upholstered Blanchfort family pew and failed to listen to the long sermon given by a curate, not through inattention but because the young man never raised his voice much above a whisper. At luncheon Lady Blanchfort had told him he ought to call on the curate and suggest he learn to project his voice. "He will like it better coming from you," she said. "And something must be done or he has no future in the Church." Felix had not agreed to this. He was not at all in the mood for assuming such a role in the village. It was hard enough to be sitting at the head of the table in the dining room.

He had spent the afternoon in the room that was to be his study but which was a mess of packing cases. He had attempted to set up his extremely expensive and complicated new microscope that he had bought in Edinburgh. Having utterly failed to put it together, he had lost his temper and taken himself off into the gardens to smoke while Eleanor and her mother went to Evensong. The evening had been enlivened a little by Lady Blanchfort playing the piano, at which she showed considerable skill. He was surprised she permitted herself the indulgence of music on a Sunday night, but found himself glad of it.

He had just begun to take his preliminary measurements when Major Vernon came in. He was carrying a quiver of arrows and a brown paper parcel.

"What's in the parcel?"

"A hind quarter of pork. I know it's dead flesh but I thought it might allow a crude comparison."

"Excellent idea," said Felix, pulling an arrow from the quiver and holding it up to the light.

"Sir Morten explained to me that there are several types of arrowhead in general use."

Felix tested the blade of the arrow he was holding against his finger.

"Sharp enough, certainly," he said, and used it as a knife to cut the string on the parcel.

"For a man who doesn't practice the sport, they are in good condition," said Major Vernon. "Perhaps he keeps them in order as a consolation for the loss of the pleasure."

"Perhaps," said Felix, taking up another arrow and peering at it. "It is a pity you did not bring a bow."

"I did consider that. But you seemed of the opinion that those wounds were inflicted at close range."

"Yes, but I was not sure of my weapon then. Not that I am now, but I should like to see how an arrow wound might differ in appearance according to the speed, force and distance at which it was delivered."

"I will get a bow. Perhaps from Mark Hurrell."

"Who can bring down a hind with one of these. I should like to have a look at that cadaver."

"With luck it may still be hanging in the larder at the Hermitage. We shall pay a visit forthwith. I certainly need to talk to him again, and at some length."

"He is my man for it," said Felix, uncovering Arthur Hurrell's cadaver. "Look at this. Look at that pointed-almond shape. It's an almost perfect match." He held the arrow close to the wound. "And if we then attempt to replicate it here..."

He seized the arrow and stabbed it into the joint of pork, then pulled it out.

"Yes, that looks plausible," he said, having studied the wound he had made on the joint and then the wounds on the cadaver.

"So we have a possible murder weapon," Major Vernon said, taking another arrow from the quiver and studying it. "Who would have thought a little blade could do so much harm?"

At this point there was a knock at the door. It was Sergeant Coxe, newly returned from Axworth.

"I might have something of use for you, sir," he said. "There is a woman in the fever hospital who will not give her name but answers somewhat to your description. A black, lace-trimmed bonnet and a red-striped apron in her possessions. She had no infirmary ticket, so she is not local. Instead she gave them three guineas straight up and asked them to take her in."

"Did they let you see her?" Major Vernon said.

"Yes, and I asked her direct if she were Esther Braithwaite but I got no answer. She seemed half dead already, if you know what I mean, sir. And they would not let me linger."

"Which is just as well," said Felix.

"I did tell the nurse if she was to say anything curious we would want to hear of it. But they have their hands pretty full, as you can imagine, sir. I felt like a rat deserting a sinking ship. That place was... pray to God it does not reach us here."

"Thank you, Coxe, that was well done," said Major Vernon.

"What do you want me to do now, sir?" Coxe asked.

"I am going out to Raythorpe again shortly. It would be useful if you came with me."

"You are going to call on Mark Hurrell, I suppose?" said

Felix. "I will be surprised if you don't bring him back in cuffs."

"We shall see," said Major Vernon, and went to the door with Sergeant Coxe, leaving Felix to the work of the post-mortem.

# Chapter Twenty

Mark Hurrell was not at home.

The fire was doused in the hearth and the drawers in the writing desk had been left open as if he had gathered up his papers and left in a hurry. On going upstairs they found a similar picture – the washstand cleared of its necessities and his clothes scattered about as if he had been deciding what to take with him.

"In the circumstances," Giles said to Coxe, "we are justified in making a search."

"Certainly, sir."

"You search upstairs. I will see to the kitchen and yard."

There was nothing of interest in the kitchen, and Giles went out into the back yard. It was ornamented by a crumbling wooden privy on one side and a storeroom on the other. Giles went in and found a room that was thick with cobwebs, many years' worth of work by industrious spiders. The light was dimly admitted by a square of mottled, dirty glass. However, there was enough light for him to notice a tangled clump of cobwebs on the floor, as if a portion had recently been pushed aside. There was a recess in front of him, also free of cobwebs, and on a high shelf was a bundle of crumpled canvas, similar to the tarpaulin that had been used to patch the roof. From the pattern of dust, it appeared to have been pushed deliberately to the back. Giles pulled it from the shelf and as he did so, it fell open in his arms, revealing that it was not just a bundle of canvas but a package containing a dun-coloured linen garment.

It took him a moment to realise what it was: a farmer's smock of the sort commonly worn in the county, with the yoke and shoulders elaborately worked in red thread. It was filthy, covered in stains that he could not at once identify.

He carried it out into the yard to see it better in daylight, shaking it out and holding it up by its shoulders to reveal its full length. It was a long smock, made for a broad, tall man, and the staining seemed heaviest on the chest. Many of the stains had a rusty reddish tint to them that suggested blood, but what sort of blood was the immediate question.

Mark Hurrell had been seen wearing a smock to protect his clothes from the more visceral aspects of his hunting activities, as a butcher would put on an apron. It was perhaps a little eccentric for a gentleman to wear such a garment, but it was a sensible choice. But why had it then been consigned to an outhouse, wrapped in canvas? This smock had been hidden deliberately.

"Is this what you were looking for, sir?" said Coxe, coming out into the yard. He was holding a quiver of arrows, similar to the one Sir Morten had given him, as well as a longbow. "Upstairs in the little back room."

They went into the parlour and laid their finds out on the table.

"Definitely blood, sir," said Coxe, peering at the smock.

"We need Mr Carswell to look at this," Giles said.

"I did hear he was working to see if he could find if a stain was animal blood or human," Coxe said. "Mighty useful that will be."

"I don't know how far he has got with that, but this might help him. It looks fresh to me in parts. Here, for example. Now, we know Mark Hurrell brought down a deer in the woods recently."

"Yes, sir, definitely. And this being stuffed away like that, you have to wonder."

"And he does seem to have cleared out," Giles said, looking around him. "We had better go and find out when he was last seen hereabouts. I saw him last on Saturday night in The Lamb Inn at Raythorpe. He was on the verge of going to see his father up at Hurrell Place."

They then called in at The Hurrell Arms where the landlady, Mrs Fuller, confirmed Mark Hurrell had hired a gig from her husband on Sunday morning.

"Did he say where he was going?" She shook her head. Giles went on: "Do you know him well, Mrs Fuller? I understand you recently nursed him and dressed his wounds."

"I've known him since we were children. He used to come and play with my brothers. My father was tenant to Sir Morten – just in a small way, mind. So he was not supposed to have anything to do with us and there were always terrible scenes when they were all found out, but my brothers were always happy to take a whipping for the pleasure of his company. He's stood by them too, for all his troubles, as if they were his own brothers, and done everything he could for them. Charlie is doing well in London thanks to him. And he gave me such a handsome brooch when I married."

"But he chose not to tell you where he was going?"

"No, sir. I asked him if he'd be back for the funeral, and he said he didn't know. He said he probably wouldn't be wanted. I suppose he had had another run-in with his father. I told him how sorry I was about Mr Hurrell, and that I hoped it would be better with his father again after it, for it's too great a thing for them to stay cold to each other, and it all ought to end now. So he said he wished it could be so, with all his heart, but it could never be. He said it was better he was gone now and that was that." She sighed. "I wish he had not gone. It would be better to stay and brave it out, for it only makes him look as if –"

"Yes?"

"Well, why are you here looking for him, if you don't think he was behind it? But I tell you, sir, there is no sweeter soul in the world than Mr Mark and he would never have done that to his own brother, never!"

~

Giles sent Coxe back to Northminster and went again to call at Hurrell Place.

On this occasion, Sir Morten saw Giles in his library, where the books were crammed up on impossibly high shelves as if they were never meant to be fetched down.

"He has left the neighbourhood?" said Sir Morten.

"So it seems. I understand he came to see you on Saturday evening. At least he said that was his intention. Did you receive him?"

"I did," said Sir Morten. "I thought, given the circumstances, that I should."

"He did not give any indication that he was going to leave?"

"No. I should have advised him strongly against it had he done so. His removing himself will only fuel the rumours which are already, unfortunately, surrounding this house – if they are rumours. His departure –" He took a deep breath. "There can be no rest for me," he said. "I have lost everything. It is the hardest blow. All my children dead or as good as dead to me, for the longer you stay here, sir, I can only see one outcome – that Mark will be found to be culpable."

"That may not be the case," said Giles. "Things are still unclear."

"But why else would he run, like a coward? Why else? If he is guilty, then –" He threw up his hands. "Forgive me. This is a trying time for me. I ought not to give in to despair. I should trust in you and in justice, should I not, Major Vernon? It may be that ruin is not absolutely upon my house after all."

At this moment a door in the corner of the room opened and a footman in his shirtsleeves came in, carrying a bucket. He froze on the spot seeing that room was occupied.

"What is the meaning of this?" exclaimed Sir Morten.

"How dare you! How many times must it be said? That door is to be kept closed at all times!"

"I'm sorry, sir," said the footman. "Mr Lightbody did not say so, and I saw him use it himself only yesterday, sir, and –"

"Be quiet! Do you think I want your excuses, boy?"

"No, sir," said the footman.

"Then get out! If you have business in here, come through the door in the hall and knock! Do you understand me?"

"Yes, sir."

"Out then, at once!"

The footman departed in some haste.

"I ought to have had that door bricked up years ago," said Sir Morten, going to the door and turning the key. He put the key into his pocket. "It creates a noxious draught. I think I can ascribe most of my rheumatic troubles to that draught and the passageway beyond it. And besides, it is one of those wretched conduits that was supposedly created for the convenience of masters but really does nothing but allow servants to take liberties. They will use this room – my private room, mind, sir – as a turnpike highway instead of going the way they ought! No, it must be bricked up, although it will be a great inconvenience to me! I imagine your excellent bride will see to such comforts for you in Rooke Court without your even having to think of them!"

"I think so," said Giles.

"She is a delightful woman. You are to be congratulated. Does she have any money of her own?"

The bluntness of this question and the turn of the subject surprised Giles, but he managed to answer, "Only a little."

"She has the air of a woman who ought to have a great fortune."

"She has no interest in that, fortunately – otherwise she would not take a threadbare husband such as myself."

"You are marrying entirely to please yourselves, then?"

"We are of an age when we may do so. Our families are happy enough with the arrangement, though."

"And she is not beyond childbearing, I would say."

"That is not something we have –"

"But you ought, Major Vernon, you ought. I wish to God I had remarried when I could. I let sentiment guide me instead of common sense. If I had done so then I might have some shred of consolation in these dire circumstances. A daughter left to see to my comfort, another son to take my name..." He shook his head and sighed.

"While we are on the question of engagements," Giles said, "might I ask you about the understanding between Miss Wytton and your late son? What was the nature of it?"

Sir Morten thought for a moment.

"It would have been an acceptable match. At one time it seemed likely, but my son, sensibly, began to see that the young woman was perhaps not worthy of the honour he had offered her. Time has proved him right. He was right to be cautious. She is not –"

"Yes?"

"I do not like to speak unkindly of her, but she is not perhaps as steady as one might wish. There is an element of flightiness, a lack of proper seriousness about her. It has grown over the years. She was inclined to flirt with my other sons, with Mark in particular. Arthur told me something had happened that made him consider his obligations to her to be at an end. That Mark had – well, you gather my meaning. Unfortunately it does not surprise me. He has no scruples whatsoever."

"Arthur implied an actual seduction had taken place?"

"Yes, Major, that was my understanding. As I said, Mark has no scruples."

"Did you not think, on hearing it, that they ought to have been obliged to marry?" Giles said.

"They both denied anything improper had taken place,"

said Sir Morten.

"To your face, sir? I assume you questioned Mark about it."

"I did not. Arthur would not have lied to me about such a grave matter, and I knew I would only have got lies from Mark."

"So you considered this enough to release Arthur from his obligations to Miss Wytton?"

"Certainly."

"You will excuse me, but I do not understand why no formal break was made. Miss Wytton seems to have laboured under the expectation that at any time the engagement would be announced."

"It was clear that it was over. She has been extremely foolish about it, but both families are clear that there was no obligation. Arthur was free to look elsewhere, and he did. Indeed, the evening you were here with Mrs Maitland, he confessed to me that he admired Lady Maria Haraald and intended to pursue the matter further. But that is now –" He turned away, overcome by emotion. "If you will excuse me."

Giles left him and spent a few minutes in the great hall making notes, wondering a little at the father so staunchly believing one son and not the other. He obviously had no real wish to accept Margaret Wytton as a daughter-in-law and had been happy to accept a blackening of her character in order to allow Arthur to be released from his obligation to her.

Just as he was leaving, a carriage drew up with Lady Wytton in. Seeing him, she put down the window, and he went to speak to her as her footman went to enquire of the butler. She was dressed in sympathetic grey and in her lap was a large basket of flowers.

"I came to see Mrs Hurrell," she said, and then added in a confidential whisper, "I do think she has a wretched life here. Sir Morten can be so difficult –" She broke off, seeing her footman return with the butler's answer. "Is she still not receiving, Patrick?"

"No, my lady."

"Well, give these to her," she said. The footman took the basket and went to deliver it. "Can I drive you anywhere, Major Vernon?"

"That would be kind. I was just on my way back to The Lamb, but I have a few questions for you, if you do not mind."

"Yes, of course."

"Sir Morten can be difficult, you were saying?" he ventured as they drove away. She again had the look of wishing to confide in him.

"Sir Morten is a tyrant. Is it wicked to say that in such circumstances?" She plucked off a petal that had fallen onto her skirts. "And Mrs Hurrell has a wretched time. He treats her as if she is nothing when she is everything. She runs that great place for him and he gives her nothing. A little pin money, but not nearly as much as she should get. If I were her – well, I don't know what I should do. I suppose her expectations for her boys keeps her there. I suppose – and this is wicked of me to say so, but now Mr Hurrell is dead, and there is only Mark left, then little Morten is almost the heir. And if something were to happen to Mark – and perhaps it might, from what I have heard... but I should not say that, should I?"

"You mean he is being spoken of as Mr Hurrell's murderer?"

"Yes, I'm afraid so. My husband is convinced of it, given how bad the quarrels have been between them all these years. He said that it did not surprise him one bit that Mark would do such a thing, especially since he seems to have lost his reason anyway when he published that book. That does happen, does it not, that people go mad and commit murder?"

"Sometimes yes, regrettably."

"I hope it is not him," Lady Wytton said. "I have only met him once or twice, and he seemed extremely charming to me. But perhaps murderers may be charming? How does one ever know?" She sighed. "Oh, how wretched, wretched all this is! Poor Mr Pierce, and now Mr Hurrell. But I hope you do not have to hang Mark Hurrell, Major Vernon, and that you will find out that it is someone else entirely. Someone I do not know."

"Unfortunately I can promise nothing," Giles said.

"No, you cannot. And we are lucky to have you here. I have read of your escapades in The Bugle."

"Might I ask you something rather delicate, Lady Wytton, about your sister-in-law and Mark Hurrell?"

"Yes?"

"I have been told that there was some impropriety discovered between them, enough to make Arthur Hurrell consider the engagement at an end."

Lady Wytton gave a little gasp.

"Between Mark and Margaret?" she said. "Oh no, no, never. Who said such a thing to you, Major Vernon? It is horrible that anyone would say that of Margaret. Her devotion to Arthur Hurrell – oh, if you could see her now! I have been thinking of sending for your Mr Carswell; she seems sick with grief, or worse. No, no, that is a horrible lie and whoever put such a lie about should be ashamed of themselves. Who told you that?"

"I'm afraid I cannot say," said Giles.

"Oh, that is bad. Edward will be furious if he hears that. His manner – well, I know he is not polished, but he does love her dearly in his own way and an insult like that would be a dreadful thing for him. Oh, I wish you had not told me that! Whatever shall I do now?"

"I'm sorry to have made you uncomfortable," said Giles.

"She says she wants to be buried with him," Lady Wytton went on. "That she will be dead within the year from grief. And as for anything at all between her and Mark – no, I'm sure of it. In fact, she is certain that he is the culprit. She was saying so only last night! You would never accuse a man you loved of murder, would you?"

# Chapter Twenty-one

Felix was not disturbed until he was writing up his notes, when the duty constable came downstairs with a message for him. It was an unsealed paper in a familiar hand. Felix read it, pulled on his coat and went upstairs. The footman who had brought the message was waiting in the hall.

"Any answer, sir?" the footman said.

"I'll come back with you now," said Felix.

It was only a few minutes' walk to Lord Rothborough's house in the Minster Precincts, but a torpid heat had built up after the rain, and it was pleasant to be ushered into a cool hallway. James Bodley was there and led him upstairs to the shuttered drawing room on the first floor.

"I'm glad you could come so promptly, sir," said Bodley. "The fact is, he's not himself at all."

"I gathered that from his message. What has happened, Bodley? I thought you were going straight to Holbroke with her Ladyship," Felix said.

"Let him tell you, sir," said Bodley, opening the door to the gloomy drawing room.

Lord Rothborough, uncharacteristically in his shirtsleeves, was sitting in the far corner on a sofa pushed to the wall. There was a litter of papers about him, which was as Felix would have expected, but it was striking that he did not seem to be engaged upon them. Rather he was gazing out through the chink in one of the shutters, so that the light caught his introspection and his stillness, as if he were his own portrait bust.

"Master Felix, my lord," said Bodley.

Lord Rothborough turned and rose at the sound of

Bodley's voice. He came down the room smiling, and embraced Felix.

"Thank you for coming, my boy," he said. "I hope I didn't take you from anything important."

"No, I had just finished a post-mortem," Felix said.

Lord Rothborough gave a brief laugh at that. "And that was what I wanted from you!" he said.

"Sir?" said Felix.

"Here," said Lord Rothborough, taking a paper from his pocket. "Tell me what I am to make of this."

Felix studied it. It was a sheet of writing paper, embossed with the words 'Villa Albinia, Firenze.' Written below was the following:

> Lady Rothborough begs to inform Lord Rothborough that she will remain in Florence indefinitely, on the advice of her medical attendant.

"It was waiting for me at the hotel at Dover. After all my efforts." He shook his head. "She did not even take the trouble to write it. That is not her hand, nor Augusta's."

"Who is her doctor?"

"Some Italian fellow. I'm sure he does not want her to return, for the sake of his income, so he will tell her anything she wishes to hear. And she never hears anything she does not wish to hear! She is so used to getting her own way in everything, that everything must bend to her will, no matter how unreasonable her demand! And this – this will hurt everyone, including my lady in the end, but will she ever admit it? No!" He flung himself down on the sofa. "Does she want to see her daughters married? No, not if it inconveniences her, not if it means being civil to me in public for the briefest space. How can she be so stubborn? Does she feel nothing for them? And poor Augusta – I must get her back here. She cannot stay with her. She is the most suggestible of all of them, and I know that she will not hesitate to turn her against me."

"But Augusta does still write?" said Felix, sitting down beside him.

"Yes, yes, the most charming, dutiful letters, but there is an absence in them. I feel I am losing her. That is the worst of it. My lady may stay where she likes and do as she pleases, but she shall not have Augusta!"

"Then you should go and bring her back," Felix said.

"It seems I shall have to," said Lord Rothborough. "And pray she will come with me. For she will not like to desert her mother, and my lady will play every trick to keep her." He sighed.

"Do you not have the right of custody under the law?" said Felix. "Given that this amounts to desertion and Augusta is not yet of age?"

"Yes, but I cannot do that to the girls, I cannot revile their mother publicly. No, this must be managed discreetly. Augusta must make her choice freely."

"If she sees you as you are now," Felix said, "I'm sure it will be easy for her. And she will want to be with her sisters."

Lord Rothborough smiled at that.

"It is a pity we do not have a handsome prospective spouse to lure her home with. I should take Arthur Hurrell with me. He might suit Augusta, and my lady could find no fault with that rent roll or lineage."

"I'm afraid that won't be possible," Felix said. "He's been murdered. The post-mortem that I –"

"Good God," said Lord Rothborough. "When did this happen?"

"Friday. He was not discovered until the next morning. He had been killed with an arrow and pushed down a hillside."

"An arrow?" said Lord Rothborough. "But now I think of it, the longbow was something of a tradition in that family. Do you and Major Vernon have any indication of who is responsible?"

"It's still unclear, but Mark Hurrell, the younger brother –"

"Yes, yes, I know the fellow."

"He may be our man."

"No, surely not?" said Lord Rothborough. He leant back on the sofa and rubbed his face. "Well, I hope for his sake you are wrong for once, but you and Vernon have an uncanny knack of getting to the truth in these matters, and there was certainly no love lost between those brothers. I saw that for myself. But oh, dear heaven, that is a miserable piece of news! What a terrible thing to happen in such a fine old family! Have you anything cheerful for me? Tell me, how is my beautiful ward? At least I can console myself with your happiness."

"She is very well," Felix managed to say.

"Then I ought to let you go home to her and not keep you here listening to my lamentations."

"Won't you come and dine with us?" Felix said.

Lord Rothborough shook his head, and reached for one of the papers on the table.

"I'm going to Holbroke shortly. And I have a great deal to do here first. It has been hinted to me that there may be a seat for me in the shadow cabinet again if I check my wings."

"You, sir?" Felix could not help saying. "Check your wings? Who said that to you?"

"Dunbar – well, not directly, he is not so insolent yet. He may be more frank with me when he marries Charlotte. That will be his privilege. But he has been pleading my cause, and since he is so much the rising man, they may consider taking on the old fool clinging to his coat-tails if he behaves himself."

"Do you really want it on such terms, my lord?" Felix said. "I'm not sure I would!"

"That is the difference between five-and-twenty and fifty."

"They should be grateful to get you on whatever terms you dictate," Felix said. "And do you trust Dunbar?"

"Charlotte trusts him, and I trust him enough to let him marry her."

"If I were him, I would not give you any quarter," Felix said. "If you are returned to favour, surely all your experience and connections will make him look raw."

"Some would say raw, others will say fresh, and that is a desirable quality. The electors love novelty!"

"He is only setting up a rival if he helps you, and from everything I have heard of Dunbar, he is fixed on power, at any cost. You should be careful."

"You have such a cynical view of politics, Felix."

"You cannot try and convince me it is other than a bear pit, not after you have been so battered over the years by men who pretend they are your friends! I do not know how you can stand it."

"It does not hurt me so much," said Lord Rothborough. "And I'm touched by your concern for me." He studied the paper in his hand for a moment and then let go of it. "Of course, this may all be moot! This business with Lady Rothborough may have sunk me for good in terms of taking office. We live in censorious times, after all, and even if we keep this out of the newspapers, it will be known and held against me. She may even stir the pot. I would not put it past her."

"Stir the pot?"

"A letter or two to the right person outlining my supposed misdeeds." He got up and went to the window, opening the shutter. "In fact, it is possible that one of her correspondents – and she has many – has told her that I may have visited a certain widow from Santa Magdalena when I was in town."

"Do you mean –?" Felix said. "I thought my mother said she would never come back to England."

"The situation on the island was unsafe for her. She was obliged to take refuge in London. This was last month, while you were in Scotland."

"But I thought that you and she had decided –"

"Town was empty," Lord Rothborough said. "But it seems we may have been seen together. An innocent walk in St James Park, that was all. In retrospect foolish, perhaps, but –" He sighed. "It was so pleasant to see her. And she is glad to hear you are settled."

"And she is going to stay in London?" Felix said.

"She has not yet decided," said Lord Rothborough. "And don't worry, we shall not make a scandal. I'm not such an old fool as that. However tempting it might be, these are, as I said, censorious times and I care too much for her to make any such trouble for her. It is wretched, for she had to leave in great haste, and as a result she is living in rather straitened circumstances. But I cannot do anything for her. She will not allow it."

"How bad are things for her?" said Felix. Lord Rothborough's idea of straitened circumstances probably meant managing without a carriage and pair and not giving dinners for more than a dozen. "Would she allow me to help her?"

Lord Rothborough smiled at that, and then shook his head.

"She will not allow that either, but I shall tell her you suggested it. She will be touched."

"So you are writing to one another?"

Lord Rothborough did not answer at once, but got up and walked down the room. He picked up a small alabaster figurine of a naked goddess and began to play with it.

"We find that we are," he said, replacing the figurine with care on the table. "And as she herself has pointed out, Héloise within the cloister wrote to Abelard. Are we not allowed some solace?"

"I don't know," said Felix.

"The fact is," said Lord Rothborough, "the marriage laws

in this country are no longer fit for purpose. My wife and I, for example: we do not have a marriage, we have not done for years – I can speak to you about this now, Felix, for now you understand what it means to be married – and it would be immeasurably better for both of us, and for our daughters, if we could dissolve that bond without recourse to sordid fault-finding. It ought to be enough that when a couple have not lived comfortably together for years, when a couple have not been intimate in any sense, when they have lost all sense of common life and purpose, that they ought to be released to seek better and more productive unions!"

"Are you planning to raise this in the House?" said Felix.

"I may do," said Lord Rothborough. "The cruelty of our present arrangements... but you do not want to hear this. I do not want to poison your well with my complaints when the institution is clearly doing you no harm. You look as if you are thriving, I must say!"

# Chapter Twenty-two

Felix returned to the Northern Office and spent the rest of the afternoon writing up the post-mortem. Major Vernon came in at a little after four.

"I have more things for you to look at," he said, and presented Felix with a bow and quiver of arrows as well as a bundle of linen.

"More arrows?"

"Mark Hurrell's. Or at least taken from his house. The man himself has absented himself and cannot confirm if they belong to him."

"That speaks volumes."

"It does and it does not. Everyone in the neighbourhood is more than willing to put a noose about his neck, but at the same time they tell me how sweet and charming he is."

"What is this?" said Felix, turning to the linen.

"A blood-stained smock. Found in an outhouse. Stuffed away on a shelf with an intent to conceal. Can you do anything with it?"

Felix picked up the smock and carried it to the window to examine it properly. "Heavens, but that is interesting!"

"Isn't it? The spattering here – it is dense."

"It looks like an arterial spurt at first glance," Felix said, "which would certainly match the position of one of the wounds, if our murderer was facing the victim. Unlike your first hypothesis." Felix laid the smock down on the table. "In a box somewhere at Hawksby I have the beginning of my comparative study of bloodstains. There is an album of samples of different stains which might be useful."

"Then you had better go home and find it," said Major

Vernon.

Felix nodded, though the idea of going back was not appealing. However, he would at least have something to keep him busy and away from Eleanor. There were a dozen or so boxes to sort through.

"There is an arrow here which also interests me." Major Vernon drew an arrow from the quiver that had been marked with a piece of twine. "This one. That must be blood."

"Most possibly," said Felix. "But why did he not clean it?"

"It looks partially cleaned. Perhaps put away in a hurry?"

"If that is the weapon, why did he not conceal it better?" Felix said.

"It does seem foolish," said Major Vernon, frowning. "But we should not be surprised at that. If he killed his brother in a rage, without much premeditation, then the details of concealing the crime may be equally haphazard."

"So what do you think happened?"

"This is purely hypothetical," said Major Vernon, picking up the arrow again. "But can we surmise that on the Friday at some point, before the rain starts, Mark Hurrell, sufficiently recovered from his wounds, takes his bow and arrow out into the woods for a little sport, perhaps to relieve his feelings? He is probably still angry with his brother. Perhaps he is wearing the smock to protect his clothes, like a sensible countryman of limited means. He has been seen wearing a smock when hunting by Mrs Maitland and Lady Maria, after all. But instead of finding a few rabbits to shoot at, he finds his brother at his prayers in the old chapel. It would be provoking to see him there, and the idea of getting some immediate redress for his public humiliation may have come over him. It may have started with angry words and gone from there. Perhaps Arthur said something that pushed Mark beyond the limit at which he could restrain himself."

"And with one of them being armed and the other not,"

Felix said, "one thing led to another."

"He has the arrow in his hand and his brother at a disadvantage for once. Hurrell does not even have his coat on to protect him. He is an easy prey and Mark has the perfect opportunity." Major Vernon then mimed plunging the arrow into Felix's chest. "Two good stabs and the deed is done."

"But not without a fair bit of blood covering them both," Felix said.

"Arthur collapses onto the ground and Mark cleans the arrow on his smock or his handkerchief, before dragging the body to the edge of the cliff and pushing it down."

"And then he buries the handkerchief, and goes back to the Hermitage and hides the smock. And puts the arrow back with the others."

"Perhaps he intended to dispose of them more thoroughly at a later date."

"Why did he not take them with him when he left?" Felix said.

"And be caught with them?"

"He might have wanted to dispose of them somewhere further away, where the connection would be harder to establish. But to leave them in the house – it is strange, is it not?"

"Very," said Major Vernon, laying the arrow down on the table again. "Well, do what you can with them now, Mr Carswell, and we shall see where it leads us."

~

Giles went to Jebb Street in order to remind himself of the circumstances of the fire, having spent some time trying to construct a plausible sequence of events that might have led Esther Braithwaite – if it *was* she – to try to burn down a warehouse. She was still a cipher to him, and now, standing in the street looking up at the timbered warehouse and the neat stone face of Wytton's Bank, he wondered what detail he was missing that would make sense of it all. Had someone already said something of which he had failed to take proper note? Had he been less vigilant than he should because of the business at Hurrell Place? To have two such cases open on his books was both stimulating and troubling. To concentrate on one inevitably meant the neglect of the other.

The door to the bank now opened, and a man was strong-armed out into the street by a sturdy looking individual in a porter's coat. With them was the clerk Giles had spoken to previously. He was now attempting to calm the man who had been put out.

Giles crossed the street to join them.

"Yes, yes, I shall go!" the ejected man said, putting up his hands and retreating a little as the porter threatened to give him a further shove. "But I shall be back tomorrow, and if you do not –"

"No, sir," the clerk replied. "Not tomorrow. You will only be disappointed and there is no point to it. Henry, keep the door closed to him!"

At which the clerk went scuttling back in, closing the door, and Henry took up his post in front of it. The ejected man eyed him, full of hostility – his fists were balled and he seemed to be considering an assault, at which point Giles thought it best to intervene.

"May I help you, sir?" he said. "I am a police officer."

The man who had been put out turned his angry gaze to him. He was a respectably-dressed man in his thirties.

"Yes, sir, you certainly may!" he exclaimed, speaking in the local accent. "This place – they will not –" He glanced around him furtively and then added, in a furious undertone, "Give me my money! And you," he said, turning to the doorman, "I should not be put out like a ruffian! You may think you are serving your master, but I'm your master! I am a depositor in this bank and I demand that –" He broke off, glancing around him again. "This is not a matter for the street, Lord help me, but –"

"No, sir, certainly it is not," said Giles. "Perhaps we should go into this coffee house and you can tell me what the difficulty seems to be?"

The man agreed and they went into the coffee house. They sat down in the privacy of a red-curtained booth.

"I am Major Vernon, the Chief Superintendent of the Northern Intelligence Office," Giles said, having ordered the coffee. "And you are, sir?"

"Nathanial Dyson," said the man. "Wool merchant. I was with Hurling and Co but I am making my own way these days." He took out a neatly engraved card and laid it on the table. "And it's a honour to meet you, sir – the famous Major Vernon, eh? I have read all about you in The Bugle."

"You should take all that with a pinch of salt," Giles said, opening his notebook. "Now, you said you are a customer at Wytton's?"

"Yes. I don't have all my money in there. But I have a tidy sum there – some of it my wife's." He rubbed his face and sighed.

"And you asked to make a withdrawal?"

"Yes, and this is what I cannot fathom. Well, I can fathom it, and the fates have sent you my way, sir, for there is a stink there, I'm sure of it. I was not so sure at first, but now..." The waiter brought the coffee and Dyson drank his down in one gulp, winced at it and then ordered another.

"A stink?" said Giles. "What makes you think that?"

"Last Thursday I went in and asked to clear out most of my money. They were very civil, as usual, and said to come back the following day and it would be ready for me. It is a matter of a hundred pounds, give or take a shilling, and I was happy to come back and collect it on Friday, except that when

I went on Friday they hadn't got it ready for me, which was vexing, but I thought I would come back today. So I did and I left it until the afternoon, and still it was not ready! Now I'm not wanting to kick up a fuss, but it's not the largest sum and they've had all the benefit of it for a couple of years, at least. They ought to have been able to hand it back to me in three days. I was not expecting the interest on it – I told them to leave that be, such that it is – not the best rate, no matter what they say – and so I left it and then, this afternoon, I am treated like a damned dog by the head clerk, and told I don't have any money in the account, that it had been closed three month ago, and did I not remember? Which of course I did not, never having done such a thing. I tell you, Major Vernon, if I'd had a hundred in cash I would have remembered it!"

"That is curious. Why did you want to take out the money in the first place?"

"Ah yes, sir, that's the interesting point and that's why I smell a stink, although I pray to God I am wrong, for it is the last thing trade in the town needs now. I heard something which set me wondering. I was in Axworth last week. I go there about once a month, buying mostly, and I was talking to customer of mine, an honest fellow, and he was convinced that Wytton's was about to –" He glanced about him again and said in a low voice, "Go down. Plumb down."

"Axworth?"

"Yes. At first I took it for an Axworth man speaking ill of Northminster, as they do, and as we do of them. But he was in earnest. Said he had heard it from a sound man, his own family doctor."

"Who also has funds in the bank?"

"No, not at all. He'd heard it from a patient. That Wytton's was about to fail, that they had not enough money to cover their deposits."

"Did he give you the doctor's name?"

Dyson thought for a moment. "I can't be sure of it.

Perryman, I think – he's a well-known man in the town. Been in practice there for years."

"But you did not speak to him in person about this?"

"No, and I know it was just a rumour, but I thought I would take my money from Wytton's just in case there was any truth in it. Discreetly. I know how these things go. And at first, I thought they were just being slow, as these places sometimes are, but then to be told I had already taken out my money and closed my account! I swear to you, sir, I have done no such thing, even though that damned clerk showed me the ledger page with my name crossed out. I was never so shocked as when I saw that!"

"I can imagine. I shall certainly go and ask them about it, Mr Dyson."

Giles left Dyson to his second cup of coffee and went back to the bank. He had hopes of seeing Lord Wytton there, but found the head clerk instead. He was at work in Mr Pierce's office.

"Mr Dyson closed his account," he said, after Giles had told him what Dyson alleged.

"Can you show me the evidence of that?"

"Of course, Major Vernon. It may take a while to find the correct ledger."

"I am happy to wait."

"As you wish, sir. Excuse me."

Giles was left to contemplate Mr Pierce's office. He would have liked to conduct a thorough search, but he had nothing tangible enough to warrant this. The clerk returned with a large ledger, stamped Depositors. He opened it at the 'D' tab and began to turn the pages.

"Do you have any recollection of this account being closed?" Giles said. "It's dated three months ago, I see."

"No, I don't. We do a lot of business, you see, sir, and I have been working in a different department."

"But it is a large sum?"

"Not for us, sir," said the clerk. He squinted at the ledger for a moment and sighed. "I think that is Mr Fred's hand. He must have done it. He would have been able to tell you."

"Do you keep a list of recently closed accounts?" Giles asked.

"No, I don't believe we do, sir."

"But you would know how much has been withdrawn from individual accounts being closed? Would it not need to be marked as a form of loss?"

"That is a matter for the Directors," the clerk said after a moment.

"Of course," said Giles. "But you would notice if there was a higher than usual number of accounts closed?"

"I don't know what you are driving at, sir."

"Well, just glancing back a few pages, here, I see that there is another account closed here, Mrs Dixon, ten guineas paid out on the ninth of June. Now when did Mr Dyson close his – yes, June twelfth?" He would have turned a few more pages on, but the clerk intervened.

"I'm not sure I ought to allow you to do that, sir, with the greatest of respect. This information is highly confidential and I am not sure you ought to see it without the permission of the Directors."

"One of whom is indisposed."

"Yes, sir, a worrying business."

"And the other? Do you know when Lord Wytton will next be here?"

"He did not give us any indication," said the clerk. "However, I do not think he would like you examining our books, sir. If you had the proper authority, sir, then it might be possible."

"It may well come to that," said Giles. The clerk looked as if he had suggested something obscene.

"We take pride in our confidentiality," he said. "I do not think you would like strange eyes looking over your financial affairs, sir."

"I should not care one whit, for I have nothing to hide. Speaking of which, if there is anything you would like to tell me, you should tell me now. Misplaced loyalty is a dangerous thing. You should consider your own future before that of your masters."

"I don't know what you mean, sir," said the clerk.

Giles did not linger. He now felt that Dyson's caution was well-founded and he knew he had to go to the source of the rumour. He also knew there was little time to waste. He had to talk to Esther Braithwaite.

# Chapter Twenty-three

"Axworth?" Lady Blanchfort had said, rather as if he had said he was sailing for the Cape of Good Hope, rather than taking an early train the next day to a nearby city. "Goodness, how busy you are, Mr Carswell!"

He had come home to find Eleanor and her mother just finishing dinner.

"We have two murders open on the books. We need to interview an important witness," said Felix, "and there is suspected Indian cholera in Axworth. I want to see if it is true and what the implications might be for Northminster."

"You are worried the district may be in danger from an outbreak?" said Lady Blanchfort.

"Yes."

"How disturbing," said Lady Blanchfort, with a slight shudder. "You had better sit down and dine, Mr Carswell. You will need to attend to yourself properly if you are to attend to the needs of others."

She rang the bell and rose from the table. Eleanor was getting up as well, but Lady Blanchfort said, "You should keep your husband company, my dear," and sailed from the room, leaving them alone together.

"Does she know?" Felix asked.

"Know what?"

"That we have –" He broke off, reluctant to even say the word 'quarrelled', and at that moment the butler came in with his dinner.

Eleanor remained in her place as he was served. She was finishing her own dessert – eating a custard from a glass with a long spoon, and watching him like a cat, her expression inscrutable. She was wearing an elaborate dress he had not seen before, with low, almost indecent shoulders and a plunging bodice that drew attention to the charms of her figure. She had put on some weight during their wedding journey – she had been too thin before, but now there was a slight and becoming roundness about her that he found most appealing. She had also put flowers in her hair, which she knew he liked. Around her neck she was a wearing a tartan ribbon with long tails which, when she had finished eating, she sat twisting in her fingers.

He had bought that ribbon for her, from a pedlar woman at the gates to Holyrood. She had kept it about her neck all that night, and he had seen it lying between her breasts when he had pushed down her nightgown from her shoulders. As their eyes met he knew she was remembering the same moment, and he knew he was being tempted.

He turned his attention to his food, and they sat in silence. But even as he ate his meat, he could not stop thinking of that night and found himself looking across the table at her again, assailed by a different sort of hunger. Then she gave him a crooked smile, that was so tender, so vulnerable and so entirely characteristic of everything he adored about her that he could not bear it any longer. He got up from his place and went and kissed her, pulling her out of her seat and into his arms. The scent of the flowers in her hair mingled with the smell of her warm skin and he felt entirely incapable of resistance.

"Let's go up," he said, and like children they ran upstairs together, hand in hand.

They did not bother to undress, and soon lay in a tangle of her disarranged petticoats. It was only a few minutes' work for both of them to reach a state of ecstatic relief.

~

The next morning, Felix met Major Vernon at the station as they had arranged. It had been a struggle to get out of bed, and he felt sapped of energy. Only as he climbed into the train to Axworth did his mind clear, and he began to understand the full significance of what had happened. They had had congress three times over the course of the night. Her enthusiasm had matched his own, and at moments exceeded his. At one point she had teased him into action again with a disgraceful lack of modesty that had shocked him and at the same time enslaved him. She had him utterly in her power. All his sensible resolutions had been completely forgotten in a night of utter indulgence. He had behaved like a libertine and she had allowed it – no, she had encouraged it.

Major Vernon was studying his new railway guide.

"We should be there at about ten," he said. "I hope that Mrs Braithwaite is still with us."

"I'm surprised Axworth has a fever hospital," Felix said. "That's quite progressive."

"Perhaps Axworth has an unsalubrious situation," said Major Vernon, "and it's a necessity?"

"Perhaps. Some places do seem cursed with a tendency to disease. It is on the river, is it not?"

"Yes, and rather marshy and flat."

"That may account for it. There is a theory that such sodden, low-lying regions are inherently noxious. Enteric fever and cholera and so on are observably far less prevalent in mountainous regions – at least according to what records we have. It may be just that such places, being remote and underpopulated, are ill-served by the sort of medical men who would bother to make a decent study of the subject."

"They are probably too busy treating the goitre," said Major Vernon.

"What was the name of the doctor?" Felix said.

"Perryman," said Major Vernon. "My source was not entirely sure. In fact this is all extremely speculative, and I would not have put you to the trouble, especially in the circumstances, but there is definitely something amiss at the bank and I want to get to the bottom of it. Fred Pierce's death may have been an accident, but the circumstances are making me extremely uneasy. The man who told me about that rumour was informed that he had closed his own account three months ago, something he staunchly denies."

"Do you believe him?"

"He seemed reliable. He had no reason to lie. He did not approach me about it. It was quite by chance that I ran across him." Major Vernon grimaced. "Thank God – for if that bank does go down there will be terrible suffering. I managed to steal a look at some of their books and there are a great many small depositors who –" He reached for his notebook and flipped through it. "Mr Dyson closed his account on the twelfth of June, allegedly, and Mrs Dixon withdrew her ten guineas and closed her account on the ninth. Two examples are not necessarily a pattern, of course, but what if it were? Small depositors' accounts closed – struck out in the ledger as if they had been properly closed by the depositor. Small depositors are not likely to ask about their funds frequently. They may simply have left them there to accrue the interest and forgotten about it. What if Mrs Dixon, like Mr Dyson, does not know her account was closed?"

"You have lost me," Felix said.

"A small depositor is likely a humble person, and easily intimidated by the bank, an easy prey. 'Yes, ma'am, you closed your account – you must remember. You have already had your money.' What if they have done this systematically to cover losses elsewhere, by fraudulently closing accounts that saw little activity, and taking their money?"

"And you think they might have losses elsewhere?"

"Why else would they attempt to burn down the bank? To get the insurance to cover losses and perhaps to cover up the scale of theft and mismanagement. Is that why Fred was so troubled? Think what he said to Lady Wytton – he was afraid for her and her family. What had he discovered? Why was he working so late at the bank?"

"Because he liked his work?" Felix said. "As you are always pointing out, it is an excellent distraction from melancholy."

"And other things?" said Major Vernon. "How is Mrs Carswell, if I might ask? Did you resolve your small difference?"

"After a fashion," Felix said, gazing out of the window. "In the sense that I capitulated utterly, and now – well, God knows what happens now! She has got what she wants and I am whipped, so to speak. And all because I have no self-control. None at all. But she was so –" He broke off. "I did not think that she would be quite so irrational, for such an intelligent woman. But she has such ideas, and she cannot see a sensible argument when it is put to her."

"She is still young. You must let her be silly. We were all silly at that age," Major Vernon said. "When I think how I was at eighteen... but perhaps you were not?"

Felix sighed.

"Of course I was, but –"

"Do not let it gnaw at you and spoil your happiness. She is what she is, and time and your example will do the work you feel you should do. She will only resent you if you attempt to correct her. I made that mistake with Laura. It was unpleasant to discover I had the makings of a domestic tyrant." He winced and rubbed his face. "Dear Lord, I have not thought of that for some time. It is funny how you push these things to the back of your mind, and then, suddenly, you are there again, confronted by the consequences of your foolishness. Having to beg earnestly for forgiveness."

"This was not domestic tyranny," said Felix. "All I proposed to her was that we take precautions so that she does not conceive a child. What is there in that for a woman to find objectionable? It's so foolish of her!"

The Major did not answer for a moment and then said, "That is no small thing to suggest. And for a young wife – you must allow her to be a little confused by such a radical notion."

"There is nothing radical about it. It is common sense. You have seen the damage endless childbearing does – to all concerned. We are not beasts of the field or slaves on a plantation, forced to it by a cruel master. We can exercise our choice in the matter, and as far as I am able I shall!" He threw up his hands thinking suddenly of the previous night's activity. "At least in theory! Oh damnation, she is a witch. She has me just where she wants me!" He screwed up his face.

"That is hardly gallant," said Major Vernon. "She is a girl of eighteen who wants to be a mother. I'm not at all surprised she was shocked by your idea. After all, maternal instinct is a powerful force. That is what you are fighting, not a girl being obdurate for the sake of it."

"Yes, yes, but why on earth would she want to be a mother now?" Felix said. "We have only just begun together. It would be such an inconvenience. It would spoil everything."

"You only think it would!" said Major Vernon. "And you sound like the obdurate eighteen-year-old, if you don't mind me saying. A child – if fate blesses you with one – is a wonderful thing, and you will find your opinion turned about. Trust me."

"Well, it's thoroughly in the hands of fate now, I assure you!" Felix said, reaching into his bag and taking out the heavy volume on fevers that he had been reading. "Thanks to my wife and her – charms."

"I see," said Major Vernon with a smile.

"Though I'm damned if I'm ready to be a father," he said, throwing the book down. "The thought of it horrifies me. I do not even like children. They are so strange. The way they stare at one. Those children of Gray's –"

"On another matter entirely," Major Vernon said, "did you find your study of bloodstains?"

"No, not yet," said Felix, frowning. "I was thoroughly distracted, unfortunately. Dear God, how could I have been so stupid? So weak! Do you know what I thought – I thought that marriage would slake that particular thirst, if you know what I mean. It only seems to make it worse."

Major Vernon laughed at that and said, "It will be easier in time, I think, and you are labouring under considerable temptation. Imagine, after all, how terrible it would be if you felt nothing! That would be cause for alarm, not this." He picked up the book on fevers and offered it to Felix. "And work, as you have already pointed out, is always a good distraction."

# Chapter Twenty-four

Busy and prosperous, Axworth was bathed in the morning sunshine and would have been pleasant had it not been for the humidity. It was almost unbearable, accompanied as it was by a particularly malodorous stench, a mixture of human and animal waste, as well as the coal continuously burning to power the many mills and manufactories. It had been some time since Giles had been to the town, and it seemed that the rate of change here was particularly violent. There was a rough-edged, unfinished quality to the place. It made Northminster, ancient and blackened though it was, seem sedate.

"I can see why they need that fever hospital," said Carswell, as the carriage stalled and started again along a main street from the station that was long and choked with traffic. "We shall both have come down with something by the time we get there."

The hospital was a small affair, placed on what passed for a hill. It sat in a courtyard with a wall about it, and was without any flourishes in its design. Its immediate neighbour was a large workhouse that was both modern and uncompromisingly severe.

"Well, that's convenient, if nothing else," remarked Carswell.

"As is the burial ground," said Giles, pointing across the fields where a newly-made graveyard was marked by a small chapel.

A suspicious porter admitted them. On enquiring for the superintending physician, they were told he was absent but he would fetch the matron for them. So they stood in the hall and waited for a few minutes until a young man in shirt-sleeves came running down the stairs.

"I'm told one of you gentlemen is a surgeon?" he said.

"Yes?" said Carswell.

"Dr Wharne is not here and I have a situation that I'm not qualified to deal with. Could you help me, sir?"

"Yes, of course," Carswell said. "My name is Carswell. Are you the only medical man in the place, Mr –?"

"Bennett, sir, James Bennett. I'm only a student, at Barts – I have just done my first year there, and I was visiting my family. My uncle is an apothecary in the town and he thought I might learn something by helping, but – well, Dr Wharne has not come in yet and there is a man upstairs who has had a fit of some sort, and –"

"Take me to him," said Carswell, and they hurried up the stairs together, with Giles following.

"He had the fit in my absence," Bennett went on. "In fact, no one was in attendance. We have but three nurses here, and the matron is a drunkard," he added in a whisper. "So he injured himself terribly and I have tried to calm him and deal with his wounds, but – this way, sir, if you would."

"This is Major Vernon, by the way, Mr Bennett," said Carswell, throwing off his coat as they entered the ward. "He is as good a nurse in this kind of situation as you will find."

"Any help, sir, would be appreciated," said Bennett.

Giles took off his own coat, for the room was unbearably warm and the windows shuttered. There was a stove in the corner that was throwing out heat. All the beds were occupied, each laden with blankets.

"Dr Wharne believes in inducing perspiration to reduce the febrile symptoms," said Bennett.

"And what do you think?" said Carswell, who had gone to the window and opened the shutter. He then threw up the casement.

"It's hardly my place to question him, but –"

"Air and light," said Carswell. "At least then we shall be able to breathe and see what we are doing. Is this he?" he added, crouching down by one of the beds where a large man was now slumped in an insensible stupor. "You did not spare the laudanum, then?"

"How could I, sir?" said Bennett. "He was raving. Though it was hard enough to get it down him. But he would have attacked me and the nurse. It was the convulsions caused by the fever."

"Shall we straighten him up?" said Carswell. They got him straight on the bed and Carswell began to look at his injuries.

"It looks as if he was slamming himself against the wall."

"He was, sir."

"Nurse!" Felix called out to the girl who was standing by the doorway, looking aghast at this invasion of strangers. "Nurse!"

"It's all right, Polly," said Bennett.

"But sir, what will Dr Wharne say about the windows?"

"I need hot water and fresh dressings," Carswell went on. "Can you manage that?"

"Go and get them, Polly," said Bennett. "You don't have to worry about what Dr Wharne says."

"But he said that I shouldn't ever open the windows. That if I did that mia-missy-ma would come in and kill us all."

"Oh dear God!" muttered Carswell. "Do you mean the miasma?"

"That's it, sir!"

"No one has proved that one way or the other," Carswell said. "So would you please do as I ask and get me some hot water and dressings? This is not the moment for scientific debate."

Polly left.

"Have you had any cases of the cholera here?" Giles ventured, watching as the two men set about tending the man's self-inflicted wounds. He seemed to have sliced at himself with the edge of a broken basin.

"Not that I have observed," Bennett said. "Most of our cases are enteric fever. We are full, though."

"We had rumours in Northminster that there was cholera here," said Carswell, glancing at the others. "What is your mortality?"

"Not good, sir," said Bennett in a low voice.

"And Dr Wharne has left you in charge like this before?" asked Giles.

"He has his own practice to see to," said Bennett. "But he has not been here much. He comes in generally for an hour or so in the morning."

"And there are no other attending physicians?"

"Dr Perry comes in once or twice a week for a little while. He is a big man here, bigger than Dr Warne, so he does not do much here, only to oblige Dr Wharne and not to put him out, since Dr Wharne is our authority on the fever."

"But you are not entirely confident in him?" said Carswell. "You will have read Malcolm on fever, and de Florence?"

"Yes, sir, I have, but he is a difficult man to have a difference with, and I'm nobody."

"You need to have the courage of your convictions," said Carswell, "backed up by your reason and reading. This is not how it is done at Barts."

"I... I... scarcely know. I have not studied this much. That is why I thought I would come here and get some practical knowledge."

"Very sound – but you must now have drawn your conclusions that this is not the way to go on." Carswell gestured at the ward. "How many nurses did you say you have?"

"Three, though they do not have much experience. But one of the patients has recovered somewhat and has been helping. She is quite able, but I do not like to see her overtax herself, though she insists upon it. In fact, here she is. Esther!" he called out.

Giles turned and looked at the woman coming towards them. She was as striking as the descriptions he had been given of her, but any bloom of conventional good looks had passed away with illness. She looked emaciated and grey in complexion, but this gave to her form a curious angular grace. She reminded him of an old carved wooden figure of a saint he had once seen in a church – St Mary, or perhaps the Magdalene. There was certainly an aura of penance about her.

He let her set down her tray before addressing her.

"Mrs Braithwaite?" he said. "Mrs Joseph Braithwaite of Raythorpe?"

She stared at him.

"Who are you, sir?" she said, at last. "What do you want with me?"

"I am Major Vernon, from the Northminster Constabulary. I would like to talk to you, if it will not tire you too much. You are Mrs Braithwaite?"

"I must work. There's so much to be done. Mr Bennett needs me to –"

"I think you should talk to the gentleman," said Bennett. "Go back to your bed and lie on it and talk to him there."

"I cannot, sir. There is a girl in that room, Lucy, she needs me. She's in pain – I must do something for her."

"Is she being treated as these others?" said Carswell. Bennett nodded. "Then take the covers from her and get her cooled down. And then do as Mr Bennett says and rest."

Carswell's manner had such authority that Mrs Braithwaite bowed her head and left the room.

Giles followed her and watched as she gently took the covers from the bed and tenderly sponged down the girl's face and neck, soothing her with quiet words. She glanced warily at Giles as he went and opened the windows, admitting what feeble breeze there was to the small room. The girl seemed to be relieved a little and fell into a fitful sleep. Mrs Braithwaite drew a stool to the bedside and sat down, taking the girl's hand in hers.

"She's a stranger here," she said at length.

"Like you," said Giles, sitting down on the other side of the bed.

"In her first place. Her mistress brought her here and left her to die, so much she cared," Mrs Braithwaite said.

"She will pull through," Giles said, "with your care. Your daughter is also called Lucy, is she not?"

"How do you know that?"

"I talked to your husband. I've seen her for myself, in fact. A bonny child. How old is she now – six, seven?"

"Seven," said Mrs Braithwaite, looking away from him and bending over the girl's hand.

"She is missing you," said Giles.

"She'll be better without me," she said after a moment. "She must learn to do without me."

"And why is that?"

"Please, sir, please, can you not just leave me be? I'll be gone soon enough and that will be an end of it. I have found a little strength now, but I'm dying. I know I am. Can't that be enough, that I will be dead to this world and facing judgement from my Maker? Can't that be enough?"

"No, I am afraid not," Giles said. "I need you to tell me why you ran away from your family. They at least deserve an explanation."

"I can't tell you why, I can't," she said, shaking her head. "Then they will know what I am and I can't bear that."

"Perhaps that is the price you have to pay, Mrs Braithwaite, for what you have done."

"You know?"

"I have worked out some of it."

"Some of it?"

"Enough to put you up in front of the Justices."

She covered her face with her hands at that.

"Can't you leave me be?" she said, with a sob. "For the love of God, sir? Let Him punish me. I can bear the fires of Hell, and I will for sure. Can't that be enough?"

"It will all come out whether you live or die," Giles said. "It is better that you give me your account of things. You are allowed to defend yourself, Mrs Braithwaite. After all, the circumstances suggest to me that there is an element of compulsion here, that you were made to act as you did, yes? You have gone against the grain, and in these cases there is often a good reason for it."

She gave a fierce shake of the head.

"No, no, it were nothing like that. Nothing. I did what I did and that's an end of it."

At this moment Carswell came in. He went to Lucy's bedside and began to examine her.

"She seems more comfortable in the last few minutes," Giles observed. "She has a good nurse."

Esther Braithwaite had moved swiftly away to the corner of the room, almost as if she were trying to make herself invisible. He wondered whether she was planning to run away, if her strength would permit it, or if her conscience would keep her there, tight-lipped and frustratingly within his sight.

"Keep her cool and washed down," said Carswell to Esther when he had finished his examination and given Lucy some more opium. "And come and find me if there is any change."

"Yes, sir," said Esther, moving back to the bedside and still looking suspiciously at Giles.

"And you and I will talk again later," Giles said, and she seemed to flinch at it.

Giles and Carswell went out into the passageway.

"Did she say anything?" Carswell said.

"Nothing useful as yet," said Giles. "How likely is it she might relapse?"

"I am frankly amazed that we found her alive," Carswell said, steering him into a side passage and speaking in a low voice. "She must have an astonishing constitution, for the treatment this quack Wharne insists on would kill the healthiest among us, let alone anyone who has enteric fever, or God forbid, Indian cholera! I cannot believe that he has been allowed such free reign. Sweating out the fevers and then bleeding them! It is madness, utter madness!"

"That was the treatment of my childhood," Giles observed.

"Yes, and we have moved beyond that now – at least all informed, sensible men have. But apparently not in Axworth. At any rate I have done what I can, at least in the first instance. There are twenty-five souls in here, though, and one or two of them, well –" He broke off and pushed his hands through his hair. "I cannot swear to it, never having seen a sufferer first-hand, but from my recent reading, I think they are showing the signs of cholera, and if that is the case... well, to be frank, then we are in for a deal of trouble."

"In what way?"

"It tends to proliferate, but by what means we do not yet know. That is the difficulty. Some say it is in the air –"

"Polly and her mia-masma?"

"Quite. Others feel it is transferred by contact – that of nurse to patient or vice versa. Scrupulous cleanliness and a good healthy situation seem to deter it sometimes, but only sometimes. It is all a question of speculation, and until we know what we are dealing with, anything we do to fight it – well, it is like fighting a ghost! And we have three nurses and a drunken matron, and poor Bennett who is running a temperature himself and should be sent away at once."

"Do you think he would go?"

Carswell shook his head.

"Where is he?" A man's voice rang out from the hallway downstairs.

"He is upstairs, sir," Bennett replied.

There was the sound of boots on the stairs and they turned to see a heavy-set gentleman stamping down the passageway towards them.

"Dr Wharne, I presume," murmured Major Vernon.

"Who are you and what are you doing here?" said the gentleman.

"Felix Carswell," said Carswell. "Are you Dr Wharne?"

"I am indeed."

"I am consulting surgeon to the Northern Criminal Investigation Office," Carswell went on. "And this is Major Vernon, Chief Superintendent of the same. We came to see a witness who is a patient here, but Mr Bennett needed some assistance and so I acted."

"From what I can see you have done a great deal more than that. How dare you, sir, come here and countermand my instructions! What gives you the right to exercise yourself so?"

"The right of any medical man who sees damage being done to the sick. Your patients are in distress, sir, and many of them are near dying. Bennett showed me the facts – your mortality rate is far higher than it should be. Your treatments are doing no good. In fact they are dangerous."

"You are outrageous, sir! That is only your opinion."

"Opinion, yes, but supported by the strongest observations of the most up-to-date authorities. And my own clinical experience of fever. Sweating out fevers and bleeding patients is grossly misguided."

"In your opinion!" said Wharne again. "And how long have you been in practice, sir, and how long have you had charge of a fever hospital?"

Carswell was about to reply when Bennett came running up to them.

"The man downstairs, the suspected cholera case – he has reached a crisis – his skin is turning blue. It must be as you said, Mr Carswell – it must be cholera!"

~

Wharne was not an easy man to convince, even when events had come to such a pass. Felix felt his energy would be better doing something for the sick than trying to make a stubborn old man see that he was a fool, but he could do nothing without Wharne's capitulation. The nurses were clearly terrified of him, but they were only simple, ignorant creatures, little more than children and entirely unprepared for the work that had been forced on them. So they stood arguing about the best way to proceed over the bed of a man having violent convulsions; whose skin had turned a leaden blue and who seemed so lost to help that Felix felt that to do anything other than make him as calm and as comfortable as the circumstances permitted was a cruelty. But Wharne had his theories and his ideas of a cure.

"There is no cure," Felix said. "I have read extensively on this over the last few weeks and the conclusion is quite clear. There can only be relief, not –"

"Calomel," said Dr Wharne. "Calomel!"

"Dear Lord, no!" Felix said. "There was a paper in the Lancet only last month, sent from Bengal, which stated that calomel had nothing but the most disastrous effect when administered. They have discontinued it entirely there."

"In a conservative doses it does nothing, I will concede that," said Dr Wharne. "But when an adequate dose is prescribed –"

"And how much is adequate, sir, in your opinion?"

"Thirty grains in hot brandy."

"And poison the patient?" said Felix, going to his medical bag and fetching out his notebook. "I have all the references here if you would care to study the literature for yourself, sir!"

Wharne snatched the notebook from his hand and threw it to the floor.

"This is my hospital, sir," he said, "and I will determine what is done!"

Felix glanced despairingly over to Major Vernon. He was at the bedside of a young man and was gently washing his face and shoulders. He carefully finished the task and came over to them.

"I regret to say that may not entirely be the case, Dr Wharne," he said. "Now that two medical men have confirmed the presence of cholera, the situation is quite altered. The recently passed statute on infectious diseases places the management of a cholera epidemic into the hands of the Constabulary of the district. It was decided that given the legal powers required to hold in check an epidemic, a senior officer of the Constabulary, superintendent or above, would be better placed to manage such a situation. The outbreak in 1834 in Upper Canada proved the utility of this approach. They reduced the mortality by as much as sixty-five percent – is that not correct, Mr Carswell?"

Felix realised he was witnessing a bravura display of invention, for he was certain from his reading that there had been no recent legislation on the subject. So he nodded and said, "Actually it was only sixty-two percent."

"Over sixty percent, at any rate," said Major Vernon. He picked up Felix's notebook and handed it back to him, with a degree of ceremony, almost as if he were conferring a certificate upon him. "And since I am Chief Superintendent of the Northern Office, equivalent in rank to an assistant chief constable, I am obliged to take charge of this unfortunate situation. I offer you my credentials for your inspection," he said reaching into his waistcoat pocket and taking out his badge. "Sir."

Dr Wharne gazed at the badge for some moments and frowned.

"In that case," he said, "I suppose I must yield to you, although I must confess I am not up to date on all the legislation. There is too much legislation, in my opinion, too much for any liberty-loving Englishman to feel comfortable with, and this particular piece of legislation is not at all to my taste. I would have argued strongly against such a measure that undermines my own profession and leaves too much control in the hands of whomsoever has climbed the greasy pole. However – whatever you say, Major Vernon, whatever you say. You are clearly a gentleman and I feel your honour will guide you to do what is right. I can only hope your subordinates are so minded."

With which he made a stately departure from the room.

"I think he will go and drink sherry with the matron now," Bennett murmured, closing the door behind him. "He often does so. I had not read of that legislation either, I must admit, Major Vernon, but it seems like a good measure in the circumstances."

"It does not exist," said Major Vernon. "It was proposed in committee but it never got anywhere. I hope I can rely on your discretion, Mr Bennett, at least in the short term? It seemed necessary given that there are lives at stake."

"Yes, of course, sir," said Bennett. "So I am to take my directions from –?"

"Mr Carswell," said Major Vernon. "Do as he says, and with luck we may remedy things a little here."

# Chapter Twenty-five

Unfortunately, the cholera victim, a joiner called John Makepiece, did not survive the night.

At a little after four in the morning, Giles and Carswell carried him out of the ward and downstairs to a chilly cellar room where a dozen other unfortunates were awaiting removal and burial. It was a terrible sight and there was only just room for Makepiece.

Wharne had gone home, and Giles wondered how long it would be before they were disturbed and he would be forced to account for his behaviour to the other authorities. He did not know if he would be forgiven for such an outrageous stratagem, but when he saw the general improvement of the patients under Carswell's care, he felt justified in it. In the second cholera case, a young woman called Mary Pepper, it was evident that his approach might mean lives saved rather than lost. She was in a dire state, but she had been isolated and watched over carefully and she was showing signs that she might struggle through.

"We need reinforcements," said Carswell, surveying the corpses.

"I will go to the workhouse and see if they can help us," said Giles.

"What will you say?"

"Oh, I will fabricate something else, I dare say," Giles said, lightly.

"You are risking a great deal."

"We both are, but the end is a good one," said Giles. "And I shall send a message to Hawksby while I am out. They will be wondering what has become of you. Now, give me your list of requirements. Mr Bennett's uncle the apothecary ought to be of use to us."

In fact, he did no more fabrication. He went and found the nearest station house and made himself known to them. Fortunately the sergeant in charge was a former constable from Northminster called Walker, whom Giles remembered had gone over to the Axworth force because his sweetheart had been in the town.

"I remember writing your letter of recommendation, Walker," he said. "And I am glad to see you are doing well."

"Thank you, sir, it has all gone well with me, especially when we joined with the county force. But I was sad you were not made Chief Constable."

"I did not want it," said Giles. "I am happier where I am."

"It seems all wrong you being only a superintendent, sir, that's all," said Walker. "Now, what brings you to Axworth?"

So Giles explained all that had occurred at the fever hospital and did not omit any detail of how he had overcome Dr Wharne.

"A desperate remedy," he said, "and I'm afraid not at all a sound one."

"A good thing you did, sir," said Walker. "No one in the town has any trust of him or that dreadful place. Only the most miserable souls commit themselves there. My mother-in-law will go halfway round the town to avoid walking past it. She says the place is cursed, and it seems she is right."

They spent a few minutes planning how to proceed, at the end of which Giles made a note to mention to Captain Lazenby that Walker ought to be promoted as soon as was possible, for he was a man of shrewd common sense and natural authority. Then, having been supplied with coffee and breakfast, he sat and wrote his letters in the comfort of Walker's little office, before setting out again into the town, calling first at the Post Office and then at Bennett's uncle's shop. This gentleman, Mr Lane, was as helpful and sensible as could be desired, and by midday, even Dr Perry had been located and brought to the fever hospital.

"I cannot say I agree with your methods," he said, on presenting himself to Giles and Carswell, "but the truth is we have been trying to remove Wharne from his post here for some time. We were perhaps not firm enough with him. The post is a well-paid one – the endowment is rather curious in that respect."

"It often takes a crisis to change matters significantly," Giles said.

"Certainly. The numbers suffering from enteric fever in the town are raised to alarming levels and now we have cholera confirmed." He gave a sigh.

"Only two cases," said Giles.

"It seems that the late Mr Makepiece and Mary Pepper knew each other before they were admitted. She was a servant in his house," Carswell said. "I find that interesting."

"You are a contagionist?" said Dr Perry.

"When it comes to the cause of cholera I do not know what I am," Carswell said. "The more I read and observe, the less clear it becomes."

"There is some truth in that," said Perry. "Perhaps we should make a tour of the wards together, Mr Carswell?"

"Certainly."

"Before you go to the wards, Dr Perry, there is another matter I would like to talk to you about. The reason why Mr Carswell and I came here in the first place, in fact. It will not take long."

"Yes?"

"We are investigating a case of fire-setting in Northminster, the target being Wytton's bank. I believe you told one of your patients that you had heard a rumour that Wytton's bank was unsound and he ought to withdraw his funds."

"I was told that, yes," said Perry.

"Who told you?" Giles said.

"A patient here. A woman called Esther. She would not give her full name. She was in a terrible condition and I was able to help her somewhat. She insisted on telling me that I should be wary of Wytton's bank, that I ought to remove any funds I might have lodged there from it forthwith. Of course, patients do say curious things in extremis and one does not always believe them. But she was full of conviction."

"And you told this to whom?"

"I told it to Richard Preston. I have been looking after his family for many years and he is a respectable merchant in the town – not a great man, but I know he has many financial interests here about. He has given me good advice in the past, and when I went to call on his wife, who had some trifling illness, I told him what I had heard."

"And where will I find him?" said Giles, making a note of the name.

"Usually in Hesketh Street – he lives above his warehouse, but they have gone to the country, to his brother-in-law's farm. For I also told them that there was fever in the town, and they thought it best to take a holiday for the sake of their children."

"And the woman, Esther, did not tell you anything about how she came by such information?"

Perry shook his head.

"But as I said, she had great conviction. There was something about her – most curious."

Carswell and Perry set out on their survey of the wards and Giles went upstairs to where Esther Braithwaite and Lucy were lodged. He found her sitting, as before, at Lucy's bedside, holding the girl's hand. Esther looked very pale, and had wrapped a blanket tightly about her. She was shivering.

"I think you ought to go back to bed, Mrs Braithwaite," he said, and to his surprise she consented. Giles helped her back into bed. "Dr Perry is here now," he said. "He will want to see you again."

"I would rather see a clergyman," she said, and suddenly clutched at his hand with both of hers.

"Mr Gray was your parish priest?" She nodded. "I cannot bring him here at once, but perhaps I can give him a message from you? He would tell you to unburden yourself to me, for the sake of your own peace of mind."

She rolled her head away from his gaze, but continued to clutch his hand.

"You saw my children," she said after a long moment.

"I did."

"Tell them, please tell them that I had to do it. I had to."

"You were forced into it, yes, I understand. I have thought that all along, Mrs Braithwaite. Someone compelled you. Will you tell me who?"

"I cannot."

"Tell me and I will bring him to judgement. He deserves to suffer for making you do this dreadful thing. Fred Pierce's blood is on his hands as much as yours."

There was a long silence and still without facing him she said, almost inaudibly, "Her hands."

"A woman?" Giles said. "A woman made you do this?"

Now she rolled her head back, as if infinitely weary, and looked up him.

"Miss Peggy," she said. "It was Miss Peggy at the big house –"

"Margaret Wytton?"

She nodded and then closed her eyes.

"God forgive me," she said.

At which her breathing became most unsteady and she was soon gasping for air. Even as Giles called for assistance, he heard the death rattle in her throat, and in a moment or two more, she was gone.

~

Dr Perry had arranged quarters for them at The Blue Bell, an inn in a hamlet that lay half a mile from the fever hospital. The accommodation was by no means luxurious, but after the fever hospital, Felix found it a pleasant relief to sit in the late afternoon sun in the old-fashioned garden. He was surrounded by the sweet scents of pinks, lavender and rosemary and the trees were full of apples and pears. Nothing was yet ripe, but there was the promise of a good harvest. Axworth and all its horrors seemed distant. He could almost imagine himself in the gardens at Ardenthwaite. The ginger cat of the establishment sat on the bench beside him and allowed him to tickle his chin.

Major Vernon came into the garden, stopping to pluck a sprig of rosemary before sitting down on the bench with the cat between them.

"Our dinner will be ready in a quarter of an hour," he said.

"I should be hungry," said Felix, "but I have no appetite."

"It might come back when you sit down to it. And later you will be glad of having eaten."

"Probably," said Felix.

They had decided that he would remain in Axworth for the next few days, at least. His services were sorely needed, for there had been further admissions during the day, some of them from the workhouse. No one was as yet showing any further signs of cholera, but as some of the enteric symptoms were similar there was no saying what might develop.

Major Vernon sniffed the sprig of rosemary and said, "I will go to Raythorpe first thing. I need to tell poor Mr Braithwaite his wife is dead."

"At least she confessed."

"Only after a fashion."

"And talk to Miss Wytton?"

"Yes," said Major Vernon. "That's a curious twist. One can only speculate what manner of secret there could be sufficient to make Mrs Braithwaite act so desperately."

"Bigamy, bastardy or whoring?" said Felix. "Theft?"

"All possible. I was thinking, though, of the arson itself. After all, Esther had considerable skill, although she failed to do what she was supposed to do. However, what if she had in the past successfully set a fire and Miss Wytton knew about it? The latter conceives that a fire will conceal what has gone wrong in the bank and cover up any wrongdoing on her brother's part. Therefore she approaches Mrs Braithwaite to do the deed."

"If something like that is the case," Felix said, "then the bank must be in a dire state. How did Margaret Wytton come to know of it?"

"That's an interesting question, for she does not seem close to her brother. There was some friction between them when I saw them together. Perhaps that is a result of the plan they conceived having failed so spectacularly. He was, I remember, attempting to pack her off to some relative. I hope he has not – I should like to talk to her as soon as possible."

"I wonder if Mark Hurrell has been found yet?"

"That would be convenient, certainly. But perhaps he has already reached the Continent and will continue to elude us for years."

"Do you think he is guilty?"

Major Vernon thought for a moment and said, "His father said a curious thing. He accused Mark of having seduced Miss Wytton and that was why Arthur Hurrell considered he was free of his obligations to her. There may be some secret history between Mark Hurrell and Miss Wytton. She went to see him several times at his house, unchaperoned, after all."

"Perhaps she killed Arthur, furious at his prevarication,

and she now hopes to marry Mark?" Felix said. "If she is capable of coercing someone into committing arson, as you think, she may be capable of murder."

"That was what I was thinking. Perhaps she was more in love with the idea of being Lady Hurrell than with either of the gentlemen. Her going unchaperoned to the Hermitage so often might be a stratagem to force Mark into marriage. Remember that if Arthur is dead, Mark is the heir to everything. Everything is entailed. Now, this is spinning a wild tale, but perhaps she hopes to force him to the altar quickly – and she may have the means to pressure him into it."

"Given that Sir Morten said Mark seduced her?"

"Quite. So she gets her Hurrell husband – then he is arrested and hanged for the murder of his brother. She is left with the name and the prospect of a handsome widowhood and more. Especially if she is with child."

"No wonder Mark Hurrell cleared out of the district, then. Do you seriously think she might actually have murdered Arthur Hurrell?"

"It's not beyond the realms of the possible, surely? After all, she is highly motivated. She is about to lose her family name and fortune in a bank disgrace, it seems. Her arson plot has been a disaster. She is angry at Arthur for having made her wait to marry. She has wasted her best years waiting. She knows Mark has a weakness for her and can be manipulated easily. She can sacrifice him to her cause because she has no true feeling for him. He is a tool, just as Mrs Braithwaite was a tool."

Felix thought for a moment.

"There is no reason why she should not have stabbed him. It does not require much strength, and he would not have been on his guard with her."

"But her character – is she that passionate, violent type who can only endure so much when circumstances go against her? Is she the sort that will fight for herself against all odds, even if it means turning to crime?"

"And as a plan, all that is fraught with risk," Felix said.

"Perhaps she is beyond caring about that. She is driven by her emotions – her need to be someone at last, when she has been denied it for so long. Imagine being kept waiting by Arthur Hurrell like that, when you have been promised paradise – to be the mistress of Hurrell Place and one of the first ladies in the county. And then to have it constantly kept from you, as if you were utterly insignificant? She has languished as an unmarried woman without any proper status. In fact, her world is full of men who have failed her: Arthur Hurrell, her brother and Mark Hurrell – if he did seduce her. Even if he only made love to her, it would have been a cause for grievance. But it is all a theory!"

"But she could have planted the arrow and that smock at the Hermitage. She went there enough times, after all," said Felix. "And if Mark Hurrell had done it, would he really have been so careless?"

"That has been puzzling me as well. Perhaps he intended to retrieve them and destroy them later?"

"Why not take them when he fled, then?" Felix said. "He is not a fool."

"But if you put a man under pressure, he may start to behave like one," Major Vernon said, getting up from the bench. "Come, let's go and see if our dinner is ready."

# Chapter Twenty-six

After dinner, Carswell went back to the fever hospital while Giles remained at The Blue Bell, with the proviso that he could be sent for if any further crisis arose. Giles, suspecting that this would be the case, drew the table and chair close to the window to get the best of the remaining light, and set about writing his letters and reports. He was surprised to have finished this task without being interrupted, despite writing a lengthy missive to Emma at Holbroke, so he took Mark Hurrell's ill-fated novel out of his pocket and began to read.

He found himself diverted by it. Hurrell's style was rough and often lurid, but there were flashes of brilliant writing that made him want to read on. The world that sprang from the pages was convincing. He did not know if it was because of his recent stays in the neighbourhood that he recognised the descriptions of those magical woodlands and the stately beauty of Hurrell Place itself, there called Breakbridge Hall. Then another house was described, situated in the cathedral close of a nearby city. This was most certainly meant to be Northminster, for a famous blue cheese and a racecourse were mentioned. This second house was significant in the tale – it was where Lady Breakbridge, the hero's mother, was staying while she saw a succession of doctors in her ultimately futile search for a cure to an illness that no one could name.

> She spent her days stretched out on an ancient couch with only a grey parrot and a faithful old servant for company. Her bodily weakness made her effectively a prisoner. She was too weak for guests and certainly too weak to see her children. Then a marvellous thing occurred – a visit was permitted, and one Sunday the younger children, accompanied by their gov-

erness, were driven into town in the ancient family coach, and after attending matins at the Cathedral, they were allowed to call upon her.

Hal had never seen this ancient house before. It seemed to shiver and creak like a ship at sea in the brisk spring wind that was taking all the blossom from the trees. They climbed up the staircase to the room where their mother was, and found her there lying on her couch, surrounded by flowers, with the parrot on his stand. She spoke to them all in turn, although her voice was no more than a whisper, such was her weakness. Then, delight of delights, just as they were leaving – for they were allowed only a few minutes with her – she called him back to her side. Why he was chosen above his sisters and brothers at that moment he did not know. He was not the last born, nor the first born, not the cleverest and certainly not the best behaved of them. Yet at that moment, he was called back.

The others went into the garden to pick flowers, and he was left alone with her and Miss Smith, a deaf old retainer, who sat with her sewing at the far corner.

"You remember who you are named for?" she said, taking both his hands in hers.

"Yes, Mama, your brother."

"Yes, my dear, dear little Hal," she said, "who was taken from us when he was just nine." Hal swallowed hard and nodded. "How like him you look now. I could think you were his ghost," she said, reaching out and touching his cheeks, "except for these roses." Her voice became even quieter. "I could think you were him, indeed, come to take me to Paradise, for I am sure he is there, just as he was, as perfect and as beautiful as you are now." She pulled him into her arms and he found himself crying as she held him, and he felt her shake with sobs too.

"You will get well, Mama," he said. "I am sure of it. And you and Bobby will come back to us at home, and –"

"No, no, I am sorry, Hal, but I shall not be coming home. It will break my heart, but I shall have to go forever soon enough. Jesus himself has told me it is my time and you must accept that, as the good boy I know you are."

"I am not a good boy," Hal said. "Papa says –"

"You are a good boy," she said, now lifting him from her breast and looking straight at him, her hands pressed to his cheeks. "For I know you will look after your brothers and sisters as you ought. I know you will not fail me."

"I will try, Mama, I promise," he said, shaking now. He felt as if she had handed him some great wooden chest that he could not lift, let alone carry. But her eyes told him he must attempt to carry it.

She kissed him and said, "Now, do you know that there is something very clever in this room, Hal? If you go to that wall, and tell it your secrets, I shall be able to hear them here. And if I tell you mine you will be able to hear them too."

"Truly?"

"Yes. Go and see."

So he went to the wall and pressed his ear against it, and heard his mother say, in the most curious voice, as if she were not in the room at all, but speaking to him as if he were dreaming: "There is a wrong that must be righted, Hal. It will be said when I am gone, when you are older, things will be said – you will not believe them, my love, you must never believe them. I am innocent."

He broke away from the wall, staring at her, but she waved him back to his place.

"And you will tell them all that what is said is not true. Do you promise me?"

Now he ventured to speak, turning his face to the wall.

"What will they say that you have done, Mama?"

"A very bad thing, that no wife should ever do. Your papa believes it to be true and he has punished me for it. I know you have been punished when you have done nothing wrong, Hal, so you will understand me, you will know how I feel. I am innocent."

"Punished?" he said, but there was no answer and he turned around to his mother again. She had sunk back onto the pillows and was breathing hard.

"That's enough for now, Master Hal," said Miss Smith, getting up. "Madam is exhausted."

He kissed her hand and left.

"It is the most fanciful scene," Giles wrote, finding what space he could in his unsealed letter to Emma to summarise what he had just read. "But striking – and surely it must refer to Rooke Court? No wonder Sir Morten found the book so offensive – as well as a tyrannical father, he is a vengeful husband. I would be interested to know your opinion of it, but I do not know where we are to find a copy for you."

He added a few more affectionate lines and then sealed the letter, thinking still of the implications of Mark Hurrell's words. Did he mean to accuse his father of actual harm to his mother in that reference to punishment? Given the barbarities inflicted on the son by the father in the name of discipline described at painful length elsewhere in the book, it was hard not to draw the conclusion that he meant something serious by it. Even the implication that Sir Morten had been violent to his wife was scandalous enough, but Giles wondered if Hurrell was not implying something else about the circumstances of his mother's death.

He went to bed, musing on it still, and was somewhat surprised not to be disturbed by any summons from the fever hospital. Carswell arrived back at about six and they had breakfast together. Carswell was too tired to make much conversation and Giles was anxious to be about his own business, so he left him to his sleep.

He reached Northminster just before nine and went straight to The Black Bull to change and shave. Holt was waiting for him with hot water, coffee and his letters.

"What is the news in Northminster?" said Giles, sitting down to allow Holt to shave him. "Any disturbances in Jebb Street?"

He had set Holt in his absence to watch for any unusual activity outside Wytton's Bank.

"Not that I saw, sir," said Holt, "and I kept at it pretty constant as you told me. I was away an hour or two yesterday afternoon – Mr Yates from the Treasurer's House wanted my assistance and I do not like to refuse him."

"No, no, you must not offend Mr Yates," said Giles with a smile. Yates was Sally and Lambert's butler, a recent addition to the household. A most superior and scrupulous character, he had been setting the house to rights while his master and mistress were away with their children in the Channel Islands.

"And that is all in hand?"

"I have never seen a house in such good order," said Holt.

"It is just as well, then, that Tom will only be staying there a few days before he goes on to Edinburgh," Giles said. Tom, his nephew, was due to start a course of study at the University, before being apprenticed as an engineer.

"It is," said Holt. "I don't think Mr Yates is too fond of young gentlemen."

"He is growing up fast. He will be less of a bear soon enough," said Giles.

"Afterwards, we looked over Rooke Court together," Holt went on as he scraped his blade along Giles' jaw. "He pities me, sir, although he is civil about it. He said something about never taking a place in a rabbit warren."

"And do you agree with him?" said Giles.

"I do and I don't, sir," said Holt. "But I'm used to roughing it. It is my Mary-Anne and Mrs Patton, and the mistress, that I worry about. It is the women who feel the wrongs of a place far more than men."

"True enough," said Giles.

"Having said that," Holt went on, standing back for a moment to contemplate his work, "there is a pretty room by the kitchen that would make a very comfortable parlour bed-sitting room for Mary-Anne and me, if you and the mistress thought it suitable, that is, sir?"

"I think I know the room you mean. Yes, that would be convenient for everyone, certainly," Giles said, getting up and washing the remains of the soap from his face, thinking again of Hurrell's book. Holt was standing behind him holding his clean shirt. "If there is time today we will look over the house together, if you like? I would be interested to hear what Mr Yates said. I am sure he had some good suggestions."

"Yes, he did," Holt said. "But they were all of the 'how I

might serve dinner for a company of four and twenty' sort, and I did not care to tell him that – well, you know what I mean, sir."

"That we have scarcely enough spoons between us for our own family use?" said Giles. "My apologies, Mr Holt. I have brought you to a sorry pass and if you and your future wife wish to take your leave of us, then we will quite understand."

"Should not dream of it, sir," said Holt, helping Giles into his coat. "Twenty-four sitting down for dinner sounds like a great deal too much work for me, although I suppose Mary-Anne would not baulk at it."

"We shall have to try and oblige her with a little grandeur occasionally, but twenty-four – I think not," said Giles, collecting up the contents of his coat pockets that he had taken out to change his coat. "So she does not forget all she has learnt at Holbroke." As he did this, his notebook fell open and he noticed the widow Dixon's address. He decided he would pay her a brief call before he went about the rest of his business.

"She will not expect that, sir," said Holt. "She's happy to be a plain cook from now on. She has scalded herself enough times on the boiling sugar. No, all she wants is a cat. She talks about nothing else!"

~

Mrs Dixon lived in a neat little house in a street near the Minster. He found her sitting with two of her neighbours, drinking tea. All three women were widows, their lush black weeds suggesting an equal adherence to propriety and fashion. There was a rustle of good quality silk as they adjusted their chairs to admit him to their company.

"Now, what can I do for you, Major Vernon?" said Mrs Dixon, having insisted on making him tea. "I must say, this is somewhat exciting. You are famous, you know."

"Yes, we have read all about your exploits in The Bugle, Major Vernon," said another of the widows, Mrs Geoffrey.

"I hope you haven't done something wicked, Anna," said the third widow, Mrs Keyes. "Is there something you haven't told us about?"

"Oh, I don't think so. And if I have, I have forgotten!" said Mrs Dixon. "So, Major Vernon, what do you want to know of me?"

"It's to do with your financial affairs. I hope you do not mind."

"No, of course not."

"I understand you have an account at Wytton's Bank."

"Yes, I have a little money lodged there. Not much. I don't know why I have it there still, for the return on it is not good. Mrs Keyes here was suggesting I move it."

"But you have not moved it yet?"

"No, no, certainly not."

She got up and went to the desk and began searching through a drawer.

"You certainly should," said Mrs Keyes. "I have heard –"

"Yes?" said Giles.

"Mrs Keyes is very sharp on these matters," said Mrs Geoffrey.

"My late husband taught me the rudiments," said Mrs Keyes. "And one would be foolish not to keep one's eye on fiscal matters, both local and national. When one has only one's capital to live upon, the interest or lack of it is everything."

"So you have heard something that alarms you about Wytton's Bank?" Giles said.

"Enough for me to advise that Mrs Dixon move out her money."

"But it is only a matter of ten guineas," said Mrs Dixon.

"Only?" said Mrs Keyes. "I would move it if it were ten farthings."

"What have you heard that makes you so uneasy?" said Giles.

"I have a little acquaintance with Mrs Pierce –" Mrs Keyes said.

"As do I," said Mrs Geoffrey. "And now he is in an insane asylum – Mr Pierce, that is. Had you heard that?"

"No!" said Mrs Dixon, returning to the tea table. She had in her hands an account book. "No, surely not?"

"I did hear that," said Mrs Keyes. "It is dreadful. And yet –"

"Yes?" Giles said.

"It did not surprise me. Mrs Pierce told me that he has been working himself into the grave trying to keep the bank afloat. She was being most unguarded, but I don't suppose she understands his business affairs and she was worried sick, and with good reason. So I have been wary of that establishment."

Giles turned to Mrs Dixon.

"What I wish to confirm is that you definitely have not closed your account at Wytton's."

"No, no I have not. See," she said, opening the account book. "This is the page for Wytton's. If I had closed the account I would have crossed it all out. Mrs Keyes has made me scrupulous, for which I am grateful, for I am sure I am far better off than I was, before she took me in hand! I was such a muddled fool about money!"

"When did Mrs Pierce say that to you, Mrs Keyes, about keeping the bank afloat?" Giles said.

"About six months ago. That is when I told you to close the account."

"You see my reformation is not quite complete," said Mrs Dixon, with a smile. "But I shall do it at once, I promise."

"Mind you do," said Mrs Keyes, "you never know what

may happen. I was reading in The Times yesterday that there has been a terrible failure in the Swedish railways. I forget the name of the company, but the whole thing has overspent and fallen into utter disarray."

"Swedish railways?" said Giles.

"Yes – oh, what was the name? Oh yes, I have it now, Major Vernon: The Stockholm and Malmo Railway Construction Company. One of the directors committed suicide."

"This was in yesterday's Times?" said Giles, getting up from his seat. Mrs Keyes nodded. "Excuse me ladies, I must go now. You have all been wonderfully helpful!"

~

"Yesterday's Times?" said Tom O'Brien. "It's still here, I think, with the other papers."

"You don't have any money in Wytton's, do you?" Giles said, while he was looking for it.

"No. Is there a problem?" When Giles did not answer, he said, "Then there is. How bad?"

"Can you hold it for a day or so?" Giles said, laying the paper on the table and opening it.

"This week's Bugle has just gone to bed," said O'Brien. "You're in luck."

"There is a part of me," Giles said, "that wants every depositor banging on the door demanding every last farthing from them. But that would hardly be conducive to public order, and I am beginning to fear the money is all long gone and there will be misery for a great many because of it. Ah, here we are – The Stockholm and Malmo Railway Construction Company."

"Oh, yes, I saw that. Has Wytton's put money into it?"

"I don't know. Have you heard any rumours? I have picked up a couple about the place. But I do know for sure they have been closing accounts fraudulently, presumably to cover losses."

O'Brien whistled. "That's a risky strategy. So they must be in a bad state."

"Hence the attempted arson."

"That's for certain now?"

Giles nodded, scanning the article.

> The company's losses are estimated to be at least ten million kroner. The company was heavily promoted throughout the Continent and this correspondent believes that there are several large investors in England and France who will stand to lose considerable amounts.

"Names no names, though," said O'Brien.

"No," said Giles. "But it's something. May I take this?"

"Certainly," said O'Brien.

"And is that sharp nephew of yours still staying with you?"

"Jerome? Yes. He's just in the print room."

"He wanted to know what police work was like. If he's still interested, I have a job for him. If you can spare him for a day?"

"Certainly. I'll get him. He'll be pleased."

"I'm not sure he will be," Giles said.

~

"All these, sir?" said Jerome, looking at the large pile of bound volumes of The Northminster County Gazette and The Northern Courier heaped on the deal table in the small back room at the Northern Office that had been designated a library. The collection was not yet as extensive as Giles would have liked, but he had been fortunate to pick up the old bound volumes of the newspapers at a recent auction.

"Yes, all of them. But you can stop at 1833. When you see any reference to unexplained fires, in any context, you will take a note, with the page number and column number, and give me a précis."

"A précis, sir?"

"A summary. Just a few words. For example, unexplained fire in warehouse in Northminster."

"I see, sir," said Jerome.

"The place of the fire is most important. Don't omit that."

"No, sir, I won't."

"If there is difficulty, go and speak to Inspector Rollins. He will make sure you get some dinner as well. I have to go now."

"Yes, sir," said Jerome. "Can I just ask one more thing, sir?"

"Yes?"

"Why?"

"We are looking for an arsonist at work some fifteen years ago. Someone who caused considerable damage but got away with it."

"Oh, I see," said Jerome. "At least I think I do, sir."

"The picture is never clear until the end. To be honest, at the moment there are so many questions unanswered," said Giles, "if that's any comfort to you. It will be tedious work, for which I apologise, but if you find what I am after, then you will have helped a great deal."

"Then I'd better make a start, sir," said Jerome, pulling his stool up to the table and opening the volume for 1820.

# Chapter Twenty-seven

Mr Braithwaite sat in silence for some minutes after Giles had finished his account of what had happened to his wife. Then he knotted his huge hands together in front of his mouth, and closed his eyes for a moment, apparently praying.

They had gone into the parlour in the small house attached to the forge, a room that was obviously little used, but all was in scrupulous order, with even a posy of flowers decorating the old oak table.

"Lucy has been keeping house as well as her mother," said Braithwaite, breaking the silence, and then, utterly overcome, he leapt from his chair so violently that it was overturned, and left the room.

Giles put the chair to rights and waited for him to return, wondering if any new information would be forthcoming.

Having composed himself a little, Braithwaite returned with a bottle of brandy and two small pewter mugs.

"I'm not a drinker, sir," he said, "but sometimes needs must. Will you have one, sir?" Giles shook his head. Braithwaite poured a measure and sipped it tentatively as if he thought it poison.

"So, you think she set that fire in town?" he said, sitting down again.

"There is no doubt that she did," Giles said. "The question is why. Now, I know this is painful for you, but can you think of any secret difficulty that might have set her on such a path? I am certain she was forced to act, and if we are to find who was responsible, then her name will partially be cleared."

"I wish I could say. But I've nothing for you. Forced into

something – that doesn't sound like my Esther. You could not force her to do anything, let alone anything that was wrong. All these years I've know her, she's never –" He gulped. "She'd never been anything but straight. That's why I married her. I thought a good woman would make me good, and I pray to God that I have been a good man, but this, this is all too..." He took another sip of brandy and grimaced at the taste again. "I hope you are wrong, sir, that I do!"

"And you can think of no connection between your wife and Miss Margaret Wytton? She never worked at Raythorpe Hall?"

Braithwaite shook his head.

"But I know they were put to nurse with her mother, his present Lordship and Miss Margaret, but that was long before I came here. And her mother died when she was ten." He gave a sigh. "I suppose you could talk to her sister – if you can find her."

"Mrs Braithwaite had a sister?"

"Half-sister. She'd been married afore, had Esther's mother, or at least all said she was married, to keep it straight. I don't think there was a husband, to tell you the truth, just a child – and that was Esther's older sister, Ruth."

"Who took her stepfather's name? Which was Apley?"

Braithwaite shook her head. "Ruth Hull. She was always called Hull."

"And you don't know where she is?"

"She went into service just after I came here. I'm glad she did, for she was – well, handsome like my Esther. Very handsome, in fact, and I was a lad of sixteen and she was the same age. I think I should have found myself in the way of temptation, because she had that way of acting that girls sometimes have, as if they are women already. You know the sort of thing, sir?" Giles nodded. "Mr Apley was glad to be rid of her," Braithwaite went on. "But apparently it was a good place she was going to. She was full of talk about being a lady's maid and then she went, and I don't know if she even wrote to her family. Esther never liked to talk about her." Braithwaite sat back in his chair as if surprised at himself for remembering all this. "But that's all I can tell you about her."

"You don't know if they have been in touch at all?"

"I don't know. I suppose she might have written and Esther not told me. She did not like to talk about her and so we did not."

"Might I look through your wife's things?" Giles said.

"I suppose you must. When shall we get her home for burial? I should like her home soon."

"I don't know. I will get an answer for you as soon as I can."

Braithwaite left him alone in their bedroom, having pointed out the large carved chest at the foot of the bed as particularly belonging to Esther. The box was full of lavender bags and carefully stored linen, but it also contained a Bible and a prayer book, a few trinkets and ribbons, and another small wooden box. This contained her marriage lines and a tiny gold ring attached to a ribbon. The Bible was inscribed "Esther Apley" in careful copperplate, while the prayer book said "Ruth Hull." Giles wondered why Ruth had not taken her prayer book away with her when she went into service. He flipped to the end to the blank pages and found another inscription: "To my little Esther, with all my love, Ruth. I know I don't deserve to be remembered, but I know you will, my sweetheart." Below it she had drawn a heart broken in two.

He carried the book downstairs and into the kitchen. Braithwaite was sitting with his children and another woman Giles did not recognise. The news had clearly just been told. Lucy was howling into her father's lap while the boy, not sure if he was allowed tears, sat on his stool, staring at the floor. He glanced up at Giles with terrified eyes, as if he were death himself and not his wretched messenger. The sight was too much for the child and he at once ran from the kitchen.

"Go and see to Jack, Lucy, there's a love," said Braithwaite, drying his daughter's face with his handkerchief. The girl left dutifully.

"This is my sister, Mrs Walker," said Braithwaite, indicating the woman who sat beside him on the settle.

"You didn't know Ruth Hull at all, did you, Mrs Walker?" said Giles.

"Yes, yes I did, as a matter of fact," she said.

"You didn't?" said Braithwaite, with some surprise.

"It was when I was working up at the Hall. When I was in the laundry – remember? She was working indoors. Housemaid, I think."

"But then she went away, to Lincolnshire or some such," said Braithwaite.

"Aye, she did. But it was before you were apprenticed, John, that she was at the Hall. She came home again after... well, nothing were ever proved, but everyone thought –"

"Thought what?" said Giles.

"That she'd been thieving," said Mrs Walker.

"I never heard a word of that before!" said Mr Braithwaite. "Nay, Alice, you have that wrong. I never heard a word of that."

"Have you seen this before?" said Giles, laying the prayer book on the table open at the inscription.

"That's Ruth's?" said Braithwaite. "I never saw that before. Why did she never show it to me? Why did she never –" He broke off and went to the window. "I feel I've been married to a stranger, not my Esther. She is lost to me forever, that's for certain, the woman I courted and married. This Esther, sir, that you are talking of, that is not my wife!"

With which he left the room to see to his children.

Mrs Walker now looked at the inscription in the prayer book.

"They must have been very close," she said, stroking the little broken heart. "Oh, my poor brother. How will he get on without her? And he said that you told him she was behind a fire in Northminster?"

"It does seem so." Mrs Walker gave a deep sigh. "Can you tell me anything more about this business with Ruth Hull? When was it you were working for the Wytton family?"

"It were fifteen years back, when I was eighteen or so. I wasn't there long. Nobody stayed long in that house. The old lord and his lady were not – well, you won't mind me saying this, sir, being a gentleman yourself – but there are some gentry folk who deserve to be treated with respect because they respect those less well born than themselves. But Lord and Lady Wytton – there was no respect. It was a miserable, cheese-paring house. I have worked in a few big places before I was married, and I can tell you, sir, there is a way of keeping servants and there is a way of losing them. Lady Wytton was in the way of losing them. It's a wonder they didn't have Ruth transported instead of just sending her home without her character."

"You have no recollection of what she was supposed to have stolen?"

"Probably no more than a lump of sugar," said Mrs Walker. "That would have been enough to do it. Poor, poor girl. She was probably hungry. We all were. Not that I think thieving is right, sir, you understand."

"No, of course not."

"It's just that when one person has so much and another so little – I suppose Ruth was tempted."

"So we are speaking of about 1825?"

"Yes. Yes, 1825, I remember because that was the summer I met my George, and the summer the rigs burned at the Home Farm. That was a shocking business. A man died."

"The Home Farm to Raythorpe Hall?" said Giles. "Lord Wytton's property?" Mrs Walker nodded. "And the cause of the fire?"

"An act of God, they said," said Mrs Walker. "But who

can say?" Her expression grew concerned as she realised the implication of what she had said. "No, no, you can't say Esther was anything to do with that, can you, sir? Surely not?"

Giles could not give her a comforting answer and so took up his hat and left.

# Chapter Twenty-eight

"I wish I could help you, Major Vernon, but my husband and sister-in-law are both out," Lady Wytton said. She was stretched out on a sofa in her shuttered sitting room. "They have gone for a drive together. Just to get a little air. I wanted them to take the children with them, but Margaret said they had business to discuss and it would be dull for them."

"Business?" said Giles. "Do you have any idea what they were discussing?"

"No, I'm afraid I don't," said Lady Wytton.

"And has there been much talk of business between them lately?" he said.

She looked up at him.

"You had better sit down if you are going to ask me such grave-sounding questions," she said. "Please. I feel quite frightened with you towering over me like that! Should I be afraid?" she added, as he pulled up a chair. "I have been, ever since Mr Pierce said that strange thing to me, and then with Mr Hurrell being murdered. It is all so troubling."

"It certainly is," said Major Vernon.

"I am glad you called. What you said to me about Margaret and Mr Mark Hurrell –"

"Yes – you told me there was nothing in the rumour."

"I'm not so sure. The thing is – well, my maid Sarah has been away visiting her sister and so Agnes, Margaret's maid, has been coming to help me instead. She is a good creature and does my hair nicely, so I must get her to give Sarah some lessons when she comes back. However, she has also been sneezing and coughing and looking very unwell. She said it was nothing, she had just caught a chill because she had been sitting out in the rain, and it was her own fault. So I asked her why she did it, and she went so quiet that I knew it was because she was ashamed of why she had done so. And then there was one of those silences – I am sure you know exactly what I mean – and then she burst out with it – that she had been made to wait outside the Hermitage, sitting in the rain while Margaret was inside – alone – with Mark Hurrell!"

"Ah, yes, I saw her there."

"You did? You found them together?"

"I did."

"I see, and that is why you thought – oh, I can see that you would. It is rather – why was she there? And that was not the only time. Agnes told me the whole story, how she had gone there at least three times, not to mention when she was made to take letters."

"And were there replies to these letters?"

"That I don't know. Why do you not ask her yourself, Major Vernon?" she said. "Would you ring for me?"

So a few minutes later, Agnes Baker came in and confirmed what Lady Wytton had said.

"Did Mark Hurrell send you back with any messages?"

She shook her head. "I don't think he read Miss Margaret's letters. Once I saw him throw one straight into the fire."

"Have you been with your mistress on any other visits?" Giles said. "Or taken letters to anyone unusual?"

"Well, there was Mrs Braithwaite," said Agnes after a moment. "Everyone has been talking about her going missing, and it set me wondering – worrying, really. Miss Margaret did have something to do with her. I took notes to her and once she even came here. I met her in the back court and brought her in, up the backstairs, to Miss Margaret's room."

"And when was this?"

"About a month ago, sir."

"And were you there when Miss Margaret spoke to Mrs

Braithwaite?"

"No, sir, I was told to go away and never tell a soul that it had happened. But I heard Mrs Braithwaite went missing, and so I –" She looked imploringly at Lady Wytton. "I know I should have said something afore, but Miss Margaret, she does like her secrets and when she tells you to do something, then –"

"Yes?" said Giles. She glanced again at Lady Wytton, looking for permission to continue.

"Tell him everything you know, Agnes," she said.

"I'm sorry, my lady, I do not like to speak out of turn or against my betters, you know I do not, but Miss Margaret – sometimes it's as if she has the devil in her. She has a way of speaking, of turning things against you that you do not know what you should do but fall in with her, or else."

"She has threatened you?" Giles said.

"Yes. She said that she would tell my lady here that –" She broke off, shaking her head. "Oh, I cannot say it."

"Oh, I am sure it cannot be so bad, Agnes," said Lady Wytton.

"You will not like it, my lady," said Agnes. "And if you hear it, you will make me pack my bags."

"Tell us the whole truth," Lady Wytton said. "Your place here is safe."

"Are you sure, my lady?"

"I give you my word. Please will you tell Major Vernon everything."

"The thing is, I have a little girl, my lady. She's at my mother's. She thinks I am her big sister. Miss Margaret got it from me and said that she will tell the whole world and his wife and you and his Lordship, and then I will never get a good place again, will I?" Agnes was now breathless with anxiety.

"How old is she?" said Lady Wytton.

"Two and a half now, my lady. Like your Miss Elizabeth."

Lady Wytton nodded and sighed.

"How unfortunate for you," she said. "And the father, he would do nothing for you?" Agnes shook her head. "Your mother has been very good to you."

"Yes, my lady, I'm lucky, I know I am. And I know I should not have lied to you about it, not because of who you are, but because you are so good and kind to everyone."

"Just to return to this business with Mrs Braithwaite, Agnes," Giles said. "You have no idea what Miss Wytton wanted to discuss with her? Did Mrs Braithwaite tell you anything?"

"No, but she was not happy about it, sir, that I can tell you. I just supposed that Miss Margaret had got something on her as well and wanted something from her. But what that might be, I can't say, sir."

"That will be all for now," Giles said. "But I shall want a full statement from you at some point, Miss Baker, about Mrs Braithwaite coming here. If you can try and remember when it was and how it all happened, I will send one of my men to take a record of it."

"Yes, sir. Has Mrs Braithwaite been found, sir?"

"Yes, I found her," Giles said. "But unfortunately, she has died of the fever at Axworth."

Both women looked shocked at that.

"There is fever in Axworth?" said Lady Wytton. "Cholera?"

"There have been some cases, yes."

"I pray to God it does not come here," Lady Wytton said. "But then, I heard this morning that Sir Morten had taken to his bed with something that sounded like a fever. And he is never ill! Oh goodness! Poor Mr Braithwaite and those beautiful children. Whatever will they do without her? What a strange, strange tangle all this is!"

At this moment Margaret Wytton herself came sweeping into the drawing room, still dressed in her widow's black.

"Oh, you are here again," she said seeing Giles, and then noticing Agnes, she held out the bonnet she had just taken off to her, expecting her to take it. When Agnes did not do so, she added, "Agnes?" as if she were a dog to be brought to heel. But Agnes did not move. "Agnes?" said Margaret again.

"Agnes has just told me some interesting information, Miss Wytton," said Giles. "And as a consequence you and I must have a serious conversation. In fact, I would like you come back to Northminster with me."

"What do you mean?" she said, throwing the bonnet onto a chair, and laughing nervously. "Are you arresting me?"

"No, I am only asking you to co-operate with me. But it would be better that this conversation took place in Northminster," he said, "for your own sake – so that everything might be clear and above board."

"I wish I knew what you were talking about!" she said. "What on earth am I supposed to have done that needs you to have such a conversation with me? I simply cannot imagine!"

"Can you not?" said Giles.

"I am afraid my brother will not be amused by this," she said, going to the door. "Let us go and see what he has to say about it."

"Very well," said Giles, and followed her from the room.

As they crossed the hall, a pair of footmen were carrying a large crate from the front door. There were several others of the same size waiting at the foot of the stairs.

"What are these?" Giles said, noticing that they were being unloaded from the carriage that was drawn up outside. This was presumably the carriage which Lord Wytton and Miss Wytton had used for their drive. It seemed an unusual cargo to have accompanied them.

"Oh, nothing of any importance," said Miss Wytton airily, heading towards her brother's study.

"Ledgers," said Giles, looking into one of the crates. "And papers too, I see. Did you just bring these back from

Northminster, Miss Wytton?" She did not answer. "Perhaps your brother would answer that question for us."

Now she took alarm and went running into the study.

"Edward! Major Vernon is here and he is being most –"

She stopped in her tracks and screeched. Giles dashed in after her to see Lord Wytton standing with a pistol pressed to his temple.

"I shall do it, Meg," he said. His voice was slurred with drink. "I bloody well shall, you know."

"No, no!" she screamed, and lunged at him so the pistol went flying from his hand and onto the floor. Giles retrieved it while Miss Wytton, in a fury, cracked her palm across her brother's face. "You stupid, stupid fool! Now you really have ruined everything!"

~

"There's no chance I could have a proper drink?" asked Lord Wytton. "Brandy? I'd take gin, at a pinch."

Giles shook his head.

"I would get some sleep," said Giles. "Your solicitor will be coming in first thing to talk to you. Your sister has seen to that."

"Ah yes, of course she would," said Lord Wytton, with a sigh, sitting down on the bench again. "Sees to everything. Thinks she's so clever. Fact is, Vernon, we wouldn't be in this pickle if I hadn't been such a damned fool and listened to her. It was all her idea. Swedish railways be damned! Should never have listened to her. Never take advice from a woman. Never." He gave a groan, and pressed his hands to his face. "If that damned Arthur Hurrell had done his duty and stood by her, then we'd never have had all this. She'd have been on her back, pushing out little Hurrells, instead of making my life impossible with her ridiculous ideas. Swedish railways!"

"So you made the investment at her suggestion?"

"Yes. And to tell you the truth, it did seem like a good a bet. But she talked it up. That was it. She can talk anything up. Little bitch."

"And you needed the money?"

"The bank was not exactly making it hand over fist and everything is so expensive these days. My wife, she's expensive, I'll tell you that! Shockingly so. She has money of her own, but the tightest set of trustees I ever saw in my life. Never could get a penny out of them."

"That must be a comfort in the circumstances, then," said Giles, "that she and your children will have an income."

"What would be a comfort now would be some hard cash on the table. Perhaps you might talk to her? She likes you. Get her to get them to ease up on me."

"In the circumstances, it seems unlikely that they would," said Giles, "and it would be highly inappropriate for me to talk to her about it."

"But you'll get her to come in and see me? I need to talk to her."

"I'm sure she will be here tomorrow," Giles said. "Now I must go."

"And there is no chance of a little drop of something, just to get me through the night?"

"I'm sorry, no," said Giles, and left the cell.

Coming upstairs he met Captain Lazenby in the passageway.

"Would you come into my office, Major Vernon?" he said. When they were alone together, he continued: "I understand you have charged Lord Wytton and his sister and you are keeping them here. Do you think this is appropriate?"

"Yes. Given he's no better than a common thief and she is – well, I am not sure the extent of it yet, but conspiracy to set a fire and manslaughter is the least of it."

"But in the common cells?"

"Surely our new model cells are good enough for anyone?" Giles said.

"They are not the occupants I had in mind," Lazenby said. "There will be a lot of talk if we fail to get a conviction, Major Vernon."

"You only need look at the books," said Giles. "Lord Wytton and his sister went and fetched them from the bank premises today, with the intention of doctoring them further or destroying them entirely. They are all the evidence we need to keep them. We have already identified many more accounts being closed without permission to disguise losses. My men have already talked to some of the account holders and they are good witnesses, respectable people who have lost their money."

"But how is Miss Wytton involved in this?"

"She conspired with Esther Braithwaite to burn down the bank."

"But she has not admitted that?"

"Not yet. But she will," said Giles. "Lord Wytton has just told me that it was her idea to invest so heavily in The Stockholm and Malmo Railway Construction Company. If he is telling the truth, she is at the heart of the disaster."

"But the Braithwaite woman is dead. What she said on her deathbed to you might be construed as merely malicious towards Miss Wytton and an attempt to exonerate herself. I am sure any competent defence will take that line."

"Certainly they will. But when I talk to Miss Wytton, I'm sure I can get the truth of it out of her. Mrs Braithwaite had a nasty secret that Margaret Wytton exploited to get what she wanted. It seems likely that Mrs Braithwaite was behind the burning of the rigs at the Raythorpe Home Farm in the summer of 1825 and that Miss Wytton knew of it."

After a diligent search, Jerome had turned up a report that confirmed the fire mentioned by Mrs Walker.

"But why would this woman Braithwaite do such a thing in the first place?" said Lazenby.

"She was an angry, vengeful sixteen-year-old with a talent for fire making. Her half-sister had been disgraced and dismissed by the Wyttons."

Lazenby frowned.

"That strikes me as a disproportionate reaction to such an event."

"Yes, I agree, but she had a passionate nature. When we are young we can be foolish and impulsive, and her anger at her sister's fate got the better of her. She regretted doing it for the rest of her life."

"But you have no direct evidence for this?" Lazenby said.

"No, not yet, but neither can I find a scrap of anything else that might cause Mrs Braithwaite to leave her family. A man died in the Home Farm fire. That would weigh heavily enough on anyone, and when threatened with exposure from Miss Wytton she became an easy prey. And when we have finished talking to Miss Wytton, with luck we will have a full confession to all this, and perhaps more. She may be cunning, but a night here will make her see things more clearly."

"That remains to be seen," said Lazenby. "There is another matter, Major Vernon, that I wanted to raise with you. I have received an" – he hesitated for a moment – "interesting communication from Dr Wharne in Axworth."

"Ah yes, that – I wanted to speak to you about it," said Giles. "What does he say?"

"That he intends to pursue the matter. It is a serious thing, certainly."

"It was a serious situation."

"But your actions appear to have been quite improper."

"That's a matter of opinion," Giles said. "There was a crisis and I was forced to act. Lives were at stake. He was incompetent and dangerous."

"That's very strong."

"I saw what I saw. And Mr Carswell's judgement as a medical man could not be dismissed. Something needed to be done. You would have done the same, sir, I think. Sometimes rules need to be broken."

Lazenby frowned at that and said, "That is not a motto I like."

"Nor do I. But in this case I had no choice. It was not done lightly, I assure you. But it had to be done."

"That remains to be seen. I am afraid I cannot entirely take your word for it. There must be a further investigation and in the meantime, I regret to say that I must suspend you from duty until the matter has been dealt with."

"I beg your pardon, sir?" said Giles.

"There is no room for discussion," he said. "That is an order, Major Vernon, and you must obey it."

# Chapter Twenty-nine

Giles sat by his empty hearth, turning over in his mind what Lazenby had said. He had listened to it meekly enough at the time, perhaps because he had not taken it seriously. He had thought, in the first instance, that it had just been said for form's sake, and once it was said, that was the end of the matter. It was a rebuke, a reminder, a warning even, that if he did not take more care he would be suspended. That was how he had carried the words from the room and out into the street, and all the way to his sitting room at The Black Bull.

Here, having taken off his boots and his coat, he had sat down at once, contrary to his normal habit. Usually he would wash and then make a few notes for the following day, standing at the secretaire in the corner. Only after that did he allow himself to relax, but on this occasion, as if winded by a blow, he had sat down and stared at the blackened bricks of the hearth without seeing them, as he realised that Lazenby had meant what he said. He had suspended him from duty until further notice, an act that was entirely within his rights, and in the circumstances, understandable. Giles knew he would have done the same thing in Lazenby's position. The matter could not be dropped quietly. There had to be an investigation of some sort, that much was clear. Lazenby, the man he had recommended for the job, was doing exactly as he ought.

What was not clear was how he had found himself to be on the receiving end of such an action. How was it that he had, without much thought, strayed into such dubious territory? To make up a tale like that, to resort so calmly to low trickery – the means had justified the end. This was an idea that he had cheerfully adopted; indeed, he had nailed it to his coat of arms.

No doubt that was obvious to Lazenby. For this was hardly the first time he had exercised such expediency, and perhaps Lazenby feared this would not be the last. He had been checked – again Lazenby was doing exactly as he should. He had proved himself the right man for the post while he, Giles, had proved himself slippery.

Yet as he reminded himself carefully of all this, he began to feel a dry fury at Lazenby's punctiliousness. In the circumstances it looked like utter stupidity. How could Lazenby not see that? He was like a general surveying the field, on the bright high ground, never leaving safety, never going down to the place of battle itself, that low, dirty and dangerous region, inhabited by devils who had no scruples at all. As such he was failing to see that the war would be lost if his men were not adequately armed. How could they fight if they were constantly checked by such peccadilloes? He had done what needed to be done, and if his hands were now dirty, so be it. That was the sacrifice that the cause demanded, and Lazenby ought to be able to see that.

And to find himself put out at such a moment, when he had got his birds in the net! Was Lazenby really not going to let him question Margaret Wytton? Who else would be able to get her to talk? He knew he had trained Coxe and Rollins well, and that their own intelligence could guide them to success in many instances, but Miss Wytton was a special case. He feared that their natural deference to a woman of her background would stop their tongues and make them squeamish in going for the kill. She could not be held more than another few hours without a formal charge, and it seemed unlikely that Lazenby would relent so swiftly. He was obviously not in a rational mood. Margaret Wytton would slip through their fingers. She could easily vanish to the Continent. She had the resources to do so. That was always the difficulty with such people. They could defend themselves so much better than the commoner sort of criminal.

He got up and opened the window to get what breath of air he could from a night so sultry and sticky that he was reminded of the humid summers of Upper Canada. Leaning out, attempting to calm himself, he realised that was what angered him most of all about this business. He wanted Miss Wytton to himself, wanted to see her crumble and admit it all. This was a cruel pleasure that he could not resist and which went far beyond any nice ideas of justice. That was the cold, plain truth of it.

Holt came in.

"Will that be all, sir?"

"Yes."

"Not hungry, sir?"

Giles glanced back as he began to clear the table of the food he had put out.

"No. Leave the wine, though."

"Yes, of course, sir," said Holt, and gave him a puzzled look. "What orders for tomorrow?"

"A good question," said Giles. "I'm not sure. Captain Lazenby has suspended me from duty."

"The devil he has!" said Holt. "He can't do that, sir, can he?" Giles nodded. "But why?"

"I took a short cut. And he may use my indiscretion to dispense with me entirely. Which is within his rights."

"He'd be a bloody madman if he did that!" said Holt. "If you'll pardon me saying so, sir."

"I appreciate your loyalty," said Giles. "But it is perhaps unjustified."

"And now you're talking like a madman, sir," said Holt, "and for saying that, I shan't ask your pardon. What could you have done to make the Captain think that he can turn you out?"

"There is a line that one ought not to cross in this

profession, and I have crossed it now, too many times to mention. Lazenby has seen that. That is the difficulty."

Holt stood with his arms folded, shaking his head.

"Nay," he said. "The Captain is jealous, sir, that'll be it. He's never been comfortable having you serving under him, and now he is picking on some trifle to get you to go. You should not stand for it, sir, that you should not! That's what the mistress would say, I know it, sir, and Mr Carswell, and no doubt the Canon and your sister as well!"

"And Lord Rothborough?" Giles said, smiling.

"Aye, certainly his Lordship. In fact he will not stand for this, will he, sir? He will get it set to rights. Mr Bodley says that his Lordship thinks as highly of you as if you were his own kin. I reckon if you were not to turn to him, he'd take it as an insult."

"Yes, yes, I take your point," said Giles.

"It's your livelihood, after all, sir," said Holt.

"And yours too," Giles said. "Though I am sure you could get an excellent place elsewhere."

"That I could, sir, that I could, but you shan't be rid of me that easily."

"You will when there is no money to pay you."

"I doubt that, sir," said Holt. "The Captain will never see this through, no matter how much he may want rid of you. If you fight your corner, sir, then all will come right."

"I suppose so," said Giles, sitting down again, exhausted suddenly. "Take the wine away after all."

"As you wish, sir. And when shall I call you tomorrow?"

"The usual time," said Giles, taking his letters from his pocket. "Good night – and thank you for your counsel."

"Aye, and you will thank me for it, sir," said Holt as he was leaving. He always liked to have the last word.

Could Holt's theory, crude though it seemed, have any merit in it? It could not have been entirely easy for Lazenby to take command in the circumstances. Giles thought he had exercised sufficient deference to make the arrangement workable. But perhaps he had not. Perhaps the occasional annoyance he had felt about the way Lazenby had been conducting things had been apparent to Lazenby. Perhaps he had been a thorn in his side, and an excuse to relieve himself of such an inconvenience, when it came, was to be seized upon. In which case, he had to seriously consider whether he wished to save himself. He had no desire to be an unwelcome irritant.

Yet there was the question of his livelihood, and it was not a small one. Holt, the working man who understood the true meaning of shillings and pennies, never having many of them to his name, had seen that clearly. Many things depended on his stipend – most pressingly his marriage. Emma had given up a wealthy man for him. She did not expect a fortune, but he had promised bread on the table. He had a small income of his own, which would have kept him quietly in lodgings, but without his salary it was not enough for a wife, let alone a wife with a maid, a manservant of his own and his wife, all installed in a ruinous property for which they had scarcely a stick of furniture. To be removed from his post at such a time was a grave misfortune. As Holt had said, he would have to fight his corner if he were not to put all that in jeopardy. Yet he suspected it would not be so much a matter of fighting as humbling himself. Lazenby would want an act of repentance and a guarantee that there would be no further transgressions. He would be allowed to continue, but not as before. Would that, he wondered, even be bearable?

Frowning at himself, he turned to the comfort and distraction of his letters: one from Sally and one from Emma. What talent these women had for letter-writing – for being as intimate and as lively on paper as they were by the fireside in a private conversation! He could not feel dejected for long with such correspondents.

He opened Sally's first – it was a long account of their

family travels in the Channel Islands, visiting various Fforde relatives, with much in the way of sea-bathing, botanising and pony-riding. There were sketches from Celia to enliven the text, a lengthy interjection from Lambert about fishing and then a scrawl from Tom, before the baton had passed again to Sally.

> We have been vexing ourselves about a wedding gift for you. But the sale of an old manor house near here has put something in our path which will suit your tastes: a fine old bed of a hundred years ago, in the best quality mahogany, and of magnificent proportions (at least six foot long) with a beautiful set of bedroom furniture to go with it. It is the work of a famous local cabinet maker, we are informed, in a simple but grand style that Lambert seconded me in approving (and he has nice tastes, as you know). It will suit whatever sort of house you do settle on, and the hangings and so forth can easily be replaced – but they are of first rate quality, with hardly any wear despite being so old. Does this sound of use?

He laid down the letter, glad that he did not have to reply at once to that, and picked up Emma's letter instead.

He turned it in his hands for a moment or two before breaking the seal. He then opened it, and settled back a little in his chair as he slipped the letter from the envelope. The letter was dated Tuesday.

> My dearest man,
>
> We are now safely lodged at Holbroke. The master of the house has returned but not the mistress, a circumstance you may or may not have heard about. It seems that she has decided to remain in Italy after all.
>
> Maria has been brave, as you might imagine, but she had set her heart on a reconciliation and is cast down by it. The ugly question of having to make a choice has now raised itself in earnest. Lord Rothborough has told her that there is no question of choice, telling her she may spend half the year with him and half in Italy, but she does not quite believe that, and neither does she have any wish to spend half her life in Florence. So

she is rather distraught. Thankfully we have become intimate enough so that she did not hesitate to turn to me. All I can do is play the old nurse, and mercifully she permits this liberty. So we take long walks, and read together, and talk, mostly the latter.

Lord Rothborough is not at all himself. The blow has fallen far harder than he imagined, and he could very much do with your counsel were it possible for you to come here. He has told me to ask you to come on several occasions. I think he may write to you.

There is one curious thing that I must mention: Mark Hurrell is in the neighbourhood. He called on Sunday afternoon, asking to see Lord Rothborough, but he was not yet back from Dover. Lady Maria saw him, in my company, and we drank tea and he was gravely charming and much affected by his brother's death.

Now, I am not sure, but it felt to me as though he was there by some prearrangement with Maria, but how that can be, I have no idea! He had been most insistent that his call was to see his Lordship rather than her, but to me he had the distinct air of a man wanting to get permission from a father to address his daughter. That evening, when we were alone, I made a vague hint to that effect to Maria, as carelessly as I could, as if it were something ridiculous. She told me I was indeed being ridiculous, and so I thought no more of it. After all, she is the last person to be involved in something clandestine.

However, on Monday, a little after we had heard the news, he came again. He is staying in the village, it seems, waiting there like a patient Holbroke spaniel to call upon Lord and Lady Rothborough, and then he had heard of that lady's decision and felt he must come again, to see if there was anything he could do. This was all done very well – one cannot fault his manners – entirely correct, and with much warmth and sincerity behind them – but it struck me again that it was the most important thing in the world to him that he should see Lord R. Why would that be? Surely he wishes to present himself as a candidate for Maria's hand!

He was here fifteen minutes at most, but I swear I saw them glance at one another when they did not think I was looking, and Maria was flushed and foolish. When he had gone, she was in a flood of tears, telling me how it had comforted her to see him, and that he seemed to understand exactly how she felt, and was it not remarkable? She is falling in love, if I am not mistaken. I want to counsel her against it. This is not the time for surrender, especially to such an unlikely candidate. It is true that he is now the heir to all that glory, but I am sure he is not entirely what Lord Rothborough would want, and certainly not what the Lady R would want. There are too many uncomfortable questions about him. But what does she see? – a handsome, passionate and intelligent young man; a wronged, misunderstood young man with fresh scars on his face, who seems like the hero from a novel, and who gazes at her as if he means to find his redemption in her. It is too powerful a mixture for a girl like Maria who has just suffered a profound emotional blow.

It has occurred to me I should go and tell him this – that she is too fragile for such an assault and that no good can come of it. Is this meddling? Am I forming a story from scraps where there is no such story? I would press her about it, but it seems cruel to do so, especially if it is only a foolish comforting dream for her. I cannot think that there has been any clandestine communication between them. She would never stoop to that, and yet he is, I sense, a terrible temptation for her. Sometimes the best among us will fall and I can understand the allure of Mark Hurrell. I should undoubtedly have fallen for him myself at that age.

# Chapter Thirty

"You are frowning over your letters," said Emma, coming into the library.

"I am frowning over my lack of letters," said Giles, getting up and greeting her with a kiss. He had been sitting in the great library at Holbroke, with a long, half-written memorandum in front of him. He had retreated there from Northminster two days previously.

"Nothing from Captain Lazenby?" she said.

"Nothing. And nothing from Inspector Rollins. Have they been told not to write to me?"

"They are probably too busy," Emma said. "You said yourself that the business of interviewing Lord Wytton and Miss Wytton would be a serious one."

"True enough," he said.

"Captain Lazenby will soon realise that he has made a foolish mistake," Emma said.

"That is debatable," said Giles. "What I cannot bear is being made to leave a job half-finished."

"And they will see that you must come back and finish it, I'm sure of it," said Emma, her hands on his lapels. "Now, Major, some exercise, I think? There is a pleasant breeze today. I can smell autumn in the air at last! Shall we ride or shall we walk?"

"Ride. Then I shall see you in your new habit –"

"Which you like very much," she said, as he wrapped his arms about her. "Maybe a little too much? Perhaps we should walk."

"Perhaps," he said, releasing her from his embrace with a kiss. "But if we ride we can go and pay a call on Mr Hurrell.

You said he was lodging at the schoolmaster's in the village?"

"Yes, but should you talk to him? If he is a suspect?"

"We shall go as friends of Lady Maria and her father – in that capacity we have a right to know why he is here. I have not mentioned it yet to Lord Rothborough, but it will have to be talked about sooner rather than later."

"Yes."

"And I would like to talk to him before he is arrested. That is surely imminent – they have all the evidence."

"But you have not told them he is here?"

"No, I didn't know until I read your letter, and that was after I had been relieved of duty."

"And I suppose the conversation will not stray onto the subject of Lady Maria?"

"If it strays, it strays. One thing cannot be talked of without the other, I dare say."

"You are a devious fox," she said, with a smile. "You want to keep him to yourself. You want to extract a confession out of him and use him to bargain your way back. You will bring his head in on a plate to show they cannot do without you."

"That would be useful, certainly. But he may not be guilty. That is why I want to talk to him. His behaviour is curious. He has a strong nerve if he did do it. And would you not prefer him to be innocent, given how charming you find him?"

"Certainly!" she said. "It would be beyond dreadful. Especially for Maria!"

The ride through the parkland was made delightful by the cooler weather and the sight of Emma in her new dark green riding habit, her veil streaming behind her as she broke into a canter. As he watched her, he could not help wishing he had the money to buy her such a fine horse, and then, remembering his situation, wondered when he would be asked to give up his own horse, the reliable and sweet-natured gelding of which he had become fond.

They made their way to the east gates, where the village lay, with its neat houses and well-stocked gardens. They asked directions to the schoolmaster's house, which was, unsurprisingly, next door to the school. It had been put down in a generous garden of its own, trimmed with an orchard's worth of fruit trees, all heavy with that year's crop.

Giles dismounted, and was about to knock on the schoolmaster's door when a pony cart came down the street.

"Oh, it's Maria," said Emma, and trotted away towards her. The women exchanged a few words, Emma turned her horse and they came down towards the schoolmaster's house together.

"I was not going to call on him," Maria was saying earnestly to Emma. "You must believe me. I was only taking some things to Mrs Watson – she has just had twins and..." But she was blushing, as if she had thought of committing the crime, even if she had not done so.

A first floor window opened and Mark Hurrell himself looked out and saw them all.

"May we have a word, Mr Hurrell?" Giles called up.

"Yes, of course, sir," said Hurrell. "I shall be down at once."

"I had better go," said Maria, picking up her reins, "had I not?" She glanced at the house and then at Emma, desperate for guidance.

"Stay," said Giles, catching the bridle of her pony. "You both should stay."

"Are you sure?" said Emma.

"Yes," he said, as the door to the house opened, and Mark Hurrell stood in the porch. "In you go. I will deal with the horses."

He returned a few minutes later, and found the three of them had gone into the orchard.

"I thought it might be more discreet out here," Mark

Hurrell said.

Emma and Lady Maria had settled on a rustic bench, under heavily laden branches and late summer sunshine. In other circumstances it would have made a fine setting for a double portrait, for it showed both women to great advantage. But Maria's anxious expression would not have suited the portrait. She had leant close to Emma for comfort, taking Emma's hand, and it was certain that the sight of Mark Hurrell was causing her both pleasure and pain. That gentleman for his part had sat down on the grass, his knees drawn up under his chin, but he did not look remotely at his ease. He sprang up again at the sight of Giles, muttered something about fetching another stool, and bolted back into the house.

Giles sat down on the clumsy stool that remained, and received a questioning look from Emma, even as Maria leaned closer to her.

"What is going on, Major Vernon?" Maria said. "What is this all about?"

But he had no opportunity to answer, for Hurrell returned with a chair and sat down, and then at once stood up again.

"I suppose you have been wondering why I left the Hermitage," he said.

"Given the circumstances, yes," said Giles. "Perhaps you could give us your account of it. I know that you saw your father last Saturday evening."

"Yes, yes, I did," said Hurrell.

"And you left the next day without telling anyone where you were going."

"Yes," said Hurrell.

"Which in the circumstances aroused great suspicion."

"I suppose it might have done," said Hurrell. "But my intention was not to evade you, Major Vernon. My business was –" He broke off and gestured at Maria. "I came here to speak to Lord and Lady Rothborough, exactly as I said to you, my lady, that first day, because – may I?"

Maria now sat up straight, disentangled herself from Emma, and nodding, said, "You had better say it all."

"I wanted to ask them to give me their permission to address Lady Maria," said Hurrell. "That was our intention."

"You and Lady Maria had formed this plan?"

"Yes, sir, we had. We had decided, in the circumstances, that it was the best thing to do, that I should throw myself on Lord and Lady Rothborough's mercy because of what happened that night."

"Which night?" Giles said.

"The night we were all at Hurrell Place," said Lady Maria. "The night Mr Hurrell was thrown out. You must remember, Major Vernon?"

"Yes, very well."

"The fact is," Mark said, "I did not leave. I was angry, especially when my father had written asking me to come, and then to be refused in so humiliating a fashion! I had been listening outside to the music after dinner, which was enchanting, and it put me in a strange mood. I could not bear to be an exile from my old home any longer, so I went in by the back way. The house has several staircases and I went in, determined at least to revisit my old quarters, unseen by anyone, for I know all the ins and outs, naturally. This was in the small hours. Everyone had gone to bed and I was in the Long Gallery, and there was –"

"I could not sleep. It was too hot," said Lady Maria. "It was entirely by chance we met but... oh dear. Oh, Mr Hurrell – it was strange."

"Yes," said Mark Hurrell, now addressing Lady Maria as if there were no one else there, "and do you remember how the more we talked, the less inclined we were to bid one another good night? I knew I should leave you be, and yet I could not."

"We went up onto the roof, in the little stone banqueting

house up there!" burst out Lady Maria. "I know we should not have done, but –"

Now she rose to meet him.

"I do not know how to put this without sounding like a fool," said Mark Hurrell, his eyes fixed on Lady Maria, "but it did feel in that moment, at least on my part, that here lay my destiny. I have always wondered what the point of my existence was, and suddenly I saw clearly that it was to be with this woman who seemed already to understand me."

"You were so frank, how could I not understand you?" said Lady Maria. "You told me how hopeless it was. That you could not even presume to imagine any future for us. You told me everything that was said against you." She walked away a little, and turned to Giles. "He was so honest that I could not but feel... I have been courted before, you see, but it was never like this. This was so strange – and he felt that too. We knew at once this might be... oh, I know it sounds impulsive, and it was, and that was why I decided he must speak first to Papa and Mama and see what they said. So that is why he is here."

"That is all very interesting," said Giles. "But you both need to be aware of some important facts. Now, Mr Hurrell, after you had left the Hermitage, we conducted a search of your property. We found a blood-stained arrow and a smock also covered with recent blood spatters. Mr Carswell has established that your brother was killed with an arrow."

"That was nothing to do with me!" said Hurrell. "Lady Maria, you will believe me. Someone must have put them there to make it seem as if I were behind it! Some foolish person, I must say, because I would never do such an idiotic thing! And seriously, sir, you cannot take their presence as any indication of their being used by me? It is purely circumstantial."

"Men have been hanged on less evidence," said Giles. "And you had quarrelled with your brother for years, and you stand to gain a great deal by his death."

"I have gained nothing by it!" exclaimed Hurrell. "I have

nothing now. Not a single one of my siblings is left to me, my father will not speak to me and I don't think that Lady Maria will after this, thank you, sir!"

"I do not believe him, Mr Hurrell!" said Maria, quietly. "I know you would not kill your brother."

"The brother who so recently and publicly provoked you, Mr Hurrell?" Giles went on. "Who horsewhipped you in front of the entire village? Who has been so cruel to you for so many years? I have that from your own father, Mr Hurrell, that Arthur was over-zealous when asked to correct you as a boy. That his punishments amounted to abuse."

"I deserved all that – I was odious," said Hurrell. "You must ask yourself this: why would I risk my life and my soul to kill my only brother? I have no one left, that is the worst of all this. They have all gone. I would do anything to have Arthur back, impossible though he was, because he was all I have left of my mother. There were times, when he was so minded, that he would laugh or say something clever and I would see her again, for a moment. Why would I destroy that?"

"And then there is the matter of Miss Wytton," said Giles. "You told me that you considered your brother's treatment of her abominable."

"That's true," said Hurrell, "but that was an opinion, not a motive!"

"It might be if you had been lovers. And I am informed that there had been some intimacy between you."

"Who says that?" said Hurrell.

"Your father. He told me that was the reason that Arthur considered himself no longer obliged to marry her. Because you had seduced her."

"I did not. I swear I did not," said Hurrell.

"So, what are we to make of all her visits to you at the Hermitage? And the letters brought by Agnes Baker?"

"It pains me to say this, but Miss Wytton is a troublemaker and if she has said that to my father – for that is the only reason I can think that he would believe it, if she had told him so herself, then –" He turned to Maria who was now looking most uncomfortable. "My father is mistaken about that. She is nothing to me. You saw us together, Major Vernon – how impossible she was to me. She accused me of killing Arthur herself, do you not remember?"

Giles nodded and wished again that he had been able to interview Miss Wytton.

"But there is nothing that happened between you and Miss Wytton that might give a casual observer, or indeed the lady herself, any idea that you had intentions towards her?" he asked. "Why would she write and visit you so assiduously in the circumstances?"

Hurrell sat down again and pressed his face to his hands.

"I'm ashamed of this – many years ago, there was between us an episode, one summer – just before I went up to Oxford. There was nothing improper in it, but I was young and I fancied myself in love with her for a while, and she may have used my ill-concealed admiration to make Arthur more attentive. It made him jealous enough to give me a good thrashing. I suppose she counted that as a result."

"That was the summer you rescued me from that dog, was it not?" Maria said, plaintively.

"Yes, yes, it was," he said. "I remember that so clearly – we walked down the meadow together, and your father was there, and I was happy for that afternoon, in a way I had never known before. It was the difference between day and night for me. And it was after that I realised I did not love Margaret, that it was only folly to think of her that way. I must have seen something then, when I helped you, some truth which –" He broke off and got up, shaking his head. "But you will say that is foolishness, will you not, Major Vernon? And you, ma'am," he added to Emma. "When a man has such a question hanging over his head, when someone has gone to the trouble to put a bloodied arrow and a smock in his house to make it look as if he killed his own brother? To be talking of... of..."

"Of love?" said Lady Maria. "No, it's not foolish. And I believe you, Mr Hurrell. I don't think you would do such a thing. Even if I do not know you very well, I know this. In this case you must be wrong, Major Vernon."

There was a powerful sincerity in the ardent way Lady Maria looked at Hurrell, and be she right or wrong, she silenced them for a moment.

"What was in Miss Wytton's letters?" Giles asked.

"A great deal of nonsense. She was trying to engage my affections, or perhaps arouse my passions. She wanted to trap me, at any rate. It did occur to me that she knew about Arthur's vow of celibacy, and she assumed then that I would one day inherit everything, and perhaps I might do as a husband after all. I imagine she was a little desperate."

"Do you know why?"

"Because she was eight and twenty, with no sight of a husband? And she had wanted that so long, with so little success. But I can't say for certain. The letters were disturbing, to be frank."

"Might I see them?"

"I burnt them. It seemed unkind to keep them."

"That's unfortunate."

"Yes, because she will deny she ever wrote such things to me. She would deny that she even came to visit me, but since you saw her there yourself, she will not at least be able to do that."

"That's true," said Giles, considering for a moment the facts that he had already established. "You say these letters were disturbing. Did she make any suggestion that you should murder your brother?"

"That *is* quite a question," said Hurrell. "But no."

"And she never spoke to you suggesting you did so?"

Hurrell shook his head.

Giles wondered, with a measure of frustration, how

things might be proceeding in Northminster. Had Miss Wytton been successfully charged with anything, or had she been released? Was she already making a hasty retreat with her brother to the Continent? He hoped desperately that Lazenby had allowed Coxe and Rollins to interview her. They might not have got a confession but they might have disquieted her sufficiently to make the sort of errors that would cast doubt on her testimony. He felt certain her hand was somewhere at work in these proceedings, but he still lacked hard evidence and could not at that moment think how he would get it.

In the meantime, the wind got up a little and rustled the leaves in the orchard, and sent the first real chill in the air that he had felt for weeks. Emma rose and took Lady Maria's arm and said, "We should go back. It is going to rain."

"Yes, I suppose we should," said Maria.

"Do you want anything more of me, Major Vernon?" said Hurrell.

"I would like your assurance that you will remain here for the time being."

"You have that. I have no reason to go anywhere else," he added, with a gesture towards Maria. "And I must talk to Lord Rothborough. Perhaps this afternoon?"

"Tomorrow," said Giles. "I should like to talk to him first, if I may?"

~

Lord Rothborough drained the rest of his coffee, and sat for a moment considering what Giles had just told him about Lady Maria and Mark Hurrell.

"Love is an inconvenient emotion, certainly," he said with a sigh, and rubbed his face.

"I'm afraid I was rather brutal with her," Giles said. "But

I thought it better she knew all the facts against him as soon as possible. Before she was in too deep."

"Maria has always been a good judge of character," said Lord Rothborough. "It is a curious thing. Stranger still, she has never fallen in love before. She had a couple of suitors in Italy the winter I was there. Both excellent young men, and Lady Rothborough was in favour of one of them. But Maria was indifferent to their attentions. It was impressive, though Lady Rothborough was not amused. The worst of it is," he went on, "in other circumstances, he would be a good prospect for her. Especially now that his brother –" He gave a brief, bitter laugh. "However, cruel though it seems, they had better not see anything more of each other for the time being. You say he is lodging with the schoolmaster and his wife?"

"Yes. I know this will not suit you, but I would prefer he remained there. I need to know where he is, at least in the short term."

Rothborough nodded.

"I understand. I will go and talk to him myself. Given that he came to see me, he deserves that. If he is innocent, and serious about my daughter, then it will be some proof of it if he stays here and keeps his distance. We will have to keep Maria busy and away from the village, no matter how charitable she is feeling. I know she would not deliberately defy me and go to see him, but she might attempt to see him by accident. I will speak to her about it."

At this moment a footman came in with a message for Giles.

"It will be Lazenby repenting," said Lord Rothborough as Giles read the message.

"Unfortunately not. This is from Dr Perry in Axworth. Carswell has come down with the fever."

# Chapter Thirty-one

At around three in the afternoon on Thursday, Felix had vomited for the second time, and finding his shirt damp with sweat, went to sit on a bench in the stifling yard in an attempt to recover himself. He was soon shaking violently and in a moment he was retching again and running for the privy. Bennett, who was clearly fighting the same battle, found him there a few minutes later, and on unsteady legs fetched out his uncle, Mr Lane, the apothecary.

He unceremoniously examined them both in the yard and then said to Bennett, "Take Mr Carswell home and do not come back, either of you. Your aunts will know what to do."

He then bundled them into his carriage.

Felix sat wrapped in a blanket, his teeth chattering, his limbs on fire and his head feeling as if hot nails were being driven through his skull, as the carriage jolted through the town.

"It's not far," said Bennett, his hand clapped over his mouth. "And my aunts..."

He got no further and they were obliged to stop the carriage for a moment while he threw up into the gutter.

Bennett's aunts, Miss Lane and Miss Catherine, soon proved themselves to be magnificent, sensible women, well-versed in the care of the sick. Felix found himself put to bed in a pleasant little room, on cool sheets that smelt of lavender.

He did not know for how long he lay there. He was caught in a state of fluctuating delirium, his body intent on purging itself with regular and painful violence, but even at the lowest ebb, he was aware that he was somehow holding the disease in check. He had a vision of himself at one point leaning against a closed door, in order that the enemy behind it should not come in, and he knew that as long as the door remained firmly shut, he would be safe and he would survive.

Miss Catherine and their loyal maid, Nancy, took turns to keep him washed down and make him drink. They had a repertoire of herbal cordials and teas that were so effective that Felix felt they were surely heirs to some suppressed tradition of white witchcraft. For where science failed, as it so conspicuously had, where could they turn but traditional remedies? And as his fever retreated a little, he found himself eager to know their tricks, knowing that there was much a modern medical man could learn from such wise old women.

"What day is it, ma'am?" he managed to ask, when Miss Catherine next came in.

"It is Saturday morning," she said. He had been there two whole nights and had scarcely known it. She began to help him up onto his pillows. As she did so, he could see that her face was wet with tears.

"Miss Catherine?" he asked. "Is something wrong –?"

She looked away, and then hurried from the room, overcome with emotion.

Felix struggled out of his bed and followed her down the passageway. There, an open door revealed the source of her grief. Young Bennett lay insensible on his bed and Felix, without taking a step further, knew it was the stillness of death. Miss Lane and Mr Lane were sitting with their heads bent, while Miss Catherine knelt, took his hand and wept over it.

Dr Perry was also there, and he turned and saw Felix. He at once ushered him back to his room.

"When?" Felix said, when the door was shut.

"An hour ago. He seemed to have improved yesterday, but then passed a wretched night. His constitution could not withstand it," Perry said, glancing at Felix. "You must get back to bed, Mr Carswell. At once."

Felix did not hesitate to obey. He was shaking. Dr Perry's

implication was clear enough. He too had improved. The utmost caution was necessary now. Dr Perry helped him back into bed.

"You must stay calm, sir," he said. "It is always difficult for a medical man to be a patient. I sometimes think we are our own worst enemies," said Dr Perry, taking his pulse. "You must be calm now, very calm."

Felix nodded, breathing hard, attempting to tamp down the anxieties that now seemed to overwhelm him.

Bennett's face in death seemed to rise up before him as he closed his eyes, and indeed his ghost seemed to walk into the room. His expression was one of utter bewilderment at finding himself in such a condition. What man of twenty could not be surprised by death?

"How are things at the hospital?" Felix managed to ask, opening his eyes.

"In a much better condition, thanks to your efforts," said Dr Perry. "And Mr Bennett's, of course." He sighed. "I shall sound your chest, I think, Mr Carswell, just to see all is well. There can sometimes be a development of congestion in these cases, as I am sure you are aware."

"And the mortality rate is down?" Felix forced himself to ask.

Perry did not answer until he had finished sounding his chest and back.

"It is somewhat improved. We have more assistance now. Lane and I have taken measures to get the place on a better footing. We have got additional help from Leeds."

"And the cholera?"

"No more than the two cases you observed, thank the Lord," said Dr Perry. "Now, rest back down, sir, and no more talking. You must concentrate on your own recovery now. The profession cannot afford to lose another good man."

Felix did as he was bid. Miss Catherine came in with one of her herbal concoctions, and Dr Perry left for the fever hospital.

Felix drank his tea and she sat down beside the bed. She took out her Bible and in a quiet voice, began to read through some of the Psalms. Felix lay there and listened without being able to make much sense of what he heard, but he was calmed in some measure by her gentle tones.

Then he slept and, in his still heated dreams, found himself in a brightly-lit assembly room, with Bennett at his side. A ball was in progress and they were looking at the young ladies who were clustered across the room, wondering who they might dare to ask to dance. Bennett, finding his courage, went straight into the crowd of young ladies and then came back leading Eleanor by the hand. She was, to Felix's horror, heavily pregnant. She seemed happy to be with Bennett; in fact they were arm in arm, heads bent together, laughing over some secret. He stood and watched them, amazed at the size of his wife's belly, assessing every possible complication that might come from the birth of such a large child, or perhaps worse still, from twins. Then Bennett and Eleanor began to dance together. He wanted to intervene, to tell her such exercise was unwise, especially that dizzy, endless turning of a waltz. But they were not to be stopped and the music went faster and faster and they went with it, turning and turning until he felt sick from watching. Then at once the scene changed, and they were in the woods where he had first laid eyes on her, the woods between Hawksby and Ardenthwaite. Here Eleanor was lying on the muddy ground in her ball gown, her face contorted with the agony of labour. Bennett appeared, yet it was not the Bennett he had known, but more of a devil now, for as he turned, his countenance seemed to suggest he meant real harm to Eleanor. He meant to take her with him...

He woke with a cry and found both Miss Lane and Miss Catherine in attendance on him. They were looking concerned, for all their soothing actions, and he wondered if this was the crisis that he could not survive, if this indeed was the end. He felt so weak that he could easily have surrendered at that moment, yet he found that a sense of indignation at fate kept him from it. He struggled to sit up, taking Miss Catherine's hands in his, and managed to say, "I'm damned if I shall go now. There is too much to be done!"

This made her smile a little, and then the door opened and he was aware of two familiar figures coming towards him. It was Major Vernon and Lord Rothborough.

# Chapter Thirty-two

"Have they buried Bennett?" Felix said.

"Hush," said Mrs Maitland, bending over him. She was right. It was painful to speak. His throat felt as if it had been scoured with vinegar.

"But?" he attempted.

"Today," she said. "Major Vernon has gone."

"I must... his parents..."

He gave up; it was too much.

"All in good time," she said. "They will understand. It will not be taken amiss, not at all."

Felix managed to nod, trying to imagine what Bennett's parents might be feeling. Even if they were sincerely religious, as his aunts and uncle had been, that could not protect them from the agony of grief. To bring a child into the world and work carefully to have him learn all he should, to see him begin to find his feet in an honourable profession, and then to find it had all been for nothing: to have the object of such hope and love snatched away, without warning, without reason. He had been so sharp: he had read impressively, and his sense of duty had been equally keen. Felix had told him on several occasions to go and rest, but he had assured him that he was not tired.

I ought to have tried harder to make him stop, Felix thought, struggling now to find his ease under what felt like an intolerable burden of bedclothes. The great luxurious bed in which he had been installed at Holbroke suddenly felt unendurable. He could only think of a coffin being let down into the earth, and his own limbs, still weak and sore, seemed to beg for the oblivion of death. Why had he not been taken?

Why had he been spared?

"You must try and be still, Mr Carswell," said Mrs Maitland. "Let me help you." She placed a cool pillow under his head, and folded the covers back neatly. "There."

He submitted, closing his eyes, trying to empty his mind and breathe steadily. Curiously he found it easier to sleep than he had imagined, and after some time he woke again, stirred by a raging thirst.

Or at least he thought he woke, for he was aware that there was someone lying on the bed beside him, also fast asleep. It was Eleanor, curled up like a cat, in a heap of crushed white muslin, her hair down, just as he preferred it. This was so contrary to what he was certain Dr Perry and Mrs Maitland would have prescribed that he thought for a while that he was dreaming.

She stirred, sat up and smiled at him, stretching out her hand to him and putting another finger to her lips to silence him.

"I'm not supposed to be here," she said softly, and squeezed his hand. "But how could they keep me away?"

"No," he said, noticing she was wearing about her neck the ribbon that he had given her that day in Edinburgh. He reached out and touched it, remembering the night he had last seen her, and wondered how it was that his body, despite the weakness he still felt, was stirred by those memories.

"Here," she said, taking it from around her neck, and putting it about his own, her cool fingers touching his still burning skin. "You should wear it. To help you get better. I think it may be magic."

He managed to smile and shake his head at that, but her hand was pressing the knot against his chest, as if she meant to impress on his heart the truth of it. She leant towards him, her forehead almost touching his, her hair brushing his face, and he felt quite powerless, his own desires welling up despite everything. How that instinct remained so strong was a matter of wonder. Perhaps it was because she seemed so full of life and health that he longed for her, as if she could somehow restore him.

"You will get better soon," she said, and kissed his cheek. "You will. You must."

Felix was now again convinced he was dreaming, but at this moment the door opened and Mrs Maitland came in; Eleanor did not dissolve phantom-like in a flurry of white wisps, but remained, her hand in his.

"Now, you must not say anything," Eleanor said to her. "I am going to nurse him now. After all, he is my husband."

"Of course," said Mrs Maitland, a little bemused. "As you wish."

~

"So you think that Mark Hurrell is telling the truth?" Carswell said to Giles. "That he is not involved?"

"I find him sincere, but the facts are still against him."

He had come in to give him an account of the funeral, but after that the talk had turned to other matters.

"Very much so," said Carswell. "How convenient to have burnt her letters! And in front of Maria he would want to distance himself absolutely from Margaret Wytton. My theory is they had conspired together to murder Arthur, and then marry, but when he saw what a good prospect Maria was, he decided to let her take the blame and..."

At this point his voice gave out and he was obliged to stop.

"You should not agitate yourself," Giles said. "I should not be talking to you about this. Here, have something to drink."

He passed Carswell a cup of tea, which he drank down in

gulps.

"Yes, you should," Carswell said. "You know what a poor invalid I make. Please occupy me."

"It's certainly a good and thorny problem. Especially as we are denied access to our usual resources."

"Lazenby be damned!" said Carswell. "What on earth was he about? If I were not in this state then I should..." After a few moments' silence, he gestured towards Giles and managed to say, "Who else?"

"A good question. I will go on," Giles said, "only if you do not interrupt me." Carswell signalled that he would not, so Giles continued. "If we put aside Margaret Wytton and Mark Hurrell and a conspiracy between them, who are we left with? Willoughby? He was keen to point me towards dark and nebulous forces. Perhaps it was deliberate misdirection. He was certainly close to Hurrell, unnaturally so, Mr Powell seemed to think. Could there be something there? But the motive?" He got up and began to pace the room. "He loses everything with Arthur's death – his closest friend and colleague in their particular struggle. He gains very little, except the risk of being discovered. And again we return to the arrow and the smock in the scullery. He might wish to frame Mark Hurrell – I gather there was no love lost between them, especially when Mark deserted the cause – but framing him so clumsily? That is what I keep returning to: the stupidity of that one act. I cannot make any sense of it!"

Mrs Carswell came in.

"I'm afraid I must ask you to leave now, Major Vernon," she said. Carswell frowned at that.

"Eleanor –" he said.

"You must rest," she said.

"I agree with Mrs Carswell," Giles said. "You have plenty to think about now, at least."

~

"It's a severe trial so early in a marriage," said Emma. "Poor Mrs Carswell."

"He's a difficult patient," said Giles.

"Most men are," said Emma.

Giles reached for her hand and kissed it.

"I hope you don't include me in that catalogue?"

"No, you were tolerable. But perhaps as a husband you will be impossible, just to test me."

"Like one of those dreadful old tales? Patient Griselda, is that it?"

"I'm glad to hear you think it's dreadful," she said.

"I'm not sure what shocked me most – the cruelty of the husband, or the submissive virtue of the wife. I longed for her to rebel."

"To up and take an axe to him?"

"Yes, perhaps."

"You like murderers too much, Major Vernon," Emma said.

"But that is how I find them. Sometimes, at least. Liking is perhaps too strong, but understanding them. The dead person is an obstacle that has to be removed by whatever means. The wrong means, in the case of murder." He sighed and said, "And to whom was Arthur Hurrell an obstacle?"

"His brother. There is a strict entail on the estate. He will get every scrap of land and every penny now, when Sir Morten dies."

"Where did you hear that?"

"Mrs Hurrell told me. That is why she is reduced to living on her brother-in-law's charity. There was no provision for her husband or his dependants. He was, apparently, an unsuccessful barrister before he died, poor man."

"Sir Morten could have given her a house and an

independence of her own, though, even with the entail."

"Yes, he ought to have done. She would have been happier, certainly. But I suppose she cannot object, because her sons are being educated by Sir Morten."

"Suffering at the hands of Arthur Hurrell and Mr Willoughby," said Giles. "Lady Wytton called Sir Morten a domestic tyrant."

"Undoubtedly he is," said Emma. "It's not obvious at first, but there are things about him that make one –"

She broke off. Lord Rothborough had come into the room.

"I have alarming news from Northminster," he said. "Wytton's closed its doors at noon yesterday saying it would not make any more payments. This morning there was a crowd at the door, demanding the bank open. Apparently there was a small riot. I have ordered the carriage for you – I imagine you will want to see for yourself what is going on."

"Strictly speaking, that is none of my business," Giles said.

"That won't stop you," said Lord Rothborough. "Will it?"

# Chapter Thirty-three

"I am not sure we should be speaking at this juncture, Major Vernon," said Captain Lazenby, looking up from his desk as Giles came into his office.

"Perhaps not, but I was wondering, in the light of developments, if you might require my services?"

"The matter has been dealt with and it is improper for you to be here."

"I have been to the Infirmary. There are three of our own in there with serious injuries, not to mention the others involved. As far as I can gather it was a serious disturbance."

"It was for a while, but it has been dealt with now," said Lazenby, getting up from his desk and walking towards the door as if he meant to show Giles out at once.

"Have you got the ringleaders under arrest?" Giles said. "It is usually the case, no matter what grievance causes the riot, that there is a type of individual who likes to stir up the situation for his own amusement. There are certain people whom I could identify for you if you have not yet got them in your sights. They are an interesting class of criminal offenders, all in all."

"We have arrested those responsible."

"There is a man called Mackie, who has connections with the housebreaking trade, and who has in the past attempted to incite civil disorder in order to distract constables from their ordinary business. From what Inspector Rollins told me, this incident has his fingermarks all over it. Has anyone yet reported a burglary? If I were you I would put extra men on the more affluent quarters – St Anne's, for example – for many of them are empty at the moment while people take their holidays."

At this Lazenby opened the door.

"I think you should leave now, Major Vernon."

"Very well; one more thing. If I might ask about Lord Wytton and Miss Wytton?"

"That does not concern you."

"It does, greatly. I understand you released them without charge."

Lazenby closed the door again and said, "This is not your case any more, Major Vernon. However, out of common civility and to satisfy your curiosity, and in the hope that you will leave quietly, I will tell you. I considered that the evidence against them was not yet sufficient to bring charges. They both gave me their word that they would not leave the district while the investigation continues. There, does that satisfy you?"

"Not at all, I am afraid," said Giles. "For a start, one does not take such people at their word. And the evidence to charge them was more than sufficient. Did you take the trouble to read it? I'm sure Rollins would have brought you his report. He takes great trouble over his reports – they are always excellently put together, and he would not neglect his duty on this occasion."

"I read his report, but I do not consider the facts sufficiently established. It was my opinion that you acted hastily in arresting them."

"If I had not brought them in when I did, there would have been no evidence left. I am certain they intended to destroy the ledgers and no doubt get away to the Continent as soon as they could. And I'm sure the Justices would have agreed with me, especially if I had been allowed to interview them both. It would not have been much work to get the full story out of Wytton, and as for Miss Wytton – what did she say to you? Did she cry copiously?"

"She was distressed by her confinement. I did not want her to become ill," said Lazenby. "And I decided that public order was better served by having such persons not kept so publicly under arrest. The rumours of the bank failure began as a result of your arresting them – that is clear enough. It is difficult to keep such a matter quiet."

"Yet releasing them did not prevent a riot!" Giles said. "And now we have two suspects at large and three of our best men injured! If you had one shred of honour, sir, you would have handed in your resignation to the Watch Committee by now. I cannot even begin to conceive that a man in your position could be so gulled by rank. Have you learnt nothing in this business?"

"I released them for the sake of public order!" said Lazenby. "And I will not waste any more of my time in justifying my actions to you, sir. Your manner is outrageous. I will not be spoken to in this fashion by an inferior officer, especially one who is suspended from duty. You will leave the building at once, Major Vernon. I hope it will not be necessary to have you removed by force."

Realising he was losing control of his own temper, Giles decided that it was best to do as he was bid. He was aware that he had said a great deal too much and expressed himself far too warmly. There was something about Lazenby that provoked him and made good sense and diplomacy impossible.

He was turning this over in his mind as he walked briskly away, only to turn a corner and come face to face with Sergeant Coxe. He smiled – it was a welcome sight.

"How excellent to see you, Coxe," he said, shaking his hand.

"And you, sir. Have you just been with the Captain?"

"Yes, and it went badly."

"You must be vexed with him, sir," said Coxe.

"As he is with me. Now, tell me, the Wyttons – what happened?"

"I did my best, sir, I truly did. I did manage to get five

minutes with the young woman before Captain Lazenby came in, but I don't think I got anything of use out of her. She's as wily as they come."

"Thank you, Coxe. You had better go and not be caught talking to me, for I am a marked man at the moment. You must do as the Captain tells you and think of your own bread and butter."

Coxe hesitated for a moment and then said, "If you say I must, sir, but there'll be no pleasure in it. And what if they don't let you back? They had better, sir, or I shall throw it up myself and find another line."

"With a child on the way?" Giles said. "I don't think Mrs Coxe would be too happy about that, Sergeant. And beside, you are one of the best we have here. The force cannot do without you. You must put your head down and bear it, and keep working towards your inspectorship."

"And could the force do without you, sir?" said Coxe, with an expression that suggested Giles should take his own advice. How that was to be achieved was quite another matter.

~

"Ought you to be reading? Won't it tire you?" Eleanor said.

"It's only a novel," Felix said.

"I could read to you if you like."

"You have already read it," he said. "It's Mark Hurrell's book. But if you want to –"

"With pleasure," she said, taking the book. "And while I read, you can drink your broth." She smiled. "Do you remember how I refused to drink my broth? That morning at Ardenthwaite. I think that was when I knew we had to be married, after I had that strange dream."

Now she placed the tray in front of him and tucked a

napkin into the neck of his nightshirt.

"Drink all of it, mind," she said, "or I shall scold you."

It was just as well he had regained his appetite, and that the broth smelt delicious. This fresh incarnation of Eleanor as the attentive but patronising nurse was not something he found he could enjoy. The thought of her scolding was unendurable, so he dutifully drank his broth. She took up the book and settled on a chair by the bed. He was glad she chose to sit there and not next to him on the bed. Her presence was suffocating enough.

"Where had you got to?" she said. "Ah yes, Oxford. 'He went up to Oxford in 18-dash'. Why do novelists do that? I always dislike it. And Blankshire and so forth. It is not even consistent. Why does he not say Blankford?"

"That would defeat his object entirely," Felix said.

"But everyone would know that it was Oxford. Just as everyone will know which college he calls St Blank, just as everyone will know Breakbridge Hall is Hurrell Place, and Sir What's-his-name is Sir Morten Hurrell. I don't understand it all. Why did he write such a strange jumble of a book?"

"He is not sure himself," said Felix. "Can you go back a chapter or so? To when his mother becomes an invalid. Can you find it?"

She began to leaf through the book. "The part where she is dying?"

"No, before that. When she is first taken ill. When she is still living with the family at Breakbridge. There was a description of her symptoms –"

"This part: 'It was during that summer, that Lady B first became ill. It was some time after the confinement of her last child'?"

"Yes, that's it. Go on from there."

Hal had a vivid recollection of her fainting during a country walk. He and she had gone to visit, as was her constant habit,

> some cottage on a charitable errand (visits that were always welcomed, as her Ladyship had that rare gift of giving alms in a way that offended no one). She had collapsed in the shade of a tree and it took him a number of minutes to revive her. In fact, for so long a space that he believed her to have actually died, and his boyish imagination had been profoundly agitated by the fear that he would be blamed for it when he returned to the house with the awful news. She had revived, but it had been the start of a serious illness which none of the local medical men seemed able to diagnose, let alone cure. He went back to his school, leaving her a convalescent, only to hear in his father's letters that she had relapsed again, with a variety of troubling symptoms – that her fingers had become paralysed and that she could no longer play the piano, that her beautiful hair was thinning and she was constantly weak and in pain, and her voice was hoarse and she could barely speak. She could scarcely eat – whatever food she was served disagreed violently with her and she had begun to waste away, subsisting on spoonfuls of tea and a little bread and butter. When he returned that Christmas, she was somewhat recovered, to his great relief, only for her to relapse again when he had gone away.

"Don't you think that's rather strange?" he said. "It's such a specific description of the symptoms."

"But it isn't supposed to be a novel, is it?" said Eleanor. "If it were nothing but a story why would Sir Morten have wanted to burn it? Isn't that the whole point? It's all true, in some way or another. Shall I go on?"

"No, not just yet. Read out those symptoms again. She faints dead away, and then?"

"Let me see. 'Her fingers became paralysed... her hair was thinning and she was constantly weak and in pain. Her voice was hoarse... She could scarcely eat – whatever food she was served disagreed violently with her.'"

Felix laid down his soup spoon, turning over the possibilities in his mind.

"There is a section later when she tells the hero that she is being punished for her sins, is there not? Can you find that part?"

"Oh yes, I remember that bit. In the house with the echo."

"Yes, that bit."

"This?"

> "What will they say that you have done, Mama?"
>
> "A very bad thing, that no wife should ever do. Your papa believes it to be true and he has punished me for it. I know you have been punished when you have done nothing wrong, Hal, so you will understand me, you will know how I feel. I am innocent."

"It's curious," said Felix. "When you put it with that list of symptoms, I can't help thinking he is trying to say something rather specific – I need a book. It's in my laboratory in Northminster. Will you ring for Jacob? He can go."

"You may send for it if you finish your broth," said Eleanor closing the book and coming to the bedside again.

"It is all but finished," he said. "Please, will you not fuss so!"

He had said this rather more sharply than he had intended.

"I am only trying to help you," she said.

"Yes I know, but –" He broke off, knowing he must not speak his mind. "I am grateful, truly I am." He reached out and took her hand. "Thank you. Now, will you ring for Jacob?"

She detached her hand, went to ring the bell and then walked over to the window. She stood with her back to him, looking out at the parkland.

"Why don't you go for a walk?" he said. "And I will sleep a little more, I promise."

"Am I so objectionable to you, Felix?" she said after a moment, without turning to face him. "What did I do that I am suddenly so – dispensable?"

"It is not you, it's just that I am a poor patient," he said. "I'm sorry to be such a wretch. When I am well again –" He said this with some sincerity, for he was as disturbed by his own change in feeling as she clearly was.

She shook her head.

"I don't think you like me any more," she said.

"That's nonsense."

"Is it?" she said, turning back to him. "Do you think I'm so stupid that I can't feel it?"

"It's this –" he said, making a helpless gesture to indicate the sick-room and his condition. "When I'm better, I am sure –"

"No, that will not make a jot of difference. You are still angry with me because I could not agree with you! You think I am annoying and stupid! I can see it in your face. And even when you try to be nice to me it sounds false! Well, I shall not stay where I am not wanted. You can be as disagreeable as you like on your own!"

# Chapter Thirty-four

Having Lord Rothborough's carriage at his disposal, Giles told the coachman to drive him to Raythorpe Hall. He conjured up various excuses for why he was going there that did not involve interviewing Lord Wytton and his sister. In the end, he settled for calling upon Lady Wytton in consideration of her welfare. She was the innocent victim here, after all. There was nothing she had done or said to make him think otherwise.

He found her in the garden, playing with her children. She looked pleased to see him, and he was glad he had come. She showed him to a little summer house and they sat down to talk.

"You have come to speak to my husband, I suppose?" she said.

"No," he said. "I came to see you. I'm not allowed to speak to your husband. I have been taken off the case."

"Oh," she said. "What do you want with me?"

"To see after your welfare. You have had an unpleasant time, I suspect."

She looked at her fingers and said, "That is true. And now Edward has gone."

"When did he go?"

"Almost as soon as he came back from Northminster. He went off in a terrible hurry. I suppose he has gone to France and that is that. Margaret said I was not to say a word about it to anyone, but I can speak to you. Indeed, I must – oh, I'm so glad you came, it has been wretched." She choked back a tear. "But I'm taking the children to my brother's tomorrow. Shropshire – my mother is there. We will be all right." She reached out and squeezed his hand. "It's all so strange. I have woken up. I think I woke up when Fred told me that I was in danger, and when he died – oh, I thought we were happy, I thought I was happy, but then you realise that there is nothing, nothing really to hold on to. I'm lucky, though – I have my children." She gestured towards the garden. "It's only sad to think what Edward has thrown away. If only he had thought to say something to me about the bank. Why did he talk to Margaret and not his wife? That is the question, is it not?"

"I suppose they have always been close?"

"Yes," said Lady Wytton. "But they are constantly quarrelling. It was strange how they went on together."

"And Margaret is –?" Giles ventured.

She pointed towards one of the upper windows of the house.

"I think she's packing and she will be gone soon as well. I was not supposed to say so, but it had to be said."

"You have done the right thing," said Giles. "And really, the information can mean nothing to me since I'm no longer in charge of the case."

"Why?" she asked, with the appealing simplicity of a child. She covered her hand with her mouth, as if embarrassed by the bluntness. "Forgive me," she said. "It seems strange when you have such a way of finding everything out."

"I did something foolish in a crisis," said Giles. "And now I must pay for it. But first, I wonder if Miss Wytton will see me," he said, getting up. "Would you show me up to her room?"

"Yes," said Lady Wytton. "But will she talk to you?"

"Perhaps," said Giles.

So Lady Wytton took him upstairs.

"I have someone to see you," said Lady Wytton, knocking on the door. "Major Vernon is here."

The door opened a chink and Miss Wytton looked out warily. Giles reached out, caught the door and swung it open.

"I imagine you were told to remain quietly at home," he

said. "But I see you are packing – without the assistance of your maid."

"You should leave," said Miss Wytton. "I know that you have no business here. I know that Captain Lazenby has suspended you from your duties."

"I came to see how your sister-in-law was. And Captain Lazenby notwithstanding, you are not going anywhere until we have talked a little more."

He stepped into the room and closed the door behind him so that she could not leave. Then he turned the key in the door and went to the window, opened the casement and threw the key out onto the terrace below. One of the Wytton children, who was playing nearby, came running over.

"Take that to your mother," Giles said, "with Major Vernon's compliments."

The child picked up the key and went running off.

"This is insupportable!" Miss Wytton pushed past him at the window and screamed: "Help! Help! MURDER!"

A moment later Lady Wytton came out onto the terrace. She held up the key.

"Lavinia, Lavinia, get Bryant and some of the other men!" Miss Wytton shouted. "He is going to kill me! Have them break down the door!"

"No, I don't think so, Meg," said Lady Wytton. "You should talk to him. It will be better for you if you do."

"She will be quite safe," Giles said.

"I will come up in a while with the key, Major Vernon."

"Lavinia – no, no!" Miss Wytton howled. "Don't go, I beg you!"

But she went, and Miss Wytton turned back into the room and looked as if she meant to attack him.

"This is outrageous. Utterly outrageous. When I tell Captain Lazenby –"

"So you will talk to him? And not flit, like your brother?" said Giles. "That is something. Perhaps that night in the cells had some effect on you."

"I shall say nothing to you," she said, taking a chair and turning it away from him. She sat down, and so Giles settled himself in a comfortable chair. "My solicitor told me to say nothing."

"Yes, that is your right," Giles said. "I will read, then, until you are ready." He took Mark Hurrell's novel from his coat and began to leaf through it.

There was silence for some minutes, and as he read, he was aware that this was beginning to unsettle her.

"What are you reading? Nothing improper, I hope," she said.

"That's a matter of opinion – Mark Hurrell's novel."

"That vile thing," she said. "How dare you bring it here!"

"You might find it interesting," he said. "I think you are in it."

"What?" Now he had her attention. She had swivelled in her chair to face him.

"Who else can this be but you, Miss Wytton?"

> There was a young woman, the only daughter of a neighbouring gentleman of ancient pedigree. The baronet, his wife and their daughter Emily lived in great comfort in a charming old house. Naturally, Emily was the intimate of Hal's sisters. His eldest brother, Richard, reaching that age when a boy becomes a man, began to see her not as the sweet companion of his sisters but as a maiden whose charm, beauty and virtue made her a suitable prospect for a lifetime's felicity. They became engaged, and Hal found himself dreaming about his brother's betrothed, and wishing that he might be Emily's husband instead.

"Does this seem familiar, Miss Wytton?"

She did not answer, so Giles went on reading.

> There was some difficulty about setting a date, some misunderstanding about the settlement. The wedding was indefin-

itely postponed and soon such time passed that Hal, learning more of the world, began to see the imperfections in Emily's character. He wondered if they were the cause of his brother's hesitations. Yet he could not be certain if it was his brother's cooling ardour that had caused her to deteriorate. An apple improperly stored will rot. Emily had not been cherished as she should. Had they wed at the proper time, and had she been given the life that all women long for, that of beloved wife and mother, than perhaps Emily would have thrived, rather than withered into bitterness.

He glanced at Miss Wytton. She was sitting awkwardly, her arms wrapped about her. Her discomfiture was clear. He read on further.

> Hal reached this conclusion after a most painful passage in the summer before he was to go up to the University. Emily turned to him for sympathy. Richard had again failed to name a date for the wedding and showed no sign of relinquishing his fellowship. A clergyman and his family had lately been installed in the Rectory that was to have been their married home. In her grief, Emily turned to foolish wiles. She sensed Hal's weakness, and as delicately as she played the pianoforte, she played upon his feelings. In a few days he was violently in love with her. He was a willing victim, that must be said, and his conduct was without doubt far worse than hers. He made constant excuses for himself, and considered himself powerless as if a disease had stolen over him. This was far from the case. He could and ought to have resisted her foolishness, but –

At this Miss Wytton gave a slight moan and waved at him to stop.

"Perhaps you should tell me what really happened between you," Giles said.

"Nothing happened. That is all malicious fancy."

"But Arthur Hurrell did neglect you?" She did not answer. "Come now, you cannot pretend he did not hurt you. I'm not alone in thinking his conduct towards you was abominable. To make you an offer and bind you to him, with all the obligations that implies? When a woman accepts a man, it is a solemn thing – and so it should be for a man."

"I really don't want to talk about this," she said.

"I think we should. The record ought to be set straight. You don't want people believing you murdered him, surely?"

"Is that what you think?"

"I don't know. It does seem more and more possible the longer I study you, Miss Wytton. You have what we call form, after all, and you seem to be unperturbed that you have already destroyed several lives. Mrs Braithwaite and Mr Pierce – both died wretched deaths. I was with both of them when they died. Have you ever seen a man who has been burnt to death, Miss Wytton?"

"No," she said.

"It is not a sight I shall ever forget," Giles said. "Half his face burnt away. His clever, handsome face. And he died in agony. I have seen many men in dreadful conditions, but this surpassed it. All because you caused that fire to be set."

"You do not know that was me," she said.

"Who else was having private conferences with Esther Braithwaite? A woman you knew was a skilled fire-setter, who had successfully brought down an entire farm and burnt a man to death in the process? No one, Miss Wytton, no one but you."

"You do not know what we spoke of. And you have only the word of a duplicitous servant that she was here at all."

"Lord, you are heartless," Giles said. "Mark Hurrell is right. That is exactly what he says of Emily."

He opened the book again. "Here we are."

> When he realised that she only used him to bring his brother to his senses, when he lay recovering from the dreadful thrashing his brother had given him for his disgraceful impudence, he knew that painful though this was, it was nothing to the injuries she had inflicted upon him. He had been used, and without any hesitation. His feelings, his misery, his pain

were nothing to her. The effect was everything. Richard had been provoked, and after he had vented his anger on Hal he had shown her tenderness and affection. He had kissed her and promised to speak to his father about the settlements.

He glanced over at her. She seemed lost in thought.

"But he didn't, I suppose?" he said. "Speak to Sir Morten?"

"He may have done," she said at last. "But it would have made no difference. Sir Morten had already decided I was not good enough for Arthur. He changed his mind. I wasn't up to snuff. I had insufficient quarterings in my bloodline and Arthur could do much better for himself." She laughed bitterly. "That disgusting old hypocrite! When he made such a spotty match himself! Nobody ever talks about that! The late Lady Hurrell, who was she? Nobody, indeed, nobody at all! A Miss Smith or a Miss Taylor or something insignificant, and she came from nowhere at all. She had no money, no family. Just her fine looks and the clothes she stood up in. My mother told me that old Sir Arthur choked on his mutton and died when he heard what his son had done! Just imagine if Arthur had done that. I should like to see Sir Morten choke on his mutton, and that's the truth of it. He deserves it."

"You were treated badly," said Giles. "It can't be easy to deal with a family like the Hurrells."

"No, no, it is not," Miss Wytton went on. "And I did love Arthur, and he did love me, at least sometimes he did."

She got up and wandered over to her dressing table, where she began to play with the objects on it, her back to him.

"Is that why you persuaded your brother to make investments in The Stockholm and Malmo Railway Construction Company?" Giles said, gently. "To make you a better prospect? If you had more money, then Sir Morten might find you acceptable?"

There was a long silence.

"It was Arthur who needed money," she said. "He wanted it for his movement. His father never gave him much. I thought if I made a fortune, then... then I would be irresistible again. After all, who else will marry a woman of seven and twenty, if she does not have a fortune to her name? All I wanted was to be married. That was all. Is that so much to ask?"

She turned back to him, and made a gesture which he knew he was supposed to appreciate as appealing and submissive.

"No, not at all. So in order to achieve this, you persuaded your brother to make these investments?"

"They told us it would not fail. It was a guaranteed return!" she said. "If you want to find who is really responsible, Major Vernon, talk to them! We were duped. They lied to us!"

"But they did not attempt to set fire to the bank, Miss Wytton," he said. "They did not cause the death of an innocent man by doing so."

She put up her hands to silence him.

"That was not supposed to happen! If he had just gone home as he should then it would not have happened! No one was supposed to die!" she said. "That was not what we wanted..." Her voice trailed off as she realised she had betrayed too much.

"You just wanted to destroy the evidence, I suppose? That you had begun to steal depositors' money to cover the losses?"

"That was all my brother's idea."

"But you suggested Esther Braithwaite for the job?"

"I may have done," she said after a moment.

"That is better, Miss Wytton, much better. Now sit down again and think for a moment. Think of the tangle of lies you have caught yourself up in. They will strangle you sooner rather than later unless you start telling the truth."

She paced about the room for a few minutes, before seizing the back of her chair.

"My brother was desperate," she said. "He had made such a mess and at that moment it seemed a good idea. After all, we both knew what Esther had done at the Home Farm."

"And you never thought of mentioning that to anyone? Given that a man died?"

"We thought it better not to," said Miss Wytton. "She would have hanged for it. It was better not to say. I did not want that on my conscience." Now she sat down and Giles drew his chair a little closer.

"Do you know why she set that fire?" Giles asked. "Was it because of her sister?"

"Half-sister," said Miss Wytton. "Ruth."

"Who worked here, for your parents?"

"Yes, for a while. Until she left."

"Until she was dismissed in disgrace. What did she do, Miss Wytton?"

"I don't remember."

"Try and remember, please."

"She took some of my mother's things," Miss Wytton said after a moment, and then added, "or so everybody thought."

"And why was that?"

"Because the housekeeper found them in her box."

"But she denied stealing them?"

Miss Wytton shook her head. "She let them all think it was her, when –"

"When someone else put them there?" Giles said. "Someone who could easily take things from Lady Wytton's dressing room. A member of the family, perhaps?"

There was a silence, and then Miss Wytton burst out: "She needed to be taught a lesson! She had no respect. Esther was the same. Always behaving as if they were as good as us –

no, as if they were better, and always speaking out of turn, as if they were somebodies and not nobodies! Esther used to come up to the park to see Ruth, and I would see them sitting together, laughing, having all their silly little secrets. They said things to me –" She shook her head. "They said such horrible things to me!"

"Yet Ruth did not betray you?"

"No," said Miss Wytton. "And that was why Esther set the fire at the Home Farm. She wanted to hurt us all. I think she wanted to burn the house down and kill me. And I could not say what I knew because it would have come out that I was the one who had put my mother's precious point de Venise collar in Ruth's box." She began to cry, and with some sincerity. It was as if she regretted this transgression far more than all her others.

"How did you make Esther agree to set the fire at the bank?"

"I told her I would tell the family of the man who died. That was enough. She said she knew her sins would catch up with her. She took the money I gave her, and said, oh so prettily, that she hoped I'd be half as happy with Mr Hurrell as she'd been with her blacksmith, because she said she'd known Paradise and now she could go to Hell for eternity because she had that in her heart! The bitch. She knew Arthur was never going to marry me. She was mocking me! Even then."

She broke down utterly, and Giles sat making notes until she was done crying.

"Did you kill Arthur?" Giles asked, at length.

"No," she said with a great sniff. "No, I did not. But sometimes I wish I had! He deserved it."

"You visited Mark Hurrell on the morning Arthur was murdered?" She nodded. "It would have been an easy matter to make a detour through the Hermitage woods to the ruined chapel."

"I did think of going to see him," she said, swallowing her

sobs and drying her tears. "But the weather was very uncertain and I went straight to Mark. I did not feel strong enough to see Arthur. He was always so sharp with me, especially if I interrupted his devotions. And what would have been the point? There is only so much of that sort of thing one can bear."

"Were you alone?"

"No, Agnes was with me. We arrived at the Hermitage just as Sir Morten was leaving."

"Did you see Sir Morten leave?" said Giles.

"Yes, but he did not see us. He went storming off, which was no surprise, for Mark always puts him in a passion."

"And which way did he go?"

"Along the path towards the Chapel. That is the quickest way back to Hurrell Place."

"And this was before the rain started?"

"Definitely," said Miss Wytton.

"And you stayed with Mark Hurrell for how long?"

"Quite a while, for the rain started and so there was no point leaving until it cleared. Mark was in a wretched state. Sir Morten had given him a terrible lecture, and then he had taken laudanum and gone back to his bed, so I sat and read something Mark had been writing – the lives of the early Celtic saints. Such horrible stories, and all written as if he thinks miracles are nonsense. I think he means to shock people again."

There was a knock on the door, and Lady Wytton called out, "Shall I unlock the door now, Major Vernon? Captain Lazenby is downstairs and asking for Margaret."

Giles went to the door and said, "Yes, if you would, Lady Wytton." He turned back to Miss Wytton. "If you do nothing else, tell him everything you have told me, Miss Wytton. It is all you can do."

He went out onto the landing to Lady Wytton, closing the door behind him.

"Does Captain Lazenby know I am here?"

"No," said Lady Wytton. "I thought of mentioning it, but then I thought you might prefer I did not, given the circumstances."

"Thank you. Perhaps there is another way I might leave?"

"If you go along this passage to the end, and then take the back stairs, you can go straight to the stable yard. There is a door at the bottom of the stairs."

And so he found himself departing by the same route Esther Braithwaite had come for her fateful meeting with Margaret Wytton.

# Chapter Thirty-five

"Arsenic poisoning?" said Giles.

"I'm not entirely sure," Carswell said. "But that roster of symptoms suggests it."

"But it would have to be supposition on his part?" Giles said.

"Yes, but he's no fool. There are plenty of printed accounts of the effects of arsenic. He could easily have compared the symptoms he remembered his mother suffering and come to that conclusion. I have sent Jacob into the office for my Chrisiston on poisons – that's the standard text. I'm sure he could have consulted it when he was at Oxford."

"But why, is the question. Why would Mark Hurrell feel the need to make such a dire accusation?"

"Because it is the truth and he needs to tell it to the world? That is what the whole book is about, surely – telling all the truths that can't be told."

"We need to talk to him. If there is any substance in this idea, if Sir Morten did poison his wife, then it casts a different light over recent events. Miss Wytton told me an interesting thing. Apparently the late Lady Wytton was of humble origins and it was considered a scandalous marriage. Perhaps he regretted what he had done."

"And murdered her?" said Carswell. "Oh dear God, perhaps we do need to reform the marriage laws!" He laughed nervously, and then in a low and pained tone of voice added, "I have had the most terrible scene with Eleanor."

"What happened?" said Giles.

"She was fussing about me and I could not bear it. Then she said it was obvious that I found her annoying and stupid, and before we could discuss it, she ran away. The worst thing is that it is perfectly true!"

"Surely not?" said Giles.

"Yes, although I do want not to feel so, I do! Every time she comes in, I feel as though there is a noose about my neck, and –" He started plucking at the open collar of his nightshirt in his agitation. "I look at her and I cannot understand what I have done. I cannot feel anything I should for her. All I feel for her is the lowest kind of wanting." He looked away from Giles, his head bent in shame.

"If you were to see a patient in this condition, so soon after such serious illness, what would you say?" Giles said after a moment.

"I cannot blame it on that," said Carswell. "That is a poor excuse. No, I have felt this before. Ever since we have been back here it has been..." He pressed his hands to his face. "I cannot remember what it felt like to love her! Perhaps I never did. Perhaps all I wanted was – you know..."

"I do not think for one moment that is the case," Giles said. "You must allow yourself a little grace. No man or woman ever found the first weeks back from a wedding journey particularly easy, even without such a trial as this illness of yours. It is a great change for both of you. It will take time to adjust. I'm sure when you are yourself again, you will feel as you should."

"And what if I do not?"

"Have some faith in yourself, for goodness' sake," Giles said.

"Ah yes, faith," said Carswell. "I've never had much of a talent for it."

"This is verging on self-indulgence," Giles felt he must remark, and Carswell glanced at him, looking suitably chastened.

"I know, but I cannot start to think how I can remedy this! I know I should give it my attention, but instead I am eagerly solving riddles in anonymous novels written by possible murderers!" With which he grabbed the copy of Hurrell's book that was lying on the bed.

"Time," said Giles, taking the book from him. "Give it time. If you cannot manage faith, try patience."

"All the copybook virtues," said Carswell.

"They are in the copybook for a reason," said Giles. "We need to learn them, just as much as clear handwriting." He turned the book over. "Mark Hurrell is going to be surprised to find two surviving copies in our possession."

"Are you going to talk to him?"

"I think we both should, if Lord Rothborough will allow him in the house and you feel equal to it. I must say, his aspiration to Lady Maria's hand speaks strongly in favour of him, but you may disagree."

"I do, and I am surprised how generous you are to him."

"Mrs Maitland thinks he has an uncommon amount of charisma. Perhaps that is blinding me."

"Then certainly we must both talk to him," said Carswell. "I only wish I had been able to look at those bloodstains again. You said that Lady Maria and Mrs Maitland actually saw him in the woods wearing the smock?"

"He was wearing a smock," Giles said. "They have not identified the one we found."

"But they might, if they were to see it? I believe these things sometimes have distinctive embroidery. That is the sort of thing women notice."

Giles nodded, and Carswell sank back on his pillows. "Perhaps in a day or two I can get back to Hawksby and..." He sighed. "But then I would be a fool. It would probably kill me."

"I'm glad to see common sense breaking out in you again, Mr Carswell. In the first instance, let's talk to Hurrell here and see what comes of it," said Giles, going towards the door. "Perhaps the sight of you in your sick-bed will make him confess all his sins to us!"

Lord Rothborough consented and asked if he might attend the meeting. He then suggested Mark Hurrell be brought up to the house after dinner.

"What did you make of him?" Giles said.

"I liked him, as I liked him when I met him before. He is not in the ordinary style and that makes him attractive. We all like novelty, after all. At the same time, his manner is entirely correct. I could not be offended by him, although I felt I should be, given the circumstances. It will be interesting to see what he has to say for himself."

~

By the time Mark Hurrell came up to the house, Felix felt well enough to get out of bed, so the conversation did not take place in his bedroom, but in the cool formality of the great sculpture gallery. Here they sat at a round table supported by an angry-looking gilded eagle, while around them the famous Holbroke Canova and other sinuous, sensual pieces writhed and danced in their white marble perfection.

"I have always wanted to see this room," Mark Hurrell said. "My mother described it to me once. She and my father had come to a reception here; I'm not sure when it was. Perhaps when they were first married."

"It is your mother we would like to talk about," Lord Rothborough. "If that is not an impertinence?"

"No, not at all. Did you ever meet her, my lord?"

"Unfortunately not," Lord Rothborough said. "I'm glad to know my family received her at least once. The dislocation between our two families has been regrettable. Politics ought not to divide neighbours."

"I do not think it was politics," said Hurrell. "My father

has no taste for society. That party the other week was an anomaly born of desperation."

"In what way?" Lord Rothborough said.

"You guessed at it yourself, my lord. Your daughter mentioned that you thought it was in order to introduce her to my brother – whom my father wished to see married." He gave a slight grimace. "A strange plan, but Arthur must have provoked him into it. The most curious thing was that my father wrote to me and asked me to come up after dinner. To receive such a summons – that was strange enough, and then to find the house en fête –"

"And your brother did not believe you had been invited, I recall," Major Vernon.

"No. I should have brought the letter with me, but I was idiot enough to think my word was still worth something. But my father did ask me to call on him that night. Why, I don't know exactly."

"Because he knew it would spark a public argument between you and your brother, perhaps?" said Major Vernon.

"I think not," said Hurrell. "He would have been distressed if he had seen what you saw, Major Vernon."

"But he might have predicted such an outcome," said Major Vernon, "given the state of things between you and Arthur?"

"Perhaps he hoped to begin a reconciliation. Certainly that was what I hoped."

"Are you sure?" Major Vernon said.

"Naturally."

"After what you had written in your novel, did you honestly think that would be possible?"

Hurrell considered this for a moment.

"I regret that and I hoped my father had begun to see that I did regret it." He rubbed his face. "As I have said before, I was half mad when I wrote that book."

"Although it relieved your feelings a great deal to have set so much down on paper," Major Vernon said.

"Yes, but I should have put it in the fire at once, instead of taking it to such extremes. I'm grateful, to be honest, that my father has managed to burn so many."

"We still have two copies," said Felix, taking his from his pocket and putting it on the table. "I bought one in Edinburgh, and Major Vernon has the copy you gave to Mr Gray."

At this point Major Vernon added his own volume.

"It was for sale in Edinburgh?" said Hurrell. "Oh dear Lord, I had not thought that – and you have read it?"

"Yes, we have," said Major Vernon. "With the exception of Lord Rothborough."

"Should I, do you think, Vernon?" said Lord Rothborough, taking up Gray's copy.

"I would rather you did not, my lord," said Hurrell.

"You should," said Major Vernon. "It has its merits. There is a raw honesty about it, although it purports to be fiction. How was it you put it, Mr Carswell? Ah yes – it tells all the truths that can't be told."

Hurrell picked up the other copy and stared at it.

"I suppose that was my intention," he said. "Though had I known what trouble it would bring me – but there is truth of a sort in it, as I felt it. But it does me no favours." He put the book down and pushed it away. "I thought, and this was the most foolish thing, that perhaps if I wrote it as it felt to me, then my family might have some conception of who I was, after all – but that was sheer idiocy. They never could read me." He dropped the book on the table and pushed it away. "This was folly."

"Certainly," said Major Vernon after a moment, "if you truly wished forgiveness from your father, it might have been better not to show him murdering your mother. Which you do, do you not?"

"It is a fiction."

"A nicely observed one," said Major Vernon. "The symptoms of her illness, in particular."

"Arsenic poisoning," said Felix. "That was what you were implying? Yes?"

"It is a fiction," Hurrell said again. "Those characters are not my parents."

Major Vernon shook his head.

"A common fault in first novels is that they have too much of the memoir in them," he said. "And there is so much else painted from life, only just disguised. Your entanglement with Miss Wytton, for example. Why would you take to the wings of fancy in this instance?"

"Because I was angry at my father. I felt he was responsible for my mother's death, even if he was not."

"Then it is nothing but a libel?" said Lord Rothborough. "And against your own father! How shabby. Come now, Mr Hurrell, surely not? You are a better man than that. At least I would hope so!"

"What drove you to think in the first place that he was responsible?" said Major Vernon.

"Because she implied it to me, and I was a foolish boy, half-mad with grief at losing her. You have read the book," Hurrell said, turning to Major Vernon. "She told me she was being punished, and I thought she meant my father was behind it. And no doctors ever could say what was wrong with her. She simply seemed to fall ill for no reason."

"And the symptoms you list," Felix said. "Where did you get those?"

"Those are what she suffered."

"You did not consult a medical text at any time?" Felix said.

"No. Why do you say arsenic poisoning?"

"Because that is what your description suggests. Small doses over a period of time, causing inexplicable symptoms – the inability to tolerate food, the congenital weakness, her hair falling out, and her hoarse voice. There have been similar cases."

Hurrell stared at Felix.

"In truth?"

"Yes."

"Dear God, I did not know. There was another thing. I did not put it in the book. I remember taking her hand towards the end and she could not bear it. Her fingernails were so sore, that the slightest pressure on her fingers was agony for her. And I remember they had curious stripes upon them, across the nail."

"That is also common with chronic arsenic poisoning," said Felix.

"So you think he may have poisoned her?"

"If this is an honest account of what happened, then it is possible somebody did," Major Vernon said.

"It is how I remember it," Hurrell said, "but I regret to say, my lord, that I did mean to libel him. I meant to blacken his name without having any real evidence except my memory of what happened. But it was all so strange, the way he took her to live at that house in Northminster."

"That would be Rooke Court?" Major Vernon said.

"Yes," said Hurrell. "She was in that curious room with the echo, and she used it to tell me she was being punished by my father. I did not know what to make of it, and I still do not! It has haunted me for years. Sometimes I feel I dreamt it all in my grief. I felt that my father was responsible in some way, but I could not understand how." He reached for the book and searched for the passage. "There is a part I left out. It did not quite happen as I wrote it. On the last day I saw her, the day before she died, she said to me: 'When I am gone, look below.' I had no idea what she meant by it. I was afraid it meant she was going to Hell. 'Look below' – she said it twice." He shook his head. "I suppose she was so unwell that she was raving. And I could do nothing to help her at all. And to think

I believed I could help her now, with this foolishness..." He pushed the book away from him.

"When I am gone, look below," Major Vernon repeated after a moment.

"Who knows what she meant," Hurrell said.

"Who indeed?" said Lord Rothborough, picking up the book again.

"My lord, I would rather that you did not –" began Hurrell, but Lord Rothborough put up his hand to silence him.

"Perhaps it is better that I do read it, Mr Hurrell," he said. "For the sake of all concerned. Yes?" Hurrell nodded meekly, but he did not look at all happy. Lord Rothborough now got up and said, "And for the sake of Mr Carswell, who has been ill, we should finish this here. But you will not leave the village for a while, I trust, Mr Hurrell?"

"No, my lord," said Hurrell, getting up also. "I have no desire to do so. And thank you, gentlemen, for your time this evening. I do not know if it helps my cause or yours."

Major Vernon closed his notebook. "There are still a great many marks against you, Mr Hurrell," he said, "that's true enough. And if there is anything further you would like to say to me, I recommend that you do so, sooner rather than later. Honesty of that sort is always well received by a jury."

"I did not kill my brother," Hurrell said. "Some malicious hand has worked hard to make it seem as if I did, but I swear on my mother's honour that I did not kill him! In fact, I wish he were not dead, no matter how difficult and inconvenient that might be for me. I even wish he were here, wooing your daughter, my lord, and I was bound for New Zealand to do – well, who knows what! I would take a dozen horsewhippings from him rather than face putting him in his tomb. That is the truth, gentlemen, but whether or not you choose to believe me is in the hands of the fates. But I think, sir," he said, finishing this little speech by turning to Major Vernon, "you are a friend of justice, and will not let an innocent man hang if you can help it."

After he had gone, Lord Rothborough said, "He speaks extremely well. There is some potential there, but I suppose we must imagine that it will not be realised. A pity. Facts are facts, after all."

"Circumstantial facts," said Major Vernon. "I think I need to sleep on it. You, Mr Carswell, certainly should."

"Yes, quite," said Lord Rothborough. "Go to bed, Felix."

Felix made his way back to his bedroom, feeling an extreme lassitude overtake him as he did. Eleanor was sitting on the window seat by the open window, gazing out into the night. There was only a night light burning, and she seemed insubstantial in the soft darkness, like something he had conjured up out of his fancy.

He stood and watched her from the doorway, wondering if he should interrupt her. With some shame, he realised that she was not at all a creature of his own making, but someone with thoughts, ideas, dreams all her own. Like a conquistador seeing a dazzling mountain of silver and gold, her beauty and his own driving lust had blinded him to the reality of what marriage was. She was an uncharted country which he had to explore, slowly and delicately, before he could begin to understand her.

"May I join you?" he asked.

"Do you want to?"

"Yes," he said, "if you don't mind?"

"No," she said.

He sank down on the window seat beside her. He found he was utterly exhausted, almost to the point of being bereft of speech, but aware at the same time that he must talk and talk well to her. So he sat and tried to think how to begin, but the words did not come. She had told him that he sounded insincere and he did not want to risk any more confusion.

He felt her lean a little towards him, like a cat seeking warmth. So he put his arm about her, and soon she had wriggled closer until she lay with her head in his lap, so that he could stroke her hair.

"I'm still angry with you," she said, at length.

"I know, and I deserve it," he said. "I have been a brute."

"Would it be so awful if we were to have a child?" she said, after another long pause.

"To be frank, it terrifies me. There is so much that can go amiss." The nightmare he had had of poor Bennett and Eleanor now flashed across his mind and made him shiver. "I don't like dancing with death."

"But you do that all the time," she said, sitting up. "What else were you doing in Axworth? Major Vernon said it was as if you were going into battle."

"But – that is different. I do not feel about work the way I feel about this. I'm not ready for it. I am only just getting used to the idea of being a husband. And as you may have noticed, I am not very good at that yet. You must give me time. Please?"

"I suppose so," she said after a moment. "But you will promise to think about it, won't you Felix? After all, I might already be – well, you know, after that night, before you went to Axworth." She got up and crossed the room.

"No, surely not?"

"It's possible," she said. "Is it not?"

"Oh dear Lord," he muttered. It was indeed all too possible.

"You are heartless!" she exclaimed, "I knew you were! I knew it!"

And she ran from the room, slamming the door behind her.

# Chapter Thirty-six

Giles found Emma sitting alone in the small drawing room.

"I have been playing the governess," she said, "and have sent both young ladies to bed."

"That's just as well. How did Mrs Carswell seem?"

"She was subdued. How was Mr Hurrell?"

"Still a puzzle."

"Oh, poor Maria. I know she is trying not to think of him, but I can see her imagination is stirred."

"It is just as well she was not there this evening," Giles said, sitting down beside her. He glanced about the room, at all its subtle luxury that suited Emma so well. He wondered how he was ever going to provide her with even the barest comforts, the way things were going on. "As Lord Rothborough said, love is a most inconvenient emotion."

"Yes, but necessary," said Emma, taking his hand. "I had a letter from your sister today," she said. "She mentioned a bed."

"Oh, yes. She wrote to me about it as well," he said, and could not help sighing.

"Do you not like the idea of it?"

"It sounds excellent, except I'm wondering if we will have a house to put it in. If I have no post, then –"

"Then we will live in lodgings on crusts. I don't need a house," she said. "You know that. Let alone beds or drawing rooms. I will give German lessons to young ladies."

"You shall do no such thing."

"Pride does not make puddings, Giles," she said, with a smile. "And I don't think you should be so gloomy. Who knows how all this will work itself out."

"You're right," he said, and kissed her hand. "Now before I forget – yesterday, you were about to tell me something."

"I was?" she said.

"Yes, just as Lord Rothborough came in. About Sir Morten being a domestic tyrant."

"Oh, that," she said.

"You said, 'And there are things about him which make one...'"

"I did?" she said. "Are you sure?"

"Perfectly. So what were you going to say about him?"

"Oh, some nonsense, probably."

"But you never talk nonsense," he said.

"I do little but talk nonsense," she said. "As you well know."

He shook his head, smiling.

"What were you going to say? Even if it is nonsense, I should like to hear it. We were talking a great deal about Sir Morten tonight."

"It was that Mrs Hurrell has to serve him his dinner in his study and wait on him, as if she were a servant. Very shocking, isn't it?"

"That was all you were going to say?" he said, sensing a brittleness in her manner that was not usually there.

"Is that not enough?" she said. "Is that not a disgusting example of domestic tyranny?"

"Yes, very. But there was something else?"

She hesitated a moment and said, "He might be one of those gentlemen who let their warm feelings carry them away a little."

"He might be?" Giles said. "Is he or isn't he?"

"Very well, he is... liable... to that sort of thing."

"You are being so coy."

"I do not want to be unkind to an old man who has lost his son."

"But you meant something by that. Warm feelings? Do

you mean he has a temper?"

"He certainly has that. Yes," she added with a gesture that was clearly meant to be dismissive.

There was something about her manner that unsettled him. It was not like her to talk for so long in riddles.

"What do you actually mean?" he said, after a moment. "This is not just about him having a bad temper, is it? There is something else."

She was silent for a moment, then said, "He is an old flirt. But you knew that. So there we have it."

"I don't think we do. Did something happen between you?"

"Not of any consequence."

"What happened?" he said.

"Is it so important?"

"Yes."

"I would rather forget it. As I said, it was nothing of any consequence."

"Then why do you wish to forget it?" he said. "Something has happened that has hurt you, otherwise you would not be hiding this from me. Has he hurt you in some way? Has he offended you?"

"It was trivial. I don't want to make anything of it."

"But something happened? What did he do?"

"Please, I really would rather not. You will be –" She broke off and got up from the sofa, walking across the room. "It's not necessary for you to know. Surely we are allowed to use our discretion in such matters? I'm sure there are a great many painful things that you have decided not to vex me with."

"Dear Lord, what happened?" Giles said, getting up. "Did he – what did he do? What happened?"

"It was nothing, really, nothing at all!" she said. "Please, I do not want to talk about it."

He turned her gently to face him.

"I think you should. For your own sake."

"And be told that –" She broke off and stepped away. "That one was a fool for allowing it to happen?" she said. "Even you, the most kind and sensible of men, will draw that conclusion. Of course you will. It is the conclusion I have drawn myself and why I don't think there is anything to be gained by talking about it. I made a foolish mistake and I have learnt my lesson. Please, can that be an end of it?"

"You are judging yourself too harshly," he said. "If I have correctly understood what you are implying, then it is his fault, not yours."

"He's a silly old man, yes, an old goat, yes!" she burst out, "but he knows no better! *I* should have known better! I should not have gone with him and I should not have talked to him as I did. It is like the spark that lights a patch of dry stubble, surely? If I had not talked as I did, if I had not attempted to amuse him to keep him happy about that ridiculous low rent on the house then he would not have considered that I was willing to pay for my reduced rent in kind!"

"What?"

"He took me to mean that I was offering myself as rent!" She choked out her words. "And attempted to collect the first instalment."

Now she began to cry, throwing herself into a chair, twisting away from him and refusing to straighten when he attempted to take her into his arms. Instead, she seemed to flinch at his touch. Bending over her, he said, as gently as he could, "What did he do?"

He sank to the floor beside her and listened to her crying. In his mind a hundred phantom versions of her ordeal played out, and he was shaking with anger. Then suddenly she turned and flung herself into his arms, sobbing furiously against him, clinging to him, so that they sat in a miserable tangle on the floor.

At length she stopped crying and managed to say, "You

will not do anything foolish, will you? It was all my fault. There is no need to –"

"I should like very much to do something foolish and violent," he said, "to tell the truth."

"I know, but you must not. Please?"

"I will not," he said, kissing her on the forehead. "I promise." She sighed at that and pressed herself a little more tightly against him. "But I shall do something, and he will be punished for it, you may be sure of it."

# Chapter Thirty-seven

Giles passed a wretched night, thinking all the time of Emma in her distress. It had been difficult to leave her to bear her burden of suffering alone. She might have told him she could manage, and knowing her strength, he was sure that she could, yet he longed for some clever magic to make her forget all she had suffered. But she would have pointed out that to be relieved in such a fashion was not good for her character.

He found her first thing the next morning, standing on the great portico watching the mists rolling from the distant parklands, as the last of the summer slipped into the start of autumn. It was a beautiful sight.

"Did you manage to sleep?" he asked, having greeted her with a kiss.

"Better than I have done lately," she said. "You look as if you did not."

"Not a great deal, no," Giles said. "But that does not matter."

She sighed. "Oh, I should not have –"

"No," he said, pressing his finger to her lips. "No, it is better told, you know that." She nodded.

"And I have been thinking," he went on, "about Sir Morten. About what can be done. I need to go into Northminster. I had an idea, last night – and I need to speak to Mark Hurrell. So I must desert you, I'm afraid. Will you be all right?"

"I'm not such a frail vessel, Major Vernon," she said, adjusting his cravat to her satisfaction. "And I have plenty to do here. Maria has many useful enterprises in hand. I shall submit myself to her management."

"She is very sensible for her age."

"No wonder Mr Hurrell admires her," Emma said. "And he would admire her even more, to see how she is carrying herself through all this wretched business."

"I think she may be rewarded for it," Giles said. "I think we may have the key to it all to hand."

"Oh, I hope so. I cannot help but like him extremely," said Emma.

"Careful, you will make me jealous," said Giles.

At this moment a young woman, mounted on a vast, well-muscled grey horse, came galloping up to the house. It was Mrs Carswell. Behind her, his own mount struggling to keep pace, was Fenton, one of the more senior grooms at Holbroke.

"I never saw a young woman so reckless on a horse," said Emma. "Surely she should not be riding such a large animal? Is that one of Lord Rothborough's hunters?"

"At least she has Fenton with her," said Giles, going down to catch the horse's bridle. "Good morning, ma'am!" Giles said.

"Oh, good morning, Major Vernon," said Mrs Carswell, dismounting with perfect ease. "Do you like my new horse?"

"Your horse, Mrs Carswell?" said Emma, coming down the steps. "Goodness!"

"I bought him in Scotland," she said. "He is perfectly noble, is he not?"

"Yes, but rather lively, I should say!" said Giles, struggling a little with the defiant horse.

"Here, sir," said Fenton. "Let me take him."

"Thank you," said Giles, glad to be relieved. Even Fenton seemed to be tested by the animal as he led him towards the stables.

"Mind you cool him down properly, Fenton!" said Mrs Carswell. "Be very particular!"

"Yes, yes, ma'am, of course!" said Fenton.

"He is as sweet as a child if handled properly," Mrs

Carswell said.

"I'm sure," said Emma, "but such animals can be a little risky, perhaps?"

"He doesn't frighten me," Mrs Carswell said.

At this moment Mr Carswell came out onto the portico in his dressing gown and slippers.

"What are you doing –?" he began, his voice still hoarse. "I thought you said when we got him that you were going to put him to stud?"

He staggered towards one of the stone benches and sat down.

"Oh, he's perfectly safe!" she said. "I know what I am doing."

"Do you?" Carswell said. "Do you want to break your neck?"

"Would you care if I did?" she said.

"Nell –" Carswell said, gesturing towards Giles and Emma. "Please!"

"Would you?" When Carswell did not answer at once, she said, "That says it all, doesn't it?"

She scooped up her habit skirt, threw it over her arm and marched into the house. Carswell rose and was about to stagger after her, but instead Emma took his arm and guided him back to the bench.

"Catch your breath, Mr Carswell," she said.

He nodded and sat there tugging at his collar, his face crimson.

"What –" he began, pressing his hands to his face.

"Hush now," she said. "Yes?" He nodded dutifully. "We cannot have a relapse."

"I should not care!" Carswell burst out. "It could not be worse..." He gazed up at Giles with wide eyes and gestured behind him, towards where Mrs Carswell had departed. "It would be better if I were dead and buried! What use am I? Why should Bennett have died and not I? That is what I cannot answer. He had a better mind and certainly a better character. He did not –" He broke off, screwing up his face.

Now Emma had her arm about his shoulders.

"Hush, hush," she said. "The fever is still playing tricks on you. You must rest, and it will all seem clearer. You should not have got up last night, I dare say."

"No, perhaps not," said Giles. "Let us get you back to your bed, Carswell."

Having helped Emma to settle Carswell again, Giles set off to find Mark Hurrell at the schoolmaster's house, trying to dismiss his uncharitable thoughts about Mrs Carswell. But it was hard not to conclude that she was still very much a foolish child who had a great deal to learn. She was certainly going to be a test of character for Carswell. Giles could only hope his friend would find the necessary reserves of fortitude to make a success of the marriage.

Mark Hurrell's quarters at the schoolmaster's house consisted of a snug bed-sitting room which he had turned into a scholarly cell. Giles found him sitting at his writing table, surrounded by papers and books.

"Miss Wytton mentioned you were writing about the Celtic saints," Giles said.

"Yes. I have been at that for some time," Hurrell said. "It was Arthur who suggested I do so. He always loved those tales, though to him they were not tales but as true as anything in the Gospels. That was the difficulty for me. The more I worked on those curious old saints, the less they seemed true to me, but more akin to fairy tales."

"In which there is a different kind of truth," Giles said. "So I have heard it said."

"And that is why I have gone on with them. And I have got fond of Patrick and Ninian and all the others."

"I would have thought your last experience would discourage you from literary pursuits," Giles said.

"I never learn my lesson, Major Vernon," said Mr Hurrell.

"That is my misfortune. But there was something you said last night that made me think – about a first novel often being an ill-disguised memoir? That is certainly true in my case. I wrote that book because I had to – it was a compulsion – and I would have been better burning it before it ever got to the printer. But I learnt a great deal from the doing of it and I hope I might write a better novel yet, more in wisdom than in anger. If the fates permit, that is – or whoever may be in charge of my existence." He finished with a gesture towards Giles.

"If you mean me," said Giles, "you should know that I have no authority at this present moment in any enquiries concerned with your brother's death. You have nothing to fear from me, Mr Hurrell. I am just worrying at loose threads, as I always do. You might say that I never learn my lesson either. So it is in that spirit I ask you if you would go to Rooke Court with me today. There are things there about which I would like to satisfy my own curiosity, and I need your assistance."

"In what way? I cannot help you with access to the property. You know how things are between my father and myself –"

"No, there is no need for that. I can come and go there as I wish. I am supposed to become your father's tenant in the near future."

"Supposed?" said Mark Hurrell, getting up and putting on his coat.

"We have not yet signed the lease," Giles said. "So you will come?"

"This is to do with my mother's death?"

"Yes."

"I was thinking of it all night."

"So was I," said Giles, "amongst other things. Shall we go?"

Arriving in Northminster, they stopped first at Hopkins' office where Mr Hopkins was glad to give them the keys to the property, and then they went to the Minster Precincts.

The old house stood looking as charming as ever, the heavy growth of creeper enfolding it like the shawl around a modest woman.

"It's curious to be here again," Hurrell said, looking up, "after all that has happened. And you are proposing to live here?"

"That was our plan," said Giles. "But my circumstances have changed a little since then."

"But you are still to marry Mrs Maitland?" said Hurrell.

"Yes, that is fixed," said Giles, "thankfully." He took the key from his pocket and unlocked the front door.

"Let us go up to the drawing room," he said, and they went upstairs to the room with the echo. "This is the room you were describing?"

"Yes, this was where she spent her time."

"You said she was lying on a couch. Where was it?"

"Here, I think," said Mark Hurrell, indicating an area to the side of the room.

"Was there a carpet on the floor?"

"No. The room was scarcely furnished. That was what was so shocking."

"So the chaise was sitting on bare boards?"

"Yes."

"Something occurred to me last night," Giles said, getting down on his hands and knees and feeling for a loose board. "I remembered that a neighbour of my parents had repairs done and the boards in one room were entirely taken up. And lo and behold, they found some scandalous love letters under the boards. The previous lady of the house had been anxious to conceal them from her husband and so pushed them into the gap between the boards." He took a small iron crowbar from his coat pocket. "And I wondered if your mother might have done something similar." Finding a loose board, he cranked it up to reveal the rubble beneath. "If she were lying above here," he said, "on her couch. Then –"

Now Hurrell was beside him tugging at the boards to the left and right.

"Dear Lord, yes! Why not?" he said. "After all, she did once catch me pushing playing cards through the holes between the boards in the nursery. Major Vernon, you are quite the wizard! Lady Maria said you were. Oh, what is that down there?"

Giles reached in and brought out a tightly folded paper. He brushed the dust from it, and saw it was addressed in faint letters to 'Mark Hurrell.'

He found himself staring at it for a moment, astonished that his own instincts – no, his fancy – should have guided him so surely.

"Addressed to you, Mr Hurrell," he said, holding it out to Hurrell.

Hurrell took it and stared down at it, his hand trembling.

"Yes," he said, and handed it back to Giles. "I cannot believe it can be so, but – you had better open it, though."

Giles went to the window and carefully unfolded it, feeling from the weight that something was enclosed within. His instinct was correct – there was a twist of paper and a lock of hair tied in a scrap of ribbon.

The letter itself was written in one of the most tortured hands Giles had ever seen, the ink thinly applied as if the writer was afraid both of making a mark and of wasting ink. It made it almost impossible to decipher. He managed to read a few words and then handed it to Hurrell.

"Do you recognise the hand?" he said.

Hurrell nodded.

"That is my mother's hand," he said, after a pause. "Although you would hardly know it. It is very deformed, but her hands were all twisted up that last time I saw her, and the date – yes, it is the day before I last saw her: April 17th 1829. I saw her last on the 18th. How much it must have hurt her to write this – oh, Lord..."

Giles gave him a few moments to read it through.

"And what does she say?" he asked.

"She says –" Hurrell said, his voice indistinct with emotion. "Excuse me." With some effort, he read from the letter.

> My dearest child, if you are reading this I will have gone to my grave and God willing, I will have found my place in that realm of Heavenly love where no one can be hurt or harmed. Pray always that it may be so, my sweet boy, and tell your brother and sisters that I will be watching you all should God in His infinite mercy grant me forgiveness for my sins and let me be with Him in that sweet place.
>
> Now, there is something else you must do for me. I know you, Mark, are the boldest and bravest of all my children and the one who is a fearless speaker of uncomfortable truths. You have suffered for your honesty and this is why I give you this awful task. You father believes that I have dishonoured him, but this is not true. You will not let them defame me. You will defend my name, and you will tell the world my fate – that I have been brought low by a man who cannot believe in my innocence, by a man who has taken such steps to punish me that he will have to reckon with the fires of Hell for it.
>
> He has been poisoning me. He told me so himself, knowing that I have only a day or so to live and no way of communicating with the world beyond this prison he has made me. He told me I was vermin and that I was to be extinguished. That poison is the cause of my illness. I have the proof now – I managed to steal a little from his coat (it is enclosed in a scrap of paper) and I beg you to take this letter to someone in authority whom you can trust, perhaps Mary's godfather in London, and God willing it will not be too late for justice to be done.
>
> I am too tired now. I can write no more.
>
> God bless you Mark. Your dearest, loving mama, Eliz. Hurrell.

He laid the letter down on the window seat, and covering his face with his hands, walked down the room, giving in to his emotion.

"When I am gone, look below!" he said at last. "Look below – oh dear God, why did I not understand her? Why was I such a fool? It seems so obvious now! Oh, God..."

He broke down completely then, and left the room.

Giles found him sitting on the bench beneath the walnut tree which he and Emma had so admired on their last visit to the house. He wiped his face dry as Giles approached.

"My own father?" Hurrell said. "Could she have been right? Could he really have done that to her? So slowly, so deliberately, so viciously? He loved her. He defied his father to marry her – it was a great passion. Oh, I know I fancied it was the case, but it cannot, cannot be the truth. I thought it was only my wicked imagination that could conjure up such things. It cannot be true. But why then would she –?"

"It is a compelling accusation," said Giles, "and there may be a great deal of truth in it. We should pursue this."

"How?" said Hurrell. "How would you ever get him to admit to such a thing? I know you are supposed to have uncommon powers in this area, but my father – he is a fortress. He has no weaknesses."

"That is not at all the case," said Giles. "There is always a way."

# Chapter Thirty-eight

"That horse," said Lord Rothborough, "should be shot. Fenton tells me it is a most dangerous animal. What on earth were you doing, buying such a thing?"

"It was nothing to do with me," said Felix. "She took a fancy to it when we were in Perthshire, and before I knew it, it was bought. I had no idea she intended to ride it. It was supposed to be for stud. She had a vague idea of setting up a breeding stable." He sank back on his pillows.

Lord Rothborough massaged his brow for a moment.

"It is all most unfortunate."

"Have you spoken to her?" Felix said.

He shook his head.

"She has shut herself up in her room. I have sent for her mother."

"I don't know if that will do any good. In fact, it might make it worse. She will blame me for that, as she blames me for everything now! Which she may as well, for it is probably true. I am obviously not at all what she wanted. I don't know what it was she wanted, but it does not seem to be me! I am nothing but a wretched disappointment who throws silly obstacles in her way. What she sees as silly obstacles, of course, which the rest of us accept as common sense!"

"For example?" said Lord Rothborough.

"She is hell bent on motherhood, which of course is only natural, in some respects – I do see that, but she is still very young and I am not ready, by any means! I have attempted to explain this to her on numerous occasions, but she fights me tooth and nail. And of course she may already be with child and there is nothing else that can be done but live with the consequences, whatever they may be!"

"I see," said Lord Rothborough, having thought for a moment. "If that is the case, then you are right – there is nothing more to be done than make the best of it. There is the possibility that since she yearns for it so much, it might be just what she requires; have you thought of that? A child often has a settling effect on a woman. It might make her grow up a little. That is the difficulty here, I think – her immaturity. And having said that, the responsibility might do you no harm, Felix. It was a useful lesson for me, certainly. It is a sobering business to face the consequences of one's actions."

"Consequences which may easily be avoided!" Felix said. "You, my lord, of all people, know that! In fact, I was thinking, after what you said to me about the reform of the marriage laws, there ought to be a revolution in all these matters between men and women! As it stands, we are all wading through a mire of superstition and confusion, and God forbid that it should ever be talked about rationally or openly! I intend to write something on the subject, in fact, when I have got over this wretchedness. If I am not up to my ears in mewling infants by then, that is."

"Excellent," said Lord Rothborough, reaching out and squeezing Felix's shoulder. "You see, it has brought your mind into focus. And that surely is no bad thing. You know I want you to become more active in the business of reform. Our society is riddled with imperfections. You need to take your surgeon's knife to them."

"But it will stink of hypocrisy to speak on such a platform, and at the same time to be stocking a nursery. That is what Eleanor wants, I think – a host of small Carswells."

"The argument is about choice, surely?" said Lord Rothborough, getting up and walking about the room. "That is the crux of it. An appeal to rational action. You wish your fellow men and women to have the choice to become parents or not. Yes?"

"Yes."

"Then, there it is!" said Lord Rothborough. At that moment the door opened. "Ah, Major Vernon!"

"I'm glad to find you here, my lord," Major Vernon said. "I wanted to speak to you. I need your assistance, in fact."

"Of course. What can I do for you?"

"I need you to contrive a meeting with Sir Morten."

"Certainly. Why?"

"We have some interesting new evidence. It seems that Mark Hurrell's instinct about his mother's death was not so fanciful. Here." He reached into his coat and laid a folded letter, a twisted scrap of paper and a lock of hair on the counterpane in front of Felix. "Under the floor in Rooke Court. Lady Hurrell was being literal when she told her son to look below. It's extremely suggestive of murder."

Felix took up the letter and failed to decipher it, so handed it to Major Vernon, who gave them a précis.

"How extraordinary," said Lord Rothborough. "What a quick-witted woman!"

"A desperate woman," said Major Vernon. "And for her sake, I would like you to contrive to see Sir Morten. In fact, I want you tell him what we have found."

"Surely not?" said Felix.

"He needs to feel threatened, yes," said Lord Rothborough.

"But safe," said Major Vernon. "Which is where you come in, my lord. If you can play the card of the concerned neighbour, who does not want any more scandal to besmirch one of the great families of the district?" Lord Rothborough nodded. "You will in effect be tipping him off, in case of future difficulty."

"I see," Lord Rothborough said with a smile. "I don't think that will be beyond me."

"That contains a white powder," said Major Vernon, noticing Felix examining the scrap of twisted paper. "Which we can assume is –"

"Arsenic?" said Felix. "I think so, and it is an easy matter to establish." Now he took up the lock of hair. "And this was with the letter?" Major Vernon nodded. "Yes, she must have been a very quick-witted woman to know that hair may be tested for poison as well. All in all, she has made a thorough case against her husband."

"He needs to understand he is in danger from this," said Major Vernon to Lord Rothborough. "He needs to feel the possibility of everything unravelling."

"You think there are other matters to unravel, then?" said Felix.

"Yes, several," said Major Vernon. "Sir Morten Hurrell is by no means the fine old country gentleman he pretends to be, and if we apply the right sort of pressure then his façade will crumble."

"I have no doubt that you will be successful," said Lord Rothborough. "Now let us go, and you can tell me exactly what you want me to do. Felix, I think you should rest."

"Certainly. I'm hoping you might be well enough in a day or two to come with us and confront him, Mr Carswell."

"I shall do my best to recover, then."

Left alone, he slept for some time and woke feeling refreshed. He got out of bed, surprised and relieved to find himself clear-headed, and was just about to ring for Jacob when the door opened and Eleanor came in. She closed the door behind her and stood with her back against it. She said nothing, and for a moment Felix was speechless.

She was dressed for dinner, in a haze of gauze and ribbons, the shoulders extremely low, revealing the gentle curve of her breast, a style that seemed to invite his kisses.

"So you are going down?" he said at last.

"I scarcely dare not to," she said, tweaking at a ringlet. "Lord Rothborough sent me a note insisting."

"Oh, one of those!" Felix said. "I can imagine what that

was like. And impossible to disobey. But he will be pleased to see you. As am I."

"You are?" she said, drifting across the room. "Don't you want to scold me?"

"If you like," said Felix.

"What do you mean?" she said.

"It might make you feel better."

"Or rather, make you feel better," she said. "After all, that is all you want, is it not, a dutiful, obedient little wife, who never questions anything at all? Don't you want to scold me into submission?"

"No! No, absolutely not! How can you think that?"

She did not answer but stood at a little side table, examining the objects upon it as if they were the most interesting things in the world.

"Let us rip up the last few pages," Felix said, remembering all Lord Rothborough and Major Vernon had said to him. "They don't do either of us much credit, Eleanor. If you are with child, then you are, and there is nothing more to be said about it. It is a natural consequence, and I have to accept that, and if I was less than enthusiastic, I apologise. I was startled, that is all, when I ought not to have been. I needed time to adjust my thinking and face up to my new responsibilities."

She turned and looked at him.

"Are you sure?"

"Yes, yes. Now, please will you forgive me?" he said, opening his arms to her. "Please?"

A moment later, she was pressed against him, and they began to embrace.

"Oh, I wish I did not have to go down," she murmured.

"I think you had better," he said.

The ardour of her embrace had begun to stir him, and he could tell from her movements that she too was feeling the warmth of physical longing. Their animal natures were threatening to overwhelm them, as always seemed to be the case. At that moment he knew that he did not want their mutual desire to get the better of them. So he carefully detached himself and kissed her forehead as chastely as he could, and escorted her to the door.

"It does not do to ignore Lord Rothborough's little notes," he said.

"I shall be wretched without you. You must get better soon, Felix. This is all so –" She threw up her hands. "So trying!"

He took her hands and kissed them, and she left, running down the passageway with her ribbons fluttering.

He went back into the room and sat down, feeling exhausted and frustrated. However, he was satisfied that he had managed to resist her charms. It would have been foolish in the extreme to indulge himself.

He was left with a tangible reminder of his own desire and as he wondered what he ought to do with it, he found himself thinking of a book by Sir Astley Cooper. The great man had recounted an experiment on a dog, where by dividing the vas deferens he had prevented the dog, then observed in coitus, from reproducing.

He wanted to consult the book at once, but it lay in a packing case at Hawksby. He tried to remember the details of it, but with little success. What he did recall was that it had seemed a trivial matter, and the dog had not suffered in any way. He remembered even marking the passage for further consideration.

If such a procedure could work on a dog, with no adverse effects on coitus, then perhaps it might work on a man. What if there might be a mild, safe form of surgical castration, which would not affect a man's conjugal relations nor his physical manhood, but in effect render him unable to procreate – would that not be the greatest benefit to human relations? It would be an end to ridiculously large families and all the suffering that caused. How many women would be glad to be freed from the endless pain and trouble of childbearing? The matter might become one of rational choice rather than a wretched lottery. He would gladly submit to an experimental operation for such a universal benefit, assuming he could find a surgeon he trusted to perform it, a man such as Mr Harper. He had the steadiest, neatest and swiftest hand Felix had ever observed at work. However, he was also a fervent evangelical who would, without doubt, find even the suggestion of such a procedure offensive. Felix had no wish to offend the man and found himself wrangling with the difficulties of turning theory into practice on such sensitive matters. Conservative opinion lay not in an unknown mob, but in the hearts of those he cared for. He had already underestimated the force of opposition in his own wife, after all. How on earth could he convince the world, if he could not convince her?

# Chapter Thirty-nine

Three days later, although feeling a little unsteady on his legs, Felix had judged himself sufficiently recovered to accompany Major Vernon into Northminster. When he arrived at Rooke Court, he found himself ushered into a small closet that opened off the drawing room. It was hardly more than a cupboard, with its door cut from the panelling and a cobweb-covered internal window admitting a dim light from the stair beyond.

"Think of it as a box at the theatre with no view," said Major Vernon. "We are lucky to have it, all in all."

And then he pressed his finger to his lips, alerted by the sound of footsteps on the stair.

"Now I think, sir, from all that was said," Lord Rothborough could be heard saying as they came upstairs, "that it was implied that these libellous objects might be found in the drawing room. Your son seemed very convinced of the existence of these objects, and Vernon took him seriously."

"You will excuse me for being so slow, my lord – I am still a little..." This was Sir Morten, sounding hoarse and struggling with his delivery.

"No, forgive me, sir, I had not appreciated your illness had struck you so hard. If I had known I should have delayed this. Here, let me assist you."

"No, no, I can manage a few stairs, my lord, I assure. And I am glad you did inform me, my lord, and I shall be forever in your debt."

"There will be no debt, sir," said Lord Rothborough. "These matters must be controlled. It is as simple as that. There is no hope for order in society if we are not allowed to control these matters to our benefit, for what benefits our interest, is in fact to the interest of all! Now, I suppose the drawing room is through here?"

"Yes," said Sir Morten, and they could be heard coming into the room.

"Ah, what a fine room," said Lord Rothborough. "This old panelling is magnificent. And it looks as if the boards have not been taken up. We are in good time. Allow me, sir? You should sit down. I can easily lift a board or two. I have the very tool. I went to speak to Hudson, my buildings man, about it. He has given me this. What a marvellous thing it is! And he is an excellent man, been with me for twenty years now. But, now, this will amuse you, Sir Morten, he told me he has a connection with Hurrell Place – his sister was in service with you at one time – married now, of course, but he was extremely proud of her having worked for you. In fact – and is this not typical of the best old family servants? – he was at pains to point out to me that if a place came up for him at Hurrell Place, he would gladly take it. And he said this to me, quite frankly! Just to remind me, I suppose, how things really are."

Lord Rothborough laughed at that, but Felix knew that was scarcely his usual laugh, and that his whole manner had become decidedly theatrical.

He turned a fraction, as quietly as he could, feeling both the stiffness of his joints and a sense of unease at being in such a confined place. As he moved, he felt the board beneath his feet wanting to sing out like a canary in a mine, but although he avoided this, he ended with his feet at a strange angle. However, he now had a view of the room through a narrow slit on the side of the door where it hung on its hinges. He could see Lord Rothborough assisting Sir Morten to the window seat and insisting he sit down. Then Lord Rothborough moved out of sight, giving Felix a clear view of Sir Morten.

Even from this distance he could see that Sir Morten looked most unwell, his complexion grey and his expression contorting intermittently. He was clutching discreetly at his belly and he reached for his handkerchief to cover his mouth. Was he retching? Felix pressed his face closer to the chink but it did not help him judge.

There then came the sound of banging and creaking as Lord Rothborough lifted the boards. This was a proceeding Felix had to admit he would like to have seen, for he could not in his wildest imaginings have pictured his Lordship engaged in anything quite so workmanlike.

"About here, sir?" Lord Rothborough was saying.

"Yes," gasped Sir Morten, who looked liable to pass out at any moment.

"Of course, it may be that there is nothing, that your son was giving way to wild fancy. Which I suppose we may say he has done already given that appalling book of his," Lord Rothborough said. "But if there is something, anything, I feel certain you would not wish it to fall into the wrong hands, and be wilfully misinterpreted."

"No..." Sir Morten said, but then made a tremendous groan. He was still clutching his handkerchief to his face and slithered from his seat onto his knees, as his body was racked by spasms. That something was amiss could not be doubted.

"You need help, sir," said Lord Rothborough.

"No, no, I am only a little.. indisposed..." He was now out of sight, but the sound of his throwing up on the floor was evident.

Felix looked across at Major Vernon whose hand was on the latch, holding the cupboard door shut.

"I must –" Felix mouthed and Major Vernon nodded, gently letting go of the latch and letting the door slowly open, just as Lord Rothborough was saying, "We must get you to a doctor, sir."

"No, no, we must keep looking, sir!" Sir Morten said, and

then caught sight of Major Vernon and Felix emerging from the closet. "What the devil...? What is going on?"

He attempted to stand, but his legs would not hold him. There was a pool of bile and blood on the floor and the stench made Felix's own fragile stomach lurch.

"What are you doing here?" said Sir Morten.

"It is as well we are," Felix said. "I think you are unwell."

He tried to approach him, but Sir Morten pushed him away.

"This is outrageous! You have been spying upon us!"

"With good reason," said Major Vernon. "Now, sir, I insist you accept help. We have a great deal to talk about, after all."

Sir Morten looked as if he were going to protest again, but another bout of vomiting overcame him.

"I will go and get help," said Lord Rothborough, going to the door. "We will take him to my house?"

"Yes," said Major Vernon.

Having got hold of Sir Morten's hand, Felix found that his pulse was fading and his hands felt cold. His lips were also cracked and burnt, as if they had been touched by some noxious substance.

"He is extremely ill," said Felix, wondering if Sir Morten had been poisoned. "I really don't think he has much time left."

"Then do your best," Major Vernon said. "Keep him alive as long as you can."

~

All the conveniences of Lord Rothborough's house were lavished on Sir Morten, and Felix did his best to make him comfortable, although it was clear some dire toxin was attacking his system. He was installed in an elegant bedroom, and seemed to have rallied a little, when Major Vernon came in.

"It's good to see that you are a little better, sir," he said, taking a chair to the bedside. "I am glad we shall have the chance to talk."

"About what?" said Sir Morten. "I have nothing to say to you, sir. Your underhand behaviour has seen to that."

"We shall see. I want to talk to you first about my fiancée, Mrs Maitland. She has made a complaint to me about your conduct towards her."

"A complaint?"

"She said that you behaved indecently towards her."

"Indecently? What can she mean?"

"She said that you demanded intimate favours from her, as payment for the reduced rent. With force."

Felix, who was sitting in the corner, could hardly believe what he had heard.

After a pause, Sir Morten said, "The fact is, Major Vernon, charming though the lady is, you only have her word for it that such a thing happened."

"I am to doubt her word, sir?" Major Vernon said.

"You might be disturbed to hear this, given that she is your betrothed, but I found her manner when we were alone together alarming, to say the least. I'm an old man, after all. I do not expect to have eyes made at me or caps thrown for that matter, but I have to say that she did both these. I am sorry to have to tell you this."

Felix wondered how on earth Major Vernon could keep his composure, but he sat calmly and said, "That is distressing to hear, certainly."

"And I regret having to tell you so, Major Vernon. But that is the way of women, I'm afraid. Over the years I have come to the conclusion that one never ought to trust them, no matter how virtuous they seem. They are not as men are."

There was another long silence. Major Vernon appeared to be studying his fingernails.

Sir Morten, who clearly liked the sound of his own voice, went on, "Was she not engaged before to some other man? I think I heard that somewhere."

At this Major Vernon got up. He leant on his chair back, his head bent, almost as if he were riding a painful blow. But then he said, "So I am to take your word that what Mrs Maitland said to me is untrue?"

"Yes," said Sir Morten. "You have my word, sir. Why would I lie? I have nothing to gain. She has a great deal to gain by lying to you. She did not get what she wanted from me and now she wishes to have you punish me by making these accusations. But we shall not let ourselves be confused by her manipulations, shall we?"

"The thing is, Sir Morten," Major Vernon said, taking a few paces up the room, "I find your word to be a dubious thing, and I am disinclined to take it."

"I tell you, she set her cap at me!" said Sir Morten. "And you must not let the lure of bodily passion delude you about her. She is certainly an attractive woman, enough to tempt a man into great folly."

"But not you, sir?" said Major Vernon.

"I am an old man," said Sir Morten. "Those pleasures are long gone. I have no interest in women. None at all. And certainly not Mrs Maitland."

"Then all the details that she gave me, which were not pleasant by any means – am I to dismiss them? They seemed all too plausible to me. I have led a dirty life, you see, Sir Morten, and know what men are capable of. I find it hard to disregard her account as a fiction."

"She has lied to you," Sir Morten said.

"Or you have lied to me?" Major Vernon replied. "After all, this is not the first time you have lied. There is a pattern to this. I asked you if you had visited your son at the Hermitage, and you denied it. Now Mark informs me that you were there, on the morning of Arthur's death, and that you had a long conversation. You discussed the possibility of his going to New Zealand."

"That is what Mark tells you," said Sir Morten, "but given his reputation, I can only think you have a disordered brain to take his word over mine. And again, why would I lie?"

"Because you are arrogant enough to believe that no one would dare question your word. But I do question it. You may be the absolute master of your domain, and no one from the rats in your attics to the fish in your ponds can ever contradict you, but I may. You are not my master, Sir Morten."

"You are a fool to listen to Mark."

"His evidence alone would not have been enough to convince me, although it was compelling. But there was a witness who saw you leave that day. Miss Wytton."

"Who will say anything Mark tells her. She is his mistress – you do understand that? In fact, it is my belief that they killed Arthur between them."

"That's a neat theory," said Major Vernon. "But unfortunately utter nonsense. And as for her being his mistress, and Mark having seduced her – that was only something you invented in order to stop the marriage. You thought Miss Wytton quite unequal to being Lady Hurrell."

"Which events have proved," said Sir Morten. "I understand she has been involved with this terrible business with the bank."

"I do find it interesting that you despised her lineage so much," said Major Vernon after a moment, "given your own choice of bride. Her family were very small people."

"What has my wife to do with this?" said Sir Morten.

"Everything," said Major Vernon. "After all, that was why you were searching the drawing room just now. You were looking for something."

"I don't know what you are talking about."

"Lord Rothborough suggested to you that there might be evidence there, did he not, concerning the circumstances of your late wife's death?"

"I was humouring him. We do humour our great men."

"I think you were concerned to hear there might be something there that cast you in an ill light."

"This is nonsense."

"Then why did you get up from your sick bed and agree to meet with Lord Rothborough? You are a sick man, Sir Morten. This cannot be pleasant for you, but it seems to have been necessary."

"I think you are indulging in fancies, Major Vernon."

"Yesterday I took up the floorboards and discovered a letter from Lady Hurrell addressed to your son Mark. It was dated just before her death and ought to have been posted. But she did not dare trust it to the post, and in the end she pushed it through a crack in the floorboards."

"What nonsense!"

"Yes, it does sound like nonsense, but she was a desperate woman. She had been unjustly accused of adultery – and denied the company of her children. According to this letter, you left her in that house to die, Sir Morten, and furthermore you hastened her death. There was, with her letter, a little paper packet containing a white powder. Mr Carswell informs me that it is arsenic."

"She was a deluded person," said Sir Morten. "And it is entirely in character that she would attempt to defame me from beyond the grave. We were not happy."

"You should have been more careful who you married, then," said Major Vernon.

"Indeed I should," said Sir Morten. "A great beauty, but she brought a curse on my family. She trapped me. That is the best that can be said for it. And she was a whore."

"Am I to take your word for that, too, Sir Morten?"

"This is growing tiresome," said Sir Morten.

"Yes, it is," said Major Vernon. "But I am interested still that you should be so exercised about this letter being found. After all, if your word is so unassailable that you can calmly accuse a woman like Mrs Maitland of telling a shocking untruth, then why should this old letter disturb you? Everyone will believe you because of who you are. But you see, that old assurance of yours, it has been assaulted. Bit by bit, year by year, it is crumbling like the plaster ceilings in that lovely old house where your poor wife, left alone, died in great pain, and with her reputation blackened."

At this, Sir Morten attempted to stir from his bed, but Major Vernon leapt up and stood over him.

"I have not finished."

"Sir –" Sir Morten began, but he seemed overcome with bodily discomfort, and he was forced to lie back on his pillows, grimacing with pain, while Major Vernon continued. He leant over him and spoke softly.

"She did not commit adultery. That was your delusion. She was as good and true a wife as anyone could be, and a loving mother. And a great beauty – such a great beauty that you could not resist her, no matter how low her connections were, no matter how angry your father was at your actions. It killed him, did it not, when he heard what you had done? So you blamed the poor creature you had made your wife, even though she had herself told you she was not fit to be Lady Hurrell."

Sir Morten put up his hands defensively and gasped, "I'm not well, man, for the Lord's sake! For pity's sake!"

"I have very little of that for you, sir," said Major Vernon. "Mr Carswell will help you, but we are not finished."

~

Carswell had struck Giles as still being unsteady on his legs, and so he had sent for additional assistance. This appeared in the august form of Mr Harper from the Infirmary, who came in and at once sent Carswell to rest. He then turned his attention to Sir Morten. When he had finished examining him, he drew Giles to one side and said, quietly, "He is certainly dying. Why are you questioning him, Major Vernon?"

"I believe he has murdered both his son and his wife."

Harper swallowed.

"He has admitted so much?"

"Not to me. I hope he might yet, for the sake of justice."

"For the sake of his soul," said Harper, "I pray that he does."

They went back to the bedside.

"I regret to say you have little time left, sir," said Mr Harper to Sir Morten. "I suggest you use it well. The Lord forgives all those who truly repent of their sins. It is not too late."

Sir Morten rolled his head away, determined not to listen.

"Think of your children, Sir Morten," said Giles, taking a chair close up to the bedside, and using a consciously gentle tone. "You may see them in Heaven if you speak to me now. Think of that."

Sir Morten shook his head, his eyes closed. He was obviously in great pain.

"Your daughters, sir," said Giles. "Those three charming souls. They would wish you to speak now. Mary, Lucy and Jane, yes?" The mention of these names caused Sir Morten to grimace. "What account of yourself will you give them, sir? What will you say to your boys, John and Francis? Or indeed to Arthur?"

"Do not speak of them!" Sir Morten said. "It is as well they died. They were too full of their mother's blood. It's better they are gone."

"Better that they are dead?" said Giles.

"Yes. We were cursed by her. She ruined us all. She ruined my name."

"And that is why you let her die. Why you caused her to die."

"'A good tree bringeth not forth corrupt fruit, neither doth a corrupt tree bring forth good fruit,'" Sir Morten quoted. "I did what had to be done. That is all."

"So you killed Arthur?" Giles pressed on.

There was a long interval. Sir Morten was clearly struggling greatly. His breathing was extremely irregular and he began to retch violently again. When, after some minutes, he was a little calmer, Mr Harper put his hand on Sir Morten's wrist and said, "You are fading, sir. You must prepare for death and the judgement that follows."

"I did what had to be done," said Sir Morten, finding the strength that sometimes comes over the dying in their last moment. He struggled upright, and pulled his hand away from Harper. "I may burn in Hell for it, but I did what I had to! I disobeyed my father when I married that whore, and she ruined my name. Seven children, and five dead, and the two left, to my name, were not worthy of it. They had to go."

"To end the line forever?" Giles said.

"Yes," said Sir Morten, speaking with the greatest difficulty, as convulsions racked his body. "At first I thought only of Mark. After he published that book, I knew he had to be destroyed before he could do any more damage. He was a wretched, wounded beast, mired in his own wickedness and beyond redemption, beyond contempt, indeed. So I planned to dispose of him. But as I did, it came to my attention that Arthur, my dear, sweet boy, was also dangerously infected –"

It seemed that he could not go on, but after a little while, he began again, in a low, hoarse whisper: "He had developed opinions of which I could not approve – appalling opinions. He was preparing to leave the Church and go to Rome, and take orders in the Catholic Church!"

Sir Morten broke off, groaning now in pain, and writhing under the bedclothes in the most alarming fashion. At length he managed to steady himself and said, "He confessed it to me!" The words came out as if he were spitting nails, and he collapsed again.

"So you decided to kill him?" Giles said.

Glassy-eyed with pain, Sir Morten looked up at him and nodded.

"I did," he said. "I had no choice."

"So you went to the old chapel, where you knew he would be praying, and stabbed him with an arrow?"

Sir Morten sank back on his pillows.

"Yes."

"And why did you choose an arrow? Because you knew that Mark had been hunting in the woods, that he had brought down a hind. You wanted to make it seem as if Mark was responsible. You had decided to exploit the quarrels between the brothers, to contrive it so it looked as if they had destroyed each other. You planted the arrow and the blood-stained smock in the Hermitage so that it would seem that Mark was guilty."

"I wanted –" Sir Morten said, and then took a great breath. "I wanted to see him hang. And by God, I still do!"

"Sir Morten, I beg you," said Mr Harper, "think before you speak. You have so little time."

"Be quiet!" said Sir Morten. "I shall not have a dissenter preaching over me! I did what was necessary. That is an end to it!"

He began to cough blood, which turned into a violent paroxysm from which it was clear there could be no recovery. Ten minutes later, he was dead.

~

Carswell returned from his rest to confer with Harper over the body.

"Arsenic poisoning, without a doubt," Carswell said. "There was a mass of undigested arsenic in his vomit. But who would do that to him?"

"I have an idea," Giles said.

# Chapter Forty

"You do not wish to see Sir Morten?" Mrs Hurrell said.

"No, just you, ma'am," said Major Vernon.

"As you wish. Do sit down."

They had been shown into a little room where she was sitting sewing by the window.

"I'm afraid I have bad news," said Major Vernon. "Sir Morten died this morning."

She gave a gasp, her hand flying to her breast.

"No!"

"The manner of his death has raised some serious questions."

"He has been ill – with the fever."

"Yes, certainly he has been ill, but that was not the cause of it. Two medical men, Mr Harper from the Infirmary and Mr Carswell here, have both confirmed that he was poisoned."

"Oh, dear Lord!"

"Now perhaps you could help us, ma'am? When was Sir Morten first taken ill?"

"Oh, I am not sure, really."

"But you have been nursing him."

"Yes."

"So can you say when it came over him?"

"Does it matter so much?" she said.

"Yes," said Major Vernon, "I'm afraid so. You see, we have to establish how it might have happened."

"I will try and assist you, but – oh dear, I'm not sure. It was about a week or so ago, but the details escape me. Please forgive me. This is such a shock, I can hardly think straight! Oh, poor Sir Morten. I hope he did not suffer too much. Did he?"

"I'm afraid it was not a comfortable passing for him," said Major Vernon. "However, he is in God's hands now."

"Yes, yes, so we must pray. I must tell the boys. It is really –"

"I think that might wait, ma'am," said Major Vernon. "There are a few more questions I must ask, I'm afraid. Sir Morten has been murdered, after all."

There was a silence, and then she nodded, and made a gesture for him to continue. But Felix noticed that she could not meet his gaze.

"I understand that Sir Morten was in the habit of dining alone when there was no company?" Major Vernon said.

"Yes," said Mrs Hurrell.

"And he liked to have his dinner brought to him in his study."

"Yes."

"And that this task fell to you. Of serving him his dinner."

"Yes, it did."

"Although this house has so many servants? Why was the mistress of the house forced to serve dinner to her brother-in-law?"

"I was glad to do it," said Mrs Hurrell.

"Although it meant you had to wait for your own dinner, which you then ate alone, with not even your sons to keep you company? They were not allowed to join you."

"They are not old enough to dine downstairs," she said. "Why are you asking me about this?"

"Because I'm astonished you stood for such treatment, ma'am. When Mrs Maitland told me this was the usual habit of the house –"

"She told you this?" said Mrs Hurrell, stiffening. "How did she know?"

"She was concerned for your welfare. She felt you were

unhappy, and spoke to the servants."

There was a little silence and Mrs Hurrell said, "She has been telling you tales, Major Vernon! She is a wicked woman – I hate to say it, but better late than never. She was shockingly forward with Sir Morten. She set her cap at him. Fortunately Sir Morten had better sense."

"And he told you that, I suppose? Perhaps when you were serving him his soup one day. I hope he let you sit down when he ate, Mrs Hurrell."

"Of course!" she said. "What strange ideas you have, Major Vernon!"

"So what exactly did he say to you about my fiancée, Mrs Hurrell?"

"That she had – oh, I do not like to tell you this, it will distress you."

"You have already been quite blunt," said Major Vernon. "Tell me what he said."

"He said that she was a fine woman but rather warm in her manner. He thought that she fancied being Lady Hurrell – a favour which he would never grant."

"Never?" said Major Vernon. "Are you sure about that? After all, she is handsome, and her family connections are excellent. She is certainly his equal in position, if not in fortune. And she is not beyond childbearing. What an ornament to this house and his old age a woman like that might be! Of course, I'm partial to her charms and it doesn't take a great deal for me to imagine another man taking note of them."

"It sounds as if you are a little jealous, sir," said Mrs Hurrell.

"Ah yes, the green-eyed monster – a dangerous thing, certainly. Perhaps you felt that yourself, each time Sir Morten cast a glad eye over some attractive woman?"

"Why should I feel jealous?" she said after a moment.

"Because of what you are to him. You have been more to

him than a sister-in-law."

"I don't know what you mean," said Mrs Hurrell.

"You are still young, Mrs Hurrell, and handsome," said Major Vernon. "It's strange that you have stayed here, a widow."

"I have never had any wish to marry again. And why would I need to? I have all I need here, and my boys are being brought up in their father's old home. That is enough for me."

"Your late husband did not leave you enough to live independently, though," Major Vernon said. "You were forced to come here and take Sir Morten's charity. And there have been conditions attached to that charity. Not merely having to serve him his dinner?"

There was a long silence but Mrs Hurrell said nothing, wrapping her arms about herself.

Major Vernon went on gently. "I know that Sir Morten was a man with particular appetites, Mrs Hurrell. I suspect that you have been made to pay a high price for your board and lodging." Mrs Hurrell pulled her arms around her more tightly and looked resolutely down. "Is that not so?"

She was shaking now, and tears rolled down her face. She began to rock back and forth to soothe herself.

"What else was I to do?" she said at last. "That first time, when he came into my bedroom, he said he meant to comfort me for the loss of my husband. He was grieving too. He said we ought to comfort one another. That there was no harm in it, and although I did not want that sort of attention..."

"You got it anyway?"

Now she looked up and gazed over at Major Vernon, her face glossy with tears.

"Yes."

"And he was a large, strong man so you could not refuse him?"

"No," said Mrs Hurrell. "No, I could not. It just had to be borne, you must understand me, I had no choice! I was with child twice from it, and that was my fault, he said, and then I lost them and that was my fault too. I could do nothing right. And all the time it was never enough. He was always carping and threatening. He said he would send my boys away, put them into trades, that they would never get anything from him unless I behaved better towards him. That he would tell them that I was wicked and immoral for allowing him to do what he did. And so it went on and on, until he met your fiancée, Major Vernon, and then, how he was taken with her! Oh my, he would not stop singing her praises! He was set on marrying her, and getting her with child, and then I would be put out entirely, so he said. All I could look forward to was a cottage on the estate if I was lucky, and my boys sent off to New Zealand so they would never see me again, and so... I had to do something!"

"Of course," said Major Vernon. "It had all become intolerable. So what did you do, ma'am?"

She shook her head. "I cannot tell you."

"You must. Everything will be better if you tell me now. You cannot carry this burden, Mrs Hurrell. What did you do when he threatened to send your boys away?"

She hesitated, and then said in a tiny voice, "I got some rat poison."

"Where from?"

"The housekeeper keeps it locked up in a cupboard in her room, but I have all the keys so there was no difficulty. And I put a little in his soup, very little, but it was enough to make him ill."

"When was this?"

"A day or so after Arthur was killed. I was surprised how well it worked. And for the first time in years I felt happy because I had struck back, and I thought, why did I not do this years ago? Why?" She had spread open her hands towards them. "I thought that then I could be free, and so I continued. This morning he asked for a bowl of gruel. It was so very simple. I sat and watched him eat it and thought how I would soon be free of him forever." She rose from her chair, and walked across the room to the window. "But now you are here and I know I will never be free!" She began to cry again and sank onto her knees, and seemed to be praying, her elbows resting on the window seat.

"What will you do?" Felix said to Major Vernon. They had gone out into the hall. "She has saved the hangman a job."

"I cannot arrest her," Major Vernon said. "I don't have the authority, but I shall have to tell Lazenby. Dear God, that will stick in my throat. Perhaps if..." They went back into the room.

"Mrs Hurrell?" said Major Vernon.

She got up from her knees and turned slowly back to him.

"You understand that I cannot keep what you have said to us in confidence?"

"Yes," she said.

"I would suggest you talk to Captain Lazenby, in the presence of a solicitor. I can recommend a good man. Tell him what you have told me. It is for him to decide how to proceed. It will be better for you if you are straight with him. A full confession is always looked on well by a judge."

She closed her eyes and nodded.

At this moment, there was a rap at the door and Lewis, the younger of her boys, came dashing into the sitting room, carrying a basket. He had a triumphant look on his face.

"Look, Mama, the first plums are ready. Parkinson just gave them to me to give to you! I have only eaten two but Morten had three! Why are you crying?"

# Chapter Forty-one

"You contrived this meeting with Sir Morten, then?" Captain Lazenby said.

"Yes," said Major Vernon.

"With the greatest respect, Major Vernon, have you understood nothing I have said to you recently?"

"Yes, perfectly. This is why I am being so frank with you now."

"In the hope I will show mercy?"

"No, I have little hope of that. I only wanted to make sure the record was straight and the facts clear. Events overtook us, as Mr Carswell has pointed out. I know I ought not to have questioned him, strictly speaking –"

"No, you ought not."

"It was not my intention to do so. I had other business to discuss with him, but when he was taken so violently ill, it seemed the only path to pursue, for the sake of justice."

"And do you think by being so frank I might overlook this?"

"No, I do not expect anything of the sort."

Lazenby picked up the account of the affair that Major Vernon had written out for him, gazed at it for a moment and then laid it down again.

"And Mrs Hurrell is sitting downstairs with a solicitor. I have you to thank for that as well, I take it?" Lazenby said.

"I advised her to come and talk to you."

"And it was definitely arsenic administered by her hand that is responsible for his death?" Lazenby said, turning to Felix.

"Without doubt," said Felix.

Lazenby shook his head and walked to the window.

"This is all most unfortunate," he said after a moment. "It would be a great deal easier on everyone if you were perhaps to consider pursuing a different occupation, Major Vernon. Then you might leave here without fuss, without any scandal attached to your name."

"I stand by what I did," Major Vernon said. "And I would rather fight for my position, if you don't mind, inconvenient though it might be. I will take the risk of being dismissed, but I should like to give my side of the matter first."

"As you wish," said Lazenby. "I will initiate disciplinary proceedings and notify you in due course. Was there anything else?"

"No," said Major Vernon, and with that they took their leave.

"Do you think you might –" Felix began as they walked down the corridor.

"Lose my post? I have no idea, but I will take the risk. I really have no choice. I need the money. I do not want to present myself as a penniless bridegroom."

"I don't suppose Mrs Maitland would mind."

"No. She threatened to give German lessons to keep me."

"A fine plan," said Felix. "You might have little cards printed and put them up in shop windows."

Major Vernon laughed. "Yes, she would certainly do that! However, I would rather she did not, so I must stay and fight this one out."

"Lord Rothborough was wondering if he could not get Lazenby sent off somewhere. India, perhaps?"

"Ah yes, one of those promotions that are nothing of the kind. That would be a little cruel. Especially on Mrs Lazenby and the children."

"But he is being such a –" Felix broke off. They had reached the door and outside he could see Eleanor's carriage. The top was down, and she was sitting, waiting for him. "Can we drive you anywhere?"

"No, thank you," said Major Vernon. "You are going home to rest?"

"Yes, as ordered," said Felix. "But we are going to Ardenthwaite. You will come and see us?"

"Certainly, and soon."

They went outside. Felix got in beside Eleanor, and they drove off.

"You see, I was not late," he said. "Major Vernon was very to the point in the meeting."

"And did it go well?"

"Not entirely. He still may lose his post. We must do something, but what?" He sank back on the seat, feeling the exhaustion of his illness in both his limbs and his mind. He needed to think, but he could not. Instead his eye fell on the pile of parcels on the seat opposite.

"You've been busy," he said. He was glad to see she had amused herself.

"Yes, there are some nice shops here – almost as nice as Edinburgh's. And all the shop men are so kind!"

"Of course they are – to you," said Felix.

"I bought a beautiful piece of old lace," she went on. "There is a shop up by the Minster full of the most delightful old things – Mr Lipscombe's. Do you know him?"

"Oh yes," Felix said. "Lipscombe is quite the antiquarian."

"The lace is seventeenth century," she said. "I have never seen anything like it. Oh, and he had some candlesticks which would look very well in the drawing room at Ardenthwaite, so he may bring them out for me to see them in place. And I asked him about tapestries."

"Tapestries! Why?"

"I want some for my dressing room. Remember the ones at Holyrood, in Mary, Queen of Scots' closet? Something like that. Mr Lipscombe knew exactly what I meant. He is a great

Jacobite, you know."

On their wedding journey they had visited all the famous spots in Edinburgh, but it was Holyrood and the romantic chambers of Mary, Queen of Scots that had enchanted Eleanor the most. He remembered her charming, awestruck enthusiasm as they had toured the rooms, and how he had stolen a kiss or two on the tightly twisting turnpike stair, near where the unfortunate Rizzio had been murdered. Afterwards they had walked in the ruined cloisters and he had wondered at that moment if he would ever be as happy again, with her leaning on his arm, gazing up at the ribbed vaults, the Edinburgh air bringing such brightness to her complexion. Now she had the same look, her bonnet framing her face so elegantly. Her hand had slipped into his as they drove through the town. "I think Northminster has a great deal more to recommend it than I first thought," she said. "Perhaps we should take a house in the Precincts. That would be convenient for you, would it not?"

"Yes," he said. "And you could make Lipscombe a rich man. But you will probably do that anyway."

"He does have the most lovely things," she said.

"We should look there for a wedding present for Major Vernon and Mrs Maitland. I don't know what, though. Lipscombe cannot sell us Captain Lazenby's resignation."

"What do you mean?"

"Lazenby is being unreasonable. A man in his position ought to see that there are situations when one cannot play by the rules. There were lives at stake. What else could he have done?"

"Oh," said Eleanor. "I'm sure it can all be sorted out. Surely Lord Rothborough will do something?"

"He will certainly try, as will I. I do not at all like the idea of going on here without him!"

"I suppose not. Even if he does set one on curious tasks," she said.

"Do you mean Stockholm?" Felix said after a moment. It was not a topic he particularly wished to raise.

She gave a sigh. "I was so certain it must mean something."

"You were right," he said. "It did. It just wasn't a cipher."

"Perhaps I may be more useful to him in the future."

"I think that very likely," Felix said. "He does not like any of his friends to be idle."

~

Giles met Emma by arrangement in the Minster Precincts, and together they walked over to Rooke Court.

She looked up at him questioningly.

"So was anything decided?"

"Not in any real sense. There will be an enquiry of some sort. He suggested I fall on my sword and I declined to do so."

"Quite right," she said.

He glanced up at the front of the house.

"There is a chance," he said, gesturing towards Rooke Court, "that what we want may become impossible."

"Yes, I know," she said, taking his arm, "but I am sure that once the facts are laid out it will be clear enough to any intelligent person that there was no misconduct on your part. Allow me to have faith in your vindication, please."

"But if that is not enough –"

"I will bear whatever misfortune comes my way. It will be an honour to do without for your sake. But let us not plan for disaster, but for success! Justice will take your part. She must, when you have been her devoted, obedient servant."

"You should not talk to me like this," he said. "I would do better for being scolded."

"Then I shall take you to task for being a pessimist, Giles

Vernon," she said, breaking free of him and going to open the hand gate. It creaked and groaned. "Another job to be done," she said.

They went up the path and found the front door open.

"Mr Hopkins?" Giles called out as they went into the hall. They had arranged to meet him there.

There was the sound of footsteps on the stairs, and Mark Hurrell appeared.

"Oh, good morning, Mr Hurrell," Emma said. "Forgive me – Sir Mark."

"I don't know if I shall ever get used to that," said Sir Mark, shaking her hand. "Ma'am, it is good to see you, and you, sir. Hopkins said you were looking over the place today. I wanted to speak to you both about it. Shall we go up?"

So they followed him upstairs. He went into the drawing room with the echo, and Giles would have followed, but Emma caught his arm and stopped him on the threshold.

"Perhaps he does not want to let it to us," said Emma in a whisper. "After what happened to his mother here, perhaps he wishes to keep it for himself."

"That is perfectly within his rights," Giles said.

She gave a rueful smile and said, "Of course it is."

"It may be for the best," he said. She sighed at that but also nodded, and they went into the room together. Giles was glad to see that the floor had been scrubbed and the boards nailed back down.

"I understand you came to some agreement with my father about an improving lease," Sir Mark said.

"Yes, we exchanged letters to that effect, but we did not sign any formal documents," Giles said. "Which is just as well. My future is somewhat uncertain. I may not be able to go through with the tenancy, at least not in the short term."

"But we still like the house a great deal," said Emma. "Might you consider holding it for us until we know we can afford it? But that is a most unreasonable thing to ask of you."

"Nothing you could ask of me is unreasonable, Mrs Maitland," Sir Mark said. "I am already profoundly in your debt."

"You are?" said Emma.

"You have given good counsel to someone I value above my own life. Maria has told me how much your wisdom and kindness have helped her, and in helping her, you have helped me. And as for you, sir," he said, turning to Giles, "I do not know how I can begin to thank you. Had it not been for your genius, I would surely be facing the noose, and instead I have been given a new life and the possibility of more happiness than I deserve. That is why I wanted to see you both. At first, I thought I would make you a gift of the property, but I find I cannot – it is tied up in the entail. But I can make you a gift of the repairs, and the rent can be a peppercorn."

"Goodness," said Emma. "Just a peppercorn?" Sir Mark nodded. "Should it not be a golden peppercorn?"

"A common peppercorn once a year will be sufficient, ma'am. And for my part, I will try to be a good landlord. I have a great deal to learn in that respect, but Lord Rothborough has promised to help me. He came and told me the news about my father – and –" He shook his head. "I do not deserve such kindness. And he is willing to consider that, at some point, Lady Maria and I may – and it seems that she – but that is all in the future. There is a great deal to be seen to before then. My aunt and my nephews, in the first instance."

"How are the boys?" Emma said.

"Fragile," he said. "They have had their share of cruelty from my father, and this is another wound. I am all they have now since their mother – well, no one knows what will happen with her. They keep asking me what will happen, and I have no good answer."

"Her prompt confession should have some effect on her sentence," Giles said. "And a good defence barrister. Given what she suffered, there are some grounds for compassion."

"I will get the best man I can for her," Sir Mark said. "And in the meantime I must be father and mother to them. It is a great responsibility."

"Perhaps it is a burden you will be able to share soon enough," said Emma. "If, as you say, Lord Rothborough is willing –"

"If Lady Maria is willing! It is a great deal for her to take on. I will be trouble enough, I dare say."

"Oh, we women like trouble, I assure you, Sir Mark," said Emma. "Adversity makes heroines of us, which makes you gentlemen admire us all the more! An excellent result, yes?" she added, smiling at Giles.

"A peppercorn sounds entirely reasonable to me," Giles said, going to shake his hand. "Thank you, sir."

"I hope you will be happy here," Sir Mark went on. "My mother would be glad to see happiness here. Her disposition was a cheerful one, despite everything that was inflicted on her. She loved nothing better than good humour and music." He went to the wall where Giles had first discovered the echo, and caressed it with his hand. "If she chooses to haunt you, it will be out of goodwill, I am sure."

Emma went to his side and laid her hand on the young man's arm, and said, "Then you must come here often and see if you can glimpse her. Yes?"

"With great pleasure, ma'am. Now, about the repairs, where should we begin? Perhaps you might show me the most pressing problems and I can get the work in hand as soon as possible."

"The kitchen is the worst offender," Emma said.

Sir Mark offered Emma his arm and they went off together, leaving Giles alone in the drawing room. For a moment he doubted what had happened. To be offered such a house, set to rights, and for so little – it meant that if he had lost his post, they would have enough to live on, and in a plain sort of comfort that would exactly suit them. They would have fruit from the garden and excellent neighbours, whom they could entertain, albeit modestly by the standards of Holbroke or even his sister's house; but with enough elegance to satisfy the obligations of hospitality. Emma would not be reduced to giving German lessons, and he would – well, what would he do? That was a question he had scarcely considered and one that he found in that moment he did not like in the least. The thought of enforced idleness was most unpleasant. How on earth was he to do without the thrill of the hunt?

"Giles?" Emma had come back to the drawing room. "Are you coming?"

"Yes," Giles said.

"Sir Mark is talking about new kitchen ranges. I'm worried he will be too extravagant. He has no notion of money, never having had any before!" She stretched out her hand to him and he took it, and kissed it. "You look worried."

"I was thinking about work."

"You mean doing without it?"

"How did you guess?"

She smiled.

"Because I know you rather well now," she said. "And you must not fret. They will never let you go. How could they? We have no one else of your genius. There would be a public outcry, a campaign in The Bugle, at least. We need our gentleman rat-catcher. It will not happen. You will not lose your post!"

"I had better get myself a velvet coat, then," said Giles, laughing. "Gentleman rat-catcher indeed."

"And a squashed hat with tails on it," Emma said. "Come now, sir! Kitchen ranges! We need your opinion." With which he was hauled off to the kitchen.

# Chapter Forty-two

"Thank God you are here! Do you know who else is coming?" Felix said, a few days later, on being shown into a private dining room at The Blue Boar and finding Major Vernon drying himself by the fire. The weather had settled into a weary period of heavy rain.

Major Vernon shook his head.

"I am glad to see you here. When Lazenby asked me to dine with him, I was a little curious, to say the least."

"Ditto," said Felix.

"How are things at Ardenthwaite?"

"Damp," said Felix. "The place is riddled with it. I had not noticed it before. I suppose it is this awful weather. We are back at Hawksby, and thank goodness! Eleanor was getting a cough to match my own." He sat down by the fire. "I should not have come out, but his message was very strange."

"Yes, quite," said Major Vernon.

"Perhaps he wishes to pour oil on the waters," said Felix, taking a glass of wine from the table where the claret sat waiting.

"One can but hope, but it seems unlikely."

At this moment, the door opened and the Captain came in.

"Forgive me, I am late. This ridiculous weather – where has this rain come from?"

"I think Northminster has a peculiar and appalling climate all of its own," Felix said. "I have never lived anywhere where the weather was so... excessive."

"Yes, yes, indeed, Mr Carswell. That is quite the word," said Lazenby, handing his wet overcoat to the waiter, and then sitting down to pull off his gaiters. "I'm glad to see you have made yourselves comfortable. I hope the wine is to your taste. I was not sure what to order. I fear I do not have your discernment."

"It is only Major Vernon who has any discernment," said Felix. "At least about wine."

"And I only know what scraps I do from my brother-in-law."

"Ah yes, Canon Fforde. A most impressive gentleman," said Lazenby.

"I think you should try it for yourself, Captain," said Major Vernon, pouring a glass for Lazenby.

"Thank you," said Lazenby.

"How is Mrs Lazenby?" Major Vernon enquired. "And the children?"

"Oh, very well, thank you, sir, or at least as well as can be expected with this weather. It seems to set everyone sniffing. I have had to call out Mr Peterson twice."

"Nothing serious, I hope?" said Major Vernon.

"No, no, nothing, but one can never tell. Children can be so fragile. We have been very lucky, of course, in general."

Felix drank down his wine, refilled his glass and wondered if this conversation was going to encompass the health of the pet mice in the Lazenby household. He knew he ought to weigh in with his professional opinion of the prevailing winds and children's chests, but he did not feel like exerting himself. He felt sour and awkward.

Dinner was brought in and they sat down to eat it. It was by no means a comfortable meal.

Conversation was kept up with a forced good cheer that struck Felix as utterly ridiculous, but Lazenby seemed determined on it. He asked a great many questions about Scotland and its customs, about kilts and dirks and the composition of Highland regiments.

Having no ready answer, Felix changed tack.

"Have you read Oliver Truro's latest novel?" he said. "My wife and I have been devouring it."

"By your damp hearth?" Major Vernon said.

"It added a great deal to the drama, I think, to hear the rain lashing at the casements," said Felix. "It is impossible to guess how the story will go."

In fact, it had been most useful in keeping up Eleanor's spirits. She had discovered soon after they arrived at Ardenthwaite that she was not, after all, with child. It had cost Felix a great deal to hide his own relief, while her grief had made her irritable. Truro's new novel had brought a welcome distraction for them both.

"There is nothing in it one might object to for the family circle?" said Lazenby.

"Nothing at all," Felix said. "In fact, my only complaint would be that the women are a little too good."

"That is my objection to his writing," said Major Vernon. "He does not seem to know what real women are like, or for some reason cannot capture them on the page."

"As some artists cannot paint cats," Felix said, refilling his glass, and realising as he did so that the bottle was now empty. He also realised he had drunk more than Lazenby and the Major. He pushed his glass away, determined to pace himself.

"I don't quite understand," said Lazenby.

"There is a pair of curious old French paintings at Hawksby," said Felix, "where everything in them is beautifully painted except the cats, which are ugly beasts that look nothing like real felines. It has been puzzling me."

"We all have our blind spots," said Major Vernon, "surely?"

"Speaking of which," said Lazenby. He got up from the table and went over to the fire. "You gentlemen will be wondering why I have asked you here tonight. In ordinary circumstances, of course, we ought to be on regular dining terms, for the sake of *corps d'esprit*, and I think it was an oversight of mine not to initiate something of this kind. Catherine, my wife, said that I ought to break bread with you, that I had been keeping myself unnecessarily apart and that had made me –" He broke off and looked down at the fire. "She is a very wise woman. I wonder what Mr Truro would make of her. She is quite the heroine."

There was a quiver of emotion in Lazenby's voice that Felix found excruciating.

"I think we need some more wine," said Felix. "Port, perhaps?"

"I think not," said Major Vernon. "You were saying, sir?"

"The thing is, sir," Lazenby said, "I have erred. It is Catherine who has made me see my faults – towards you in particular. She has been an inspiration."

"Then let us toast the ladies!" said Felix, taking up his glass and attempting to change the tone entirely. "You like Scottish customs, Captain, so let us send for some more claret and drink their health decently!"

"I don't think Captain Lazenby is in the mood for toasts, Mr Carswell," said Major Vernon. "Please go on, sir."

"Thank you, Major Vernon," said Lazenby, adjusting his stance, rather as if he were about to give testimony of his salvation at a dissenting house altar rail. "I went to Axworth. I felt I should see the situation for myself. It was an interesting – no, a shocking experience, but my mind was still set against your actions, despite all I heard and saw there. So I went home, and naturally my dear Catherine asked about what I had seen. She had heard rumours of the gravity of the situation there and so I told her all that had happened. And her words – my angel's words – were: 'how fortunate that Major Vernon is so quick witted and Mr Carswell so dedicated. You are lucky to have such colleagues.' And of course, I pointed out the difficulties in the situation, but she would not be moved and she told me, with the greatest respect, that having seen the evidence with my own eyes, I ought not to judge you so harshly, indeed, that I ought not to judge you at all."

"I see," said Major Vernon.

"I prayed about it, and the answer was clear enough. My wife was right and I had made a grave and hasty mistake about your actions. There are indeed situations where we must act unconventionally."

"So you are dropping the inquiry?" said Felix.

"Yes, yes, I am. And I hope you will return to your post forthwith, Major Vernon. There is certainly a great deal to be done, and it is not easy to replace you."

"Hear, hear!" exclaimed Felix and downed the last of his wine. "That is worth a toast, surely?"

"Too late for me," said Major Vernon. "And I think Captain Lazenby might prefer to go and see all is well at home."

"Yes, indeed," said Captain Lazenby, and after a round of hasty goodbyes, he departed.

"That I hardly expected," said Major Vernon, sitting down by the fire.

"It's splendid news," said Felix. "And I like him better for it. Although" – and now he could not help laughing – "that was awkward."

"Yes, what a mortification for him!" Major Vernon said. "I am not sure I should have managed that."

"Given you never do anything wrong, it must be unimaginable for you," said Felix. "For the rest of us flawed mortals, we are quite used to humbling ourselves."

"Not at all true," said Major Vernon, smiling. Then he rubbed his face and said, "But I am grateful to him. I had no idea what I was going to do with myself. Idleness is no pleasure for me."

"I know what you mean. Mr Harper will not let me go back to work yet. It is quite ridiculous."

"He knows what he is about."

"He is in league with Lord Rothborough – it's a sinister

development," said Felix. "Are we sure there is no more wine?"

"You talk as if you are deprived."

"I have to restrain myself with ladies in the house," said Felix, leaning forward and stirring up the fire. "But it is probably just as well that I keep my wits about me."

"Certainly," said Major Vernon. "You never know what may happen next. Just like one of Truro's novels!"

# Epilogue

## September

"A great success, Mr Carswell," said Lady Blanchfort. "You must be pleased."

"It does seem to be going well," said Felix, watching as the floor filled up for the first waltz after supper.

It had been Eleanor's idea to throw a ball at Hawksby to celebrate the marriage of Major Vernon to Mrs Maitland. When she first proposed it, he had wondered if this would be quite the thing, as the wedding was to be a quiet affair. Nor had he, at that point, been much in the mood for dancing, still feeling the full languor of his convalescence. But as the day had approached, his health had improved, and when Major Vernon and Mrs Maitland had expressed their own delight at the idea, Eleanor's ball had become less an object of dread and more something to anticipate.

Now, after a lavish and lively supper, they had returned to the large drawing room which made a perfect ballroom. The musicians were retuning their instruments and the order was set for more dancing. Eleanor was walking down the room with Lord Milburne, encouraging everyone to stand up. Dressed in pale gold, with gilded ears of wheat, grape leaves and indeed grapes in her hair, she looked like the presiding goddess of the harvest, descended from Olympia to do the honours of the night.

"Would you like to dance, ma'am?" Felix said, remembering himself.

Lady Blanchfort considered a moment.

"Yes, why not? After all, I have been a widow for six months now. No one would consider it improper to dance with my own son-in-law in a private house, would they?"

"In my opinion, it would be improper if you didn't," Felix said. "I cannot comprehend our mourning customs sometimes, especially for women. We stray too close to those barbaric customs in India where widows must throw themselves on the pyre."

"Hardly," said Lady Blanchfort. "A little decorous seclusion is not comparable. And in my case, since I was not a good wife, I can at least attempt to be a good widow."

He was surprised by such a frank admission.

"But you will still dance?"

"I must, since you insist, Mr Carswell."

"Felix," said Felix.

"As you wish, Felix," she said with a smile, and took his hand. "Eleanor looks very well tonight, given her disappointment of a few weeks ago. It's good she had this to occupy her."

"But you don't think it a disappointment?" Felix said.

"I was too young at one and twenty. You must be careful."

"That is my –" Felix could not go on as the music had begun and the business of their dance must start. As he put his arms around her and they began to waltz, he realised quite why the dance was considered so shocking in some circles. There was an intimacy here that he had not anticipated. He felt both alarmed and, to his shame, a little excited by it, especially as they began to turn and turn about in the rapid movements demanded of the dance. She was so like Eleanor, the same rare, pale, red-headed beauty, and yet she was unlike her. Her maturity piqued him in a way he knew it should not. What had she meant when she said she had not been a good wife? That implied a great many sins, and he found himself imagining the most lurid ones. He had drunk a great deal of champagne and the heat of the ballroom and the feverish, repetitive motion of the waltz was beginning to have a curious effect on him. That she was enjoying the dance struck him too. He did not think he had ever seen her so unburdened, and at the end of it, she was breathless and smiling, with a lock of hair trailing down her cheek in a careless and most appealing fashion.

"Dear me!" she said, flicking open her black lace fan and turning a little from him. "That was rather fast."

He led her from the floor in the direction of the open window. "Thank you, though. That was most agreeable." She caught her breath, and added, "What were you going to say before we began?"

"That I am being careful. As you suggest."

"Not the easiest undertaking," she said.

"No," he said, thinking of all the nights of late when he had been obliged to resist Eleanor's charms. His convalescence was reaching the stage at which it no longer served as an excuse.

She leant a little closer and clasped his hand for a moment.

"If you find yourself in difficulty," she said in a whisper, "please do not hesitate to seek my help, Felix. I wish only to be a friend to you."

Then suddenly she had gone, slipping away into the crowd, leaving him wondering whether she meant what his disorderly, frustrated mind thought she meant, as Eleanor approached. She was glowing from the exercise and patting her wheat ears back into place.

"How nice of you to take pity on Mama," she said. "I am surprised she agreed to it."

"There was no pity involved," Felix said. "She is a good dancer. Almost as good as her daughter." At this Eleanor sank down in a deep, playful curtsey, like a ballerina acknowledging her audience. Felix hauled her back to her feet and said, "I don't suppose you have a single dance left for your husband?"

"No. I am completely engaged. Who would have thought this neighbourhood could muster so many excellent men to dance with? I'm astonished!"

"And so few unmarried girls. How did you manage that?"

"There are plenty of those and they all have had their chances. If the gentlemen prefer me, then –" she shrugged. "I must say, it is the most agreeable thing in the world to give a ball rather than simply go to one. We ought to make a habit of it. This room is perfect for dancing. In fact, if we were to knock down the wall between the morning room and that funny little room next door, we might get another nice drawing room out of it, where we could set up the card tables and so forth."

"And charge a shilling for admission like the Northminster Assemblies?"

"No, of course not. Ah, here is Mr Gray for his galop!" she said, turning to the young man who was approaching them.

This Mr Gray was the younger brother of Mr Gray at Raythorpe, whom he much resembled. He was a barrister, down from London on a visit.

"I feel hesitant to claim it, Mrs Carswell," he said, "seeing you here with your husband."

"Oh, Mr Carswell doesn't mind," said Eleanor, taking Gray's hand.

"Thank you," said Gray, more to Felix than to Eleanor. "Oh, and I have a message for you, sir, from my nephew. He hopes you will come for his sixth birthday."

"Certainly."

"His mother was convinced he would never walk without a limp," said Gray. "But he will be ready for a dancing master soon enough, thanks to your husband, Mrs Carswell."

"I only began the work. It is Mr Harper who finished it," Felix said. His illness had prevented him visiting Johnny as much as he would have wanted, and Mr Harper, with his infinite kindness, had taken over the case. He had improvised a most ingenious, light-weight frame that the child was able to bear with much more equanimity, with a result that he had recovered more quickly than anyone could have hoped.

"It is a shame not to see Mr Harper here tonight," Gray said.

"He does not dine and he certainly does not dance," Eleanor said. "He takes his goodness too far. I feel sorry for his wife."

"I think she is quite in agreement with him," Felix said. "But if she wished to go out, he would – and put aside his principles for her."

"A model husband, then!" said Eleanor with an arch smile. "Come, Mr Gray, the dance is starting. We must get to our places."

~

"How old is Lady Blanchfort?" Emma asked.

"About our age," said Giles.

They had sought a brief refuge from the ballroom in a cool little anteroom after an energetic waltz. Emma's cheeks were delightfully flushed and matched the roses that patterned her gown. As they sat down together, Giles found himself wishing he might take her straight upstairs and at last make her completely his wife.

"She makes an alluring widow, don't you think? She suits the weeds."

"Do you think she might be looking for a husband?" said Giles.

"Oh, certainly. But since I have taken the only suitable one for fifty miles about," said Emma, "she must sit and pine. For a long time, as well, for where and whenever will anyone appear who is your equal?"

"She did not look as if she were sitting and pining when she was waltzing with Mr Carswell."

"No, she did not. I had better keep Charles away from her. He is always falling in love these days, and an older woman like that – very dangerous. There has been some girl over the summer who broke his heart, and when I told him about Lady Maria and Sir Mark he looked downcast, as if he had been holding the idea of her in reserve. What am I to do with him?"

"He will be safely back at Oxford soon."

"Where he can flirt with Rome and think of becoming a celibate?" Emma said, and gave a shudder.

"It will be interesting to hear what Oxford makes of Arthur Hurrell now," said Giles.

"Or Mr Willoughby," said Emma.

"Will we have an English pope in forty years' time?" said Giles.

"How curious that would be," said Emma.

The door opened, and Lord Rothborough came in.

"I see you don't care for the galop either, Major and Mrs Vernon?" he said.

"No, we don't," said Emma. "That last waltz was quite enough for me."

"I think Mrs Carswell means to dance through her slippers," said Giles.

"And Maria," said Lord Rothborough, sitting down with them. "Sir Mark has given her carte blanche in his absence to dance as much as she pleases."

"Oh, it has come to that," said Emma, smiling, "that such things must be discussed?"

"It has," said Lord Rothborough, leaning back. "And who am I to stop them, when they are so sensible in their sentimentality? Of course, there is no question of there being any formal betrothal at this point. Lady Rothborough has seen to that, but I have given them liberty and it has not been abused. In fact, I am consulted and considered to such a degree that it is not good for me. In the meantime, I had a letter from Sir Mark about the trial."

"He is still with his aunt at the Assizes?" Giles said.

"Yes, they have instructed Penrose as you suggested. We can only hope for an outcome that will not damage the boys too greatly now."

"You still have them with you at Holbroke?" Emma said.

"Maria insisted. She has already begun to smooth them out nicely," he said. "But sometimes I wonder if it is too much responsibility for her. She has taken on a great burden cheerfully. I can only hope there is time for her to flourish a little more, to be idle and silly and all those things we need."

"I think Sir Mark feels that too," said Emma. "Why else would he give her carte blanche tonight?"

"I hope so," said Lord Rothborough, getting up again. "I wonder if she will spare her father a dance? And you, Mrs Vernon – if I may, Major? Will you take me for a quadrille?"

"Yes, certainly, my lord," said Emma, standing up also. "We should not hide ourselves away in here, should we?" she added to Giles. "Given the feast is in our honour."

"No. Then I will ask Lady Blanchfort to stand up with me," said Giles. Emma smiled at that. "So she may not pine."

"What's this?" said Lord Rothborough.

"Oh, nothing," said Emma. "I'm only feeling excessive pride in my new husband."

"So you should," said Lord Rothborough, offering her his arm. "Come, a quadrille!"

They walked away to the door, with Emma glancing back at Giles with a most playful smile, that made him glance at the clock. It was a little after midnight. In less than two hours they would be able to go to bed.

~

"Ah, you've not gone up yet!" said Felix, finding Major Vernon in the hall. He opened the door to his study. "Can I tempt you with a dram?"

"A small one," said Major Vernon.

"Yes, of course," said Felix. "I know your habits." Felix put a glass into his hand. "To Mrs Vernon!" he said, raising his glass.

Major Vernon raised his glass, took a nip of his whisky and then looked about him.

"This room is coming on."

"I think so, though it has been quite a bother getting the bookshelves made as I wanted them, but we are nearly there."

"You will soon be settled," said Major Vernon.

"Like oil and vinegar in a flask," Felix said.

"Do you mean you and Mrs Carswell?" said Major Vernon.

"We are different substances, and I have not quite worked out how one might keep us amalgamated. You and Mrs Vernon – well, you have undergone a chemical transformation some time ago now, it seems to me. You and she are no longer separate things, but a new compound. Eleanor and I, on the other hand – oil and vinegar."

"From what I know of chemistry, which is not much, of course," Major Vernon said, "some compounds take longer to form than others. Is that not so?"

"You are right," said Felix. He put down his glass. "Come and see my new microscope. I have finally got it set up to my liking and I have to say it has been worth the trouble. I have made a couple of slides to compare animal and human blood. The result is very intriguing."

He turned up the lamp and began his demonstration. In a few minutes they were absorbed in the magical effects of a top quality lens, examining the subtle differences between the blood of a human male and that of a pig, until the clock chimed the half hour.

"You must excuse me," said Major Vernon. "Mrs Vernon will be wondering what has become of me."

"Oh Lord, yes, of course," said Felix, hurrying him to the door. "My best wishes again to you both, sir."

They shook hands warmly; Major Vernon turned towards the staircase, and with his customary energy began to climb the stairs two steps at a time.

Felix returned to his study, and went back to the microscope. As he did, a squeak of protest came from the floor, and he discovered that he had accidentally stepped on the tail of Lady Blanchfort's cat who had claimed the room as his own domain. Felix scooped him into his arms, murmuring an apology, before depositing him in the armchair where Byron had made a habit of sleeping. He supposed he ought to go up to bed. The chances were that Eleanor, having danced so much, would be too tired to desire his attentions. Yet he lingered at his bench, looking at his slides, enjoying the peaceful pursuit of knowledge and the undemanding companionship of a cat.

~ THE END ~

# Dramatis Personae

## Northminster

Major Giles Vernon: Chief Superintendent of the Northern Investigation office

Mrs Emma Maitland: engaged to be married to Major Vernon

Holt: Major Vernon's manservant

Lord Rothborough: local grandee and natural father of Lord Rothborough

Lady Maria Haraald: Lord Rothborough's youngest daughter

Felix Carswell: consultant surgeon to the Northern Office of Investigation

Eleanor Carswell: Felix Carswell's wife

Lady Blanchfort: Eleanor's mother

George Pierce: director of Wytton's bank

Frederick Pierce: George Pierce's son and a bank employee

Noakes: a watchman

Captain Lazenby: Chief Constable of the Northminster and County Constabulary

Mr James Harper: Chief Medical Officer at the Northminster Infirmary

## Hurrell Place

Sir Morten Hurrell: a wealthy baronet, owner of Hurrell Place

Rev Arthur Hurrell: Sir Morten's heir and Rector of Langdon

Mrs Edward Hurrell: Sir Morten's sister-in-law

Mark Hurrell: Sir Morten's youngest son

Rev John Willoughby: an idealistic young clergyman

Mr Powell and Mr Stapleford: University of Oxford undergraduates staying at Langdon Rectory

## Raythorpe Hall and village

Lord Wytton: country gentleman and director of Wytton's bank

Lady Wytton: Lord Wytton's wife

Miss Margaret Wytton: Lord Wytton's sister

Braithwaite: a farrier

Esther Braithwaite: Braithwaite's wife

Mr Gray: the Rector of Raythorpe

Mrs Gray: Mr Gray's wife

## Axworth

Mr James Bennett: a medical student

Dr Wharne: physician at the Axworth Fever Hospital

# About the Author

Harriet Smart was born and brought up in Birmingham. She attended the University of St Andrews, where she read History of Art, and married a fellow student. She now lives with her husband in an eighteenth-century house in Northumberland.

Harriet has an M.A. in screenwriting. She has published twenty novels as well as helping to design the creative writing software Writer's Café and the e-book editor software Jutoh.

She has been writing the Northminster Mysteries since 2010.

You can follow Harriet at www.harrietsmart.com and BookBub.

Printed in Great Britain
by Amazon

84698177R00215